In Need

Daisha Alicea

PAGE PUBLISHING
Conneaut Lake, PA

First originally published by Page Publishing 2024

ISBN 979-8-89315-346-0 (pbk)
ISBN 979-8-89315-362-0 (digital)

Printed in the United States of America

Chapter 1

Love, what a funny feeling. It can make you do strange things, things that you would never have done otherwise. It's an all-consuming feeling that takes your breath away, but if not treated with care, love can be dangerous. Love can kill, not physically but spiritually and emotionally. It can leave you with a feeling of despair and pain that would not only change you but, sometimes, make you the killer.

I fell in love with a beautiful beast. A man who with his eyes can make you crumble and with his touch can make you believe in angels. His beauty transcended above all else; his strength and His will were admirable. He was dangerous in the way that most men envy, and He was my life since the moment I saw him. I knew that there was something about him that made me want to be close to him, be with him, and be there for him in any way that he needed. Most say I was in love, even infatuated with him, but that doesn't seem to do the feelings I had for him justice. I wasn't in love with Christian; it was something so much stronger; I was in need of him.

The sound of my alarm blaring makes me groan as I lay in bed. I turn to shut it off. Not that it makes any difference. I've been awake for hours, even if I wanted to sleep in some more. I couldn't move past the fact that today is the first day of senior year.

Senior year of high school is the year I'm supposed to enjoy life to the best of my ability before I go off to college. I should be anxious to rule the school and party all year, but the reason I'm anxious right now has nothing to do with the fact that I am almost done with the hell that is high school. The reason my brain can't shut down and my body is consumed with fear has everything to do with the fact that after this year, I will be queen. High priestess, if I am being more technical, but queen of the covens in New Orleans regardless.

A high priestess is basically a queen to the witches, which is something I obviously don't want to do. At the end of the year, I will have to make the vow that generations of women before me have made. To protect and serve the witch community as their "queen" as long as I live or until I have a daughter who can take over for me. My mother is a high priestess now, and usually, one waits until they are twenty-one to receive such honor, but for special circumstances that no one will tell me about, I am to be crowned on my eightieth birthday, May 13, at midnight.

I groan as I get out of bed and look in my closet for clothes to wear to go to school. I decide on a pair of blue ripped jeans, a white V-neck T-shirt, a red ball cap, and red Nikes. I comb my hair and let the black curls flow down over my chest instead of putting it into a ponytail. My eyes find themselves as I stare at the mirror in my own bathroom; the dark brown of my skin contrasts nicely with the hazel color of my eyes and my body, a slim figure of the height of five feet five, and curves that wrap around me like a road on a map. After one good look in the mirror, I walk out to face the day.

My home is big and beautiful, one of the perks of being the highest family of the witch community and my father being the mayor. A two-story house with six bedrooms, four bathrooms, and practically anything you can ask for. The walls that decorate the house are white and neat, matching most of the furniture that inhabits it.

As soon as I get out of my room, I see my brother coming out of his, right across the hall. My brother, Alexander, is my fraternal twin, and we have the same eyes and brown-colored skin. The similarities stop there. I'm short, while my brother is a giant, standing at six feet four, just like our father. As soon as he sees me, he smiles.

"You ready?"

Alex is my best friend, my main confidant. Maybe it has to do with us being twins, but I trust him with my secrets and my life. He knows how hard this year is for me, it's like a ticking time bomb until I have to give my life away for something I don't even know if I want.

"Define ready."

He wraps his big arm around my shoulder, and we begin to walk down the steps.

"It's going to be fine, Lexi."

"Easy for you to say," I can't help but roll my eyes at him.

I am jealous of my brother because he's a man. According to witch law, a high priestess is supposed to be the oldest child of the new generation and highly encouraged that it's female. No man can be a high priest. It's ridiculous because if the woman rule went out the window, Alex would be the perfect leader. He's smart, works well under pressure, and people love him. On the other hand, I am just the cheerleader who wouldn't be able to lead a horse to water.

"Hey, you know I am here for you." Alex nudges me as we get to the bottom of the spiral staircase into the marble foyer.

I can smell pancakes and eggs coming from the kitchen before my foot even touches the last step. Alex and I move to enter the kitchen, and we get blinded by the flash of a camera that I know belongs to one person.

"Mom," I groan as I try to blink, trying to make sure I am not left blind.

Once I can see again, I see my mother standing before me dressed in a black pencil skirt wrapped around her long brown legs, a white buttoned-down shirt, and her brown curly hair in a bun, making her look just like the queen that she is.

My father is at the kitchen table drinking coffee and reading the newspaper with his reading glasses around his hazel eyes. He doesn't need to look up to say, "Rose, you're going to blind the children."

"It's their senior year. Alexis and I need a photo." My mother smiles at us before she turns to sit at the kitchen table.

Alex and I headed to join our parents and start eating the breakfast that our mother had made. Most mornings, Lindsey, our maid, makes our food because Mom is too busy with the witch stuff, and Dad is the mayor of this lovely town. However, my mother insists on making us breakfast every year for the first day of school and seeing us off. It's a tradition, and my family doesn't break traditions, ever.

My mother sits next to my father and smiles brightly at me. "So, Alexandra, are you excited? In just eight months, you will become the new high priestess." Her question gave me a nervous pit in my stomach, and I immediately stopped eating. "I remember the months

3

leading up to the ceremony, and my heart raced with anticipation. Of course, I was older, and I had your father, but honey, I can already see how great you're gonna be." She grabs my hand and gives it a squeeze as she continues to babble on. "I know you said you don't want to make it a big deal, but the dress I have in mind for you is already waiting for you at Anthony's, and he will make all the necessary adjustments."

I hear her talk and just nod my head. I can't bring myself to tell her or my father that I am actually terrified to be a high priestess. I know my mother has such high hopes for me, and I want to make her happy. It's not that I can deny my destiny, but I'm so scared to do this. I am so young, and to control and lead all these people, protect them, I just can't.

My brother looks at me and then clears his throat, "Hey, Dad, you ready to see me dominate the field this year."

This gets my father's attention, and he places the newspaper down and takes his glasses off. My mother, being the high priestess, always mentions magic and witches, and sometimes I feel like my dad zones her out. However, whenever someone mentions football, my father becomes all ears.

"You know I am. I can't wait to see all the college scouts fight for you." He proudly smiles at him, and for the next several minutes, my parents are gushing all over Alex and how he's going to get a football scholarship.

Alex is the star quarterback of our school football team, the Knights. He's so good that he's been the quarterback for three years now. He's always been great at everything he does, just like the rest of my family. This is my family: the beautiful queen, the smart mayor, and the talented quarterback, and then there is me—the spoiled teenage girl who freaks out the moment she is put in any position of power.

I nudge Alex under the table as a thank you for turning the conversation away from me. We finish our breakfast just in time, and there's a honk outside, our ride.

Before I looked out the window, I already knew who it was: Paris, my best friend. Alex and I say goodbye to our parents and rush out of the house because there is one thing about Paris—that is, she is not the most patient girl around.

I take the front seat of Paris's BMW car, and Alex takes the back with Jordan, our other friend. As soon as I come in, I already hear Paris screaming at Jordan.

"Can you stop kicking the back of my seat, you fucking jerk?"

She turns around and swats him in the leg.

"I wouldn't have to kick your seat if you knew how to fucking drive," Jordan says, and even though I can't see him, I know he's rolling his eyes.

Paris and Jordan have always had a love/hate relationship with emphasis on the word hate. We all became friends before we were even born. All our parents are in the same coven, so it was like we were destined to be. However, despite that, Paris and Jordan are always at each other's throats. I feel it has something to do with how different they are and how alike they can be. Paris is very outspoken and says whatever is on her mind, no matter what the consequences. She is a free spirit with tattoos all over her body that make her controlling mother go insane. Her bright red hair is a perfect image for her fiery attitude. I guess the tighter her mother tries to pull her leash, the more out of control she gets. Paris doesn't care about anyone's opinions and always finds a way to fight for what she wants, and in that way, I envy her. She is way more brave than I will ever be.

Jordan is the opposite. Although both of Jordan's Indian parents are controlling as well, he doesn't resist them. In fact, he gives in. Well, at least that's what he wants them to think. Jordan lives a whole secret life from his parents, where his parents wait for him to be this smart, responsible gentleman of a witch, but that isn't the case. Jordan likes to live his life on the edge, sleeping with almost every girl at school, using his magic for his own benefit, which is against the rules, and bending the rules however he sees fit. He's charming and sweet and can practically talk his way out of anything.

But outside of their differences, there are similarities. For example, they both hate their parents. I guess it has to do with how controlling they are and how Paris's father left her when she was just twelve years old. They are both rebels in their own ways, and they both have commitment issues. I always thought that they might end up together or that they already had secret feelings for each other because they argued like a married couple.

I look at Paris; her long red hair is in a ponytail at the back of her head, so you can see the star tattoo behind her ear and all the piercings she has surrounding it. She has her signature makeup on black eyeliner that makes her brown eyes pop, foundation, and a red lip. Her body is decorated in a black skintight skirt, black thigh-high boots, and a long-sleeved red shirt. She looks at me and smiles.

"You ready for the last year of hell?"

I put on my seat belt and smile back at her. "Are you ever ready for such a thing?"

"That's my girl." She laughs and then begins to drive again. "Now let's go get Angel."

Angel is our other friend. We haven't known her as long as we know each other, being that she wasn't originally in our coven or that she got to New Orleans our freshman year. But she definitely lives up to her name. Angel's family practices healer magic. She can heal anything that is living with just a flick of her wrist. She uses her powers when she can. That is without raising suspicion to any of us. The funny thing is that if you didn't know she was a witch, you would think she was an angel, with her angelic voice, long blonde hair, pale skin, and her dark green eyes that look just like an emerald stone. But it's not just her beauty and healing powers that make her seem like an angel. It's also her morals. Most people try to do good, but most fail from time to time, not Angel. She lives by a set of roles and morals, and I don't think I have ever seen her steer away from them. She is kind, caring, and always does the right thing even though it might be inconvenient.

As we drive to Angel's house, we see her walk down the steps of her porch with such grace that makes her look so angelic. The sun bounces off her hair as she trolls down the walkway in a white skirt, light blue top, and white flats.

"Good morning," she says as she smushes herself into the car.

Paris starts to drive to school while we all discuss the plans for the year to come. Everyone talks about homecoming, football, and of course, all the classes we will have to endure to graduate. No one brings up the high priestess thing, and I am glad they don't. I try to push it into the back of my mind as long as possible and focus on the new school year. I don't want this to put a damper on all the things that my senior year is supposed to be about—applying to colleges, school, trips, and even the prom.

The drive to school is short, and the search for parking isn't as bad as it usually is since we got here earlier than most.

"Look at it," Paris says as we all pile out of the car, and she looks at the school. "Hell, in all its glory."

"With your driving, I'm surprised we're not in real hell." Jordan snorts next to her, which grants him a slap on the chest. "I'm just saying whoever gave you your license had no regard for the safety and lives of others."

Jordan is six feet two, has short black Indian hair, and beautiful brown eyes and is as fit as they come. He is handsome in that quite obvious kind of way. The way you can't really deny, but you know he can get any girl he wants with just his pearly white smile.

Alex laughs and puts his hand on Jordan's shoulder. "Alright. Let's go before she actually kills you." He then turns to me and smiles. "Text me if you need me. I'll see you at lunch."

I give him a small smile, and he's off with Jordan right on his tail.

"I definitely will." Paris grins as she watches my twin brother walk up the steps to school.

I groan, and now it's my turn to slap her. She knows how I feel about her saying stuff like that about Alex, not him. I love Paris. She's my best friend, but I know how she is. Paris has a reputation. She's beautiful and full of life. She is as bright as the sun attracting men from afar, but she lets them close enough, and then, just like the sun, she burns them. I want Alex to go as far as he can get from that. I see the way his eyes light up whenever the girls come around, and I am pretty sure that they light up for her. I don't want him to get burned. I won't allow it.

Paris rubs her arm where I slapped her and grins. "I was just kidding, Lexi. I know how you feel about our friends and your fine-ass brother."

I raise my hand as a warning, and she just laughs. "Come on. Even Angel thinks he's hot."

I turn to Angel, who is now beet red. Angel is someone I don't have to worry about. She is in no way interested in dating anyone. She's really into her magic and school to even notice guys. She's never had a boyfriend or even been kissed, for god's sake.

Angel just looks straight at the school as not wanting to answer the question, "I think we should go in. We don't want to be late, right?"

"I agree," I say as we watch up the long steps into the school.

Our school, Ridgeview High, is a fairly decent school. It was built in the 1940s after the castle that was built here before was destroyed. Back then, the castle that was here was, a castle for the high priestess and her family. At the beginning of the 1800s, the high priestess and the high family were treated like gods by their coven, the covens they protected, and even the humans. Humans would worship all witches, and our alliance with them was as simple as it could be. We help the humans with their needs, and they protect us and keep our secret from people outside of New Orleans. It was a great time of peace in witch history, but sadly, it was short-lived. According to my grandmother, in the 1940s, that all change when the vampires came into town, killing humans and witches alike, trying to find a special magical amulet that was entrusted to the high priestess centuries ago. A lot of people were murdered in cold blood for the amulet, and eventually, we had to call in the help of the werewolves that are the vampire's mortal enemies. The war ended, but not without a ton of bloodshed. The humans blamed the witches and werewolves for the deaths, and we were forced to hide our gifts from the world. The castle was turned into a school for humans and supernatural alike, not that people know we are any different from them.

As soon as we get in the school, we see the swarm of new freshmen running like chickens with their heads cut off to find their lockers. I can't help but remember how it felt to be naive at that time where finding my locker was one of my biggest problems. We go and find our lockers that we have had of high school right next to each other. That's actually how we met Angel. Her locker was right next to us, and the next thing we know, we were all best friends.

I open my locker and settle most of my stuff in there, just leaving my AP lit book out since it's my first class. My head is basically stuffed inside my locker when I hear Paris gasp.

"Who is the hell is that?"

I stick my head out of locker and look in the direction we just came in. Right at the entrance of the school is the most breathtaking guy I have ever seen—tan-skinned, decorated in a tight white shirt that hugs his large biceps, black jeans wrap around his long, tall legs. He clearly is taller than most people in the hallway. He towers over everyone. His face lifts from a piece of paper he has in his hand, and he starts to look around. A chiseled jaw, perfect lips, and dark brown eyes adorn his gorgeous face, and for a second, I feel like I am dreaming. His tan skin shines under the school's shitty lighting, and his wavy black locks fall on top of his forehead slightly in an almost framed way.

There's no way this guy is real. He looks like he was sculpted, like he's God's own little piece of art. I know I am not the only one who noticed because every girl in the hallway has stopped to stare at him, and how could they not? He's gorgeous. This stranger's energy has captivated everyone in this hallway as he makes his way through the crowd. His dark brown eyes scan the hall, and unbothered by all the looks cast on him, it's almost as if he doesn't notice them. He's looking for something, his locker maybe, I don't know, but his eyes stop midsearch as they cast themselves on me.

For a second, I am too busy staring at his face to notice that his eyes are fixated on me. However, when I make contact with the dark pool on his chiseled face, I can feel them burning into my own. My heartbeat starts to race, and my breath gets caught in my throat. I can feel my palms get sweaty, and the heat on my cheeks starts to rise. His eyes linger, not wavering as they make their way up and down my body. I feel as though my skin is on fire, and he's all the way across the hall. I bite my lip on instinct, uncomfortable with the attention, and immediately, he zeroes in on my lips. My stomach curls as I take him in, wide broad shoulders, biceps the size of mountains, and a sharp jaw that makes his face even more attractive.

The stranger must get tired of looking at me because he turns his direction back to his paper before settling into his locker, which is five feet away. I don't know why I stare or even why I am so fascinated with him, but my eyes stay on him for so long, I almost miss the warning bell.

I take a deep breath and resist the urge to turn around to look at him again.

"Angel," Paris's voice brings me back to reality, "I think our little Lexi has a boyfriend," she jokes as I shut my locker.

Angel laughs. "I see that."

"What are you talking about?" I try not to let my cheeks heat up as I feign ignorance.

"Don't act dumb. We all say what happened just now," Paris says as I start to turn to go to class, trying to avoid this conversation. It takes superhuman strength to resist the urge to turn around and look at the mystery boy, but I accomplish it. "You and that new boy just had the most intense staring contest. It made me blush."

"You're exaggerating," I scoff.

"Whatever you say. Just be careful before Jonah gets jealous."

Jonah, that's a name I haven't heard in months, Jonah Stevenson, my former friend and ex-boyfriend. Jonah and I have known each other for years. He's one of my first normal friends. By normal, I mean completely human. We met when we were younger at a playground. Usually, my parents, especially my father, hated that Alex or I had any human friends, and he said it was too risky. But then again, my father has always been kind of paranoid. Eventually, though, my parents accepted our friendship, and that blossomed into something more. Something about his boyish charm got to me and made me all gushy inside. He was my first love. He was my escape from the witch world. With him, I could be just a normal teenage girl, and that made me happy. I really wanted to hold on to that feeling forever. But last spring, I had to break it off. I thought it would be better if I did it before my coronation. We were both devastated, especially him, since I couldn't tell him the real reason I had to leave him, but it was for the best. I haven't seen him all summer, and a part of me doesn't know how I'm gonna feel when I do.

I push that thought out of my head and try to focus on getting to my first class.

"I just looked at the guy Paris. Now let's get to class before we're late." The words leave my mouth harsher than I intend it, but I can't just put them back in.

My legs move quickly under me as I try to walk past everyone to get to class. Embarrassed and a slight sadness accompany me when I get to the class with Paris and Angel not left far behind. The class is filling up, but there are four seats in the back, and we occupy three.

"Hey, I didn't mean to say that about Jonah," Paris points out, her brown eyes staring into my own, and I can tell she's being sincere. "It was insensitive."

I give her a small smile. "It's just I tried not to think of him this summer. I miss him, you know."

It's not Paris's fault that I broke it off with Johan, and it isn't her fault I'm feeling this way. I knew we had an expiration date. I just hate that I hurt one of the only people who cared for me—the real me, not the person I'm supposed to.

"We know, but you made the right choice," Angel interjects.

I can't help but look at her quizzically because, last year, when I was debating if I should break it off, she was the one who told me to work it out. She was the only one who believed we could make it work. I wonder what changed her mind.

As if she can read my mind, she says, "No matter how much you love someone, sometimes it just can't work." Her voice laced with longing.

Mrs. Jenkins has been my teacher for years. She's one of those teachers who just follows her class throughout the years. Usually, that kind of thing isn't allowed, but she is one of the best, so that gets her some pull. She's also a good friend of my parents. They all went to school together. She's blonde, short, and very cheerful. Everyone in the school loves her.

She looks around the classroom and smiles. "Well, we'll wait a couple of more minutes, and then we'll start."

I play with my pen in between my finger while I hear Paris and Angel talk, but I cannot really hear what they are saying because my mind is miles away from here. My coronation, although it's months away, I still hear the clock ticking on my future. *YOU SHOULD BE*

GRATEFUL! my subconscious screams at me, and I know she is right. I should be. Most witches would kill to be the high priestess, but then again, I am not most witches. I love our heritage and what we stand for, but to be in charge of everyone it's too much power, too much opportunity to fuck up. I am so scared to ruin everything. My mother, my grandmother, and every woman before them have done such a great job upholding the legacy, but I know myself. I am nothing even close to them.

I'm an average witch, and even then, sometimes, I can't even seem to control my powers.

In the midst of my thinking, I hear Mrs. Jenkins speak, "Well, look who it is."

Everyone's eyes, including my own, gravitate toward the front of the room, and there, at the door, is Jonah. My heart drops to my stomach. There he is. His blue eyes search through the room while he still has that same boyish smile on his face that he has always had. His dirty blond hair is longer than the last time I've seen him, and somehow, he looks bigger, as if he has been working out. There's something about him that seems different from before, but I can't quite put my finger on it. I try not to stare, but it's practically impossible. This is the first time I have seen him since we broke up last year. He's been gone all summer, and even though we promised to remain friends, we haven't spoken to each other since that night. A part of me wants to say hi and go up there to hug him, but an even bigger part of me, the part that feels guilty, wants to sink into my chair and disappear.

Jonas stops to look at me. His blue eyes look darker somehow. He doesn't do anything but stare for a couple of moments, and then he gives me a small smile and looks at the chair next to mine.

Before I even know it, Johan starts to head over to us. "Incoming," I hear Paris mumble under her breath as he takes his seat.

"Hello, ladies."

"Hey," we all say in unison.

He starts to take a notebook and pen out of his bag while I play with my pen nervously. What do I even say to him? Hey I'm sorry I dumped and just stomped all over your heart, and even though you deserve an answer as to why I did what I did, I am not gonna give it to you. I shake my head. Maybe this is a bad idea.

I can feel him staring at my hand that is holding the pen. "Hey, this doesn't have to be weird."

I look at him and give him a nervous smile. "Who said it's weird?"

"If you shake that pen anymore, it's gonna sue," he says, and a little smile creeps on my face as I let go of my pen. "Look, it's okay. We're friends. I don't want this to feel awkward any more than you do."

My face starts to relax. He's right. It's only weird if I make it weird. I miss him, and I want to talk to him like nothing ever happened. I want some normalcy in my life. I need some balance. So I suck it up, smile and ask him about his summer.

Chapter 2

NEW KIDS ON THE BLOCK

My stomach rumbles as soon as I enter the cafeteria. My head has been preoccupied with thoughts of deep brown eyes ever since this morning. I've tried my best to ignore it, but for some reason, those eyes stay in the back of my mind as if they're haunting me, imprinting their memory so deep that all that remains is that visual.

I pay for my lunch of a bacon burger and a bottle of water and then go search around for my friends. The cafeteria is crowded. People are already seated; others are running around like chickens and with their heads cut off. It doesn't take long to spot my friends. Everyone has already been at our usual table since we were freshmen—everyone, including Jonah. I take my seat in between Paris and Jordan and listen to interject myself in their conversation, trying to get the mystery man's eyes out of my damn brain.

"What are we talking about?"

Paris looks at me, his brown eyes full of excitement. "There you are. We were just talking about having a party on Friday. The wicked witch is out of town, so it would be perfect." The wicked witch is what we call Paris's mother. Paris's mother is one of my mother's best friend, mostly because they both grew up in the coven together, but at times, it almost feels as if she actually hates her daughter.

"I can get us the beer and liquor," Jordan says in between his bites of pizza.

"Sounds fun." Alex nods. Then he looks over at Angel. "You coming?"

Angel blushes, probably from the sudden turn of attention toward her. "I don't know. Doesn't seem like a good idea." She shrugs. "You all know how my mother can be." She avoids eye contact with Alex.

Angel's mother is a nice, sweet woman. She has a heart of gold, just like her daughter, but she is even more sheltered than she is. She doesn't believe in Angel doing anything bad, and to her, bad things involve parties, wearing tight clothing, or even makeup. We like to call her the nun because of how conservative she can be. Not only is she like this, but she also likes to follow Angel or check up on her from time to time. I think it's creepy, but Angel insists it's because her mother loves her and just wants the best for her. I insist that her mother is a stalker.

"Angel, you can just say you're staying at my place," Paris says. "Tell her some bullshit that I am scared to stay alone without my mother."

"She's just gonna say that you should stay with us." Angel shakes her head.

"Then make something else," Jordan puts in.

Angel looks slightly uncomfortable, and I know that she doesn't lie, but there is something else. I can't quite put my finger on it. I get the feeling again that she's hiding something.

"Hey." I grab her small, delicate hand from across the table. "You don't have to come. But if you decide that you want to then, we can help you deceive your mom. It won't be the same without you, Angel."

She looks me in the eye and nods slowly. I can feel Jonah staring at me, but I decide to ignore it as I retract my hand. I know it's just a habit, but I turn my attention to my burger. I don't look, so I don't even notice when Anitta makes her way to the table.

When I look up, she's directly in front of us in her cheerleading uniform, her invisible devil horns, staring down at us with those big brown saucers that she calls eyes. Her black hair is in a sleek ponytail on the top of her head with a black-and-white bow on it that matches our school colors. The uniform compliments her fair skin and contrasts perfectly against it. One might even call her pretty if she wasn't so evil.

"So I see you guys didn't get the memo," she says, and just hearing her voice after so long makes me want to vomit.

Anitta and I have been at odds since I can remember. Her mother and my mother went to school together, and they hated each other. Somehow, it came down to us. Anitta hates me with a passion. She has done whatever in her power to make my life miserable. She would steal my toys, call me names, and flirt with my boyfriends. Anything that was remotely mine she wanted, and that included cheerleading. Ever since I was younger, cheerleading was the one thing that made me absolutely happy. It takes my head from the mess that is my life to an imaginary world where I only exist, and everything is fine. It was the one solace in my chaotic life. Anitta saw that and decided to join the squad freshman year, and now she has become the head cheerleader. I hate to admit it, but having the one thing I love to do, which has nothing to do with magic and witches, be poisoned by the actual devil doesn't make it fun anymore.

If I was being honest, I don't actually know why Anitta hates me. It's almost like one day, her small five-year-old mind decided that I was going to be the target of all her hate, and she never let up. I don't know what I did to her. My mom calls their family the rudest humans alive, and if it wasn't her job to protect the city and all its inhabitants, she would probably have Dad evict them. She was a little drunk off wine when she made that comment, but somehow, I wish she would go through with it.

I look at her and try to give her a genuine smile, deciding right there and then that I will not play her hateful games. I have bigger things to worry about than petty childhood drama.

"Hey, Anitta, how was your summer?"

The look she gives me is one full of pure disgust, as if everything I do to her repulses her, and maybe it does.

"Oh, shut up, Lexi. Why aren't you wearing your uniform?" she says, her voice laced with annoyance. "I sent an email to all the girls this summer, specifying that I want everyone to wear their uniforms Mondays instead of Fridays." She points to me and then moves her finger to Angel and then Paris. "Do you guys have any explanation for this?"

"Why would we wear our uniforms on Monday when we've always worn them on Fridays?" Paris says, her lips pursed at her. "It's just stupid."

"You're stupid!" Anitta says so loudly that people from other tables start to look over her.

As much as I hate her, it's nothing compared to how much Paris hates Anitta. Paris hates everyone—that's a fact. She's very careful about who she lets into her circle. But Paris and Anita always go head-to-head, and there has been angry tension between them for as long as I can remember.

"What did you just call me?"

The look on Paris's face is the one most people should fear. The look of anger mixed with a tad of irritation, usually when she has that look on her face, a smart person would duck or even run and hide, but not Anitta. She matches Paris's glare with one of her own, and if no one intervenes now, it will be bad for all of us.

Angel, as if she can read my mind, gets up real quick and interjects herself into the conversation, "What she means is that it's a tradition. We have always worn our uniforms to school on Fridays. Why change it?"

"Besides, our games are on Friday most of the time. It would just make sense," Alex puts in.

"I am the head cheerleader," Anitta solidifies. "If I say that we're wearing our uniforms on Mondays, that is what we're doing. I don't care if it's tradition or makes more sense. My word is law."

Paris just laughs, and I know she wants to rile her up. "And if we don't do it?"

"I will drop all of you from the squad."

Now it's my turn to laugh. "You wouldn't. We're the best dancers on the squad, and you know it."

It's true, and I'm not being cocky, but Angel, Paris, and I have always pushed ourselves more than the others. We stay after practices and help with the routines, and we are the only few of the girls that actually have any background in gymnastics. Anitta wouldn't drop us because she wants her squad to be perfect, and if we leave, it would be anything but.

She looks at me, and I know she's not gonna deny it. She rolls her eyes. "Just don't be late to practice tomorrow."

With that, she turns away to walk away. Her long ponytail sways behind, almost waving at us.

"I hate her," Paris says between her teeth as Angel takes a seat back down.

"Join the club."

I roll my eyes as I see Anitta walk to her table with the rest of the cheerleaders. Hate is a strong word, and I wish I didn't feel so strongly about her, but I can't help it. She just gets under my skin. Purposely, I might add.

As I stare at her, I can't help but look at the table next to Anitta. There are two cute boys sitting there, and I don't recognize them. This town isn't too small, but new people stick out like a sore thumb. One of the boys at the table has blond hair and ocean-blue eyes that are framed by a pair of black glasses. He's dressed in a *Star Wars* T-shirt and is reading a book. The other one has a short brown buzz-cut on the top of his head, and his eyes are dark. Tattoos cover almost every inch of his melanin arms. Both men are extremely muscular and big. They're sitting down, but you can tell that they are not lacking lengthwise.

"Who are they?" I say, curiosity getting the better of me. They can't be brothers. They look nothing alike. However, they're both new.

My friends all look over at the table. "The one with the glasses is in my creative drawing class," Jordan states. "I think his name is Devin. He just moved here last week, from my understanding."

"What about the hottie next to him?" Paris says and makes it a point to lick her lips.

Jordan's face hardens, just for a second, before he turns to look at the table of newcomers.

"That's Jackson," Johan says. "He and his friend Christian also got here last week. I had to show them to the office during the second period."

"Who's Christian?"

Johan looks around to see if he can spot him, but there is no one else at their table. However, entering the cafeteria is the new guy I saw earlier today in the hallway.

I can feel the heat on my cheeks start to rise as soon as he enters. It is as if my body knows he's here. The hairs standing at attention on the back of my head are proof of that. He takes long strides across the room, commanding it with his presence. Most of the eyes in the room are on him as he makes his way to the table with the other two new boys. But again, it's almost like he doesn't notice all the stares, or maybe he doesn't care. I'm sure he's used to it by now.

It was so hard to focus in class when all I could think about were his eyes. Brown eyes—almost everyone I know has brown eyes—but yet his eyes were the only ones that made that's big of an impact. Every time I tried to focus on something on the board or something the teacher was saying, his eyes came into view, and I was as lost as I was this morning when I first saw him.

"That's Christian," Johan says, and I can feel his eyes studying me, but I can't tear my gaze away from Christian.

Christian sits at the table, facing my direction. The lighting of the outside glass windows shines on his face, and I can see these features more clearly than before. He has perfect eyebrows, a thick neck, and a dimple on the right side of his cheek. He's breathtaking.

I don't know what it is about him, but I've never been so fascinated by the way someone looks. Maybe it's his aura or the confidence that comes off him in waves.

"You're staring," Paris whispers quietly in my ear, bringing me back to my surroundings.

I take a bite of my burger and look to my left to see Johan still staring at me. I give him a small smile, which he returns. A part of me wants to give him a hug, and the other part feels like I am making a mistake by even sitting here with him. But I push both thoughts out of my head.

"So about this party on Friday," I say, trying to pull into the prior conversation we were having before Anitta stopped by. "Who are you inviting?"

"Everyone," Paris says, her eyes gleaming with excitement. One thing about Paris, she loves throwing a party.

"Even Anitta?" Alex asks.

"I don't see why not." Paris shrugs her shoulders. "We're charging $10 at the door, so it would be fun to take her money. Besides, if I don't invite her, she'll crash anyways. This way, I have the upper hand."

"Well, good, because if Anitta comes, that means that cheerleaders will come, and there's still a couple of them I need to cross off my list," Jordan says, and everyone at the table rolls their eyes.

Jordan started a list when we were freshmen, and basically, it's a list of all the girls at school he wants to sleep with, and he crosses their names as he goes. At first, when he started the list, we all thought it was a joke, but as the years gone by, the names were getting crossed off. Just last year, I think he crossed off fifteen names by the time of the junior prom. It's disgusting, and one will question how he gets so many girls to sleep with, but to most girls at this school, Jordan is a ticketed prize. With nice smooth Indian hair, beautiful ebony skin, and huge biceps, he's the top guy at this school—other than Alex, of course. Everywhere we go, girls fawn over my brother, but unlike Jordan, he pays them no mind. He's not that type. Also, it's not like the girls who sleep with Jordan don't know about the list or what they're getting into. They see it as a prize, some type of accomplishment, to sleep with a guy like Jordan.

Jordan is a charmer, just like Paris. Both set their eyes on something, and with the right words, they can win it over.

"Ugh, you're a pig." Paris rolls her eyes.

Jordan winks at her. "Don't be jealous, babe. You'll get your turn."

This makes Paris scoffs as she grabs a fry from my tray and throws it at him in disgust.

"Jordan," Angel exclaims, "I think your list is wrong, unethical, and just plain…nasty." Angel's green eyes fill with disgust. "How are you going to find the right girl if you're always sleeping around?"

I can't help but smile at Angel's mothering comment. She's so innocent it's cute. But we all know that being someone's husband isn't what Jordan wants, not even close. Jordan wants to be a rich playboy who travels the worlds, scoring tail in every country—his words, not mine.

As Jordan tries to explain to Angel that he will never get married or settle down, I zone out again. My thoughts take me to the future. Getting married isn't something that I've thought about. Not something I've strived for. I don't know how I would even have time to get married. If I'm gonna be high priestess, I don't even think I'll have the time sleep, let alone date. Besides, what guy would want to marry someone who's busy all the time taking care of everyone else's problems? My mom had my dad before she even became high priestess, but I know it's tough with my father being mayor also. They barely have time for each other.

Midway through Angel and Jordan's conversation, the hairs on the back of my neck stand up again, and I get the sudden feeling that I'm being watched. As I look up from my tray, my eyes immediately lock with Christian's. We're sitting directly across each other with just a walkway and a table in between us. His friends surround him, talking and joking around him, but he's not engaging. Instead, his attention is set on me. Brown eyes bear into my soul, and he doesn't turn away. He doesn't smile, and he barely blinks; he just stares. It's almost like he's looking through my soul. It's unnerving; however, I don't look away. I can't.

My heart skips a beat, and I swear, for just a second, the world stops. Everyone and everything turns into a blur, and all I can see, all I can focus on, is him. I have never felt the magnetic pull that I'm feeling right now—an electric charge that is coming from him, almost as if I need to get close to him or I'd combust. The feeling overwhelms me, and before I know it, I'm standing from my chair and making my way over.

"Where are you going? We still have ten more minutes of lunch." Alex's voice is nothing but a distant whisper compared to the nervous thumbing of my heart.

I don't answer him as my feet carry me toward Christian's direction. The more steps I take to his table, the more nervous I become. My hands are sweating, and my heart is about to come out of my chest. I don't know what has overcome me. This isn't me. I'm not the girl who just walks up to strangers. Instead, I'm the opposite. I am the girl who stays to herself.

I make it to the table in no time, and three pairs of eyes stare up at me, neither of them looking surprised to see me.

"Hello," is the only word I can get past the thump in my throat. This was a bad idea. I am not brave enough to do this with Christian's eyes looking at me.

"Hello, luv," the one with the glasses, Devin, I think, says in a British accent. His mouth breaks into a charming smile as he looks me over. "What can we do for you?" He has that cute boy next-door thing going for him, except for the giant muscles he has under the short sleeves of his *Star Wars* T-shirt.

"My name is Alexandra Coleman." I smile at him kindly. "I just wanted to welcome you guys to the school, and you know, stuff like that."

I can feel my cheeks heat up, but I don't dare look over at Christian. Now that I'm this close, I don't think I can look directly at him, especially when I can feel his eyes burn into the side of my face.

"Well, it's nice to meet you, Alexandra. My name is Devin." Devin continues, "This is troublemaker Jackson, and"—he points to Christian, whom I now, with a prayer, turn—"this devilish handsome lad here is Christian."

I lock eyes with Christian, and it's almost like the breath was knocked out of me. His stare is way more intense up close. I rub my hands on my jeans. I can feel the sweat start to accumulate. He's much more handsome up close. His skin is flawless, and I can see specks of gold in his eyes. I have never seen something so breathtaking in my life. For some reason, I know I never will again.

"It's nice to meet you." I try not to stutter as I look at him.

His full pink lips turn into a small smile when he sits straight in his seat. "Coleman, like the mayor?"

His voice is deep, low, and smooth, and it speaks to something inside of me. I don't know what's wrong with me. I'm practically panting at the sight of his large hands that interlock with each other on top of the table.

I start fiddling with my own hands, trying to distract myself. "Yeah, he's my dad."

"Oh, how's that Alexandra?" Jackson speaks up with an easygoing smile. His eyes aren't just dark, but they almost look black. He has dimples on both sides of his face that soften the sharp edges of his face. "Being the mayor's daughter must suck."

"It's not all bad, and you can call me Lexi," I add. Hearing my full name always makes me cringe. "That's what everyone calls me."

"Why?" Christian asks, and the question throws me off. "Why does everyone call you Lexi?" His tone is curious as his eyes never leave my own.

"It's my nickname. I don't really like my name all that much." Why does he care? My mouth continues nervously, "My brother, his name is Alexander, but everyone calls him Alex. We're twins, and our parents wanted to play on our father's name. His name is Alexis. So that's where Alexandra and Alexander come from." Word vomit, that's what this is. My anxious rambling, trying to fill in the silence. "I hate it, though. Alexandra just sounds so stuck up and pretentious, so ever since I was seven, I told everyone to call me Lexi although my parents refuse to. They're stubborn in that way. It's frustrating."

I stop midsentence because Christian's face breaks into a bigger smile, and if I thought he was beautiful before now, he's just plain gorgeous. The other boys just gape up at me, probably confused by my oversharing, but Christian's eyes just glisten in amusement, almost as if he finds this funny. Great, he probably thinks I'm an idiot. I can't focus when he looks at me like that, so I'm grateful when Devin pulls my attention towards him.

"So," Devin says, trying to break the silence that has come over us, "I heard your town has quite a supernatural history." He pushes his glasses off the bridge of his nose.

I blink at him. "Of course, it does. It's New Orleans. Home of witches and goblins and all that jazz." I try to play it off like a joke. "It's all a myth obviously," I lie, something I have become accustomed to doing to keep our secret under wraps.

"Do you really believe that? I mean, centuries of supernatural myth and legends, you don't think any of it is true?" He looks at me quietly. How did we get here? This conversation took a turn.

"I mean, I've lived here my whole life, and I haven't seen anything remotely supernatural. It's just a scheme to get tourists out here." I can't help but nervously bite my lip as they all look at me.

I know I am a horrible liar. I just hope it doesn't come through. "Believe me, I would know. I'm the mayor's daughter, right?"

Devin nods, and I can't tell if he believes or not. "I guess."

"You don't believe in vampires, witches?" Christian asks, his tone deep and calm. "Werewolves?"

The way that word leaves his mouth brings a chill up my spine. I don't know why, but it does almost as if there's an underlying meaning behind it.

I shake my head, my mouth dry and unable to make up words at this moment. Christian raises an eyebrow but doesn't push the issue. It's weird. Suddenly, I feel like I am stuck in a pit of quicksand, and it's dragging me deeper and deeper to my embarrassment.

"Hey." Johan comes up behind me, interrupting the conversation with a smile on his face. "You ready to go?"

He holds my black book bag in his hand, and I watch as he looks over at the table of boys suspiciously.

I give him a small smile, thankful for the escape. "Well, it was really nice to meet you, guys," I say to the boys. "Um, I hope you guys have a great first day. If you have any questions, I'm available."

I look at Christian one last time. *Please have questions.*

"See you around," he says, but his eyes are on Johan. I don't know why, but he almost looks angry, his lips pressed in a tight line and eyes narrowed, but Johan doesn't seem to notice.

I just brush it off and grab my bag from Johan before we head to the door. As we get to the exit, Johan opens the door for me to walk out, and when I turn to thank him, I see Christian's brown eyes follow me out.

My last class, which is art, ends right on time, and the sound of the alarm signifies the end of a very long day.

"The day is finally over." Angel sighs as we walk down the hall to the exit. This day has been a lot, and if I am being thinnest, I really just want to go back home and hide in my room. "Oh, by any chance, do you have the syllabus for AP lit? I didn't get one."

"Yeah, it's in my locker." I point in the direction of my locker all the way to the end of the hallway. "You go ahead to the car, and I'll meet you there."

"You sure? I can wait."

I shoo her away. "I'll be right behind you."

She nods and walks out the door to the parking lot. I head to my locker in the now-empty hallway. I can hear the sound of my steps as I walk on the marble floor. Once I get to my locker, I put in my combo, and as soon as the door opens, a piece of red paper falls to the ground. I pick it up, expecting it to be a regular flyer like the ones they had last year for school dances and events, but it isn't. I read the words that are the paper, and I almost have a heart attack.

Back in the day, they would cut tongues for lying. Would you like yours sliced in pieces or just a clean cut, my queen?

I look around in panic, hoping this is just one of Jordan's and Paris's pranks. But neither of them is to be seen. In fact, no one is in the hallway. My heart starts racing, and my head is clouded with questions. I look down at the paper. The words are typed out, so I can't even tell if it was Paris by her handwriting.

As I rush down the hall in a hurry, trying to shove the piece of paper in my bag, I run into a wall—more accurately, a wall of muscle. I lose balance, but before I can fall on my ass, a pair of hands grip my arms, keeping me upright. The smell of pine and man overcomes me as I look up and see those brown eyes that have been plaguing me all day. Christian.

He looks down at me. He's in a cutoff black shirt and gym shorts instead of the outfit he had on before. He is covered in sweat, and his brown hair is soaked, almost like he just came from the field or even the gym.

"Alexandra." His brown eyes lock with my own.

"Christian," I say, and my voice is above a whisper. "I'm sorry, I didn't—"

My apology gets caught in my throat. Being in his vicinity makes me nervous, not to mention the letter that it's burning a hole in my bag.

"What's the rush?" he asks. I turn and look at my locker and then back to him, my heart beating a mile a minute. I feel like I'm going to have a panic attack. "You okay, Alexandra?"

I try to nod, but it doesn't move. I'm frozen as the words on that paper echo in my head like a warning. Someone knows my secret, and they're not happy about it.

"Hey," Christian says, his eyes bleed into me, as if he's just realizing there is something wrong. "I can hear your heart. It's beating fast," he says softly, as if it's more of an observation.

I don't know how he knows that, but I do know that I have to leave. He is so close that I can smell his scent—pine, I think it is. There's no one in the hallway, the school seems empty, and he's holding onto me like he can't let go. I know I should be nervous, considering he is practically a stranger, but weirdly, all I can think is that letter and how I need to go home.

"I'm fine," I lie. "I have to get home," is the last thing I say before I peel myself out of his arms and dodge his curious face as I bolt out of there.

Paris's car is already fully loaded by the time I get to it, with Angel sitting in the front with Paris and the boys in the back. I slam the door shut when I get in the car and clutch my bag tightly.

"Did you get it?" Angel asks as she turns to look at me.

At first, I don't know what she means, and then it hits me. The reason I went to my locker in the first place: the syllabus. I shake my head.

"I forgot. Can I give it to you tomorrow?"

"You okay?" Paris looks at me through the rearview mirror.

"Did you leave a note in my locker?" I ask, ignoring her question. She shakes her head. "Jordan?" I ask him, and I am hoping he says yes.

"Like a love letter?" He looks confused. "Look, you're hot and all, but it would be like fucking Alex if we ever did it."

Alex punches him in the gut. "Shut up." Then he turns to look at me, his face full of genuine concern. "What's wrong?"

I look at Alex as I am retrieving the letter from my bag and handing it over to him. Everyone in the car takes turns reading the letter, and they all have the same reaction: deafening silence. We all know what this means, that somehow my secret is out, and someone knows about witches. Or even it's the witch who is playing this as a sick joke, but regardless, it sounds like a threat. One that I can't take lightly.

"Someone actually left this in your locker," Angel says from her spot in the front seat.

I nod.

"You have any idea who?" Jordan asks.

I shake my head, words failing me at the moment.

"Maybe it's a prank," Paris points out. "Some other witch is trying to mess with you."

"It doesn't seem like it's a prank."

"Besides, why would someone want to mess with me?" I ask, trying to keep my voice calm. I want nothing more than all this to be a prank or some messed-up joke.

"You're going to be queen, Lexi," Alex says as if it's the most obvious thing in the world. "People want what you have. The power you're going to possess, the things you can do for our people. People tend to be jealous of stuff like that, especially witches."

"It's probably a prank. I wouldn't read too much into it for now," Paris adds. "Don't let this stress you out when it can just be a jealous witch with no life and a boatload of bitterness in her.

On the car ride home, that's what I try to think about: how they're probably right, how I may be reading too much into it because that's what I am always prone to do. So I take a deep breath and try to think of anything else. One question does remain in my head, though: How did Christian hear my heartbeat?

Chapter 3

I lean my head against the door. I shut my bedroom door and take a couple of breaths. Today has been such a long day, and I am glad it's almost done. I look around my room, trying to steady my heart, before I notice a book on top of my bed. I grab the book in my hands and see that there's a letter attached with my mother's penmanship.

> My sweet baby girl,
>
> With starting your senior year, you are almost ending a chapter in your life and beginning another one. Your grandmother gave me this book when I was a bit older than you. In this book, you will learn everything there is to be an amazing witch and an even better high priestess. Be cautious with this book. The spells in here can be dangerous when put into the wrong hands. I love you, my sweet Alexandra. I can't wait to see all the great things you will do with it.

I have seen the book a few times. My grandmother has shown it to me. It's our family's spell book. It was passed down from generation to generation. It's a brown leather book with different types of papers in filing its contents. This book has been passed around for generations since the first high priestess, to my mother, and now to me. When I was just child, I would have given anything to read it in its entirety. Now I can't help but hesitate to open it up.

I love magic. I love the idea of my powers rushing through all my veins as I practice casting a spell, but now the weight of it all crushes my shoulders, and it's almost like it's hard to breathe. I caress the cover of the book, in here lies my past and my future, the history of my family and all the things we can do. I take a deep breath and open the book, losing myself in the words written by the great witches before me.

I wake up to complete darkness with the spell book still in my hands. I look around, and it's late. The alarm clock on my bedside table reads 12:30 p.m. I don't even remember falling asleep. I missed dinner, but I don't seem hungry. I sit up and immediately notice that there's a smell around the room, one that wasn't there before—a unique smell. It's almost like the smell of the forest. I feel the midnight breeze coming through the window, which is weird because I don't remember opening it. My mom probably did when she came in. I walk to the window to close it when I see a figure.

"Hello," I say loud enough that it echoes around the now empty street. No response, just staring. I repeat again, this time more forcefully, "Hello."

The figure is in a hoodie and stares at me for a moment longer but doesn't respond. I grab my phone to shine the flashlight or call someone. But by the time I grab my phone and head to look out the window, the figure is long gone, with no trace of them anywhere. The first thought that comes into my head is that maybe the same person who sent me that letter today was just out my window, but I quickly dismiss it because, again, that is a rabbit hole I just don't want to go through. I look around the street, and nothing comes up at first. I think maybe I imagined it, or I am just tired, or my mind is playing tricks on me after the day I have. So I close my window, lock it, and climb into bed, hoping that my brain will turn off and that all thoughts about this letter, mysterious figure, and my coronation will just go away.

Chapter 4

FRIDAY NIGHT-LIGHTS

Friday comes along, and I haven't gotten another letter, so I am beginning to assume it was just a stupid prank, and I can sleep at peace. There have been no more mysterious figures outside my window or sound tree branches breaking. So when I walk into school today with Angel and Paris by my side, I decide to put it in the back of my head for now.

Tonight happens to be the first football game of the season, and for the first time in months, I am in my cheerleading uniform, roaming around the halls of school. My hair, which is normally curled brown hair, is straightened and held away from my face by a white and black bow. My cheerleading uniform, matching the bow with our school colors, is tasteful, a long-sleeve top, not showing any more than an inch in the midriff area, and a skirt that stops midthigh.

Across the hall, I see Christian, and like every morning for the past three days, my eyes immediately gravitate towards him. It's almost a routine. Every day, I go to my locker, and he's there; he is at his. Getting his book like every normal student in school, yet I can't help but be fixated on him. No matter where I go, he is always in my line of sight, in the cafeteria, on my way to class, or even in the parking lot. My body has become hyperaware of him, and the hairs on the back of my neck always stand at attention when he's near.

Today, Christian isn't alone. His friend Jackson accompanies him to his locker, and they both laugh as if they have no care in the world.

Christian is wearing our school's football jersey, which I just learned yesterday. He is now our new running back. He runs his long fingers through his dark brown curls as his eyes roam the hall. I've noticed he does that plenty. When he thinks no one is looking, he looks around, almost as if he is always on alert, waiting for something to happen.

Jackson, who also has a football jersey on, happens to glance over at me, and before I notice, he's whispering in Christian's ear with a grin plastered on his face. A second goes by, and Christian turns to me, and the moment our eyes meet, a lump forms in my throat.

This has happened multiple times since we first met. Our eyes will lock for what seems like forever, and every time, I feel my body start to heat up, and my heart starts to accelerate. It's almost like I have an intense schoolgirl crush that decides never to go away even though I know I shouldn't. I can't have feelings for anyone, not with my coronation months away, yet I find myself always thinking of Christian, even when he's not around. I have had a total of two conversations with him; however, my mind and body seem to go haywire when he's near. I can't explain it, and I definitely don't want to explore it. I think.

"What do you think?" Angel's voice sounds like a distant echo in the wind even though she is just a few steps away from me. Her voice pulls me from the magnetic pull—that is, Christian and his eyes. I look over to find a pair of green perplexed eyes looking back at me. I must have zoned again. Damn it.

"What did you say?"

Paris shuts her locker and looks over in Christian's direction. "Angel was asking you if you wanted to meet up at my house to get ready for my party, but it seems like your mind is elsewhere."

"I'm sorry."

I can feel heat consume my face. This isn't the first time that the girls have caught me staring at Christian, and I, for some reason, doubt that it will be the last time.

"I would love to."

"Why don't you go talk to him?" Angel asks.

I shake my head. "Why would I do that?"

"Don't insult us." Paris rolls her eyes. "You are practically drooling. Just go up to him, invite him to the party, and get it over with."

31

I shake my head because even though a part of me is tempted, I know that I can't. There was a reason that I broke it off with Johan. I can't date right now. Especially, I can't date a human. It wouldn't be fair to either of us. Christian just piques my interest because he's a new student, not because I want to be with him.

"You know I can't."

"It's a party. I am not asking you to marry the guy, but obviously, he caught your interest, and that doesn't happen to you often." Paris grabs my shoulders and gives a squeeze. "So stop overthinking and just talk to him."

Before I can even object or explain to her all the ways this is a bad idea and that I should ignore her advice, Paris and Angel walk away to class. I stand at my locker, contemplating what to do. I refuse to look at Christian across the hall. I know I shouldn't. I know that this is the responsibility thing to do, to walk away and try to fight whatever it is that makes me want to be close to him. I don't even know him, and I have a feeling that if I take Paris's advice, I won't be able to turn back. Johan's face pops up in my head, and the hurt that flashes before his eyes when I tell him that we can't be together anymore tips the scales for me, and I decide to just walk away from this.

My feet aren't even able to move before Christian pops up in front of me. His muscular frame blocks my view of my classroom. He's so tall that I have to take a step back so I can look up at him.

"Christian" is the only word that comes out of my mouth as his deep brown eyes look me over.

"Ask me," he says. His voice is calm, but I can't help but think of it as a command.

I raise my eyebrow at him, confused as to what he's saying. There's no possible way he overheard Paris. The hallway is crowded with students, making entirely too much noise, and he is standing almost twenty feet away, not to mention Paris isn't even being loud. That can't possibly be what he means, right?

"Excuse me."

Christian leans on the locker, and I can't help but catch his scent of trees, almost as if he is just in the woods. "Ask me to the party, Alexandra."

"How did you know about that?"

He shrugs his shoulders and looks at my head, ignoring my question. "You changed your hair."

"It's game day," I say as if that just explains why my hair is suddenly straightened. The warning bell sounds overhead, signaling that I'm going to be late if I don't get moving, but I can't bring myself to move when Christian is so close. His presence is overwhelming. He's so close, and his frame can swallow me whole. "How did you know about Paris's party?"

Again, another shrug. "Are you going to invite me?"

"You're ignoring my question." I roll my eyes in annoyance. Why is he deflecting?

"You're ignoring mine," he volleys back at me, his eyes never leaving my own, challenging me to invite him, almost as if he can see I'm at war with the mere thought of it. Johan's face creeps back in my head, but immediately, I push it away. I don't know what it is about Christian, but now that he is so close, I forget about my how plans to ignore him and give in.

"Fine, the party is at Paris's house tonight at ten. Would you like to go?"

A small smile adorns his lips as he nods. "See you then."

Just like that, he leaves me in the hallway without saying another word with one thought remaining. He never answers my question.

Chapter 5

The sounds of the people occupying the bleachers are deafening as the football team takes the field again. The score is 39–34, with the other team ahead of us. The energy is electric as the lights beam on both teams on the field. It's been a close game, but now our team has the ball with twelve seconds left. You can sense the competition in the air, and our team's need for a win. If we get one more touchdown, we win, but the other school's defense is giving our school, the knights, a run for its money.

All night, I haven't been able to take my eyes off Christian and my brother. They're really good together, my brother being the quarterback and Christian always knowing where to go to catch Alex's throw. Something about the way he moves with such grace and force, taking control of the field. I am in awe. His friends Devin and Jackson aren't far-off either. They are all in sync, defending each other and fast as lightning. I have never seen anything like them. Alex's arm has gotten better than last season, if that is even possible, and he's practically a canon. The scouts are going to eat him up this year.

I have been having fun also, cheering in front of so many people. I forgot how exhilarating it is. My smile has been huge since I've stepped onto the field, and I don't think it's going anywhere soon. In the bleachers, I see my parents, my father's booming voice above all others as he screams at our team.

"Let's go, knights. Let's go," we cheer as the next play starts to go.

Immediately, the ball is in Alex's hands as he looks for an opening, and he finds one with Christian who's dodging players left and right. Alex throws the ball, and like magic, Christian catches it, and he's off. Running as fast as he can, but a player from the other team, number 67, chases after him, and it looks like he's going to catch him.

It's nail-biting, and before I know it, I find myself mumbling, "Run faster, Christian."

Seconds after those words leave my mouth, Christian runs at least two times faster than before rushing through the field, leaving number 67 in the dust as he runs the remainder of twenty-two yards, and as he scores a touchdown without anyone even coming close to him, and the crowd goes wild.

The team chases after him in cheers as the losing team leaves the field with their heads hung low in defeat. Even the other cheerleaders around me are screaming, but me, I stand still. An unsettling feeling fills my body as I think of what I just saw. How did he all of a sudden get so fast? It was almost like he was an animal moving through that field. Is it a coincidence that he moved that quickly after what I just said, or did he somehow hear me? Everyone is cheering, from the bleachers to the cheerleaders and the football team, but when I look across the field, I see jersey number 1 frozen in place, looking in my direction. Even though I can't see his eyes from this far, I know Christian is looking back at me.

Paris's house is a big colonial along the edge of town. It is the perfect place to have a party because there are not many neighbors, so no one will make any noise complaints. By the time we head upstairs into her room, it's almost nine o'clock, and the party starts about ten to ten thirty, so we have some time to get ready. Paris takes a shower first while Jordan, Alex, and Johan get everything settled downstairs while celebrating their first win of the year.

Angel starts to unpack her bag to get ready to go to the guest bathroom but stops before she leaves the room.

"Lexi," she says, her voice barely above a whisper.

"Yes." I look up to see her at the door.

Her green eyes find mine, and they're filled with something like sadness. "How did you know leaving Johan was the right thing to do?"

I look at her, a little taken aback by the unexpected question, but it doesn't take me long to answer because, to this day, it haunts my thoughts.

"I guess I kind of felt like there was this piece of my life, a big piece in my life, that I was hiding from him," I explain. "At first,

I thought it was going to be okay, but the closer I got to the coronation, the more it became clear to me that it wasn't fair to him. I couldn't lie to him anymore and have him expecting something that may never be. He's human. He couldn't understand what I would have to go through. Besides, he shouldn't have to share the burden of keeping a secret that isn't his from everyone he has ever known." I take a big sigh, the feeling of sadness creeping through my voice. "I couldn't do that to him."

She nods, and the silence that takes over the room is thick, like there is a secret or a connection I am not making.

"Why do you ask?"

Angel fiddles with her clothes, avoiding eye contact with me. "I just figured lies are never good. Might has well end it than hurting an innocent person."

Something about her tone, the way the words come out her mouth, and the look of sadness and understanding in her eyes. It's at that moment that I know that we aren't talking about Johan and me. She's hiding something, something she doesn't want me to know. I can sense it.

I think she realizes that she says too much because before I can ask what I want to. She shakes her head and says, "I am going to shower," as she practically runs out of the room.

I wait until Paris comes out and showers after her. While I soak under the hot water, I can't help but think of Christian, the fact that he is such a mystery. I know nothing about him, and by the looks of it, I never will. It seems like the more I try to pay attention to him, the more I get confused. All I tend to see is that he's surprisingly fast and moved here with friends, which in itself is bizarre. I have never seen anyone run that fast, and it seems like I am the only one who noticed. I want to talk to him and figure out what's there. Maybe if I knew him more, I can steer clear of him because something inside me tells me that if I get too close, I'm asking for trouble, yet I can't walk away.

After the shower, I get dressed. My outfit for the night is a red velvet halter top that pushes my boobs all the up to the sky, with buttons down the center, a pair of skinny black jeans, and red heels to match. I apply the basic makeup, along with winged eyeliner and red lipstick that makes it look like I kissed a beautiful red apple. I look at my hair, and for some reason, Christian's words come to me: *You changed your hair.* So instead of flat ironing my hair again, I let the curls fall and cascade down my breast as I pull some of it behind my ear. I pin it down with bobby pins. I look in the mirror and take a breath. I try to convince myself that I got all pretty because it's the first party of the year, not because I want to impress Christian.

But I fail.

Chapter 6

The party is in full swing at around eleven thirty, and by now, I have had a couple of drinks. The music is bumping in the living room, coming off Johan's speakers while almost everyone in our class is dancing. The party was mostly for the seniors, but a couple of juniors have been invited and some freshmen as well, but they are actually working at the party, passing out cups, cleaning, and standing at the door. I have seen this redheaded freshman boy with glasses clean the counter and even offer people drinks, anything to feel close to the seniors, I guess.

I head into the kitchen, where there is mostly no one in there except a couple of girls taking selfies and Johan leaning on the counter with a red solo cup in his hand.

He looks up when I come in. "Hey." He has a dazzling smile covering his face as he takes me in. The same smile charm, but now that I look at it, it makes me feel nothing compared to the one smile I got from Christian on the first of school.

"How come you're hiding in here"? I shake my head, trying to push away the thoughts of Christian. He didn't even show up. Why ask me to invite him if he wasn't going to be here?

"The music is giving me a major headache. But I'll be fine."

"I have Tylenol," I say, and I'm about to ask him if he wants me to go get it, but I just stay quiet because of the look he's given me. He looks me over and gives me that same look he always gave me when we were together, like he was in love. I try to avoid his eyes, but they stare deeply at me, and it almost makes me feel uncomfortable.

"You look amazing tonight." His words are laced with what can only be described as longing.

"Johan." My voice is soft, but with that one word, I hope he gets the point and drops it.

He shakes his head and looks down at his cup. "I mean that just as a friend, Lexi." His eyes look away, but not before I see the pain behind them. "I know where we stand." He then takes a long gulp from his cup, drowning his words.

This is a bad idea to be friends with him when it's clear that there's something here. I know that I will always love Johan; he was my first love. The boy with the sweet smile and kind heart, and I'm aware that I'm being selfish by keeping him so close, but what am I supposed to do? Cut him off, hurt him even more than I already did. That wouldn't be fair to him. None of this is fair to him. It's a complicated situation that we're in, and it's either let him go completely or hold on to a piece of normalcy y that I have.

"Congratulations on winning the game."

I try to steer the conversation from the awkward silence that has taken over the space between us.

He gives me a small smile that doesn't quite reach his eyes and whispers, "Thanks."

Seconds later, in comes Paris stumbling through the door. "Oh, there you are."

She puts her arms around me and gives me a drunken smile. The smell of the alcohol in her breath is nauseating, so much so that I am tempted to give her a breath mint. Her red hair is sticking to her forehead with sweat, and her shoes have somehow have disappeared off her feet.

She looks me up and down and frowns when she notices my empty hands. "Where is your drink?"

"I have had enough, and I think so have you."

"Oh, shut up." She rolls her eyes and then points at Johan, a frown appearing on her signature red lips. "I mean, what kind of man doesn't make sure his ex has a drink in her hand? I mean, I know it's over, but be a gentleman."

I cringe at her words, hoping that Johan doesn't take it the wrong way. I look over at him, but he seems to find the whole thing amusing.

"I'll go get her one," he says, a big smile taking over his face while Paris is barely standing steady next to me. I'm a lightweight, and so is she, and we both drank plenty.

Johan goes around the counter to make me a drink while Paris looks at me and smiles. "I need to go find Angel, baby girl." Then she leave a sloppy kiss on my cheek and heads out the door the same way she came in, with a smile on her face and not a care in the world.

"Still want it?" Johan comes back with my drink in hand.

I shrug. "Why not?" I take it out of his hand. I want to be as carefree as Paris is right now, so I take a big swing and smile.

I finish that drink, grab another one, and practically chug that one up just as fast.

"Well, okay." Johan laughs, and as he says this, a song comes up, and instantly, I smile.

"Perfect Strangers" by Jonas Blue fills my ears. I love this song, and Johan knows it.

Johan looks at me and offers his hand. "Wanna dance?"

Maybe it's the alcohol or the fact that I would do anything to feel like it did before, last year when we were just kids enjoying each other's company. Where I didn't hurt Johan, where thoughts of my coronation plagued me wherever I went, or even to a time before my attraction to Christian started to take over my life. So I smile at Johan and say yes because the one thing I want to do now is forget about life and enjoy the moment.

Next thing I know, he pulls me close and walks me to the living room where everyone is careless, enjoying the first party of senior year. He leads me to the center of floor, and our hips start to sway.

The alcohol in me makes me brave, and I am swaying my hips and throwing away every thought in my head. Johan's return, my coronation, the letter, and Christian fly out of my brain, and immediately, the only thing I know is the rhythm of the music. Johan spins me around a couple of times, and for some reason, I giggle and fall into his chest. When I look up, his eyes are on me, and for a second, I think he's gonna kiss me, but instead, he spins one more time, and I bump into Angel.

"Where have you been?" I ask her over the loud music because I haven't seen her since the party started, but before she can answer, Paris comes up beside us.

"Why aren't you dancing?" she says as she sways her hips, and we both join her.

I can feel the eyes of the boys on us, but I don't care. I'm having fun.

I don't remember them coming around us, but Jordan, Johan, and Alex are all dancing too, and for a second, it feels like it's just me and my friends on the floor. All the pressure of my life flows away with the music, and all I care about is this moment, with them dancing and having fun. I want this to last forever, being fun teenagers, drunk and together. So I enjoy it and try not to think about yesterday or tomorrow but now, and it feels good, so freaking good.

I wrap my arms around Paris and Angel. "I love you, guys." The words come out slurred and drunk, but I can't mean it more.

"Ugh, I lovre youuu too," Angel slurs her words, and it's cute because she never drinks, so when she does, she's easily intoxicated.

Paris kisses my cheek. "This is going to be our best year yet. I can feel it."

And we all jump around and sing the song at the top of our lungs until it finishes.

When the music ends, reality starts to set in. We are not alone, and I frown a little, wishing I could hold on to that moment for a little bit longer. I feel the hairs on the back of my neck stand, and instantly, I look around the crowd while my friends keep dancing around me. I know he's here. I can feel it. I search around the room, and right in the corner, there he is, surrounded by people, yet he stands out like a sore thumb, Christian.

Immediately, I'm stuck. My feet won't move. The blur of teenagers dancing is just that, a blur. All the alcohol rushes to my head, and I can feel my cheeks get hot from the drinks. My eyes can't leave his. He looks really good, wearing a pair of black jeans that hang at his hips, a tight white T-shirt with a leather jacket that covers his toned, muscled arms. I think about having my fingers trace each and every muscle on his body. The thought of touching him makes my insides curl, and it almost feels wrong to even imagine, so I push the thought out of my head.

He looks me up and down, and my stomach drops from his stare. He's here. He really came. After I didn't see him for a while, I assumed he wasn't going to come, but now he's here, and his eyes aren't leaving my own.

I take deep breath, gather all the courage the alcohol in my body will allow me to, and walk over to him.

With each step, my body warms up, and before I know it, a smile has reached my face as I make my way up to him. "You made it?"

"We decided to stop by," he says over the loud music. *We? Who's we?* I don't see his friends anywhere. Maybe they walked away before I could see them. How long have they been here? "You looked like you were enjoying yourself." His long finger points to the dance floor.

I blush. He saw me dance like a complete idiot. "I was," and I have to scream because the music somehow has gotten louder. Maybe this was a bad idea? Inviting him here.

"Do you want a drink?"

He shakes his head lightly. "I don't drink."

I bite my lip, not knowing what to say. I was hoping he would say yes so I can take him into the kitchen, where there's more privacy and less noise.

Christian's brown eyes rake over the party and then to my pouted lips, and a look of understanding crosses his features. "Do you have water?"

I smile and lead him into the kitchen. Immediately, as we enter the swinging door, the music is significantly quieter. It's practically empty, except for the one couple in the corner swallowing each other's tongues.

I grab a glass and fill it with water. "Ice?"

"No thanks."

I hand him the cup, and for a second, our fingers touch. I feel a rush circulate through my body. If I didn't know what magic felt like, I would assume it felt like this: that one touch brings my skin to tingles. All the hair in the back of my neck stands up, and my heart starts racing. It's almost electric. I pull my hand away quickly, too drunk to be able to process what just happened.

"Thank you," he mumbles.

"Of course." I look down at my hand. Now that we're alone, I really do fear that I made a mistake. I thought that the alcohol would make me brave, but if I am being honest, I am still intimidated by him. What am I supposed to talk to him about? How do I even start a conversation? My nerves start to get the best of me, and after a couple of more seconds of silence, I break and blurt the first thing that comes to mind.

"The game," I think loudly.

He looks at me, puzzled, most likely thinking I am a crazy person. I internally groan. That was not as smooth as I had hoped.

I compose myself and elaborate further, "You were really good at the game. Congratulations on the win."

"It was mostly a team effort," he says, and I can't help but roll my eyes.

The team was great, but almost every touch down he made, and I can't tell if he's faking humility or if he actually is humble.

"Of course." I smile at him, and I can't stop the sarcasm that inhabits my voice. Christian looks me over, his eyes searching for something in mine before he looks directly at my lips. I can't help but take advantage of this and admire his face for how close he is. There's no scar, no freckle, not even a damn pimple. He actually looks perfect. His eyelashes are long and decorate his deep brown eyes, like curtains to the window of his soul. Then there are his lips, plump and pink. From here, they look so soft, and for a split second, I think about what they will feel like against my own.

Quickly as that thought comes, I toss it to the back of my brain because I am not trying to date him. I can't date. I am just figuring out why I am so drawn to him and how to make it stop. *Yeah, keep on telling yourself that.* My subconscious rolls her eyes. What am I doing with Christian? Why did I actually invite him? Most importantly, why do I never want him to leave?

"What's your deal?" The words escape my mouth before I can filter them out, but I honestly don't care. I need to know. The way that this boy fascinates me, the fact that I can't stop thinking of him, it isn't normal, and I need to know why.

He looks taken aback by the question. "What do you mean?"

I roll my eyes. Can he be so dense? "I mean, what makes you, you? I know nothing about you, not your last name. Where did you come from?"

Why do I care so much? I don't say the last question out loud, but I want to.

For the first time since I have given him his drink, he takes a sip of water, avoiding the question. Or perhaps thinking of a response. He takes a couple of beats before he says, "I'm not that interesting."

"I doubt that."

"Why do you say that?"

"I just know." I know that there is something under that surface, something drawing me in. There has to be.

Christian shakes his head and takes a step toward me. "I know nothing about you."

"You know more about me than I do of you," which is true. He knows where I'm from, my last name, and my family.

"What's your last name?" I ask before he does what I've come to notice is his number one talent: deflecting.

He smiles a slow, sexy smile that almost knocks me off my feet. "Castillo." His Spanish accent creeps through as he says his last name.

"Christian Castillo," I say it.

Tasting the alcohol and his name on my tongue, it's intoxicating, just like being around him.

"My turn to ask a question." He takes a step closer, and this time, his scent of pine infiltrates my nostrils and leaves me light-headed. "How long have you been cheerleading?"

"Nine years. Where were you born?"

"Florida." He takes a couple of more steps, getting closer. Heat radiates off him in waves. It's practically making me sweat just being near him. "Is that guy you were dancing with, Johan?" Christian urges my eyes to look at his own as if he can find the answer to his next question in them. "Is he your boyfriend?"

This time, the question surprises me. I didn't realize he was watching me for so long. I almost don't answer, just because it feels wrong speaking of Johan when I know he's just in the other room. It feels like I'm betraying him, but I know if I don't answer, he won't let me ask him any more questions, and the need to get to know him is overpowering all my senses right now.

I shake my head slightly. "He's my ex."

He nods. His face is unreadable, so I can't tell if he's content with that answer or annoyed. I don't know why I hope for it to be the former, but I do.

"You always dance so closely with your exes?" He gets closer, and this time, he lowers his face so he is inches away from my own.

We are practically breathing the same breath. That's how close we are. His smell encircles around us, making me almost dizzy. I look into his eyes. They're attentive, but something lies beneath them, a gleam of jealousy, maybe, although I don't know what he will be jealous about.

I shake my head because that's all I can manage at the moment. He's so close I can't concentrate. It's too much. I want to touch him so badly my hand starts to twitch. My eyes make contact with his brown ones, and for a second, I am lost in them. They're so deep, and I swear I see a gleam of gold in them.

He stares down at me. "Breathe, Alexandra."

And as if the words were the keys to the lungs, which all the air was in, I let the breath I didn't know I was holding escape my lungs and in between the air that encircles us.

God, why is he so close? Why can't I talk? My head is spinning, and I don't know if it's the alcohol or if it's the proximity of Christian. But a part of me feels as if he's doing this on purpose, trying to distract me from getting to know him more.

So I take a step back, but he follows. "Why are you here, Christian?"

"I was invited," he says casually, and it makes me jealous how he can have such an effect on me, and I have none on him.

"Is that all?"

"Do you want it to be something more, Alexandra?"

Again, the words fall out of his mouth with such ease it annoys me.

I ignore his question because I myself am not even sure of the response. "I told you, you can call me Lexi. I don't like Alexandra."

He shrugs his shoulders and places his hands on the counter behind me, caging me in.

"I do." His voice is deep, and he looks at me as if I am his prey or next meal. It's uneasy, but not in the worst way.

Before I can say anything else, his right-hand moves to a strand of my hair that has escaped from behind my ear. He twirls it around his index finger as he examines it closely.

It's too much. He's too close. It's overwhelming, suffocating, and intoxicating all at once. I don't know whether to pull away or move in closer. I can feel my heartbeat start to race and the alcohol making its way through me, but I feel something else. The control I have on my magic is starting to loosen involuntarily. Maybe because I'm drunk and distracted, but I don't feel the strong hold on my powers as I did before.

"I like your hair better this way," Christian says.

It's almost as if he was saying it to himself instead of me. I want to tell him I don't care, but I had a feeling when I did my hair tonight that it would get his attention.

He's avoiding my question. "Christian"—his attention turns back to my eyes—"you didn't answer my question. Why are you here?"

His eyes search mine deeply as if he's pondering. He wants to answer the question or ignore it. It takes a beat, and then, before I know it, he grabs hold of my chin and speaks into my lips so softly I'm not sure I hear him correctly.

"You."

The word registers in my head, but I don't have time to unpack what I'm feeling.

I don't know what it is, if it's the proximity or his touch or maybe even his confession, but my palms get sweat, and before I know, I feel my magic start to rise.

The glass that Christian had before shakes on the counter next to me. Both Christian and I look at it, him with a confused look on his face and myself with a horrified one. I know I'm doing it. I can feel my magic getting out of control.

"What the hell?" Christian says as the cup shakes harder, and the water inside starts to boil. I try to stop, try to breathe and calm down, but my mind is running a mile a minute, and I can barely concentrate.

I know the cup is going to shatter, but I can't stop it. This is the first time I have ever exposed my magic in front of a human, not that he knows what's exactly going on. He doesn't let go of me as he goes to grab the glass.

But I stop him. "Don't," I practically yell. If the glass shatters, it can cut him, and that's the last thing I want. His eyes look up at me, and although I expect to see panic or confusion, I see the opposite. I see understanding. It confuses me. Why is he not freaked out? A cup shaking and rumbling next to us while water boils in it, and he's looking at me like it's a regular day.

I don't get a chance to analyze what I'm feeling or what's going on because the door swings open hard as hell, revealing Paris, Johan, Devin, and Jackson right on the other side.

I'm startled by the sound that I try to take a step but realize I can't because of the counter. I look at the water glass to see the boiling has stopped, and so had the shaking, almost as if it never happened. I look at Christian to see if maybe I imagined the whole scenario, but he's no longer looking at me but at Johan, whose face is laced with anger.

Johan looks at Christian, then at me, and then back at Christian as he is putting two and two together. He looks hurt, mad even, and without thinking about it, I quickly take a step away from Christian. Christian notices and follows me as if he's marking his territory like a dog.

"What's going on here?" Johan's voice is calm, too calm/

"There you are, Castillo?" Jackson grins and then looks at us. "I thought I saw you walk in here, but I didn't realize you weren't alone. Want to play a friendly game of beer pong?"

Johan's eyes are burning into me, and I can feel the room spinning, all the alcohol making its rounds in me at that exact moment. The magic that I didn't intend to use taking a small toll on me isn't helping.

"Lexi?"

"Um," I say, my voice caught in my throat. What the hell am I supposed to tell him? I don't even know what was going on. A minute ago, I made a glass shake to the point of almost shattering, and now it's almost as if it never happened. I think I'm going crazy.

"We were talking." Christian looks at Johan, and for a second, it's like he's angry. "Is that a problem?"

"When you're alone with her while she's drunk, and we know nothing about you? Hell yes," Johan says or practically shouts. Johan takes a step toward Christian, and I know this isn't going to end good, if I don't intervene.

"I'm not drunk," I say as the room continues to spin, faster this time. I need to sit down. The drinks I had before have taken their toll. I've never had jungle juice before, but I am pretty sure I am not having it again.

Paris laughs, her usually pale cheeks red, and she's wobbly. I know she's far gone as much as I am. "Want a shot?"

"What the hell do you think I'm gonna do to her?" Christian says, and I see his hands form fists by his side. I don't like where this is going. His jaw clenches, and suddenly, he's in front of me, blocking Johan from my view.

"Let's not make this into a problem, gentlemen," Devin intercepts, and his accent makes me smile.

Johan takes a step toward Christian. "I don't know you or your intentions."

It's like neither of them is hearing the rest of us. It's just them and their egos occupying the room, and if I am being honest, it's frustrating.

Christian echoes his movements. "Right now, my intention is to punch you. That good with you?"

Now I have to intercept. This is getting out of hand. I walk in between them both, placing my hands in the air. "Stop it," I say a little too loud. My stance is wide, and my feet are far apart, trying to balance myself and keep myself from face-planting.

"You're drunk, Alexandra," Christian says. "Let's get you to sit down," and he goes to take ahold of me, but Johan grabs me first.

"Don't touch her." I can smell the drinks on his breath. He's been drinking a lot. And so have I by the way the floor is starting to feel wobbly. I try to think of all the drinks I consumed, and it doesn't even feel like that much, but I guess I wasn't taking into account that I haven't eaten anything in hours, and the last time I drank was months ago at Paris's beginning of summer bash. This is a mistake, the drinking, this argument, all of it.

"What's your problem, dude?" Paris asks Johan. "He's just trying to help. Let him be her hot knight in armor shining."

"I can help."

Jackson laughs as I lean into Johan. I feel like I am gonna be sick. "You're drunk too."

"Let her go," Christian says, and his voice sounds icy cold. It brings shivers down my back, but lately, I have noticed that his voice always seems to do that.

I don't understand how this all went so south so fast. It's confusing and making my head want to explode.

Johan holds on to me tightly, and it hurts, so I try to push him off me, but he doesn't budge.

"I am not drunk. Stop acting like kids."

Even though the words come out of my mouth, I don't believe them. Anyone with eyes can tell I am wasted, but I refuse for them to act as though I am the last toy in the toy box and act as though I am not even here.

"I got you, Lexi," Johan whispers in my ear as I turn and make eye contact with Christian.

He looks pissed, his jaw clenched, and eyes narrowed at the arm Johan has my waist. It's almost like he wants to rip me off him.

I don't know why, but Christian's mean glare sparks something in me, and as much as I don't want to hurt Johan's feelings, a part of me doesn't want to make Christian feel that way either. So with all the strength I can muster up in my drunken state, I push Johan off me and stand in between the two of them.

"I'm fine."

"You're not fine," Christian says, and his voice sounds annoyed. I should be the one annoyed. They are the ones being jackasses.

Johan moves in to grab me again. "Don't talk to her."

"You touch her again and. I will rip your hands off."

All I hear is a ton of screaming after that comment, but the only thing I can make out is my voice saying softly, "I'm gonna fall."

Seconds later, I feel my head hit a hard surface.

Chapter 7

I'm running barefoot in a dark forest. My feet move fast from under me, carrying me away from something in the night. The crunching sound of the leaves that seem to grow louder under my feet echoes around the forest as my heart races a mile a minute. A light wind breezes through the flowing, long white dress that adorns my body, giving me goose bumps all over my skin. I'm panting, running, out breath, and I keep looking behind me. I can feel like something is gaining on me, but I can't quite figure out what. I weave through trees as if my life depended on it. *Why am I running? Most importantly, who am I running from?*

I can hear the sound of my heart thumping in my ears as I make it down the dark, steep hill. I trip over my own feet and end up rolling down the hill. My body flips over itself as I make my way down the slippery ground. My head hits the bottom hard, but I don't have time to assess the pain. I stand up quickly, not wanting to risk getting caught by what's chasing me. I look up at the top of the hill to see nothing, but instead, I hear a howl in the close distance. I take off fast, but I can feel something dripping down my forehead. Before I touch it, I know what it is. I'm bleeding. It must have been from the fall, but I don't care. I have to go. No destination, just away from here and now. The sense of urgency overcomes me.

Panic and fear fuel my body and scrapped up my legs as they force me to move and create space between me and whatever is chasing me in these woods. Whatever is behind me is gaining quickly. I can feel it. Whatever it is, it's getting closer, and I'm panicking.

A voice in my head tells me, *Run faster, Alexandra. They're coming.*

I know that voice, the deep tone, and the way it makes the hair in the back of my head stand at attention. It's Christian. How is he in my head? Why is he telling me to run? I run as fast as I can although the hit to my head is taking its toll. The loss of blood makes me dizzy, and I can't help it. I now start stumbling and bumping into trees, using most of my energy to keep me up and from falling. Blood drips down my face, and it's getting harder to see straight.

I lean onto a tree, trying to steady my balance and catch my breath, but it's no use. I feel my legs start to fail me as I start to fall down.

I can't, I say to my thoughts, hoping Christian can hear me, hoping he'll come and get me, hoping he can save me from whatever I am running from.

I see a shadow coming toward me, and for a second, I think it's the same thing that I heard howling. I stay there, my upper body leaning on the tree, trying not to pass out. The dark shadow gets closer, walking as if I were prey and they were a predator. A human form begins to take shape, and in a couple of seconds, it comes into view, a familiar face appearing.

"Johan," I say weakly.

A small part of me can't help but be relieved. Another part is confused as to why he's here, but I don't have the time nor the energy to question it.

He walks toward me but doesn't say anything. His footsteps are light as air, and I don't hear the leaves crunching under him. He gets to me, and his once-blue eyes, full of light, are now dark and hollow.

"You're bleeding, babe," he says as he touches a speck of blood from my forehead.

Did he call me babe?

"Help me." My voice is small as I watch him examine the blood on his finger, as if it's the most fascinating thing he has ever seen. His eyes don't look at me, and he just sits there, not helping me up.

"I can't," he says, still not looking at me, still staring at the drop of blood in his hand.

I hear the sound of rustling trees in front of me, and suddenly, a huge wolf pops out. It's the biggest wolf I have ever seen. Its fur is pitch black, and it stands about six feet tall. His stance is threatening as he stops and looks at Johan and me and growls. My vision is blurry, but I can see his sharp teeth. This is what I was running from. It has to be. A werewolf was chasing me down the woods, but why?

The wolf's fur is pitch black and almost blends into the night if it weren't for its brown eyes with gold specks. Something too familiar about them, as if I've seen them before. Before I realize it, I know who they belong to. Those eyes that mesmerize me. They make me weak, and my heart pounds like a drum when they bear into my soul. Those eyes belong to him.

Christian.

I wake to blinding sunlight on my face, and I sit up to see that I am in Paris's bed. The room is empty—no sign of anyone being in here other than myself. I groan as I remember my dream and all the questions it raises. However, I don't have time to pick it apart due to a massive headache that plagues my head because of last night's activities.

The memories of last night swarm through my mind like a tornado as I get out of bed and head to the bathroom to brush my teeth and grab a painkiller from the cabinet. Christian came to the party; he was here talking with me. The things he said, the feelings he provoked, the magic in me that he spurred, it was all too much, yet not enough. I don't know what it is about him, but my curiosity is getting the best of me. Even though I know I should stay awhile, especially after last night's magic incident and the confrontation between Christian and Johan, a part of me, the selfish part, doesn't want to.

My feet take me downstairs to try to find someone else in the quiet house. As I reach the end of the white steps, I see Alex and Jordan sleeping on the adjacent couches in the living room. The house is clean, which is odd because, after last night, I would have assumed this house would be littered with red solo cups and spilled alcohol.

"Look who's up." Angel gives me a huge smile as I enter the kitchen.

She's at the stove stirring eggs in a bowl, and I am immediately envious of how she doesn't look like she has a hangover. Her blonde hair glows from the sunlight beaming off it. Her angelic face is clean, and she looks all out cheery. While I, on the other hand, am pretty sure there's still dried-up mascara under my eyes.

"Good morning."

The smell of the food is making me sick. I take a seat next to Paris, and if it wasn't for the loud groan she's let out, I would think she was dead with her head lying on the counter.

"I am making breakfast," Angel states the obvious.

I shake my head. "No offense, Angel, but I can't eat that. I feel nauseous just smelling it."

"That's what I told her." Paris picks her head up, and she looks, as I feel, just like shit. Her red hair is piled on her head in a mess that I can only compare to a bird's nest.

"Oh, stop your complaining." Angel sets her bowl down and walks over to us. "I can help."

"I doubt that."

Angel rolls her eyes and places her hand on my temple. "What are you doing?" I say, alarmed by how close she is.

"Shh." She closes her eyes, and a slight warm glow comes from her palm, the same one that always comes whenever she does her healer magic. "Heal," she says, voice soft. In seconds, the headache and nausea are gone, and I feel instantly better.

"Did you just take away my hangover?" I ask as she walks over to Paris to do the exact same thing.

She nods. Of course, she did, healer. She can't help but see people in pain. It's her healer instinct to help those in need. I'm kind of envious. I don't even have my gift, yet Angel is so in tune with her powers it's crazy. I didn't even know that she can do that.

"So you're telling me that this whole time when I was practically dying from hangovers, you can do that?" Paris looks at Angel as she makes her way back around the counter. "You think you know a person."

Angel smiles. "I didn't know I could cure hangovers until this summer."

"What happened this summer?" I ask her as I grab a strip of bacon from the plate, suddenly famished.

"Um." She glows beet red as she flips more bacon. "Someone came to me in a drunken state, and all I wanted to do was help. It just came out of instinct."

I can feel that she's not telling the whole truth. I don't know why she would withhold anything from us. She's been acting weird lately. The open and honest Angel that I knew and loved is being distant, and I don't know why. I eye her suspiciously but don't say anything because I don't want to ruin the moment by confronting her.

"Any plans today?" Paris asks as she shadows my movements by grabbing some bacon.

"Not much. I'm going over my family's spell book again."

"Good morning, ladies." Alex comes into the kitchen with Jordan in tow.

"Good morning," we all say in unison.

"You ready to leave soon. I want to hit the gym," he says after he grabs a plate Angel made for him. I don't miss the way that she practically shoves it in his hands, making him frown.

"Can I get a ride with you guys?" Jordan asks as he steals some food from Paris' plate. "My car is still in the shop."

"Sure."

"Get your own food, jackass." Paris slaps his hand off her plate and rolls her eyes.

"Your jackass." He winks at her and blows her a kiss as he walks around the island in the center of the kitchen to go get some coffee.

"You disgust me."

"I love you."

Paris rolls her eyes and turns to whisper at me, "So are we gonna talk about what happened last night?"

The images of Christian and me up and close come up in my mind, making me blush as I remember his proximity, "What are you talking about?"

"Don't do that," she says as she rolls her eyes again. "I got drunk, not amnesia."

I look to see if anyone is paying attention to our conversation, but I just see Alex and Angel on their phones while Jordan is way too focused on chewing.

"I don't know. We were just talking, and I was just asking him questions, he was asking me, next thing I know, he's coming close to me, making me distracted."

"What did you ask him?"

"His last name? Why did he come?" I bite my lip, thinking of his answer: *You.* What does that mean? Maybe I do affect him. Maybe a part of him is as intrigued as I am. Perhaps this isn't so one-sided.

"What he asked you?" Paris pulls me back from my thoughts.

"He asked how long I've been cheerleading and if Johan was my boyfriend?"

"I told you," she says, slapping my arm, and when I look at her all crazy, she elaborates, "I told you that he liked you. Why would he care if Johan was your boyfriend or not?"

"Maybe he was just curious."

Paris rolls her beautiful brown eyes, annoyed with me. "A curious man does not act like he did last night. They were both acting as if you were the last meal."

I start to blush because I know what she's saying is true. The way Christian and Johan were acting was as if I were their property, it was surprising. Don't get me wrong. It was annoying and kind of insulting how they just up and decided to ignore me and talk about me as if I wasn't there. However, at the same time, the fact that Christian was actually fighting for me brings a smile to my face. Johan, on the other hand, and I need to talk. I have never seen him like that, not even when we were dating. He was never the jealous type. The way he was acting was unacceptable. We are just friends, and I don't know what other way to put it for him. Maybe being around him as much isn't such a good idea.

"Who's they?" Alex asks, looking between Paris and me.

"Christian and Johan were fighting over your sister last night."

I shoot Paris a look. What is wrong with her? I love my brother, and he and I are as close as twins can be. I haven't even mentioned Christian to him. I know how close he is to Johan. When Johan and I called it quits, even though he encouraged it, I know that it hurt Alex not having one of his best friends around as much he used to be. Before Johan and I ended, they were inseparable. Now Johan and Alex haven't talked all summer with him being at camp, and a part of me can't help but think it's my fault knowing that Johan wouldn't have even gone if it wasn't for me. Ever since he's been back, he hasn't been the same, and I know that has taken its toll on their friendship. I know Alex loves me and will always choose me above all else, but deep down, I know he wishes it was different with Johan. Christian and him are on the team together. I don't want to say anything until there is something to say.

"It wasn't like it," I tell Alex quickly.

He raises a perfectly arched eyebrow at me. "What was it like?"

"It's not important," I say, biting my lip. I grab my phone and look at the time. "We should go, though, before Mom has a fit."

He looks at me quietly but doesn't say anything. He just nods and walks out of the room. Everyone else's eyes are on me when I look back forward.

"What?"

Angel looks at me with a mug in her pink manicured hand. "I don't ever think I've seen you lie to Alex."

"It wasn't a lie," I say too loudly, making me sound suspicious. "Besides, you weren't even there, Angel."

"We didn't have to be. Johan told us everything yesterday while he was faded as fuck," Jordan says in between bites of his food. "That dude is never gonna get over you."

That ping of guilt I always feel when I think of Johan just got bigger. The thought of Johan never getting over me is a thought I don't want to face. I don't like the idea of him pining for me forever. I want him to be happy, happy as he was when we were together, maybe even happier. I want him to find a girl and fall in love. I want him to be close to Alex and Jordan like they were before. I want him to forget about me.

"Leave her alone," Paris snaps at Jordan, and she turns to me as she rubs my back. "Lexi doesn't have to tell Alex everything, and it's not her fault Johan is some lovesick puppy who can't get a hint. She's single. He's single. She can do what she wants, and if he doesn't like tough shit."

My heart warms. Paris always has my back, even when I don't even have my own. She's someone whom I know will always be there for me at any time. I can count on her entirely.

I head out of the kitchen to grab my stuff and say goodbye to everyone, promising to see them on Monday for another week in hell, and then I'm off with Alex.

The car ride is silent as we drive through the highway, no music, no words just the sound of the cars around us and the wheels on the road. We drop off Jordan, and it's even more silent. I can feel the tension, and I know it's because of me. I know it's because I lied, and he knows it. I just don't know what to say. How do I explain what this is if I don't even know what it is? I'm just as confused as him. I don't want to put something in his head that I don't know what's gonna happen.

"Alex," I say, my voice soft as we reach the red light a block from our house.

His hazel eyes, which mirror mine exactly, look into mine. "It's nothing. It's just a small crush. If it ever becomes something, you know I would let you know."

He searches my eyes for any indication of lying on my part, but there's none. Finally, he just sighs and turns back to the street. "I know you wouldn't lie to me."

Hours later, after I am showered and taken a nap, I head into the basement with my family's spell book in hand. Our basement is like any regular basement; however, this one has magical ingredients, a magic book, and tools that can enchant abilities.

It is the one place in the house where I feel more like myself. Maybe it's the way the bricks cover the wall hide noise from outside, or it's the comfy old couch that somehow still smells like my grandmother and is filled with memories of her telling me stories from when she was high priestess. This place feels like home, always, not like the rest of the house, which seems too impersonal with its white walls and white furniture.

I grab the spell book and look over the spells. They range from anything like making plants grow faster to causing pain on others to creating whole earthquakes. The pages are filled with the legacy of my family, and with each spell I look over, I feel my intimidation grow larger by the second.

Midway through the book is a page on gifts that have been bestowed to my family from the ancestors. The reason my family became the high family centuries ago was because we have had a special gift given to us that sets us apart from other witches. Not only are we capable of immense magic, but we are also given a little something extra that sets us apart from the witches in our coven. The page is completely covered front to back with the name of each witch of our family and a spot next to them for their gift. For example, my mother and grandmother have the same gift. They can stop time while my brother can freeze things with just a single touch or a wave of his hand. Well, I haven't gotten my gift yet.

According to Grandma, there's no specific timeline for a witch to get her gift, but the fact that I'm becoming high priestess soon and I don't have my gift just solidifies the notion that I am not good enough to be queen. I know it, and it's about time my family learns the truth just as well.

I examined the page deeper, looking at all the gifts that witches in our family have had. It ranges from invisibility to even the power of levitation. Of course, the spot next to my name is blank, staring back at me. However, something else catches my eye. Right under my mother's name and before Alex's and mine are two names that have been scratched off. I try to make out what the names were, but whoever crossed them off did a job at hiding them because it's completely unreadable.

I don't know why that is because last I checked, Alex and I are the only witches of our family after my mother. She is an only child, and Alex and I are her only kids. It must be a mistake, but I don't get too much time to analyze it because my phone vibrates right next to me.

How are you feeling?

I look at the name on my phone, and I almost have a heart attack, Christian. When did he get my number? I try to recall the events of last night, but nothing comes to mind. I do not remember giving him my number. I was drunk, but not that drunk.

Better. How did you get my number? You
shouldn't drink that much.

I can't help but roll my eyes. Who does he think he is? My father. In true Christian fashion, he avoids the question.

For your information, I didn't drink that
much, and last time I checked, I'm old enough

to decide what's my limit. Have you always been
this good at straying away from the question?

I think the floor decided your limit last night.

And yes, I can't help but smile as I read the message, so he has
a sense of humor.

Was that a joke, Mr. Castillo. Didn't know
you had it in you.

It's a one-off. Didn't know you had backtalk
in you either.

Meet me tonight.

The next message comes before I have time to type out a
response. My teeth automatically go to my lip. He wants to see me.
Butterflies fill my stomach as I type out my response.

Are you asking me or telling me?

I'm telling you that I will be outside your
house in an hour. See you then, Alexandra.

My heart does a summersault. What the hell? He's coming here,
to my house, to pick me up. Usually, the demanding type of guys
aren't really my type. I've never been one to be ordered around. But
the fact that I get to see him trumps all that. I place my phone down
and start to get ready. Anxiety courses through my veins for the next
hour. I try to ignore the fact that I told myself I wouldn't date this
year because he's human, and I can never be together. It just one
night, but even I know that it's not true.

Chapter 8

An hour later, I am dressed in ripped jeans, a graphic tee featuring the Tupac in poetic justice, a leather jacket, and a pair of black Converse. My hair is down, the curls flowing perfectly as I pinned them behind my ears with a simple twist. As I look at the vanity mirror in my room, I notice the letter that I got on the first day of school.

I still have no clue how that piece of paper got in my locker and who put it there. Someone knows I'm a witch, and they are not afraid to let me know that they do.

I put the letter in my dresser and run downstairs to wait in the kitchen.

"Well, someone looks like they're going out." My father comes into the room in a buttoned-down shirt with the first couple of buttons open. His hair's a mess, and he has his reading glasses on. He's been working. His hazel eyes look tired, and his body looks like he's ready to drop.

The job of a mayor is never done, Alexandra. My father's words, which he told me once upon a time, come to mind as I watch my dad look through the fridge for food.

"I asked Mom before she left. Is that okay?"

My father grabs a yogurt and an apple, trying to keep his great physique intact. My father's encounter with junk food is as rare as it can ever be. "Of course it is. You're young. You should enjoy it."

I grab him a spoon from one of the drawers, "You look beat, Daddy. You should probably rest some before you keep on going with these mayoral duties." I offer him a small smile.

"I wish I was dealing with mayoral duties." He sighs as he opens the yogurt and starts to eat it, finishing the small container in about fifteen seconds.

"What are you dealing with?"

My father only ever works weekends if it has to do with something about the city, and it needs his tending to right at the moment. Yes, he always answers phone calls from his office when called, but other than that, if it isn't important, he usually lets it wait until Monday so he can help Mother out with her job.

I've always admired my parents' ability to be there for each other, even in spirit. Neither of them deems their job more important than the other. They work together to solve problems from both the witch world and the human. It was almost scary how good they were at it—helping each other, always having the right answer, and being able to resolve any conflict with just the simplest of ease. I also respect how my dad, even being a witch, protects the people the best he can. He makes sure he can help in any way possible.

"Helping Mom?"

"You know it." He takes a bite of his apple, and while still with food in his mouth, he says, "Most of the time, I think I have it rough, but then I look at your mother's caseload, and I am so grateful."

"Mom can do it all."

He nods. "Indeed she can, and soon, you will be able to do it all as well."

For some reason, his words send a warning to my head. *No, you can't.* The voice in my head mocks me as I think about the book and all the witches before me. Maybe I should tell him, tell him that I'm scared, that I don't think I can live up to the family name. Maybe he will understand. I open my mouth to say something, and the door rings.

"I think those are your plans," he states, pointing at the window.

"I don't have to go, Daddy." I take in his tired appearance over again, messy hair and bags for days under his hazel eyes. "I can help you. Just tell me what you need. It would be good practice for when I take over."

He shakes his head. "No, I want you nowhere near this, and hopefully, by the time you take over, we would have this situated."

The way his words bring a shiver up my spine. He's hiding something. I know he is. Usually, my father has a smile on his face, but it's almost like he's stressed out.

"What do you mean?" I ask.

His hazel eyes search mine, and for a second, I think he's going to tell me, but instead, he plants a fake smile on his face and begins to walk out of the kitchen and to the door.

At first, I just look after him, confused as to why he's keeping me in the dark, but then it suddenly dawns on me that on the other side of the front door is Christian. A boy is here to take me out, and considering that my father wasn't the nicest when Johan and I were dating, I can only imagine how he'll react when he sees a complete stranger on the other side of that door.

I start sprinting after him. "Dad, you should get back to work."

His long legs have already carried him to the door, his hand already on the knob. "I can take a break. Besides, I haven't seen Paris or Angel in a while."

"But—"

Before I can stop him or even warn him, he opens the door.

Christian stands there, his back turned at first, then he turns at the sound of the door opening. He's dressed in all black: black leather jacket, black V-neck shirt, black jeans that hang at his hips, and black shoes. He makes a simple outfit look like a suit and tie, and I swear my heart skips a beat.

"Who's this?" my father says, his apple still in his hand as he stares down Christian. His eyes bounce from Christian's black Mustang back to Christian.

Christian looks at my dad and pulls his hand out for my father to shake. "Christian Castillo, sir."

My father looks at his hand for a second and then shakes his hand. "Alexis Coleman." He holds Christian's hand a second longer than usual. "Firm handshake," he says as he finally lets go. These are not the reactions I was expecting.

My father then looks at me, a smile on his face. "So where are you two going on this fine evening?"

I open my mouth to answer, but no words come out. I was expecting my father to drag him in and almost threat him like he did to Johan. Instead, he's being nice. He doesn't know Christian. He knew Johan since we were six.

"I plan on taking your daughter on a date, if that's okay with you, sir," Christian says once he realizes I am not going to answer.

Both my father and I look at Christian. *Did he say date?* I look at my dad, not knowing how he is going to react. "Are you asking my permission?"

Christian nods. "Of course, sir. She's your daughter."

Excuse me. My dad nods slowly and then gives a slow smile, not his mayor smile, which is for photo ops and portraying politeness, but his actual smile, this one filled with approval. I am dumbfounded.

"Have her back by eleven, and everything should be fine." He pats Christian on the back and then looks at me. "He's a good one," he whispers as I walk by to go out.

Walking down the pathway out of my house, I can't help but think how bizarre that is. My father rarely likes any guy who tries to get to me. It took him forever to warm up to Johan, and I have known Johan for half my life. But two minutes with Christian, and he's all smiles and pats on his back. First, my brother and then my father. *Don't forget you.*

"How did you do that?" I ask.

"What do you mean?"

I point back at my house, still in disbelief. "My dad, he usually doesn't like anyone."

"I've been told I'm pretty likable," he says, and even though I am not looking directly at his face, I can hear the smile in his voice.

"So this is a date?" I ask as he leads me to his car, a solid black Mustang, parked at the curb. Little butterflies fill up my stomach in anticipation of his answer.

He opens the door and smiles at me. "Isn't that what I said?"

I look at him for a second before climbing into the car. If I didn't know better, this image right here would be dangerous—a dangerously hot guy, opening the of his black car, looking at me like that, while I have no way of knowing where I am going. It's already dark, and the moon reflects perfectly off his tan skin. I bite my lip and climb into the car because even though there's a small part of me is anxious, another part of me, a great part, is excited.

Christian climbs into the driver's seat and starts the engine, ready to drive.

"You must really like the color black," I point out, looking at the black interior of his car.

He drives off the curb and down the street. "It's my favorite color."

"Oh, like pitch-black darkness?"

"Like a calm dark night sky in the middle of the night."

I nod my head. "Mine is red."

"How come?"

"I look good in red," the answer comes out quickly and does not make me realize how shallow that must have sounded.

I expect him to call me out on it, but instead, he turns to stare into my eyes and says, "You do?"

Chapter 9

About fifteen minutes later, we end up at the park, which is practically abandoned at this time. We get out of the car, and as Christian gets something from the trunk, I look out to the park, wondering why we're here. There's a slight wind that makes the leaves on the trees move just a little.

From the corner of my eye, I see something move in the trees. The sudden urge that I am being watched makes my skin crawl, and my nerves run wild. I try to look closer, but from the parking lot, it's pretty impossible to tell if my mind is playing tricks on me or if I actually saw something.

"Ready?" Christian's voice makes me jump as he walks up to me. He has a picnic basket and a blanket in his hand.

"Are we having a picnic?"

"You and your questions." He smiles and starts to lead me through the park until we get next to the pond.

The moonlight reflects in the water, and the sound of crickets is the music that surrounds us tonight. The slight breeze is perfect for a summer night, and it seems like the grass was cut recently—perfect setting for a moonlight picnic.

I try not to burst with happiness as my cheeks heat up, watching Christian place the blanket on the ground and pull an electric lantern and food from his basket. The effort he put into this is almost unbelievable. All this for me, a girl he badly knows.

"No one has ever done this for me before," I say softly, more to myself than to him, but he catches it.

He looks up at me, and for a second, he almost looks nervous. "Is this too much?"

"No," I say quickly, and I take a seat down on the blanket as he mirrors my actions. "It's incredible," I beam up at him. The butterflies in my stomach have created a swarm where they reside, making me feel all giddy inside.

One minute, this man is dodging my questions, and the next, he's setting up a picnic for me. I don't think I can process all this as fast as it's happening.

"I got strawberries, blueberries, crackers, cheese, juice, and water. If you're still hungry after this, we can pick something up before we get you home."

"What is going on?" I say because my head is on a whirlwind. At first, I didn't think Christian even noticed me, and now I am on a date with him.

He looks at me confused, so I elaborate, "Why are you doing this? Set all this up for me."

"I like you," he says as casually as ever as he pops a blueberry in his mouth. "I thought it was kinda obvious," he adds as I am still trying to process what he just said. I don't know if I should be pumped, confused, or relieved. Maybe all of them. I try to think of all our interactions, and none of them show me that he likes me other than last night, and even that is questionable.

"You don't know me, Christian," I say finally because it's true. We have barely had conversations except for my drunken one last night, and that one wasn't even long.

"Isn't that what a date's for."

"But why me? I don't understand. How could you like me?"

"I don't," he says as he pops another blueberry in his mouth, staring out at the night. "Like isn't the right word, but I definitely feel something for you," he says as if expressing his feelings is something that comes naturally to him.

"Wait, what?"

I heard his words, but it's almost like their too good to believe them. He's Christian, confident and handsome. I see how the girl gawk when he walks by. He can have any girl at school, so why me?

He looks me up and down. "Alexandra"—his eyes bare into mine—"you can't tell me this is one-sided, or else, you wouldn't be here."

I study his face. The planes and sharp lines, the perfection that should be studied. He looks like he was born for magazines, movies, and art, not here, not with me.

I can't even respond to his comment because he's right. It's almost as if Christian had some invisible string pulling me closer to him with every look and every word. I can't explain my feelings myself, so why should I expect him to do so?

"You ask a lot of questions," he says it differently, not like he's teasing me but more like an observation, like he's making a note of it himself.

"I'm a curious, girl." I grab a strawberry, and when I look up, my eyes go directly to his, which are staring at me.

Before I can process what's going on, his hand comes up to my face to caress my cheek. His hand is so warm that without thinking, my cheek leans in. His touch is electric, soaking something inside me. My breath catches as I stare back into his brown eyes. He's being serious. We don't know each other, but I know that what I feel about him isn't just a schoolgirl crush. It's stronger, and it scares me to think that I can feel like this about someone who I know nothing about. It's something about him that makes me want to be close to him— something that forces me to be close.

I try to think of reasons why I should pull back, why I should walk away. This is going too fast. I just met him this week. I'm a witch; he's a human. This can never work, but I push those thoughts away from me. I decide to enjoy the moment, enjoy him.

"I can't explain it. You intrigue me, Alexandra." His eyes search my own. "You're not what I expected you to be." The words breathe into my parted mouth as they leave his.

Expected? What does that mean? I want to ask him what he means by that, but I stay quiet, my head spinning with a whole lot of other questions, neither of them coming out.

He pulls away slowly, and it's like the world comes rushing in. The sound of crickets, the calm breeze of the night, and the reflection of the moon all hit me at once, and I am brought back to reality. My cheek still tingles from his touch, and my heart still can't go back to its normal beat.

"What did you expect?"

"To be honest, I expected just a normal teenage girl. Focused on boys, school, and probably the next party coming up," he says, his eyes focused on the pond. "The moment I saw you at school, I could see your beauty radiating above everything else. But just because a person is beautiful on the outside doesn't mean they are the same inside."

"What changed your mind? You've only known me for a week, and I could count the number of conversations we've had on one hand."

"I could feel it." He now grabs two water bottles from the basket and hands one to me. "Senses it, better yet. Something about you, I don't know what it is, makes me..." He hesitates, trying to find the right words.

"Want to be close," I finish his sentence without even thinking about it. I feel it too. Something pulls me into him, and I can't seem to control it.

Christian looks at me, his eyes conveying understanding. "Why question it? You feel it too."

"I know nothing about you," I say more to myself than to him because it's true. I can feel so strongly about someone who I met just this week. I literally just learned his last name yesterday, yet I've felt as I've known him longer. A part of me feels safe with him, if that makes sense. Like I'm supposed to be with him right at this moment in time.

"I'm not that interesting."

I raise my eyebrow at him. That's not gonna fly. Does he really think I'm just gonna act like it's okay? I know nothing about him. Just because I feel something around him isn't enough. I want to know more. I want more.

I watch as he starts to pull on the grass beside us, and after what seems like forever, he gives me a reluctance, probably figuring out I'm not talking until he does. "What do you wanna know?"

"How could you run so fast?" The question comes out of my mouth as quick as a bullet, as if I have been thinking about it for a while. I have seen fast running, track star running, and believe me, that was nothing like that. The way he ran, fast as lighting, almost like an animal. The way he went faster after I whispered to myself within a football field away for him to go faster. It was almost like he could hear it. Call me crazy, but that's too big of a coincidence.

"I've been in track and field for as long as I could remember," he says as if he's been programmed to say that. Again, I raise my eyebrow. I hope he doesn't think I am just gonna fall for that.

"Wanna try that again?"

He shrugs his shoulder. "I don't know what you want me to say. It's the truth."

"You're lying," I say as I look into his eyes, which try to avoid contact with my own.

He sighs and looks at me. "You think I am lying about running fast?"

"Nope, I know you are lying."

"Everyone has their secrets." He looks deeply into my eyes as if he is talking about me and my secrets, as if he knew I was hiding something.

I nod, not wanting to push it. I have secrets I would rather not have some light shed on. Maybe I'm looking into it. Maybe I want there to be another reason because if there was, then I could be with him. I do not have to let him go like I did Johan.

"Strawberry?" he asks as he puts a strawberry in his hand and offers it to me.

I give a small smile and go to grab the fruit, but he pulls back. "Nope," and then he offers it up again. Confused, I go grab it again, and again, he pulls awhile. "Nope." And this time, he points the strawberry to my mouth.

He wants to feed it to me. My heart drops, and at first, I hesitate, but slowly, I start to move in. I look at him as he places the strawberry at the tip of my mouth, and I take a bite.

Who am I? This isn't me. I would never let some guy feed me strawberries, especially one that I don't know, no matter how hot I think he is. Paris is gonna have a field day with this.

I sit back as I enjoy the strawberry, my favorite. I close my eyes to savor the taste, and when I open them, I see Christians eyes watching, and instantly, my cheeks heat up. The way his brown eyes search me up and down makes the butterflies in my stomach flutter like crazy.

His eyes stay on mine as he opens his mouth to say, "You are so beautiful. It's breathtaking," he says the words with ease as if it is the easiest thing he could have possibly said.

My breathe catches in my throat, and for a second, it's like time is frozen.

The rest of the night, we end up talking about school and how he's adjusting. I can tell he's trying to dodge all my personal questions, so by the time I am ready to go home, I know nothing more about him than I did before the night began. Yet he asked me so many questions about myself that I am afraid he knows everything about my life—almost everything, anyway.

I help Christian clean up, and we start walking toward the car. I carry the checkered blanket while he carries the basket, both of us admiring the beautiful silent night that surrounds us.

"Did you have a fun night?" he asks as we make our way to the parking lot.

"I did." I smile. "Thank you." My cheek is still buzzing from the simple touch that he gave me earlier, and I feel myself on cloud 9 as I try no tot break my face from the huge smile that is straining my lips.

"I did also. Maybe we can go out another time. I heard there's— what the hell," Christian says as we look at the side of his car, confusion coating his words.

The blanket in my hand falls to the ground as I take in the scene in front of us. The back window is smashed, and on the right side, Christian's car, in red paint, reads, "LIAR, LIAR, PANTS ON FIRE. THE FUTURE QUEEN IS FULL OF LIES."

This must be the same person who left the note in my locker on the first day of school. The figure that I saw outside my room, and again, tonight in the bed of trees. I can't pretend anymore. Someone is after me, and worse, they are getting bolder by the second.

Fear starts to overcome me, and I can feel my body starting to shake. Christian is still looking at his car in disbelief, and I can't help but feel bad. He had nothing to do with this. He just wanted to take me out. The guilt and the fear all start to accumulate inside me, and

70

I can feel my hands tremble at my sides. My mind goes to the letter, the figure outside my room, and the fact that the same person could be here right now, watching. It's too much.

The lights in the parking lot start to flicker, slowly at first, but grow as fast as the drum that has replaced my heart. I can hear myself starting to hyperventilate. My chest moves up and down at a rapid pace while my breathing can hardly keep up.

The car turns on, but there is no key. Me and my magic are overwhelmed by fright. The alarm goes off, accompanied by the radio, and shortly, it looks as if the vehicle is possessed. The park is now a huge light show, and I can't stop it. I know it's me. My magic is out of control, but I can't stop it, not while I'm panicking. My powers are heightened. I can feel it in my blood, the rush of my powers making its way through, then out, and then back again.

For a second, I forget that Christian is here until I feel his large hands on either side of my face. "Breathe, Alexandra, breathe." His words attempt to soothe me, but they don't work.

One of the park light bulbs goes out, and then another, and then another one. He tries again, this time squeezing the side of my face slightly, urging me to look into his deep brown eyes. "It's okay, Alexandra. Breathe. Just breathe."

My heart is pounding in my chest while I fight hard not to cry. This is really happening. This is my life. The letter wasn't a prank. This car paint job isn't a prank. This is happening to me.

I look around at the scene I have created, the flashing lights, the car, and all the broken bulbs. I can't take this. My magic has never felt this, never so out of control.

Again, Christian squeezes my face, and this time, my eyes go to his. The golden specks in his eyes are darker and filled with concerned. Behind Christian, another light goes out, and the sound of the alarm still continues, but he doesn't turn in that direction. His eyes stay fixated on me as if this doesn't faze him. He's not worried about what's going on out there, but he cares about me.

"Alexandra." His voice is calm in the midst of this chaos. "Just breathe. You're not alone."

In his eyes, I see the urge to get me to the stop—the need.

I don't know if it's his eyes or his tone. Maybe it's the way he holds me that finally brings me off the edge.

Slowly, the lights stop to flicker as my heart rate goes back to normal, my body stops shaking, and the car turns off. As everything goes back to normal and I get ahold of my powers again, I notice my heartbeat regulates, and now I'm left with one realization. Christian is right in front of me. His hands are making contact with my skin, and his eyes are staring into mine. I start to smile at him, and then another realization comes in. He saw all this, the light, the alarm, all of it.

I take a big step back, away from his grasp. HE SAW ME DOING MAGIC. My head starts to spin. What are the odds of him thinking that I did that? Maybe I can blame it on a faulty power line? But how would that explain the car? This is bad, really bad.

"You okay?" He looks me up and down, a small frown appearing on his lips.

"Yeah." I bite my lip. I have to get out here before he asks more questions. "I think I should walk home. It's such a beautiful night," I say even though it's late, and I don't want to. But if I step into the car with Christian, he's going to ask questions. He's going to want to know what just happened and why I had a panic attack, and I can't do that.

"You wanna walk?" He looks at me, confused. The drive here was a good ten-minute drive. It would take already an hour to walk. But anything is better than the awkward car ride that awaits me if I stay.

I nod. "Yeah, why not?" I tried putting on a cheerful tone to my voice as if that's really what I want to do. I think I succeeded.

"I'm not letting you." He shakes his head as if his word is law.

"Excuse me?"

"You heard me, Alexandra. I am not letting you walk. It's 10:30 p.m., and it's pitch black," he says as he picks up the cloth that I dropped and opens the passenger door for me to climb in, ignoring my request to walk.

"I can handle myself. I'll be fine." I cross my arms, a little offended.

"I didn't say you couldn't. I promised your father I would have you home by eleven, and I am a man of my word." He walks up to me, his head towering over me as if I was a little child. "Now the way I see it, you can get in the car willingly, or I'll make you get in the car. Either way, I am keeping my promise to your father."

I roll my eyes, bossy much. Who does he think he is? He can't just order me around. I would love to see him try. I turn my heel, and before I even take a step, I am over his shoulder, getting carried like a disobedient toddler.

"What the hell is wrong with you? Let me go." I slap him back, which is surprisingly hard. "Christian, I swear to God."

The blood rushes to my head, and a small part of me wants to tell him off. Another part doesn't see the point in resisting. He's a giant compared to me. If he doesn't want to let me go, he won't.

He doesn't budge, put me in the car, and slams the door behind me. He gets in the car after me. "Now was that so hard."

I try to open the door, but he puts the lock on. "Ugh," I groan in frustration. I unlock the door and try to get out, but he reaches over me and slams it.

"Why are you so stubborn? I said you're coming with me."

"I can ask you the same thing!" I shout back at him. "Are you always used to getting what you want?"

"Actually, yes," he confides.

A war of wills has started in the car. I don't wanna stay, and he doesn't want to let me leave. He stares me down, and I do the same to him. He doesn't understand. I can't be here. This was a mistake, and if someone is after me, soon enough, they will find him too. That's how it works in my world. I may be naive in a lot of things, but not this.

Christian's glare softens as if he can read the emotions on my face. "We don't have to talk," he says, his voice completely changing from the harsh tone he had earlier. Now he's calm but stern. "But I'm not letting you walk home alone."

I look him over, and if I didn't know better, I would say he's worried about me. Is he not curious about why his car window and his light are smashed? Did he now put two and two together?

I nod as he starts the car and drives me home. I try not to think about the park incident or anything else, but I just focus on the smell that has filled the car—his smell. It smells like pine and man mixed in one. The smell fills my nostrils, and it's so familiar it makes me feel comfortable. I sit back and start to feel the effects of all the magic I use today. It almost felt like I went haywire. I wasn't in control, and that never happens.

Since I was a child, my mother taught Alex and myself to keep our emotions in check so nothing like this would happen. Lately, though, when I am around Christian, my body and powers aren't my own. Yesterday at the party and tonight. Rare occurrences.

My eyebrow is heavy as I look outside the window, and I can actually feel how tired my body really is. The next thing I remember is the sound of a knock on a door as I lay in Christian's giant arms.

Chapter 10

It's noon by the time I get out of my room. I've been up for hours, cleaning, folding clothes, and even studying anything to keep me from checking my phone or calling Christian. I woke up from the same dream I had the night before, and I'm starting to think it means something, but I have no idea what.

Yesterday was a mistake. I should have never gone out with Christian. I know how this is gonna end, and no matter how I feel, I can't put someone else through that. I can't be selfish, not this time.

I head downstairs to see my parents are already gone, and the only people that inhabit the house is my brother, who lies on the couch playing video games, and myself.

As soon as I enter the living room, Alex jumps off the couch, turning off the TV.

"We need to talk." His voice is stern and serious, unlike himself.

"What's up?" I expect him to ask me about my date, or maybe even worse, Christian probably called him to fill him in on all the details of his confusing night.

"I went to your room to find the spell book when I got home last night," he says, and I see him dig in his pocket, showing me a piece of paper folded up, and before he even tells me what it is, I already know it's contents. I've read that note over and over again.

"Why did you keep this?" He shows the paper that was in my locker on the first day of school.

Words fail me, so I stay silent, not knowing how to exactly explain that I'm terrified.

"Lexi, what?" he repeats, his voice more stern than before. I can see it in his eyes, worry filling them to the rims.

"Why are you doing through my things?"

"Lexi, I swear to God. If you don't tell me, I will tell Mom and Dad." His voice is laced with anger and annoyance. I know he's serious, so I take a seat on the couch and look up at him, preparing myself to tell him.

"Alex, I don't think it was a prank!" I shout out of fear.

After I got the letter, I kept it because deep down, I knew it wasn't a prank. That I was being watched, and most importantly, I might be in danger. "Something happened last night that solidified it."

"Last night, what happened last night?" His eyes look worried, but he stays silent as I explain everything. How I swear I saw someone in the trees watching me, how Christian's car got vandalized, and even how I lost control last night and nearly caused a minor blackout.

"You can't tell mom or dad, Alex. They would freak out," I add.

Knowing my parents, they will keep me under house arrest until the end of time, and I don't want that.

"With good reason, this is serious."

"I know." I nod because this is my new reality, but I know my parents, and if they even get a whiff of this, I would be in solidarity until they found who was behind this. I need to figure this out myself. I'm going to be queen soon. What would it say to the witch community, to my parents, and more importantly, to myself if I have my parents fight my battles?

"Lexi."

"I'm going to figure this out. I need to."

"Not alone. If you don't think it's not a prank, then it's a threat." He waves the letter around. "Whoever is doing this has made it clear that they don't care about making their presence known, which makes them dangerous. If you insist on doing this without our parents knowing, then you're not doing this alone."

Chapter 11

Monday morning, Paris comes and picks us up. Everyone is really talkative today, but I am dreading going to school. By the end of last night, I had two missed calls from Johan, six missed calls from Christian, and a text from Christian, saying we needed to talk. Neither of those conversations seemed appealing to me, so my plan for the day is to avoid them as much as I can.

"Lexi, I have a bone to pick with you." Paris looks at me through the rearview mirror as she pulls up to the school parking lot. "You never called me after your date with that mysterious Christian."

I shrug my shoulders as if it's no big deal although I was freaking out about a couple of days ago. "It was alright."

"Just alright?" She parks the car and turns to look at me. "What do you mean just alright?"

"Just that," I say as I open the door to get out of the car. I don't want to talk about this, especially not now.

"Well, does that mean I have a chance?" Jordan jokes as he blows me a kiss in a joking manner.

Alex slaps him in the back of the head. "Boundaries," he mumbles.

We enter the school, and as soon as I walk in, the boys go their separate ways as always, and us girls go straight forward to go to our lockers.

I stop in my tracks when I see Johan leaning on my locker all the way to the end of the hallway. I'm tempted to walk away, just go to class without going to my locker, but I know I need my books. I can't just forget them. Johan looks up from his phone as if he can sense that I have entered the building and smiles when he sees me. Fuck!

Angel sees Johan shortly after I do and pulls Paris to her side, stopping her in her tracks. "We can just meet her in class."

Paris follows her line of vision, and a mischievous smile appears on her lips. "I need my book."

"You can read off mine." Angel rolls her eyes and drags Paris to class as I walk up to my locker. "Good luck." She gives me a small, encouraging smile.

My feet stay stuck, unmoving for a couple of seconds before I take a deep breath and then head up to the locker to this dreaded conversation.

"Lexi." Johan leans off my locker, giving me access to open it.

"What's up?" I say without looking at him. I look through my books and grab my AP lit one before closing my locker back up. I am not in the mood to talk to him, to talk to anyone, actually.

"I tried calling you yesterday, but I guess you were busy." He rubs the back of his neck as he always does when he's nervous, something I learned from years of being friends. "I wanted to apologize. I was drunk, and I shouldn't have grabbed you that way." He gives me a shy, apologetic smile that doesn't have the same effect on me that it once did.

"That's what you wanted to apologize for."

I look at him, confused. I mean, he shouldn't have grabbed me like that, but that's not what bothered me. What really bothered me was the fact that he thought he had the right. The right to act like I was his property that he was defending. We aren't together, and I don't know how else I can put it so he can understand it. I don't want to be cruel to him, but at this point, I have to figure out a way to nip this in the bud.

"Yeah, it's just I don't trust that guy." He scratches his neck again. "I know you can defend yourself, but something about that guy gives me the creeps. In one week, he has gotten you alone in a room, drunk. That doesn't say much about him."

If he only knew that I went into the kitchen, willing, that it was me that led Christian there. I was the one who wanted to be alone with him. I can't tell Johan that. I can't tell him that I have feelings for some other guy when I can see he still has some underlying feelings for me. So I bite my lip and say nothing.

"You forgive me?" He holds his hands up in between us in a begging motion. "I really didn't mean any harm. I just wanted to make sure you were okay," he says in between pouted lips.

I sigh. I have to get to class, and I honestly don't wanna have this conversation anymore. I have bigger things on my plate at the moment. So I give him a small smile and say, "Don't worry about it."

"Really?" He gives me his world-famous smile. "This is why you are my favorite," he jokes, and he looks behind me for a sec. The smile plastered on his face wavers, and then he turns to me again. "Let me walk you to class."

I should say no. I know that I should, but the hair on the back on the back of my neck stands up, and I know that means one thing. Christian is here. I don't know how my body knows it, but it does, and I can't speak to him.

I give Johan a smile and then turn to the way of our classroom. Immediately, as I turn, I see Christian at his locker, his eyes staring daggers at Johan's hand that's placed on my lower back, leading me through the sea of students. He stands at his locker for a couple of seconds, watching us with a glare that intimidates the shit out of me. I watch as he slams his locker shut, scaring nearby students and he begins walking over.

"Alexandra," he calls my name out. His eyes stare directly at me, and he raises an eyebrow when I don't stop.

I bite my lip and look at Johan. I don't want to talk to him because I know it's gonna lead to more conversations and eventually something else, and I can't do that. I can't have him a part of my life, not after this weekend. I need to focus on my magic, and I don't want another situation like Johan to arise.

I was stupid to believe that it could be different, that this would be different, but that was a pipe dream. I am who I am, and right now, if I have Christian in my life, he can be put in danger, and I don't think I can live with that.

Somehow, Christian reaches my classroom before me, and he stops in front of us, blocking Johan and me from getting into the class. He stares at me, his eyes glued on my own. Those breathtaking brown eyes look angry, really, really angry.

"What are you doing?" he snaps, and his voice makes me jump slightly.

Before I can even speak, Johan answers for me, "We're going to class." His voice is calm, but the way Johan grabs my waist, I know he's anything but. "If you don't mind getting out of our way," he emphasizes the word *our*.

"Alexandra, what are you doing?" he repeats, disregarding Johan's comment completely.

I don't know how to answer the question because he's staring so deeply into my eyes. It's almost as if he can read my mind, and he knows I am avoiding him, using Johan as a shield because I am too big of a coward to talk to Christian. It's childish. I know. However, I panicked, and I have no other ideas.

"She obviously doesn't want to talk to you. Now move. We're going to be late."

This brings Christian to turn and look at Johan, and if looks could kill, Johan would be dead in a heartbeat. Narrowed eyes, clenched jaw, and stern frown decorate Christian's face as he looks over at him.

"You don't speak for her, and if I were you, I would take my hand off her before I fulfill the promise I gave you a couple of nights ago," he threatens, referring to the night in the kitchen and how he told Johan he would rip his hands off his body if he didn't keep them off me.

Johan just smiles. "I would love to see you try."

For a second, I think that Christian is going to. He takes in a deep breath, his fist clenched at his sides. It almost looks as though he's trying hard to contain his anger. However, the warning bell goes off, and somehow, it breaks me from my trance. I pry myself out of Johan's grasp and look at Christian.

"Please move. I have class," I say the words as sternly as I can, even if I just want to run right out of school.

He studies my face for what seems like forever. Looking for an answer or a reason to make me late, I don't exactly know, and frankly, I don't have time to care. He stays put, his eyes never leaving my own as he stares deep into them. "Please," I whisper.

This must have convinced him to leave me alone because he just nods and takes a step toward me. "I will see you later, Alexandra."

The promises hang in the air long after he's moved away and gone down the hallway.

"That guy is crazy," Johan mumbles under his breath as he enters the classroom first, but I don't quite pay attention to him because all I can think about is how when Christian walked past me, I was immediately enveloped by his smell—pine and man, his personal fragrance. As I take my seat in the back of the class, my stomach drops slightly, and I realize that may be the last time I ever smell it.

After lunch, I walk to the bathroom. The day has been Christian-free since this morning, and I am hoping to keep it that way. The more I stay away from him, maybe he'll get the hint, even if it's not what I want in the slightest. It is what we both need. As I wash my hands, I can't help but think about our date, what he said, how he smelled the way he touched my face. I wish things were different and that I could try with him. I want nothing more. I can't risk it, though. I can't expose my secret to a human. It's not only mine to tell; it's also my family's. I would never put them at risk just for a boy, no matter how mesmerizing that boy is.

While drying my hands on the paper towels I have in my grasp, some of which fall to the ground. I bend over to pick it up, cursing myself for being so damn clumsy. The hairs on the back of my neck stand, and I freeze for a second as I crouch down. It's almost as if I can feel Christian's presence, but I just shake my head and just ignore it because I am truly losing my mind.

As I stand up to discard the paper towels, my heart practically jumps out of my chest. There, in the reflection of the mirror, stands Christian right behind me. Piercing brown eyes and tall stature stare back at me. What the hell is he doing here in the girls' bathroom?

"You've been avoiding me, Alexandra." His voice is deadly as he makes eye contact with me through the mirror. His glare is cold, and I can feel the anger that radiates off him.

At first, I think it's a mind trick. My brain must be playing with me because I feel guilty for avoiding Christian. However, my heart immediately races as I turn to look at him and realize this isn't an illusion. He's really here.

"What the fuck are you doing here, Christian?" I try to peek under the stalls of the bathroom to see if anyone is here, but his body is so big and close that I can barely see anything past him.

"We're alone," he says, reading my mind again. "I locked the door as well," he says nonchalantly as if he didn't just lock me in a bathroom.

"Excuse me?" I screech.

I look at the door that's about ten feet away from me. If I run, I can make it, I think.

"Don't even think about it," he says as he glances at the door and then back at me. Again, reading my mind. "Why have you been avoiding me?"

"I haven't," I say, barely getting the words out.

I need to get out of here. I try to take a step to the left, closer to the door, but he's right there, fast as lighting, blocking my path.

"You're a horrible liar."

"Do you spend a lot of time hanging in female restrooms?" I cross my arms over my chest and raise my eyebrow, trying to redirect the conversation, just like he does to me.

Christian gives me a small grin that, under other circumstances, would make me melt. "This is a onetime affair, I promise. I was desperate."

"Desperate?" I echo, trying to look into his eyes, trying to see why he cares so much.

He takes a step toward me. "You weren't answering my calls. You avoided me today in the hallway. I was worried."

Worried? My heart pings, and I can't help but feel butterflies in my stomach as I look at this boy in front of me, this gorgeous boy who's worried about me. He's wearing a gray T-shirt that makes his biceps look perfect. He's insanely beautiful, and I know he knows it. It almost makes it hard to concentrate when he speaks like this—like he cares for me.

"There's no need to be worried. I'm fine." Another lie. I am not fine. I am freaking out, not only because of what's happening in my personal life and the creepy notes but also because when Christian is this close, talking to me like I matter to him, I almost want to cave—

to tell him about me and my family, the impending time clock that looms over my head, and the fact that I am so scared that I have no idea what to do. I barely know this man, and somehow, I want to trust him with the scariest parts of me. It doesn't feel wrong, but it should.

"What happened Saturday night?" He stares into my eyes as if he can try to read the answers from behind them.

My heart skips a beat. There it is. The question I was avoiding. How am I supposed to answer that? How am I supposed to act as if everything is okay? When I feel as if the answer is plastered on my face? He makes me feel transparent, something I cannot be with him.

"I don't know what you're talking about. I have to go to class," I say, trying to walk past him again.

Before I can walk out, he grabs my elbow and pulls me to his side.

Christian towers over me a good foot, but he leans in close, so close, that I swear I can feel his eyelashes on my forehead. Heat radiates off him, warming me up, but his touch on my elbow is what sets me on fire. My heart starts to race, and my breathing is hard. Being this close to him is distracting. His smell is intoxicating. It infiltrates my nostrils, making me feel almost dizzy.

The hair on the back of my neck rises, and it's almost as if every nerve in my body is alert. I'm paralyzed. Under his stare, I can't say anything, can't move. The world has stopped, and the one thing I can think about is Christian and his fingers imprinting themselves on my skin.

"Don't lie to me." His voice is dangerously low, as if he was mad.

I shake my head slightly. "I'm not." My voice comes out smaller than I intended, but I can't help it. He's so close. I look up at his eyes, and immediately, I regret it because I know that I'm going to get lost in them.

"Alexandra." He looks at my lips for just a second and then back at me. "I don't like being lied to." He pulls me in a little closer, and our chests are now touching. His hand on my elbow is sending a wave of shivers down my back while his voice sets fire to my entire body, making it hard to concentrate. "I also don't like annoying pretty boys touching what's mine."

"Yours," I echo, and I am actually surprised the word can come out of my mouth with how dry my throat has become. I know he's talking about Johan, but the fact that he called me his has my heart beating out of my chest. He said it as if it was common knowledge. It definitely isn't.

"How am I yours?"

He shakes his head. "I'll answer your question when you answer mine. What happened at the park, and why are you avoiding me?"

"That's two questions," I joke because the energy in the room is filled with a tension that envelops us both and almost makes me forget I am here at school.

"Don't play with me, Alexandra." His words almost come out like a growl, animalistic even. Making me take a step back, I look into his eyes, and they have changed in color; instead of dark brown, they are almost black. The gold flecks in his eyes are brighter. "Tell me what I want to know."

"I can't," I say, distracted by his eyes that I don't even realize that the words have come out of my mouth. I curse myself silently and hope that he ignores it, but he doesn't.

"What does that mean?"

Before I can even answer his question, a knock startles us both. Christian looks at the door long enough for me to get out of the spell. He may not be a witch, but he certainly has power over me.

I pull my arm from his embrace. "Now if you excuse me, I have to go to class."

I unlock the door and walk out before he can say or do anything to make me go back on my decision. As soon as the door shuts behind me, I already miss his presence.

The rest of my classes are a blur. I don't remember anything that was taught, and frankly, I don't care. My brain is in shambles after everything, but the only thing that is clear is Christian. His smell still lingers in my nose and how his touch is still imprinted on my skin. It's insane how someone, whom I barely know, can have such an effect on me and my thoughts. It's terrifying.

Chapter 12

"What's wrong with you?" Paris screams at me as soon as we get into the playhouse. The door slams behind her as she glares at me with her famous death stare. Her dark brown eyes can burn holes into my face.

The playhouse is an abandoned house at the edge of the bayou. We found the place when we were just ten, and ever since then, it's been our hiding spot. No one knows about it, not even our parents. It's our escape from everything going on. It's the only place other than our homes where we can do magic freely without any consequence, where we can be ourselves.

The playhouse looks like shit from the outside, but on the inside, it's decked out. Jordan even hacked the light company to give us electricity and air-conditioning. We have a fridge, couches we got from the pawnshop, TVs, anything you can think of we have it, except for a way to calm a very mad Paris down.

"How could you not tell us that someone has been terrorizing you?" Paris continues with the same rant she had the whole time in the car on the way here.

"Because I knew you would act like this," I say as I take a seat next to Jordan on the black leather couch in front of the TV. "And it happened last night."

"Act like what?" She stands in front of the TV. "Like my best friend has been keeping secrets from me. Like some dick face has been sending paintings on people's cars. Did you want me to act calm? I want to kick your ass."

Alex comes from the kitchen with a soda. "Are you happy? You did this." I point to Paris.

"They needed to know." He shrugs his huge shoulder and gives a small apologetic smile. "We need help figuring this out."

"Paris, I'm sorry I didn't tell you. I'm sorry I didn't tell any of you." I look at Angel, who is sitting on the recliner, and Jordan, who's next to me. "I just figured there's nothing you can do about it."

"We can figure out who's doing it," Jordan says.

Alex takes a swig from his drink. "And why."

"But who can it be?" Angel asks the question that circles through all our minds.

"This is serious, Lexi," Angel says as she rubs her cross pendant that hangs on her neck. She looks nervous, and now I can't help but be even more anxious.

"She doesn't see that!" Paris shouts. "This is not a prank. No one says this as a prank." She turns to me and points. "What if something would have happened to you, Lexi? What then?" She runs her perfectly manicured fingers through her red hair. "All because you wanted to act tough and handle this shit on your own. That's not what a leader does. A leader knows when to ask for help, and the fact that you thought you couldn't tell us or trust us fucking sucks."

"I'm sorry." I bite my lip, guilt eating up at me. She's right. I wasn't thinking like a leader. I didn't think how this can affect others. How would it affect the community in general if something happened to me?

Jordan rubs my shoulder, trying to console me. "It's okay. We know now." His kind gesture makes the guilt that has a hold of me lessen just a little.

"I just wanted to believe that this was a prank. I didn't want to think that it was a real threat or that someone was out my room or even that I was being followed. I mean, for Christ's sakes, I'm supposed to be a queen in less than a year. I wanted to hold on to being a teenager for a moment longer. I didn't want all this to be real. I was scared."

Silence fills the room. No one knows what to say. And they are probably feeling sorry for me and probably thinking of how to deal with their anger.

"Who do you think it could be?" Angel asks, moving next to Paris, to calm her down.

I shake my head. "I have no idea."

And I really don't. I have no idea who would purposely do this to me. I am not the nicest person in the world, but I have never done anything to warrant this. It could be a witch that wants to intimidate me or even a human who somehow figured out my secret and is now trying to terrorize me. I honestly have no idea.

I don't get much time to really ponder on it because a knock comes from the other side of the front door, and we all stand up in alert. No one knows about this playhouse, absolutely no one. In the time that we have been hanging around here, we haven't even seen anyone near it. So the fact that someone is knocking on the door makes everyone nervous.

"Who is it?" Alex screams at the door.

"Open the door and find out," a familiar voice that I can't quite place says from behind the door.

Paris looks out the window reluctantly and then rolls her eyes. "What the hell," she says as she turns and glances our way and then opens the door.

In comes Jackson, in all his tattooed glory, with a huge smile on his face. "How's it going?" His skin is glistening and covered in sweat. He has basketball shorts and a T-shirt. He looks like he just came from a run.

"What the fuck," Jordan cussed as Devin comes from out of the kitchen with a bag of chips in his hand.

"You guys should probably lock your doors." He pushes his glasses off the bridge of his nose. His blond hair is kind of a mess, and like Jackson, he is just as sweaty. "I'm sorry, but I was starving." He gives off a shy smile as he raises the bag of chips.

"How did you find out where we were?" Angel asks, staring at our newcomers suspiciously.

Jackson laughs. "Well, you know, the occasional spying, following you around stuff like that," he says calmly and looks over at Angel as he sits on the couch and puts his feet up.

"You followed us here?"

"You guys need to go." Alex takes the bag of chips from Devin while Jordan kicks Jackson's feet off the table. Jackson looks so nonchalant as if this is his place and we are the guest.

"Can't do that, mate," Devin says, and you can tell he is actually a little uneasy with how the situation has transpired.

Paris puts a hand on her hip and stares Jackson down. "Why the hell not?"

"Boss's orders, beautiful," Jackson says to Paris but looks at Jordan as he puts his feet back up on the table, almost daring him to move it again. I can already tell Jackson likes trouble. It oozes off him, probably because he has the strength to combat any trouble that comes his way.

"Who's your boss?" I ask although a part of me already knows the answer. I can feel the hairs on my neck on command as he enters the room through the open front door.

Covered in sweat like the rest of them, Christian leans on the door as he surveys the room, as if we are the ones who came into his space.

"I am." His eyes pinned on me as he closes the door behind him and makes his way to the center of the living room. "I told you we need to talk."

"So you're stalking me now?" I scoff in annoyance at how he doesn't seem to grasp the concept of me wanting to be away from him.

"I told you I'm desperate. I followed you to the bathroom. Do you really think I wouldn't follow you here?" He looks at Jackson and then at his feet. "Can you act civilized? Get your feet off the goddamn table," he commands.

I expect Jackson to disobey him, but he does the opposite. He rolls his eyes and does as he's told.

"Let's just cut to the chase, shall we?" He stands up and claps his hands. He looks around the room. "I am not much for being subtle, so let's just rip the Band-Aid off. We know you're witches," he says and just smiles like he didn't just drop a bomb.

My heart drops. Did he just say they know? How could they know? I mean, other than what happened Saturday night, did Christian tell them? But he said he knows that we're all witches. How is that possible? Everyone is silent, letting the news settle in. It's my fault. I know it is. That night at the park, Christian saw what happened, and then he told me them and somehow put two and two together. Of course, he did. He's not stupid. I should have known.

"Just to clarify"—Devin takes a step forward and puts his finger up—"we've known before we got to town."

"Wait, what?" Alex puts his hands up, confused like the rest of us. I have exposed us, the one thing I was taught not to do, and I did it. "Someone needs to explain what's going on here."

"What do you mean before you got to town?" Angel asks. "What are you doing here?"

"In town?" Christian looks up at me. For once, he doesn't give eye contact, almost as if he is nervous. But he also acts as if no one else is here. "We're here for her."

"What's that supposed to mean?" Alex's fist at his sides, and it looks like he's about to charge, and it doesn't give me time to unpack Christian's comment.

"I won't ask again." Alex gets about an inch away from Jackson's face. "Answer the question."

"Or what?" Jackson gives him a cocky grin.

Alex looks pissed, squaring up to Jackson. I know my brother, and I know when he's about to throw a punch, and it looks like it will be in any second now. Jackson, on the other hand, looks almost happy about this altercation, like he's provoking Alex on purpose.

"Jackson, stand down," Christian says, his voice stern. He doesn't keep his eyes off me or turn to see what exactly Jackson and Alex are doing behind him.

Jackson gives Alex one last look and then scoffs. "You're no fun, Castillo." He moves behind Christian and leans on the back wall of the crowded living room.

The tension in the room can be cut by a knife. All this for what, for me? I don't understand.

"Wait, were you the ones behind the letter?" Alex asks, desperation and annoyance coating his words. He looks in between Jackson and Christian, who pay him no mind.

I know in my heart that Christian couldn't have done any of this. He or his friends aren't behind this; they aren't. Even though I have known Christian for a total of one week, I know that he isn't capable of this. I can feel it in my bones. Besides, why would his own car be vandalized? It doesn't make sense.

Christian just shakes his head, ignoring everyone in the room except me. "We're here to protect you, Alexandra."

"Protect her from what?" Paris interjects.

"Let's just say they're some people who aren't so happy that she's gonna be queen," Devin pipes up.

"Why is that?" I ask, curious.

This is getting too real too soon. I am barely thinking through this. It's almost as if the information enters my head, but I can't process it quickly enough.

"Man, you guys ask a lot of questions." Jackson rolls his eyes again. "Do witches ever know anything?"

Jordan ignores Jackson's dig and just asks, "What qualifies you guys to protect her?"

Christian looks at me, his eyes staring into my soul for the first time he gets to the playhouse, and all he says is, "She knows."

Immediately, every pair of eyes turns to me, and for a second, I'm perplexed. I don't know anything. In fact, I probably know less than anyone here.

What could he possibly mean by "She knows"? I try to think of the indication he's given me, but I have nothing. I stare back into his eyes, those beautiful brown eyes with golden specks in them, and it suddenly hits me. I can't believe I haven't put it together, the dream, the one I keep on having every time I close my eyes. It makes sense how he heard me at the field, how fast he ran, how he can hear my heartbeat and move into places so swiftly. But most importantly, those eyes sold it. I have been having the same dream for days now. My subconscious is telling me what I know deep down, yet I don't listen. Christian isn't human at all; however, he isn't like me either.

"He's a werewolf."

Chapter 13

"Hallelujah!" Jackson claps his hands as he jokes. "She's got it."

"I don't understand," Angel interjects, but my heart is racing with all this information. "What do the wolves have to do with the next queen of the witches?"

"Usually nothing," Devin explains and takes a seat on the couch where Jackson was. However, he sits at the edge of the couch, almost like he doesn't feel welcome but wants to make himself smaller. "But this case is special."

"How so?"

Devin clears his throat. "See, my mate Christian and your friend Alexandra are destined."

Destined? I look around and see my friends are just as confused as I feel right now. What does he mean Christian and I are destined? Destined to what? First, I find out he's a werewolf, and now this. Who said the hell surprises are a good thing because when I meet that person, I will punch them in the throat?

Everyone is asking questions, overwhelming me with their voices. It gets hard to even think. I am still trying to wrap my head around the fact that Christian is a werewolf. A real-life werewolf. I know they're real. I've read the stories, and I've done the research, but to have one here in front of me is a different story. I feel lightheaded with all this information. It feels like the world is spinning. So when Christian offers to take us outside and talk, I don't object.

I step on the porch and take a deep breath. The sky is beautiful. The sun is setting, causing an orange-reddish background. A light breeze comes across my face, and I just take it all in, trying to enjoy the silence before Christian tells me what he has to say. All this is too much, werewolves, people coming after me. I just wish I could go back to last year to a time I didn't have to worry about anything.

"You okay?" Christian sits next to me as I take a seat on the porch steps, clutching my knees to my chest, almost like a safety blanket.

"You just told me people are after me because I'm becoming queen. What do you think?" I say, my voice laced with sarcasm. I don't mean it to come out that way, but my mouth has a mind of its own.

"Fair point."

Silence fills the air for a couple of seconds, neither of us knowing exactly what to say in this situation. Christian is most likely trying to give me space as I try to wrap my head around the whole thing. At this moment, my life feels like a stupid movie, a horror movie, to be more specific.

"So you're a werewolf?" I sigh, still can't believe I didn't put it together. He's a pro, technically a giant with muscles as big as my head. Of course, he isn't completely human. "Like you can actually turn into a dog."

From the corner of my eye, I see Christian smile. "I can turn into a wolf," he says matter-of-factly.

"Whenever you want?" I ask and watch as he nods. "So on Friday on the football field, you heard me when I said to Run faster, didn't you?"

Again, another nod.

I know that there was something about him, something magical. I learned from research that werewolves have amplified hearing and smell. Not only that, but they're strong, as strong as a vampire. But it's in their wolf form where they are their strongest, faster than anything with teeth that can tear through bones in one bite.

"Why didn't you tell me you knew?"

He looks out at the trees that border the house. "I wanted to gain your trust first. I wanted you to be comfortable enough with me," he says. "I thought maybe you would tell me yourself."

"So you came all the way to New Orleans to what protect me?" I stare at the side of his face. "Why?"

"Like Devin said, we're destined."

I roll my eyes. "Just because you repeat it doesn't mean I know what you're talking about."

"How much do you know about this town's history?" he asks, and before I can answer, he mentions, "The war that happened in the '40s."

"The war with the vampires over the amulet." I remember my grandmother mentioning the Great Vampire War multiple times. It was the one time in history that the witches and werewolves teamed up against the vampires. My grandma brings it up almost every time she comes over, always noting that this was an important part of both of our races.

"Yeah." His eyes stay straight, not even bothering to look at me. "When the dust settled and the war was won, our ancestors decided that something like that could never happen again." He starts to explain, his voice soft as if he was telling a child a bedtime story. "So many people died and got hurt over something as silly as an amulet. So they came to the conclusion to join our races, werewolves and witches, an alliance sort to say."

An alliance? I've never heard of such a thing. My family would have mentioned something this important, wouldn't they? The word alliance has never even been said in my house.

"They found a witch," he continues to explain, "Freya, who predicted that in the future, there would be a high priestess born a twin and an alpha born with a moon birthmark." Christian raises his shirt to show his hipbone, and right on it is a crescent-moon-shaped birthmark. It's about an inch on his hip bone. It's dark brown, and it contrasts against his caramel skin beautifully. As for the twin aspect, Alex and I are the first twins to ever bless our family, so my mother always reminds me.

"It is to be said that this alliance will be the greatest display of power ever seen in the supernatural world. That no one would dare threaten any of our kinds again." I hang on to every word. "And just to make sure it was to work, my great-grandfather and your great-grandmother sacrificed themselves to the witch. She used their blood to cast a spell. This spell would make sure that we fell for each other and that our love would be so great it could unite our two worlds, leaving them unstoppable and completely protected."

It's like the words he says break into the deepest thoughts in my head, but I don't quite register them immediately. I am a soon to be high priestess born a twin, and he has the crescent birthmark. It is clear that Freya's vision was about us. It's too big of a coincidence not to be.

"After the war, the wolves headed down to Florida, training to become better fighters, faster, stronger, and smarter. Anything to make sure a tragedy like that would never happen again. We became one with our wolves' sides and swore to protect any witch that comes onto our path."

I am speechless. It's too much. Not only are there people coming after me now, but I know my ancestors played super matchmaker for me before I was even a thought. I am destined to be with Christian. That explains why my feelings are so strong for him and why I felt that pull toward him ever since I saw him.

A realization hits me deep in the gut. "So when you took me on the date and went to the party, you were doing it out of duty." The words leave my mouth with much disappointment because although it has been a short time, I know I care deeply for him. I would hate if this is one-sided.

"Growing up, my mother would tell me this story over and over until I was tired of it. I used to think it was a myth. I didn't think someone can make me feel anything for anyone." He turns to look at me. The sun behind him makes him look like a mirage. "I swore I would do my duty, even if I liked you or not, but then I saw you that day at school, and I knew that I was a goner. It was like I wasn't really living until I met you." His words make my heart skip a beat. The way he looks intently at my eyes makes sure I know that the words he's saying register in my soul.

"My senses were heightened. I don't know how much you know about wolves, but when wolves fall for someone, it's like their whole life becomes that one person. We want to protect you and be there for you. It's like a need, like I need to be near you, need to see you."

"That's the way I feel," I say breathlessly because hearing him confess all this has me in a whirlwind of emotions.

"I don't know much about magic, but I do know it can't make you feel something you don't want to. We were destined to be since the beginning of time," he states matter-of-factly. "The spell our great-grandparents did just made sure we would find our way to each other."

I soak in his words, trying not to overthink them. It's a ton to process, but I can't unpack it all now. There's more pressing matter at hand.

"So who exactly is after me?" I put his confession in the deepest part of my mind so that I can fawn over it tonight when I am alone.

"We don't know exactly." He looks back at the woods. The crickets are starting to sound, and I know my parents will call me soon. "My guess is vampires. They would be affected the most when the alliance is solidified."

Solidified? My mind pours over that one word and what it means. I don't have time to analyze it because there's so much running through my brain.

"So they're after me because of the alliance."

"That's part of it, I guess," Christian says. "I didn't realize the threat was real until Saturday with the incident at the park. Do you want to tell me about this letter and figure your friends talked about?"

"It's not a big deal."

Christian's head turns to my face, and I immediately know that was the wrong answer to his question. "Alexandra, we have to be honest with each other for this going to work. Your life is at risk. I don't think you get how seriously I take all this."

I nod in agreement. The only reason I didn't tell Christian everything before is because I assumed he was human, and it would be putting him in danger by staying in his life. Now I know he isn't human, but I am still hesitant about Christian knowing everything. He doesn't strike me as the kind of guy who would just let things be. However, if he is right about the alliance and everything that comes with it, I have to trust him. I described what the letter said, what I saw outside my window, and the night of our date. He stays silent after I discuss everything, almost as if he's going over it in his head, combing through the information and looking for clues.

"That's why you were spooked," he says more to himself than to me, "the day we met, and I ran into you in the hallway. You had just found the letter."

I nod. "I think I ran into you, but yeah."

For the first time since I met Christian, I see his cheeks start to turn red like he's ashamed. He diverts his eyes back to the trees that surround the house. "The only reason you ran into me was because I placed myself in your way."

"Why would you do that?" I raise my eyebrow. I remember looking in the hallway that day. It was empty, and then out of nowhere, I bumped into Christian. I was too distracted to even think about it then.

Christian's cheeks brighten up more. "I had just got done running laps on the field. I was going to leave school, but I smelled you."

"I have a smell." I look at the sight of him being embarrassed; it's adorable. This huge man, with gorgeous hair and breathtaking eyes, is blushing right in front of me, and I can't help but smile regardless of all that is happening in my life.

"It's one of the first things I noticed about you." He nods. "Your scent is like a mixture of roses and vanilla."

The vanilla, I understand. It's my soap. I've been using the same soap since I can remember. The roses, I can't quite comprehend that. I don't have anything rose-scented.

"You smell like pine and man, if that makes sense." I don't know why I say it. Maybe because I know he was embarrassed or the fact that there was silent. However, it's true. Every time I am near Christian, I smell pine. I've come to know that it's his scent.

He's quiet for a beat, and he suddenly breaks out and laughs, like actually laughs. The sound is music to my ear, and the next thing I know, I am laughing right along with him. I forget that there's someone coming for me. I forget the letter and mysterious figure, and I just focus on this moment right here. I laugh when I haven't laughed what seems like forever.

I don't exactly know how I feel about this whole alliance thing. Just like everything in my life, I don't have a choice. However, I understand the duty that has been bestowed on me, and that isn't my biggest concern, at least not now. What confuses me is that my parents never mentioned this to me at all. You would think I should know something so big, but they kept me in the dark. Surely, they must have known, especially my mother. Why would she keep it from me?

My phone pings, and I know who it is before I check it.

Christian looks at the message and sighs, bummed that our time is cut short, just like myself. "Let's get you home."

"But." I start to protest. I have so many more questions I want to ask him. I want to talk to him and discuss our different "species." I feel as though the weight of having to carry this secret around has finally disappeared; however, it has been replaced with the atomic weight of the fact that someone, indeed, is after me. I can't ignore it, even if I want to. I will always be looking over my shoulder.

"We should probably go back inside."

"Christian."

I don't want to leave. I want to stay here where I know I'm safe. No one can find me here. No danger can come for me.

"I know," he says and stands up. He lets out his hand for me to grab, and I ignore the electricity that passes through me as we touch. "I got you," he mumbles, and I know he isn't about talking about this moment right here. In fact, I know he's talking about all the moments after this one.

The next couple of weeks are pretty normal. After Christian confessed everything, he's been around me 24-7. He walks me to class when he can, and if he can't, he'll have Jackson or Devin do it. We had two abandon our old lunch table because Christian and his friends eat lunch with us every day, so we ended at a larger table. He insists on driving me home every day, and if I go out, he wants me to let him know. At first, I was glad to have him around all the time, but when we're alone, he's always talking about ways to keep me safe or ways to keep me in the house. We never talk about anything else. He still has this wall up even though I figured it would come down once all our secrets were out in the open. I thought I would get to know him better, but it's like having a bodyguard, not a friend or whatever you would call us.

My friends aren't any better. Paris and Angel are always around, sleeping over or texting me, walking me to and from practice to see if I'm okay. Angel practically holds her breath every time I open my locker, hoping there's not a letter falling out of it. Alex has been fully protective mode as well, demanding he knows where I'm at and with whom. We have looked through our entire spell book, trying to even get a glimpse of all Christian has said about the past that involves both our families. We always find nothing. Not to mention, every time I try to even speak or bring any of this up with my parents, they are always gone or distracted before I can even get the word out.

In the past month, they have both been so busy looking at their emails and phones, having members of our coven coming in at all times of the day and discussing matters in secret. They have done this before, but now it's more apparent to me that they are hiding something.

The good news is that since that night a month ago at the park, nothing has happened. No figures, letters, or painted messages. Almost as if this secret threat has vanished, leaving the rest of us always on our toes, always waiting for the other shoe to drop, especially Christian. I have been held hostage by my fear and his protectiveness, unable to enjoy my last year of normalcy before my life turns upside down.

So today, a day before Halloween, I sit down with everyone and decide to do something about all the suffocating they have all been putting me through.

"I can't live like this anymore," I blurt the words out as soon as I sit down, not being able to hold them down for even another second.

"Like what?" Alex asks, his eyebrow perched up before he takes a bite of his salad.

"Like something bad is gonna happen to me at any moment," I say as if it isn't obvious. "You guys look after me as if I'm a child, and the only places I've been lately are home, school, and occasionally the playhouse. This isn't living."

"The priority is to make sure you're safe," Christian grunts, and I can't help but roll my eyes.

Bossy Christian has been here for the last month, and the adorable Christian that was with me in the playhouse has since vanished. Next to me, Christian is wearing a plain gray T-shirt and a pair of black jeans. He's gorgeous as always, his brown hair perfectly tossed up on the top of his head. He looks as always breathtaking, and if it weren't for the annoyance creeping in my blood, I would take a moment to drink it all in.

"I haven't gotten a threat in weeks. No one has been outside my window. I'd say I'm safe."

"You don't know that."

"I know that I don't want to live in fear anymore."

I can't remember the nights I stayed up in my room just thinking of all the bad things that could happen to me, losing sleep, looking over my shoulder for a threat that happens to never strike. I'm tired of it. This isn't the way I want my life to unfold. I only have so long until I give my life away to witchcraft and the covens. I want to enjoy life before then.

Angel speaks up, a small smile plays on her lips, and her green eyes look to my hazel ones. "We don't want anything to happen to you, sweetie. You have to be careful."

"Look, it sucks for now, but better safe than sorry, babe," Paris adds.

I shake my head. "Don't you think if there was a real threat, my mother would know about it? She's the high priestess."

Every time I try to talk to my mom or ask her about any of this, she's too busy. However, then I realized Christian and his friends came here because they heard about a threat. Wouldn't my mother hear about that also? I mean, if there was a real threat, a real reason why someone would come after me, I doubt she would keep that from me. She would do the opposite and make sure I was prepared and safe at all times.

"Yes, I got some threats, but the person or people who sent them didn't follow through, and I can't spend the rest of my life, especially the rest of my senior year, living like a hermit."

"There's still a risk, Lexi," Alex says.

"A risk that I lose my sanity," I say sarcastically as I roll my eyes. They are not listening to me; instead, they are just doing what they think is best for me.

Christian looks at me. "There is a real threat, Alexandra. I don't know what you want, but this is what's best for you," he says, like the decision is final, and I am supposed to take it, as if I am a member of his pack, and his word is law.

"Shouldn't I have a say on what I think is best for me? After all, it's my life."

"If you want to talk about how to keep you safe, then I am all ears."

He raises his eyebrow, and I can see that he's frustrated. Well, he can join the club. I've been here for weeks. He doesn't take me seriously; none of them do. It's almost as if I am talking to a wall, and the wall just keeps on getting thicker and thicker.

So the next words that come out of my mouth aren't exactly planned, but they come out of their own free will, regardless.

"I want to throw a harvest party," I blurt out.

Everyone stares at me in silence, all of them emotionless. Harvest Night is one of the biggest nights of the year for a witch. The harvest takes place on Halloween. It's an old witch holiday representing our gift to the ancestors for bestowing us with magic. Back in the olden days, witches would sacrifice other witches as a token of gratitude to those before us. Nowadays, it is a big excuse to party, eat, drink, and the occasional magic. When I was younger, our parents would tell Alex and I that on Halloween, our ancestors spirits would rise from the dead and give us blessings. I don't know if all that's true, but the magic that runs through our veins is always heightened on Halloween. It's like our bodies can feel the presence of our ancestors "rising from the dead," and it fuels our magic for the night.

"I already texted Mom earlier, and she told me she didn't mind. My father and she are spending the night with the round table discussing business anyways," I continue, taking their silence as my cue to explain everything quickly. "Before you guys say no, I'll be at home. You guys will be there, and I invited almost everyone from the senior class, humans and witches alike, so if someone were to attack me, they won't do it in front of humans. No one wants to get exposed."

"Lexi." Alex shakes his head, and I'm sure he's about to come up with a ton of reasons why this is a bad idea, but I won't let him stop me. I already planned everything out.

"Alex, in less than seven months, I will be the high priestess," I say, trying to plead to his empathetic side. If he can't respect my choices, maybe he can sympathize with me. "That means I have seven months left of senior year, seven months to be irresponsible, and importantly, I have seven months to just be me before the chaos sets in. I just want to be normal for a couple of months. Is that too much to ask for?"

I look into my twin brother's eyes. I can't pull this party off without his support.

"But you're not," Christian snaps. His voice is loud, so loud that it makes me jump. "You're not normal, Alexandra," he says as he stares me down. "You are going to be the next queen. You're not just some average teenage girl."

"I understand that, but I want to have a life before I succumb to what it is to be queen." I think of how my parents always talk about the good old days, the days when they were foolish kids heading off to college, ready to cause trouble. I want that. I want to have fun and make memories that I can carry with me through the long years to come.

"It's dangerous. There are people after you. This isn't something to be taken lightly." He eyes me like a child. "Why can't you see that?"

On the table, I see him clench his metal tray, his knuckles practically white from how hard he's holding it. I know he's angry, and I also know that it is taking him a lot to control his anger. Werewolves are known for their temper. Its genes are passed from generation to generation, which is a downside to their species. They can't always control their emotions.

"I haven't had any threat."

"Why do you think that is?" he says, his voice sharp as a knife. His brown eyes are now almost black. "Because they haven't had an opportunity to get to you. They can't access you. We have been watching you 24-7. No one has the chance to come to you."

"Well, I am not living in fear anymore, Christian," I snap back at him. He is not my father, nor does he own me. I will do this whether he likes it or not.

"Maybe she's right," Devin interjects, his voice is calm in the midst of Christian's and my annoyed tones. I almost forgot we were in the cafeteria, that we were surrounded by our friends. Neither Christian nor I look away from each other, despite Devin clearing his throat and continuing, "It's just one party, mate. We'll be there."

Jackson clears his throat and agrees with Devin. "I need a good party. I've been getting antsy lately, anyways."

"No," Christian snaps at his friends, and the whole table shuts down. At first, I'm shocked at him for raising his voice, and then I'm even more pissed that he thought that this decision was up to him.

"I wasn't asking permission, Christian. I was telling you," I snap back at him, crossing my arms over my chest as he stares me down. His eyes are so intense that if I weren't so mad, I'd be intimidated.

The whole table stays silent, probably shocked by the show-down in front of them. This is the first time Christian and I actually fought or even disagreed on anything. In the last month, I have taken his side on everything. He wanted me to stay in. I didn't complain, and I stayed at home. There were parties I was invited to, and he thought it wasn't best I'd go, so I hung out with Paris and Angel, watching movies. Everything he asked of me, I did, no questions asked, but not this time.

I am not backing down. This is my decision. It's my life, and if I want to throw a party and have fun for one night, that's totally in my right. He doesn't control me; no one does, and the fact that he thought it was okay for him to even think he did is wrong. We may be destined or whatever it may be, but last I checked, this is my life, not his.

Christian's breathing is hard. "I know you weren't because you already set everything up without even consulting anyone else," he says, and before I have time to respond, he pushes back from his seat, causing it to fall as he gets up, not even bothering to look at me when his voice hardens as he mutters. "Do whatever you want, Alexandra. It's your life, right? We're just here."

Chapter 14

After school, I head to cheerleading, my mind yearning for a distraction after what happened at lunch. I haven't seen Christian since then, and honestly, a part of me misses having him close by. I got used to him walking me to my class, being around me, someone to talk to. It was addicting, and I didn't realize how much I liked it until he was gone. I know he's mad, but I truly believe I am safe from harm, and he can't take away the last year I have to be just me—the last year I have to just be Lexi.

On my way to the gym, I see Johan at his locker. I haven't spoken to him in so long. It's almost awkward on the rare occasions I do set my eyes on him. He's kind of distanced himself from all of us about a couple of weeks ago. Maybe because Christian and his friends are always around, or maybe it's because he doesn't feel like he belongs anymore. Most likely, it's because of me. Maybe he's just trying to stay away from me, but I know Alex misses him. We all do. He was that one friend who had nothing to do with the magic world, a complete breath of fresh air.

So before I know it, I walk straight up to his locker. "Hey, stranger."

His eyes widen in shock, but he still gives me his boyish smile. "Hello there."

"So I'm throwing a party tomorrow night at my house. I was wondering if you would come." I smile at him, his blue eyes looking darker than usual.

"Are costumes required?"

"They are highly encouraged."

"So in other words, if I don't show up in a costume, you will beat me up like you did when we were eight and I stole your candy?" He laughs.

I smile fondly, remembering that one Halloween. It was one of the only Halloweens that my parents actually let us dress up and go trick-or-treating. Alex, Johan, and I went as s'mores. Alex was the chocolate, Johan was the crackers, and I was the marshmallow in the middle. That year, we got so much candy it could feed a small village for a week. Johan was convinced that I stole some of his candy, so he stole all of mine, claiming it was his. I got so mad that I pushed him on the ground and started punching him. Our parents got involved, and looking back at it, I laugh. Five minutes after the whole debacle, he gave me a lollipop from his stash, apologizing, and everything was forgiven.

"Maybe something about Halloween brings out the crazy in me," I joke, and he just laughs.

"Very well." He closes his locker and places his book bag over his shoulder. "Can I bring a date?"

"Of course." I smile bigger and relieved because a part of me thought he would never get over me. Not to be cocky or conceited, but I was worried that his feelings for me would be permanent. I am happy he found someone else. Johan, more than anyone, deserves to be happy.

"Well, we'll be there."

"Can't wait." I wave goodbye and head to the gym.

When practice is over, Paris drive Angel and me home. "Is it me, or was the queen of mean being way too nice today?"

"I noticed." Anita, who's usually the meanest person I know, was actually quite helpful today. She gave compliments and didn't yell when some of the girls didn't land their stunts. It was unsettling, to put it lightly.

"Someone is getting laid."

Angel scoffs. "Why does your head always go there? Maybe she's just happy."

"Happy because she's getting dick down."

"Paris," Angel screeches.

I can't help but laugh at their interaction. It's so them—Paris saying something inappropriate, and Angel freaking out. It's normal.

"Ugh, whatever." She rolls her eyes. "So has your boyfriend talked to you yet?" Paris turns her attention to me as she stops at a red light.

"He's not my boyfriend." I check my phone and sigh—nothing. He must be really mad. "But no."

"Just give him some time to blow off steam," Angel says.

I shake my head. "I just don't understand him."

"What's not to understand?" Paris says as she makes a turn. "He wants to protect you. And it frustrates him that you won't let him. It's simple, really."

"I don't need protection." I can't help but roll my eyes. She's defending him. He's acting like a child, throwing a tantrum because I won't do what he wants. It's frustrating. All of them are frustrating.

"You think you don't need protection," she corrects. "Someone did break into your locker and gave you that letter. Someone did follow you to the park. That is not normal stuff, dude."

"Stuff like that doesn't just go away," Angel interjects. "You're just being stubborn."

"I'm not stubborn."

"Yes, you are," they say in unison, their voices sounding like a chorus to an annoying song.

"Look, Lexi," Paris says as she pulls into my street, her tone serious. "The only reason I'm going to this party is because you really want me to, and if something were to happen, we can prevent it. But I honestly think that this is a bad idea."

"Nothing is going to happen." I throw my hands up, pissed to have to explain the same thing over and over again. "And let's say something does happen. Someone comes after me. It's the harvest. My magic will be heightened."

"Yours and everyone else's," Angel adds. "What if the person after you is a witch and not a vampire?"

I never thought about it like that. That could be a possibility, especially since there haven't been vampires in New Orleans since the war. My anxiety threatens to creep through the dark cracks of my mind, but I won't let it.

"I'll be fine."

"I hope so." Paris shakes her head. "Anyway, Angel, I found a costume for you online, and we're gonna pick it up tomorrow before the party."

"I don't need a costume. You know that I have one."

Every year, Angel dresses up as an angel—every year.

"Yes, don't worry. You're still gonna be an angel, but my version." I see Angel bite her lip in the rearview mirror, and I smile. "How about you, Lexi? You need a costume."

"I'll look for one tomorrow. I just wanna shower and go to bed tonight," I say as she pulls into my driveway.

"Well, I'll send you ideas."

"Thanks, I'll see you guys tomorrow. Love you."

They smile at me in unison and say together, "We love you more."

I get home, and the house is practically empty. Alex is probably still at practice, so I decided to go straight up to my room. As soon as I enter the house, the smell of Fabuloso fills my nostrils. At the end of the foyer is Trina, our housekeeper. She cleans and cooks for us whenever my mom can't be around, which lately is a lot. She gives me a small smile as I give her a small greeting before heading up the stairs. Trina isn't a woman of many words. She's a middle-aged woman, just like my mother, with a strong work ethic. Her black hair has a few gray strands from up-and-coming age. She's a petite white woman, and all I really know about her personal life is that she was raised by a witch but never had powers of her own. My mother met her when she became queen and offered her the job. She's been with us ever since.

Once I reach my room, I decide to get into the shower. A cascade of warm water is exactly what the doctor ordered. As the water runs through my hair and down my body, I can't help but think of Christian. I hate that we fought, I hate that he isn't talking to me, and I hate most of all that I actually want him to be all over me like before. What does that say about me? A girl who doesn't know what her life is without a man and that I don't feel complete without him.

When I get out of the shower, I immediately notice the black gown laid out in my bed, a crown right next to it. It wasn't there before I got in the bathroom. I walk over to my bed to examine the dress. The material is lace, and it felt like heaven through my pruned fingers. The gown is long and has a halter type of top and a skintight bottom. The crown is gold with red jewels decorating it. Red heels lay on the floor, and there's a note on the mattress next to the crown with a message typed out.

Dress as what you aspire to be.

My mother must have dropped it off and must have left afterward, maybe even had Trina lay it on the bed. That would explain the typed-up note. She must have got this dress today because it's brand new. She must have bought it after I said I wanted to throw a party.

I place the dress neatly in the closet and put all the crowns on the dresser. Although I know I am going to regret it, I check my phone, hoping that I missed a text or call from Christian, but I was wrong. Instantly, a frown covers my face. I was hoping he would at least see if I got home okay. I debated calling him for about two minutes until I decide that a text message is the best way to communicate.

Still mad at me?

And almost instantly, I get a response.

Yes.

I sigh, throw my phone on the bed, and go downstairs to make something to eat, knowing that the conversation we need to have cannot be over text.

As I descend the stairs, the scent of sugar cookies makes its way through my nose and ends at my grumbling belly—sugar cookies that are as familiar as a warm hug and always make me yearn for the person who makes them. I know she's here before I even make it into the kitchen. Her presence is always known in this house by her soft humming that fills the empty halls of this so-called home.

The smile on my face is probably the realest I have smiled in ages as I look at my grandmother Rosa wiping the kitchen top. Her gray hair is pushed back into a bun, showing off her brown eyes, which are accompanied by a few wrinkles around them from smiling too much. Her caramel skin shines from the sunlight bouncing off the window, and her big, genuine smile appears on her face the moment she sees me enter the room.

"There's my favorite granddaughter."

I rush into her arms and immediately feel the warmth that her body always radiates. I embrace her fully, trying to stop the tears from my eyes from springing. I have missed her deeply, and after the last month, I needed her more than I would ever probably admit.

My grandma has always been the burning flame in a cave full of darkness—the supportive voice that always quiets my doubts. My grandmother has a way of speaking that makes you believe that you can do anything.

As a retired high priestess, she's respected heavily in the witch community, and the way she commands any room she enters with grace and poise always grants her admiration. Even more than that, she is a fountain filled with knowledge that never runs dry.

"Grams," I say as she pulls me away from her body to examine me head to toe.

"Oh, you get even more beautiful by the day. It must be from our side of the family." She winks at me, her smile infectious. She pulls my brother up from his chair, from the kitchen table, which I didn't even notice in his presence, and holds up both our hands as she looks at us, love filling her eyes. "Remember what I always tell you two. You together are unstoppable. You are the future of our community."

"You mean Lexi, Grams. She's the one who's gonna be in charge. She's gonna change the world. I am just her twin brother."

I look up at Alex. I note something off in his voice, a little bitterness or even sarcasm, but it's there. I hear nuances of his words and the tone in his voice.

My grandmother squeezes our hands, bringing my attention back to her. "I said together." She sounds persistent, as if she is hinting at something, but I have no idea what. Ever since we were little, my grandmother would tell us that we were a force to be reckoned with. I always thought that she meant we were our own support system, but right now, I'm not so sure. It feels like she means more.

"Mother."

In comes my mom and my father in tow into the kitchen fresh out of work. My mother looks tired as if she has been working for days straight with no rest.

"I thought you were coming tomorrow."

She walks up to Grandma and kisses her cheek while my dad goes in for a bear hug.

"I thought a day earlier wouldn't harm anyone."

"But we agreed, Mother." My mom grabs a wineglass and then a bottle of wine setting it on the table. She looks rundown, and I feel so bad. That light that usually fills her eyes has vanished and, in its wake, has left behind bags under her beautiful eyes. My father looks no better; his hair is a shivered mess, and I swear he looks more stressed out with each passing day. He also grabs a glass and sits next to my mother. He sighs loudly as if his day wasn't any better.

"How was work?" I ask them both as I stand on the other side of the marble-covered island that takes place in the middle of the kitchen.

Dad nods and then takes a gulp from his wine while Mom just says, "Work was work," with a fake smile on her face.

I look at Alex. His eyes meet mine, and I know he's thinking the same thing as me. My mother has had the same response to that question for as long as I can remember. Whenever work is brought up, she has always given one answer. I have the best job in the world. I can't complain. Her nonchalant answer and the fact that Grandma is here when she ever comes back to New Orleans for Christmas, Thanksgiving, or my birthday makes me wonder if something is wrong.

"Grandma, what's with the surprise visit?" Alex reads my mind and changes the subject, trying to figure out why everything is weird.

My grandmother looks at my mother and father, and they both raise any eyebrow at her as if warning her to be quiet. The energy in the room has been replaced with something I am starting to know all too well, a secret.

"I don't need a reason to visit my grandkids." She smiles, but it doesn't reach her eyes.

Alex raises his eyebrow but doesn't question it anymore, but to me, that answer doesn't seem legit. They're hiding something, I can sense it.

Grams makes dinner, and we all sit in the dining room table to enjoy the meal. My parents and Grams talk about how Florida is treating her or how school is going for us, but no one mentions anything about work, the harvest, or their favorite topic for the last couple of months: my coronation. It's like they're avoiding something, tiptoeing as if Alex and I won't notice. It's kind of insulting to think that they think of us so little they figure we won't realize something is up.

"How come no one told me I was destined?" I ask because, with all three of them here, I need answers.

The room goes quiet. My father, who's at one end of the table, stops. Alex and Grandma, who are directly in front of me, turn to my mother, as does my father, who is at the end of the table. He has stopped eating, and we are all waiting for my mom to say something, looking at me. No one says anything for a while, probably thinking about what to say next or how to avoid it.

At this moment, I know all Christian has said is true. The looks on their faces of shock confirm it. The more silent they stay, the angrier I get. They lied to me, all three of them. They raised me, telling me all the histories of our family, but they forgot to tell me the biggest one of all. Their silence now is a slap in the face, as if they don't care about giving me my answers.

"No one is going to say anything?"

"Who told you about that?"

My mother is the first to say anything. Her eyes going back to cutting the piece of chicken on her plate. Her voice is calm and collected, and somehow, this angers me more.

"Christian," I turn to Dad. "You remember him right, Daddy?" I say, recalling the night that Dad stood at the door and talked to Christian before our date. It suddenly hit me why he wasn't weird about it, and he was okay with Christian taking me out; he knew. He knew exactly who he was then, and he didn't say anything. My blood boils just thinking about it. "You knew, didn't you? When he came to pick me up? You knew exactly who he was?"

"Yes, as soon as he said his name, I put it together."

The betrayal stings. A small part of me was hoping that Christian was lying or maybe embellishing the truth. That's probably why it took me so long to actually ask my parents. I didn't want to think that the same people who taught me how to control my magic and who dressed up as Mr. and Mrs. Claus when I was a child would lie to me about something like this. I couldn't believe it. It's true. They neglected me from the truth about my future for seventeen years without any regard for me.

I turn to my mother. "Why didn't you guys tell me?" I ask again, this time determined to get a damn answer from someone. "How come I had to hear from a complete stranger that I am destined to be with him?"

"We were going tell you," Mom says as she continues to eat her dinner as if this is just a normal conversation.

"When?" I scoff. "On my way to my wedding?" I can't help but roll my eyes.

Grams looks at me, her eyes and voice soft. "Don't be mad, Alexandra. We figured the less you knew, the less overwhelming it would be for you. You have enough on your plate."

"Are you kidding?" I throw my hands up. Not only did they set me up and didn't tell me, but now they are dictating what is too much for me.

"Lower your tone, Alexandra," my mother says, a warning in her voice, but frankly, I can't care less.

"You lied to me my whole life, and now you want me to lower my voice?" I give her a humorless laugh. "You're unbelievable."

My mother looks at me. "We did what was right because I am your mother. End of discussion."

"Mother of the year." I roll my eyes.

"What did you say to me, young lady?" my mother shouts at me, and I see the vein popping out of her forehead. Her anger mirroring my own, but frankly, I do not care. "I am your mother, and you will respect me. I don't care how you feel."

"Like all of you respected me!" I yell back. "You lied to me for seventeen years. You all did." I point to all three of them. "And what, you expect me to be okay with that? No, I want answers." I slam my hand on the table, and I can feel it. The magic is building in me slowly, but it's there. I know I'm gonna blow if I don't calm down, but I can't, not now.

"Alexandra," my mom seems shocked.

"Go to your room, young lady, now!" my father says sternly.

"Why do Christian and his family think there's a threat to me?" I ignore him and look at my mother. "I know you know what I'm talking about."

"Alexandra, I will not discuss such things with you in the state that you are in."

"So there is a threat."

"No!"

"Liar!" I yell louder. The magic is running through my veins just like that night in the park, but this time, I'm not scared. I'm pissed.

"Rose, just tell her the prophecy," my grandmother says, and immediately, I turn to her.

"What prophecy?"

"Stay out of this, Mother!" my mother snaps, and my grandmother just shakes her head, refusing to look me in the eye when I try to stare her down. What prophecy are they talking about? Christian and I, or is there more that I do not know?

The feeling of lack of knowledge and ignorance fuels my anger even more. They are still hiding something, still lying, leaving me in the dark as if I was a child with no say. Do they not understand that this is my life? How am I to accomplish anything if I don't have the pieces to the messed-up puzzle that is my life?

"What is she talking about? What prophecy?"

"It's nothing."

My hand slams on the wooden table in anger, and the hold I have on my emotions and magic loosens. "Stop lying."

"Lexi, calm down." Alex looks at me, concern in his eyes.

Alex was never one to rock the boat, even now when we know our parents have been withholding information. He doesn't act on emotion, not like me. I am all feeling, all impulse. Even now, I know he's right. I do need to calm down before my powers go haywire. I can feel it coming.

However, I don't care. I am too annoyed to give a damn, "No, they're hiding something. You know it, and so do I. They need to fess up."

"Alexandra," my mother stands up from her chair, her hands planted firmly on the table, her stance demanding. One I know all too well. "You will go to your room RIGHT NOW."

"No."

I am tired of people telling me what to do—Christian telling me where to go and what to do for the last couple of weeks, my friends telling me I need to stay put and be protected, my family lying to me for years and now telling me that I need to calm down, be a good girl, and go to my room. I'm tired of it, all of it. I am not a little girl anymore. The need for answers feeds my magic that courses through my brain, and suddenly, the lights start to flicker, just like that night in the park.

"What's going on?" My dad looks up at the lights, perplexed. They all do, except Alex.

Alex studies my face, and whatever he sees staring back is enough confirmation for him to say, "It's Lexi."

"Alexandra, you need to control your emotions. Don't let your feelings take control of you."

"Stop telling me what to do." The words come out of my mouth, but the voice sounds unrecognizable from my own—deeper, madder, almost vengeful. "What prophecy?"

The table starts to shake under my palm, and the glasses and plates start falling to the ground, spilling the food and the water. "Tell me."

I look at my mother. I can't stop what's going on around me, but frankly, I am too heated to think of anything else. The table shakes faster as I think of all the years they have kept me in the dark, all the years they didn't tell me anything. It's wrong. They were wrong, and I want them to admit it. I just want the truth.

I know what I am doing isn't right. I know I should at least try to regain control of my feeling—to control my magic and be the good witch I was raised to be, but that girl got no answers. That girl was ignorant of the fibs that surrounded her life. That girl is gone.

"Alexandra." My dad gets out of his chair, and so does Grams.

"She needs to calm down," she says. "She's gonna blow out the circuits."

"Tell me," I repeat again and again until it's the only thing I can think about.

The picture frames that decorate the wall start breaking, and everyone uses their arms to cover their heads from the broken shards, everyone except me. It's like I'm possessed almost. The power cursing through my veins is too much, using my anger as fuel, taking over me until I feel the rush of my magic and its effects. It's like I am not in my body anymore. I can feel what's happening. I know it's coming from me, but I cannot stop it.

"Alexandra, take deep breaths, honey. You need to calm down." Another picture frame breaks, and another. "Control it." The lights flicker faster, and my chair starts to rise from the ground and up into the air. I am levitating, or at least my chair is.

I can see myself in the reflection of the dining room mirror. I don't look like myself, my hair standing up as if I have been electrocuted, my eyes darker than they have been, almost black even. I look pale and drained of any light, like a shadow of myself. My family stare up at me, all of them look panicked. It's like I'm here but not really here. I see all of them look up at me, confused, scared, and alarmed. I am in the air while the lights are flickering, the table is shaking, and the wine glasses are shattering.

I see my grandmother grab my brother by his shoulders. "You need to stop her. Only you can," I hear her say.

"I can't." He shakes his head.

"Rose, can you get her down," my father says to my mother.

"Not without hurting her!" my mother yells, and I can see her eyes look up at me, and I can see worry run across them. "Alexandra, stop it. Come back to us."

The vase in the middle of the table breaks, and the shaking of the table increases and goes faster than before. I can feel it, the powers taking over me, the magic overcoming me and my anger. I'm no longer in control. I've never felt like this before. I'm scared. I try to breathe. I try to calm down, but it doesn't work in the slightest.

"You have to stop her, Alexander, before she hurts herself!" my grandmother screams at Alex as his eyes look over at me, laced with concern and fear.

"I don't know how."

"Alexander!" my father shouts.

"You come from the same power source. You can stop her if you will it, Alex."

He shakes his head, panicking and anxious as he looks at me. He doesn't know what to do, neither do I. I am no longer the one pulling the strings in my body, no longer the one pushing the buttons.

In one motion, he places his hands up, his eyes still staring into mine. "Prohibere!" he screams loud, the Latin word for *stop*. Nothing happens. He looks at my grandmother, and with a reassuring nod from her, he tries again. This time, he plants his feet firmly on the ground, his eyes never leaving my own as he yells to the deepest parts of me. "Lexi, prohibere!"

As soon as the word leaves his mouth, something happens. All of a sudden, the anger that fueled my magic has simmered down, and my chair crashes to the ground so fast that I fall out of it and hit the floor. As I look up, I see that the lights have stopped flickering, and they are rushing to my aid. My mind is no longer fogged up, the shaking is down, the breaking of glass is complete, and I feel my blood start to cool down. My body feels weak as I look at the concerned looks on my parents' faces. I can't speak, too stunned.

My eyes grow heavy, and before I pass out, I see Alex pass out right beside me.

Chapter 15

I wake from my recurring dream to find that I am in my own bed. The sun shines through the curtains of my room, and the alarm clock next to my bed reads 10:52 a.m. I haven't slept in months, and it feels weird to do so.

The events of last night are still fresh in my mind: the yelling, the lies, and the loss of control all circle through my mind, accompanying my head with a splitting migraine. I still can't comprehend how I lost control so quickly. My body still feels somewhat weak, and sitting up seems like a chore.

"Well, look who's up," a familiar voice fills my ears.

I see Christian at my desk in the far corner of the room with the chair looking at me. He's in a white T-shirt and blue jeans. His midnight black locks sit on his head, looking messy as if he's been running his fingers through them multiple times. Yet he's a sight for sore eyes.

"Christian, what are you doing here?"

Christian is in my room. I look down at my clothes. I'm wearing a One Direction concert tee I got when I was fourteen and a pair of gray sweatpants. Both of which have several stains and wrinkles.

"You didn't show up to school," he says as he gets up from the seat. In his hands is a picture frame, and before he even places it down, I know that it's a picture of Alex and I, as kids, dressed as princesses and princes for Halloween.

"I got worried."

I try to ignore the flutter of my heart as I hear him say those words.

"My parents let you in?"

"No, they have no idea I'm in here." He shakes his head and takes a seat at the edge of the bed beside me. "I was going to knock on the door, but I heard your parents talking about what happened last night. They seemed upset, so I wanted to make sure you were alright."

"So what? You climbed up the side of my house, onto the roof, and into my room," I joke, but it's not a joke because while I am smiling and being sarcastic, his face is serious. That is exactly what he did.

I steal a glance at my window. I live on the second floor. I was about to ask him how the hell he accomplished that, but the werewolf thing came to mind. Enhanced supernatural abilities that make him run faster, jump higher, see and hear better, and be stronger than ten human men combined. It was probably a cakewalk for him.

"Are you hurt?" He takes my small hands in his giant ones. Shivers run through my body, as always, when he touches me. His eyes examine my hands and arms intently, looking for something. I don't know what, but he doesn't find it.

"What are you looking for?" I say as he looks at my neck and finally cupping my face as his thumb caresses my cheek. He hasn't been this affectionate with me since the playhouse, and I try to revel in that feeling.

"Your mom was cleaning up glass when I got here. I wanted to make sure you didn't get cut."

"Oh." The sound of breaking glass and my family's screams echo in the back of my head.

"Did you do that?"

My cheeks heat self-consciously at his question. "Yes," I say, ashamed.

Christian's brown eyes search my own, almost pleading. "Did it hit you anywhere?"

Being this close to him, I can see how clear his tanned skin is—no imperfections whatsoever. His shoulders seem tense, and I can see the outline of his biceps and the veins on his arms. Christian is so beautiful it's distracting. He's trying to see if I am okay, and here I am, checking him out. The nature of our relationship: Christian taking care of me and my head is too busy being in the clouds.

Again, I shake my head as he moves my head slightly to the right and then slightly to the left as if he didn't just check it.

"Are you still mad at me?" I say as he finally lets go of my face.

"Yes."

I look up at him to find his brown eyes watching me. "I don't want to live—"

"Let's not talk about that right now." He puts his hand up, interrupting me. Then he gets up and walks up to the end of the bed before taking a seat on it, creating distance between us. "What happened last night?"

I pout as I already miss the warmth that comes from him. "I thought you heard my parents."

"I wanna hear your side of the story."

I bite my lip. I don't want to tell him. I can't. I'm too ashamed. This is the third time I that I have lost control. What kind of future queen does that make me? I feel weak and useless. My anger fueled me to the point that the dam that holds in my powers broke and caused chaos.

"Alexandra, what happened?" Christian's soft voice brings my attention back to him and away from my thoughts. His tone isn't commanding or nonchalant but instead filled with care. His voice is softer than I've ever heard it before, and it pulls at my vulnerable heartstrings. "Are you okay?"

"I lost control." I play with my fingers that lay on my lap, refusing to look up at Christian. "I don't know how. I confronted my family for lying to me and not telling me about you. I asked them why they were lying and what they were hiding, but they avoided everything I said to them." I sigh. Memories of last night have not stopped playing in my head since I woke up. I can still my reflection in the mirror. I didn't recognize that girl, that witch with incontrollable power, being erratic.

"My grandmother mentioned something about a prophecy, and my mother just dismissed her. I felt like a child, not heard, and one thing led to another, and I got furious. I was in the air, our dinnerware broke, and the table shook so hard I can still hear it in my head."

I look up slightly from my lap to see Christian, listening to me intently, no emotions shown on his face. No words, no judgment, just letting me say what I have to say.

"I was so mad, Christian. I didn't recognize myself. I couldn't stop it when it got too far. I remember seeing my parents worried faces, and all I can think about was how they lied and how it all went left so fast. Alex had to will me to stop." Realization dawns over me. Alex fainted before me. "Alex," I say before I rip the blanket off my bed and try to get out of bed.

"Whoa."

In a second, Christian comes from the end of the bed to me. "Lie back down. You should take it easy."

"I have to check on Alex."

What if he hurt himself? He could have hit his head when he fell, or I could have hit him or anyone else with broken glass. I would never forgive myself if I hurt any one of them, regardless of how I felt. That was never my intention.

"He's fine," Christian says as he places the blanket over my legs again. "They all are."

I take an exhale, the breath I didn't know I was holding in, relieved.

"Are you okay?" He sits back down next to me.

"Yeah, just a little run down. I don't know what happened. It's like I wasn't me. The magic was so strong it was like I was there, but I wasn't. It's never been like that before. I can feel my powers in me running through my veins. After last night, it's different. It's not as strong, but it's definitely different from before." I try to explain the shift that has taken over my body and mind, how I feel different from when I woke yesterday, how I don't feel like fully back to myself before I was able to ignore it, a slow hum in my body. I try to find the right words to discuss how this really feels. "It's like a current, electrifying me." I look at my hands. I can imagine the magic under my skin. Little bolts of electricity are moving in me, ready at any moment. It's like my body has been asleep for years and has finally awakened.

I try to ponder on my feelings. I am pissed, hurt, but mostly confused. Confused about last night and why my parents would go out of their way to lie to me. It doesn't make any sense.

"I just feel like there's this part of my life that I don't know about, and it sucks, and now this."

I raise my hands, and I look at Christian, my eyes fill up with tears. "I'm scared, Christian."

Without a second passing, he pulls me in his arms. He is letting his big arms envelop me and soothe me from the feeling of being broken. His hug is strong and all too real. Quieting the noise outside this room, outside of us. My fear doesn't go away or dissolve, but it does take a backseat in my mind and lets me sit in this moment.

"Maybe you should talk to your mother about this."

He pulls away after about a minute, but it still feels too soon.

I sigh. After last night, I don't know how I would approach her. We were both mad at each other, yelling and screaming. That has never happened before.

"I don't even know if she would have an answer for me."

"She's coming up," Christian says, getting off the bed and moving toward the window.

"Don't leave," I barely whisper.

I am not ready to face the reality that awaits outside my door. With Christian here, I can prolong it for a bit more. I don't know how to explain it, but Christian doesn't make me. He just gives a small reassuring smile while he hides in the closet, the door closing the exact moment my mother opens my bedroom door.

"Alexandra."

She runs to my side, her hands on either side of my face as she examines my eyes. She looks the exact opposite of how I feel. Her hair is brushed and pulled back in a bun. She's in a dark blue pantsuit and minimal makeup that enhances her already natural beauty. She looks whole and put together as if the events from last night were just a bad dream that has faded away for her.

"Oh, thank the ancestors, you're okay."

She hugs me tightly, almost cutting circulation from my lungs.

"How's Alex?" My voice is small, too embarrassed by the events that transpired last night. I don't even look her in the eye. My mother is the high priestess, always in control, always demanding perfection. She taught me how to control my emotions so events like the ones that transpired last night wouldn't happen, and yet it still did.

"He's okay, playing video games downstairs." She holds onto my hands. "How are you feeling?" Her thumb runs on the back of my palms.

"Mom, I'm so sorry about last night. I was so angry. I couldn't control myself. My powers were all too much. I"—I look at my hands—"I lost it. Everything you taught me about controlling my emotions went out the window."

She nods for a second, pondering my words or perhaps her response, and after a beat, she says, "It's okay. All that matters is that you're okay."

"Mom, but I don't think I am." I shake my head. In fact, I know that I am not. "That just doesn't happen. It was like my powers were in charge of my body, not me. I feel possessed. Something is wrong with me?" My words come out smaller than I intended, and I know you can hear my fear coming out, making itself known.

"Of course not, baby." She squeezes my hands. "There is nothing wrong with you. You are a young witch who is coming to the full effect of your powers." A small smile appears on her lips, but it doesn't seem genuine. "It's normal. We all lose control from time to time."

I shake my head. She's not getting it. This wasn't a normal occurrence. I was not in charge. I was not myself. "Mom, this isn't like when I was young, and Alex and I would close doors one accident. I almost destroyed the dining room." Why isn't she taking this more seriously?

"Honey, you're okay now. That is all that matters. Now I'm gonna let you get some rest before your big party tonight." She kisses my cheek, ready to go, and leaves me here with looming questions.

I don't care about the party right now. Why can't she see that?

"Mom." She gets off the bed.

"Alexandra, don't exert yourself," she warns, and I can see it. Behind her eyes, an emotion passes through them before she erases it from her face. "Your father, grandmother, and I will be out most of the night at a gala at the mayor's office, and afterward, we're gonna visit some of your grandmother's old friends and have round table meetings. We are going to be busy." She grabs the knob to walk out. "We might stay the night there, so please be careful."

"Mom," I say, trying to urge her to stay, to listen to enlighten me. Something is happening to me, something isn't right, and I know she knows. Why can't she just tell me?

"You know the rules. No drinking, no drugs, no boys staying over that aren't Jordan or Johan, and definitely no magic in front of humans." She points her finger at me. "Is that understood?"

"But, Mom."

"Alexandra, is that understood?" She ignores everything I've said completely. Her voice is stern, and I know that this is final.

I am never gonna get the answers from her that I needed. She's evaded every question or ignored it as if she never heard them. If I wanted to find out what I needed to know, I was gonna have to go around her and figure it out on my own.

So I bite my tongue and give her a world-class smile, willing the anger out of my voice before I speak, "You got it, Mother."

My mom smiles back and closes the door behind her. As soon as she does, I take a big sigh and throw my head back on the pillow. Feeling defeated, what can she be hiding? What can be so big that she can't tell me the truth?

Christian opens the door to the closet, and I almost forgot he was there. I hear him walk around the bed and feel the bed shift as he lowers down on it. We stay silent for what seems like forever. All that you can hear in the room is our breathing.

"Be my date tonight," Christian speaks so low that I am not even sure I hear it.

I open my eyes to see him looking down at me. "Are you asking or telling me?"

"Telling."

"I thought you didn't want me to have the party."

"Oh, I still think it's a bad idea." He sighs and runs his fingers through his hair as he watches me sit up.

I can't believe this. The only person more stubborn than myself is Christian. That's something I know all too well. So hearing him now, saying he'll be my date, almost sounds too good to be true.

"I know that you have been feeling overwhelmed and like you're not in control of your own life," he explains his reasoning. "I never want you to feel that way with me. I don't want to take control of your life or make you feel unheard. I want to protect you. I need to protect you."

In this moment, his voice sounds so sincere that the smile that graces my face is all too real.

I know it's hard for him to do this because although I may not know much about Christian, I do know that he loves control. He strives off it. So giving me a say for tonight, even though he's completely against it, makes me care for him so much more. He listens to me unlike my parents. He does. He knows how important this night is for me, and he's letting me have it.

"Thank you." I place my head on his broad shoulders and smile brightly at him. I hope he knows how much this means to me and how much I appreciate it.

"Alexandra." His big hand grabs onto my own as we both look outside at the sunlight balancing off the trees. "If something happens to you"—shakes his head as if the thought is unbearable and looks down—"I wouldn't forgive myself," he mumbles the last few words.

"As long as I'm with you, I'm safe," I reassure him, and as the words come out of my mouth, I truly believe them. When I am with Christian, I am safe, safe from danger and my own fears—safe from myself.

Chapter 16

Christian decides to stay for the afternoon, both of us wanting to stay in the cocoon that is my room. He lies next to me in bed, watching movies and enjoying each other's company. My body is completely aware of him here. I can barely focus on *Die Hard* with him being so close. He has had my hand in his since we started the movie, his fingers running back and forth on my knuckles, leaving goose bumps in their wake. Shivers run through my body every time his knee bumps into my own or even when I sneak glances at him.

A single piece of hair hangs off his head and onto his forehead, and the only way that I can describe that look on him is romantic, like the love interest in a romantic novel with the big muscles, dimples, and breathtaking eyes that you can get lost in for days at a time. Christian is one of those men, one of the men that they make movies about and one of the heartbreak songs that make you want to lock yourself in your room and give in to your feelings. His long eyelashes, perfectly sculpted nose, and sharp jawline make my knees grow weak, and I don't think they ever won't. His long legs are landed out in front of him. He looks comfortable even though the bed looks so small under him. However, that is just Christian. Bigger than any bed, any room, anything.

Christian grabs the remote with his free hand, shuts off the TV, and turns to me. "You know you have been staring for the past five minutes, right?" A knowing, smug grin shines on his face.

I should feel embarrassed, but I am not. I like staring at Christian, trying to find imperfections where there seems to be none, memorizing his face so I can dream about it later on. "You know this is the first time since our first date that we've actually hung out together without worrying about threats."

"I'm sorry about that."

"Make it up to me. Tell me more about yourself." I know almost nothing about Christian, yet he has seen the ins and outs of my life for the past month. It is only fair I get an exchange of information.

A heavy sigh comes out of his mouth. In the time I have known Christian, I have noticed a couple of things. He's controlling, detail-oriented, protective, and he hates to talk about himself.

"I told you I'm not that interesting," he mumbles under his breath.

"Let me be the judge of that."

He searches my eyes, and when he sees that I'm not letting up on this, he lets go of my hand and lies his head down on the pillow so that I am looking down at him. "What do you wanna know, Alexandra?"

I try not to grin too big at the small victory and ask my first question of many. "Are you the alpha for your pack?"

"Not yet." His eyes stare right at the white ceiling above us. "My father is the alpha. He's training me to be his successor, though."

"How's that?"

"It's alright, I guess. I've been preparing for this my whole life, giving orders, taking care of my people," he said in a calm, unhurried voice. "It's all I know."

"So when you give orders, do people actually listen?" All I know about werewolves is their powers and their need to be in packs; other than that, I am utterly clueless.

"They have to. It's wolf law." He places his arm under his head to prop his head up, his eyes still trained forward. "Us werewolves aren't like regular people. When our alpha gives an order, something in our brain goes off. We have to do it, and if we don't, it hurts."

"They hurt you." I try to hide the shock that accompanies those words, but by Christian's raised eyebrow, I know that I failed.

"No, it's not like we actually get beaten. Our bodies are built differently. We're wired to follow orders. It's literally built in our DNA. When you try to disobey an alpha, your brain sends a trigger to the weakest point in your body, your head, your knee, maybe even your heart, and it exploits it."

125

I try to imagine having to obey every little thing my mother says. Doing what she wants me to do with no question. There's a reason Christian is so controlling. It all makes sense. That is the only way he knows how to be.

"What is your weakest point?" I wonder out loud.

He shakes his head. "I always follow orders, Alexandra." His tone, something like regret, creeps into his voice. "I wouldn't know my weakest point."

"You said following orders is wolf law," I point out. "Are there any other laws?" I urge him to continue, curiosity getting the better of me.

"Most of our laws are based around loyalty. Don't cause intentional harm to your pack members. Don't conspire behind your pack's back. Always put the pack first. Alpha word is law.

"Us werewolves aren't only different from humans physically. It's emotionally, spiritually, and mentally also," he explains, lost in thought. "When we experience a loss or any pain, the feeling almost paralyzes us. We don't just get angry. We get ballistic. We don't just get sad. We get depressed. We don't do like. We love. Every emotion we have is enhanced to a different degree. We never feel anything halfway. It's either all or nothing with us," he said with a quiet intensity that makes me hang on every word he says. "So betrayal stings more than it would for humans. That is why loyalty is so important to us."

Does he have strong feelings for me? I know how I feel about him. Does he feel the same way, maybe more than I do? I think about that night in the playhouse when he told me we were destined. How he said his feelings for me were real. He never really acknowledged it after that day. We never talked about what exactly we were. We just acted like it wasn't this huge thing clouding over us both.

I don't know what to say. Maybe I need time to process something so big. So I reach in between us and grab his hand. He wraps his fingers around mine, and immediately, I feel the heat coming off his body. We stay like this for a while, neither moving nor saying anything, absorbing what he just said. Is he thinking the same things I am? How we're so complicated? Or is his mind just blank.?

I want to ask him, but I don't, maybe because I'm scared of the answer, maybe because I might feel the same way.

"I have another question?" I bite my lip as I look up at the long eyelashes that decorate his face.

"I would be surprised if you didn't have one," he jokes as he fully turns toward me. His body is facing mine, head in hand, as he looks me over, and a small smile decorates his face.

"Are you scared to take over?"

Christian stays silent for a second, pondering the question. I almost think he didn't hear me ask it. "If I am being completely honest, no." His tone is certain and makes me take him at his word. "I grew up watching my father take charge of any situation that came his way. He's brave, strong, and, most importantly, cares for my people more than anyone. I know I should feel nervous in stepping in his shoes, but I'm just excited to be able to do what I have been trained to do, to be able to follow in his legacy."

Excitement—that's what he feels when he thinks of talking over. I envy him for that. I envy that he sees it as the honor that it is and not the burden I claim it to be. However, our situations are different. Christian knows he's worthy of following in his father's footsteps. Christian looks at all his father does as alpha and welcomes the idea of becoming like him. I, on the other hand, don't. I have been dreading taking over because, deep down, I know that I will never be as good as my mother, never live up to the legacy that she helped build.

"When you turn into your wolf form, is your fur black?" I recall the dream. I have been having a month now, the one where I am running in the forest. The black wolf that always comes at the end has Christian's deep brown eyes with specks of gold.

Christian blinks for a second, probably surprised by the question. He nods. "How did you know that?"

"I have dreams."

Before I can say anything else or elaborate on my dreams, he interrupts me, not allowing me to finish my thoughts.

"You're in the forest running," he finishes for me. My face must show a total look of confusion because he explains further. "I've had the same dream every night since the first day of school. I'm running after you in a forest," he says, his eyes never leaving my own as he continues, "I don't know what I'm running from, but all I know that, in this dream, I have the strong urge to get to you, almost like you're in danger."

I try to recall the dream. It's the same every night. I'm running through a bank of trees in a white dress. The overwhelming feeling of being chased succumbs me, and it almost feels like I am fighting for my life. I remember the howling of the wolves and my falling on my face. I even call to mind Johan coming up to me as I bled from my head, unable to help me. Then Christian appears, and all of a sudden, I awake. Christian and I are having the same dream, but the questions still remain. How is that possible, and why? Does this mean something? Is my subconscious trying to tell me something?

Christian stays with me into the late afternoon, saying he has to leave to handle some business, and after much begging, he decided to also get a costume for tonight. After he leaves, I relish in my thoughts. I got to spend the day with him. We watched movies. He told me about his younger sister, who's apparently more stubborn than I am. He brings up Devin and Jackson fondly and tells me that he's known them since he can remember and that he would be nowhere without their support. Christian even mentioned his parents and how they drive him crazy, but he knows they mean well. He opened up to me today, and my heart grows in size as I think of how much that means. He trusts me.

I set up the party at around six with help from Angel, Paris, and my brother. We hang fake cobwebs on doorways, fake eyes are placed on tables that contain punch and candy, and fake skeletons are in every room on the first floor. We have a speaker, a great playlist, and liquor, all ingredients for an amazing party. Neither of them mentioned the events of last night, and I am very grateful for it.

"So you spent the day together, and he didn't even kiss you," Paris says as we're making spiked punch with gummy worms in the kitchen.

I nod. A smile creeps on my face as I try to keep my voice from sounding like a tween girl talking about her first crush. "But we talked."

I don't care that he didn't kiss me. I didn't mind the talking. It's all I wanted. I wanted to get to know him, see behind the complicated mask, and look at what was all underneath, and today was a start.

"Oh, that's so much better." She rolls her eyes, and the sarcasm is practically dripping from her voice.

"Paris, everything isn't physical," Angel mentions. Then she grabs the candles, but instead of lighting them up with matches, she says the word, "Ignis," and suddenly, all the candles in the kitchen lighten up at the same time.

Angel turns to give us a satisfied smile and then looks directly at Paris. "She feels an emotional connection with him. Talking to him is more important than any touch he can give her. He's letting her in, and that's better than anything else."

"Exactly," I agree with Angel and then grab a gummy worm from the kitchen counter and toss it to Paris in a joking manner.

"How would you even know, Angel? I thought the mere thought of boys was prohibited to you."

Something passes through Angel's green eyes, a look of guilt or maybe even regret. I don't have time to analyze it because she immediately blinks, and the look is gone like it never appeared in the first place. "I'm just saying, I understand."

"You have a secret boyfriend we don't know about."

She shakes her head, and the word *no* comes out of my mouth so loudly and quickly that it makes my eyebrows rise. She's hiding something. She has been since summer. The Angel I know doesn't lie, so it's for me to believe that is, but hey, I didn't think my parents would lie to me, and here I am. I want to ask, but it's clear it's something she doesn't want to discuss, and who am I to push her?

"Right." Paris's voice sounds skeptical as she washes her hands in the sink before shrugging her shoulder. "Whatever you say, Angel Cakes. Your costume is upstairs. Let me show you."

Angel and Paris leave the kitchen at the exact moment that Alex comes in with a box of leftover decorations.

"The house is all ready to go."

As soon as I make eye contact with my brother, yesterday night came into mind, specifically the memory of me in the air and Alex spelling me down. I can feel my face heat up from embarrassment as I look at him. It must think I'm an idiot for putting him in that situation. It could have gone worse, the glass that broke could have hit someone, cutting them. He could have hit his head when he fell. All the worst possible scenarios play through my mind like a whirlwind, almost destroying my brain in its wake.

"Thank you." My voice comes out low and sheepish. I don't know what to say and how to react around him at this moment.

"How are you feeling?" Alex asks.

He places the box down and walks over to where I am sitting at the kitchen island.

"I should be asking you that. You were in that position because of me, you fainted because of me." He must think I'm an idiot.

"Don't put that on yourself."

"It's the truth, Alex." I look at my brother, irritation crawling its way through my voice, threatening to lash out. I am not annoyed at my problem, not exactly anyway. I am annoyed that he's acting like this isn't a big deal, just like my mother, pushing it under the rug, acting like it's a normal thing that happens.

"Don't act like what happened last was something we can just brush off. I levitated in the air like I was possessed. I couldn't stop."

"Lexi, you didn't mean for that to happen."

"Does that even matter if I meant it or not? I did it," I snap without thinking, and I immediately regret it. I don't mean to lash out. It just comes out.

"I'm sorry," I apologize and grab his large hand.

"I'm so sorry you were in that position. I'm sorry for snapping at you. I'm sorry for all if it Alex."

He nods, slowly agreeing with me. He waited for me to continue, and when I didn't, he says, "Your eyes were clouded, almost all white," fear crept into his voice as he describes what he saw. "I try to look into your eyes, and for a spilt second, I didn't think I'd be able to pull you back." He grips my hand tightly, almost like he doesn't want to let go. "I felt it in my blood, Lex, the power that was surging out of you. It was like we were connected. Ever since last night, my magic is…"

"Different," I complete his sentence.

I lie my head on his shoulder, and he lie his head on my own. Our hands stay entwined, both of us staying silent in understanding. We're no longer the same witches that we were yesterday morning. We both feel it. Our magic has maximized within us, cursing through like bolts of electricity fueling our bodies. The question is, though, What happens now?

Chapter 17

I place the crown my mother placed on my bed yesterday on my head. I didn't do much to my hair but let the natural brown curls flow down my back. The red jewels in the crown complement my red lipstick well. My black dress fits me like a glove, the black-styled halter top clings to my curves perfectly while the lace falls perfectly to my feet. I look different, grown almost. Music plays out of the speaker downstairs, and I can hear people talking and laughing. *This is what you wanted*, I remind myself. One night, with no worries and no problems. Just a night of being young and myself, so enjoy it.

I take in a deep breath and take one last look in the mirror before I decide that it is time to join the growing party that is taking place in my house.

As I walk down the stairs, I see Paris at the Botton of the stairs, with Jordan playfully flirting with her.

"The devil is a liar." He's practically drooling as he eats her up with his eyes.

Paris is dressed in a red latex dress with a sweetheart neckline. The dress is as tight as it can be. Her red hair is down to the end of her back, and on top of her head are red horns. She's the devil.

Next to her, Jordan is dressed in a black suit and tie with black shades hiding his eyes. I know for a fact that he and Alex are dressed exactly alike. Men in Black is their costume this year.

Paris snaps her fingers in Jordan's face and points to her face. "My eyes are up here," she calls him, but I don't miss the slight blush that appears on her cheeks from his attention.

He scoffs. "Don't flatter yourself. I was looking at your face, and by the way, I can still see your pimple. You didn't hide that well, idiots."

"Just crawl in a hole and die," she groans and swats his arm, and then she looks up and notices me. "You look amazing, babe."

"The hottest girl at this party," Jordan whistles as he takes my hand, and as I take the last step, I smile and thank him for the compliment.

The decorations look great as they are surrounded by people in costumes having a good time, drinking and dancing in the living room, and talking in the foyer from what I can see with one glance. Everyone looks like they are having a good time. The party isn't completely in full swing, but a good number of people are already here. Music is playing, and the Halloween decorations look great in the lights. Right here, I make a promise to myself that I'm gonna enjoy it and that I won't let anyone or anything ruin this one night that I set up. No coronation thoughts, no looking over my shoulder for a potential stalker, no more mama drama. Just my friends and me, illegally consuming alcohol and celebrating an old witch holiday.

Paris and I say hello to a few people before we head into the kitchen, where we find Angel. Paris picked out Angel's costume, and I am surprised she got her to wear it. Every year, Angel dresses up as an angel, but this year is no different. She's an angel in a matching white latex dress, just like Paris. Her blonde straight hair is in a ponytail in the back of her head, and a halo graces her head. She looks different but is still beautiful, as always.

I look at her, and her lipstick is smeared, and her cheeks are flushed red. She's drunk. The party started an hour ago, and I can tell she has more than one to two drinks.

"Angel." I walk up to her, placing my arm over her shoulders, trying to stabilize her. "Having fun, are we?"

Her green innocent eyes light up when she sees me. "Lexi, I was looking for you," she says, and I can smell the tequila coming off her breath.

"I left you alone for ten minutes," Paris says loudly, trying to speak over the music. "Here you are in the kitchen with two of Ridgeview's eligible bachelors." She looks over at the guys across the island.

Paul and Justin, both of them, play for the football team. Paul is huge, six feet five tall, with dark skin, dangerous brown eyes, and muscles the size of tree trunks. He is the definition of tall, brown, and beautiful. Justin, on the other hand, is a skinny, charming white dude, about five feet eleven, with a charming smile and blue eyes, red hair, and adorable freckles. Paul and Justin are polar opposites, Paul being dangerous and a player who is just trouble while Justin is really sweet, funny, and shy.

Justin gets beet red when Paris mentions to him that he should ask Angel to dance instead of just starting. He can't keep his eyes off her, but then again, he's always had a thing for her. Last year at prom, he asked her to be his date at least once a day for a week before he got the hint that she wasn't interested. He sent her flowers, chocolates, and anything he thought would catch her eye, but Angel insisted on going solo. She never gave him a chance.

He doesn't even get the chance to ask her because as soon as his mouth opens, Alex pipes up from the corner with a drink in hand and sunglasses on top of his head. "Angel doesn't dance." His eyes stay trained on Justin, looking him over as if he was an enemy. I don't know how long he's been standing there, but his stance is intimidating, his glare icy, completely unlike the charismatic brother I know.

"Yes, I do," Angel says, her lips pursed, a hand on her hip matching Alex's icy stare.

"Not with him." Alex glare turns to Angel, but she doesn't wave under it. Instead, she gives him one right back.

My eyes volley between Angel and Alex, and I can't help but feel as though I have missed something important. The tension between them is thick, filled with anger and something else that I can't point out. It's confusing. I know Alex is protective of me, and sometimes that extends to my friends, but it feels like something more. Is there something I'm not seeing?

They participate in a stare-off that lasts a couple of seconds too long before my brother rolls his eyes and places his glasses back on his face. "Do what you want." he says, and the annoyance is clear as day in his voice. He takes a swig from his drink and then just walks out.

"What was that about?" I turn to Angel.

She just shrugs it off and takes another shot basically dismissing me. I know that I won't get a straight answer. Lately, Angel has been closed off, and none of us know how to unlock her.

As I leave the kitchen, I think I hear Paris tell Angel, "We need to talk," but the music is filling my ears, and I could probably have heard it wrong.

I try to find Alex, but it's like he disappeared in thin air. The living room, which had now turned into a dance floor, is filled with people whom I recognize from school, some classmates from different grades. He's not here, but in the far side of the room, I see Johan, all alone with a drink in his hand and bumping his head to the music. He's dressed in a gray button-up shirt, with his sleeves rolled up, and dark jeans. I pout a little because a small part of me wanted him to indulge me with the costume theme.

"What happened to the costume?" I walk up to him.

His eyes brighten up just a little when he sees me, and he smiles brightly. "I am in costume." He pulls out fake plastic fangs from his pocket.

"A vampire." I eye him weirdly. The costume doesn't necessarily scream vampire, but at least he tried.

"Yes, ma'am, specifically Edward Cullen." He puts the fangs in his mouth. "I've been reading up on vampires lately, and my new girl thought it would be cute to be Edward and Bella."

"Reading up on them?"

I raise my eyebrow. I've known Johan my whole life. The lure of supernatural life has never quite allured to him, so the fact that he's researching them is strange.

"Yeah, it's for my college essay. I wanted to write about what New Orleans is most known for, and of course, supernatural beings is one of them." He shrugs. "I'm starting on vampires, then wolves, and ending with the spooky wild witches of the South," he jokes, his eyes dancing with amusement.

Johan never believed in anything remotely supernatural while we were together. That's why it was so hard to lie to him. Lying to someone who doesn't even know or believe that this world exists just felt wrong in a way. The fact that he's actually getting into it now that we're not together is unbelievable.

"Well, that's interesting," is all I could say and nod. I don't want to talk about this anymore. "So where's your date?" I change the subject.

He looks around with a small smile on his face. "She's around here somewhere." He searches for a couple of seconds. "There she is."

I turn to see Anitta come toward us with a huge smile on her face. She's dressed in flannel, jeans, and almost no makeup, which is totally unlike her. As she makes her way over, I can't help but feel like I got slapped in the face. I know I shouldn't, but I feel betrayed. Johan has known me practically my whole life. He knows how Anitta has tormented me and practically tried to ruin my life. My ex—no, scratch that—my friend is now dating someone who made it her mission to ruin my life. I can't believe this.

I watch as Anitta comes up, gives him a small peck on his mouth, and interlocks their fingers. This is so wrong.

"Hey, Lexi." She smiles at me, and I almost think it's genuine. "Thanks so much for the invite. It was the perfect opportunity to show the world that we are a couple." She eyes me, and I can read through her act so quickly. She wants to make me jealous. "Right, babe?" Her voice comes out honeyed, like she's forcing herself to be extra sweet just for my benefit.

"Well, isn't that great?" I say, trying not to let the sarcasm come out of my mouth. I think I succeeded.

I'm not jealous. Johan and I were never meant to be. People from different worlds and different backgrounds could never understand me fully. I know that. I also know that he would date someone eventually. In fact, I hoped he would. However, the sight of him with Anitta feels like a stab in the back, almost as if he knew it would hurt me. I scratch that thought because it's my personal feelings. No matter how disrespected I feel, it doesn't mean that was his intention. Johan isn't the type of guy to hurt my feelings out of spite. He's too nice of a guy.

"So did you bring a date, Lexi?" Anita asks, and her intention is obvious. She's rubbing it in my face. Trying to prove something, she can get what she wants even if it was mine. She got Johan over me, and she wants me to know. She wants me to relish in all of it.

The hairs on the back of my neck stand at attention, and before I know it, Christian's voice makes its entrance into this conversation.

"She did."

I feel his hand make contact with the small of my back.

My heart skips at the touch. He's wearing a black tux with a white button-up shirt that has the first couple of buttons undone. His curls lay perfectly on his head, and a gold crown with red jewels sit on them. He looks breathtaking, and I can't help but smile as I notice his costume matches my own.

"You look beautiful," he whispers in my ear before he looks over at Johan and Anitta.

"Christian Castillo." Anitta looks at Christian up and down—sizing him for a second. "I'm impressed, Lexi. You don't wait long. He's been here for what, two minutes, and you're already dating." She smiles, but it doesn't reach her eyes. "Didn't want another girl to have a chance in taking him, huh?"

I open my mouth to tell her off or tell her she can suck it when Christian voice beats me to it. "No other girl has a chance," he says, his voice calm but direct.

"So you guys are a thing?" Johan says, wiggling his fingers between us. The smile that he had is gone, leaving his face expressionless. He awaits an answer, and that's when I realize I don't know what to call Christian.

"It's a little bit more complicated than that," I say, trying to read his face. "But yes." I nod my head, and for a second, I feel Christian grab my waist and pull me in tighter into his side, almost like he's claiming me like his own.

"Well, we should all go enjoy the party," he says dryly as if this conversation is a waste of his time, and before anyone can say anything, he practically drags me away from them without so much of a backward glance.

Chapter 18

Christian drags me outside to the backyard, away from the people and the music. I can feel him vibrating under my grasp as he maneuvers us to the center of the yard. He's upset, and I have no idea why.

My backyard is about half an acre long, full of grass, and a patio in the center covered in lights, which we only use for cookouts. A rock path leading to a shed and a tree with a tire swing still attached since Alex and I used to play when we were younger. We walk to the patio, and his face is completely serious. He lets go of my hand and paces back and forth on that patio, leaving me standing at the center, staring at him, confused.

"Everything okay?"

The twinkle lights that hang off the patio reflect off his perfect tan skin as he looks down over at me. His brown eyes are practically on fire, an indication that he is, in fact, upset.

"You invited your ex." His tone is cold, and I see his fists clench at his sides as he avoids eye contact with me.

"I didn't think that it would be a big deal."

He huffs out and goes to run his fingers through his hair before he realizes he can't because of his crown.

"Of course you didn't." He shakes his head, annoyance just oozing out of his pores.

"Johan and I are just friends," are the only words that come out of my mouth.

The realization that he's jealous hits me like a ton of bricks. How can he be jealous of anyone? Look at him. Does he not see how crazy I am about him?

"You're blind if you think that pathetic human sees you as just a friend." The sentence comes out of his mouth as a breathy explosion of words. "I see how he looks at you, Alexandra. He wants you."

"He has a girlfriend." I try to defend my point, but I can tell that whatever I am saying is falling on deaf ears. I want to say he's being ridiculous that he doesn't need to be so vexed, but I know it's his words from earlier that come to mind. Wolves don't get mad. They go ballistic.

"I wouldn't care if he was married. I know what I saw," he barks out. Christian takes steps toward me, stopping when he gets about an inch from my face. His sudden proximity surprises me as he says through gritted teeth, "Do you still have feelings for him?"

"Of course, I don't."

Christian shakes his head. "Don't lie to me, Alexandra. I saw you guys dancing at the party at the beginning of the year and that day in the hall. I see the way he looks at you when he thinks no one is looking, and I know that you care for him as a friend, but what I need to know if there is something more. If being around me is something you are doing out of duty, you need to tell me."

My heart softens when I hear the vulnerability in his voice. His brown eyes search my face, looking for an answer, and I see a slight glimpse of fear in them.

I break the inch of distance between us and place my hand on the left side of his suit, right above his heart. "I like you, Christian, not because of duty, not because we're destined, but because I just do." I urge him to look into my eyes. "You are who I want, not Johan."

Christian doesn't say anything at first. His face is completely unreadable as he contemplates what I just said. I can feel him under my hand, his heartbeat beating so fast I think it's going to jump out of his chest and into my hand. My own heartbeat responds to it, to him. I can feel myself getting lost in his eyes again, and I fear I will never get found if I go too deep. This is how it is with Christian, electric. My body reacts when he's near, my mind empties when I am with him, and my soul feels at home amidst all the chaos. I have known Christian for a small amount of time, but if I'm being honest, even through my great days with Johan, I have never felt the way that I feel with Christian.

"Christian, what you and I have confuses me sometimes. I don't exactly know what to call us or what we are." His brown eyes glisten in the moonlight as he looks down at me. "But I do know how I feel about you. That is actually the one thing in my life that isn't complicated. I didn't mean to hurt your feelings. I'm sorry."

"Alexandra," he voices my name like a prayer on my lips as he leans his head down. The smell of pine infiltrates my nose, and I welcome it with open arms. "You need to know that I am not doing this out of obligation. I like you. I like you so much. It consumes my every thought and every breath that escapes my mouth." His words are passion-filled as they leave his mouth, making me dizzy with the meaning behind them. "I wouldn't be able to handle it if you wanted that human but settled for me because you can't have him."

"No one is settling. Not even close." The words barely come out louder than a whisper because I am entranced in his spell. His words, his hands wrapped around my waist, and the shock it sends up my spine. His lips are so close that I can practically be salivating for a taste.

I don't miss the way his eyes flick to my lips and then back up to my eyes. He wants to kiss me. I want to kiss him. He leans in slowly. A ghost of a kiss falls on my lips as a scream comes from inside the house.

I jump up and take a step back, but immediately, Christian pulls me in closer as he looks over at the house. He tucks me into him, protecting me from invisible danger. He listens in with his keen sense of hearing and then just shakes his head.

"Someone fell in the kitchen and spilled punch." He loosens his grip on me slightly, and I hear him mumble under his breath, "Way to ruin the moment."

"I heard that." I poke at him, trying to lighten up the tension that has filled around us because of our almost kiss.

I try not to let my head spiral at what was about to happen and how badly I wanted it. I was about to drool. He's like a drug, and the more he's around, the more I want him. I think I would have spontaneously combusted if he had kissed me.

He gives me a cheeky smile and kisses my forehead. "It's good that we didn't kiss."

"How come?" I look at him surprised, and I can't stop a pout from forming on my lips.

"Because, if we kissed here, after just discussing your ex, I would be thinking about him."

When he looks at the weird, perplexed look on my face, he elaborates, "I would be secretly hoping that he was watching as I slammed my lips onto yours. I would force my tongue down your throat and make a whole show out of it, making sure that he watched as I claimed as mine. Like a dog pissing on a tree, I wanted to mark my territory."

He describes in my ear, and each word that came out of his mouth in that territorial tone makes me go weak at the knees. My insides curl as I try to imagine what he just said happening. Excitement bubbles up in my stomach, and I wish he would. I wish he would kiss me. I wish he would do exactly what he said. I wouldn't care who was here or who wasn't.

"That sounds passionate," I say, breathless.

Christian chuckles and pulls me in closer. "Cariño, when I do kiss you, passionate won't be the only word you'll be using." He grins as he winks at me, almost causing me to pass out. "Now let's go enjoy your party."

We continued the night with our friends, dancing, laughing, and having a great time. I stay away from alcohol, trying to stay coherent as I am the host even though Paris is trying to shove some down my throat. I feel the effects of the harvest in the house. Everyone's magic is heightened, including my own. It's unavoidable the surge running through the atmosphere.

Jackson and Devin come over, and they are dressed as each other. Jackson is wearing fake glasses and a button-up shirt tucked into his pants. He has makeup, I think, covering the tattoos that normally cover his arms. Devin has contacts on and is dressed in tattoos with fake tats all over his arms that look nothing like the ones Jackson has on his. In the kitchen, they decide to play beer pong with Jordan and Alex, and they are whopping their asses.

I tell everyone I'll be back as I do my rounds, making sure that everything is okay and everyone is having a good time. When I pass the living room, I make eye contact with Johan. He eyes me as I enter, and his eyes stay glued on me as Anitta talks to one of her friends sitting beside them. The light that is usually in his eyes is gone and replaced with something else, but I can't exactly say what. I give him a small smile and a wave, and he mirrors my action with the same amount of enthusiasm.

I had the dining room closed off, trying to limit the party to the kitchen, the living room, and the family room. The sliding door to the dining room has been closed all night with a sign attached saying is, "Off-Limits Room." I stand outside the door, my hand hovering over it. The events enter my mind like a tidal wave, almost knocking me over. I debate, opening it. It's a party, and I promised myself that I was going to enjoy it. So why am I looking for a reminder about what happened last night? I should walk away and try to get back to the party, but for some reason, I can't, so I open the door and slide in the room. I close the door behind me slowly as I look at the room.

All evidence of what happened last night is gone, the broken class and picture frames, all gone as if nothing happened except for the broken mirror that hangs from the wall. One single crack splits the mirror. I was so gone yesterday that I don't even remember that happening.

I place my hand on the table, in the exact spot I was sitting. I try to pinpoint the exact moment where it all went wrong. I have never felt that much power ever in my life. I look at my palm. The memory of the table shaking is imprinted under my skin. I can still hear the screams of my family begging me to stop.

"Excuse me, Alexandra," a woman's voice snaps me out of my deep thoughts.

My head snaps back to find a girl standing right there. She's about my age or probably a couple of years older. She has black curly hair that slightly resembles my own, caramel skin, brown eyes, and a heart-shaped face. She's slender and tall, about five feet ten. She has no costume; instead, she's dressed in a leather jacket, white shirt, heels, and black jeans.

"Hey." I don't recall hearing the sliding door open. I must have been so deep in my mind to ignore the sound. I watch as she moves from the corner of the room, almost as if she's coming out of the shadows.

I just recognize that she said my name. "Do I know you?" I search her face, and I can't quite remember if we met before; however, something about her feels familiar.

She shakes her head, and a small smile forms on her lips. "I don't want to bother, but I just had to meet you." Her long legs walk toward me, shortening the distance between us. She pulls her hand for me to shake. "I'm Robin." I glance down at her perfectly manicured hand and red nails before taking her hand in mine.

The moment my hand makes contact with hers, a zap passes through my body, and it makes me jump back and let out a giant yelp that is drowned out by the music that plays outside the door. She's a witch. There's no doubt about it. Although I have never met her, I can feel it in my veins.

I have never felt that before—the automatic jolt when touching another witch. Usually, I can feel the magic, like a sixth sense all witches have, but with Robin, it's more than that. Something in her response to something me.

"Whoa." A huge smile is sprawled across her face. "Did you feel that?" she says, her voice is a mixture of sweetness with a tad bit of eagerness.

I can blame it on the harvest for the fact that a tingle climbs up my spine as soon as we touched. I can chalk it up to the many things I've come to realize I don't know about my magic, but one thing is clear: Robin has powerful magic, just like me.

"What the fuck was that? Who are you?" I don't mean for my voice to come out as panicked and choked up as it does, but I am trying to get over the shock.

"I told you. I'm Robin."

I don't get a moment to ask her to elaborate before the sliding door that opens the dining room slides open with such force that I'm scared it might break. On the other side of the door are Christian, Jackson, and Devin standing before us, eyes wide and alert as if they were expecting trouble.

Christian's eyes survey my body, most likely looking for any indication that I am hurt. He must have heard me screeched like a banshee. He doesn't hesitate. As soon as he sees that I am okay, he rushes at werewolf speed and pushes Robin to the wall, away from me.

"Who the fuck are you?" he growls, his eyes never leaving Robin as he stands in front of me with a clenched fist and a protective yet threatening stance. Devin and Jackson close the door behind him and stand as if they're taking guard.

I try to move past Christian to see if Robin is okay. His push is anything but gentle, but she stands in front of us, just as okay, with a smile never wavering. Her eyes, however, betray her. They stare down Christian, narrowed and full of something that can only be described as anger and hate.

"You must be Christian," she speaks in a controlled voice.

I tuck myself into Christian's side. "This is Robin." I squeeze his hand, trying to reassure him that everything is okay, but he doesn't budge. His eyes stay fixated on her as if she is prey and he is the predator, ready to pounce if she makes one wrong move.

"We came to pay our respects to the future high priestess." Her glare is icy as she stares Christian down.

"Who's we?" Christian asks as his fists ball tightly.

Robin doesn't say anything just stands there, as if she didn't hear the question, rolling her eyes in annoyance, almost as if Christian was beneath her.

This doesn't settle well with Christian. "Answer me," he barks out, and the sound of his voice makes me jump up in my place.

"I do not answer to you yet, you mutt." Anitta's smile has disappeared and replaced with a scowl. She takes a step toward Christian, not intimated by the look of him. "I answer to her." She stares Christian down while her finger points straight at me.

"Who exactly are you, and why are you here, Robin?" I try to stand straight to give the illusion that I'm taller than I actually am.

"I'm a witch just like you. My coven and I practice ancestral magic. We're here to join the alliance."

"What alliance?"

"Yours." She wiggles her finger in between Christian and me. Did everyone know that Christian and I are destined? Great! But that doesn't make sense. Our alliance isn't even forming yet. I'm not queen yet, and he isn't alpha.

"That doesn't make sense. Why now? The alliance doesn't form yet." I sound skeptical. "Why are you really here?" I cross my arms. She's lying.

"That's the truth." She puts her hands up in surrender. "Isn't the wedding on the thirteenth of May."

When she says this, Christian's entire demeanor changes. He went from his threatening stance to standing up straight and grabbing my waist. "Alexandra, we should go to enjoy the party." His voice is softer, and he tries to lead me to the door.

I shake my head, confused. "That date is my coronation and my birthday." I look over at Robin. She must be mistaken. "There isn't a wedding."

"Oh, I see," she says as if she just realized something. "Look, I'm not trying to cause any troubles, but I am not a liar nor am I mistaken. You should ask your friend here about it." She gives Christian a quick glance before she looks back at me. "I just wanted you to know that I'll be there." She takes a step closer to me, her eyes gleaming with something I can't decipher as she says, "I wouldn't miss it for the world."

She smiles and then turns on her heel, walking out of the room leading us here. For some reason, her last sentence rings in my head. She said it almost like I was missing something. She knew something that I wasn't aware of.

I shake the feeling off as I look over at Christian. "What is she talking about? What wedding?'

Behind Christian, Devin and Jackson turn around to open the door and leave. "I think you guys got it from here." Jackson's voice is filled with a tone of avoidance as he tries to leave the room.

"Claudere."

I raise my hand and shut the sliding door before any of them can get out. The door closes hard, which I didn't expect, but the magic that fuels me today is powerful.

The boys turn around slowly and quietly while I stare down Christian. "What are you hiding?"

"Alexandra, I don't think this is the time or the place for this."

"For what?"

And right as those words come out of my mouth, I already know. Robin isn't the one who is mistaken. I was. *Most when the alliance is solidified.* The words Christian had said to me the first time he told me he was a werewolf. He knew. He knew this whole time.

145

"We're getting married in May, aren't we?"

Christian looks down at his feet, averting my eye contact, and he nods slowly.

"You guys knew?" I ask Jackson and Devin, already knowing the answer. They all look ashamed, and they should. They all lied to me again.

I can feel the anger starting to boil up in me. Not only did my whole family lie to me, but now they are too. I'm getting married soon, and no one bothered to tell me, not even the groom.

"Whatever." I scoff and turn to leave through the other door across the room.

"Alexandra." Christian goes to grab my hand, but I snatch it back without a second thought. "Let me explain."

I roll my eyes and push him away from me out of anger. "Explain? You want to explain how you and your friends lied to me. You knew exactly how I felt about my whole family lying, yet you did the exact same thing. You can't say anything that's gonna make it better, so don't even bother."

His face is unreadable as I turn away from him and storm out of the door, annoyed that I put so much trust in him and he ends up being just like everyone else.

Chapter 19

I spend the next hour trying to avoid Christian, who refuses to leave the party because he swears he needs to protect me. Meeting Robin and finding out that I am not only gonna be queen in a couple of months but also a wife doesn't exactly put me in a party mood. I try to act normal, but my head is completely scrambled.

Paris seems to notice as she returns from her game of beer pong. "You okay?"

"Yeah." I try to smile, but my lips barely tilt up.

"You sure?" She raises an eyebrow at me, her eyes searching my face, and knowing Paris, she can already tell that I am lying. "This party was your idea, and I feel like you are the only person here who's not having fun," she points out. "And pretty boy is all the way across the room staring at you, but it's almost as if he's scared to get close."

I steal a glance at Christian who's at the other side of the kitchen behind the beer pong table, his eyes glued on me. I want to be mad at him, and a part of me is, but another part wants to walk over to him and just get in his arms. I feel so weak. He lied to me, just like my parents. I shouldn't feel this way. He's like everyone else.

"What's up?" Angel comes over with Jordan and Alex in tow. Her blonde hair is a mess, and the halo that was once on her head has disappeared. "Why aren't you taking shots with us?"

"The question is, why are you still taking shots?" Jordan laughs as Angel tries to steady herself in between Alex and him. "You are drunk."

"And you're a man whore."

"Angel."

We all look at her, shocked, because this is probably the first time I have ever heard Angel say anything mean about anyone. For a second, we are quiet, but suddenly, the laughter fills the kitchen, starting with Jordan. A real laugh climbs up my throat as I join in because, strangely, this is probably the best thing that has happened tonight.

"Yeah, you are drunk." Paris laughs.

I try to grab a water from the cooler behind me, but as soon as my hand opens it, the cooler is slammed shut. I look up to see Christian with a solemn expression on his face. "Alexandra, you need to get everyone out of here."

Immediately, I shake my head. Who does he think he is? "I'm not doing that."

"Alexandra."

"Christian, I said no."

"Dammit, Alexandra!" he practically shouts, making me jump, and everyone stares at us. He doesn't bother to look around at the audience he has caused. "This isn't a joke." He glares at me.

I cross my arms over my chest, purse my lips, and stare him down. I am not shutting down this party, and he cannot make me. I don't understand what his problem is, but I should be the one that is mad. He deceived me, not the other way around.

"Dammit," I hear him mutter under his breath when he sees that I am not going to break. "Devin, shut down the party."

"I said no." I try to stop, him but it doesn't matter because Devin moves into motion, kicking all the guests out of the kitchen. "Christian, who do you think you are?"

"I smell blood," he says, his eyes burning deep into mine, his tone completely solemn as he adds, "A lot."

My heart drops as I watch Christian and Jackson head out of the kitchen and toward the stairs.

The anger and betrayal felt seconds ago have subsided, and immediately, I'm on high alert. I follow them without hesitating, hoping that this is just a misunderstanding or something small, but deep down, I know that it's not.

It's dark on the second floor of the house, and with everyone leaving downstairs, it gets quieter by the second. With each step I take up the stairs and down the hall, my heartbeat grows louder in my ear, making me very aware of how scared I actually am. I hear Angel, Paris, and my brother's presence behind me as I catch up to Christian and Jackson, who have made it to the end of the hall.

Christian puts his hand on the knob to the bathroom door, but instead of opening it, he turns to back at me. "Are you sure you wanna be here?" Concern drips from each of his words when he asks that question.

I nod hesitantly. I am not sure I want to see what is on the other side of that door, if I am being completely honest. However, this is my party, my house, and if something happened, I need to know.

"I smell a lot of blood, Alexandra," he warns.

I look into his eyes, and I can see it—a bit of fear hidden behind the pretense of being calm and collected. He's just as scared to see what is behind that door, and he doesn't want me to be here. He doesn't want me to see.

"Open the door."

He opens the door, and what we all see makes me want to crawl under my bed and never come out.

"Jesus." I hear Jordan behind me as we all crowd the door to the bathroom. In the middle of the floor, there lies Paul in a pool of his own blood. I can't tell if he's unconscious or maybe if it's something worse. His Aaron Donald costume is soaked in his blood, and I swear I don't see his chest move.

The guest hand soap that is usually on the sink has been dropped on the floor, including the shower curtain. The sink is running, and so is the shower. I don't know why, but it is.

"Is he...?" *Dead.* I can't get the word out, but we all know what I mean. The thought that Paul is dead upsets my stomach, and this scene displayed in front of us isn't helping. He looks like he was just using the restroom, and something horrible happened.

"Not yet," Jackson says as Christian and him walk toward where Paul is, careful not to step on the pool of blood. "His heartbeat is faint, but it's still there."

"I'll call an ambulance." Alex pulls his phone out in a hurry, dialing the number at an impressive speed, but Christian's voice stops him.

"Don't," he says and then signals Jackson to come over to his side. "Jackson, look." He moves over Paul's body and shifts his head to show a head wound where it seems to be the cause of the blood. There seem to be two punctured holes at the base of his neck, almost as if he was stabbed by prongs. The markings look recognizable, something I am sure I have seen before in one of my mother's books, and suddenly, it hits me. Paul wasn't stabbed. He was bitten by a vampire.

I try to process this while Alex and Christian argue back and forth about what we should do. My head is spinning. A vampire was in this house, and none of us knew. He sneaked upstairs and hurt Paul while we were all having the time of our lives right below him. How could this have happened? Why Paul? My head is spinning a mile a minute. Thoughts clouded my head like an incoming storm, but one thing is for sure: we can't let Paul die.

"How are we gonna explain to the police that some guy died in your house? Nay, how are we gonna explain that a vampire tried to kill someone in your house, the mayor's house?" Jackson rolls his eyes at my brother as I check back into the conversation.

"We can't just let him die," Paris snaps, and she's right.

We can't. However, Jackson is right as well. If we call the cops, questions will be asked, questions we can't answer. It would shed a light on my father, not to mention if this got out that a vampire entered the high priestess house, I would send a wave of panic through the witch community.

I try to think about what my mother would do in this situation and try to enter her frame of mind. My mother would tell everyone to calm down, close the room off to essential personnel, and figure out a plan, but what? How am I supposed to save Paul and make sure we protect top-tier secret? I look around at my friends, all wide-eyed and scared. Alex keeps arguing, running his hands through his hair while Jordan is pacing in the hallway. Paris argues with Jackson, and right beside her is Angel, who was insanely drunk just minutes ago. Now she looks like she's in shock, her eyes fixated on Paul's body, never wavering. She looks how I feel, completely terrified.

"We are not calling the cops," I say, trying to keep my voice stern and calm even though my insides are freaking out. I look over at Paris,

Alex, and Jordan. "You guys are going to go downstairs with Devin and make sure everyone is gone. No one else can know about this."

"He's gonna die," Alex says, his voice full of panic.

"No, he isn't. Angel is gonna help him." She is our only choice. We can't call the cops, and we can't let him die.

Angel's eyes widen as the words leave my mouth. "I've never brought someone back from almost dying before." She has gone pale, all color draining from her face as she looks back down at Paul.

"I believe in you, Angel." I stand in between her and Paul and place my hands on top of her shoulders. "You can do this. You are the only one that can help." I try to make her understand that it's her or death.

"Maybe we should call an ambulance. They can help."

"He'll die before they get here, and you know it," I tell her. I know this is a ton of pressure on her shoulders. I hate that I am the one who has put her in this situation, but I can't let him die. "I need you, Angel. He needs you." I point to Paul, who is running out of time.

Her green eyes make contact with my chocolate-colored ones, and after a beat of silence, she just nods. She starts to kneel in the blood like it doesn't faze her. She is directly parallel to his head as she places her hands lightly over the wound and starts mumbling a spell. The glow from her palms appear, and I silently pray to all my ancestors that this works.

I turn back to Paris, Alex, and Jordan, who still haven't left, whose eyes are glued to the one person who can save Paul.

"Go, I'm serious."

Once they leave, I muster up my courage to then again look at Paul. Christian and my friends warned me about this. They told me something would go wrong. I was so stubborn, worried about how I would spend the last couple of months before my coronation, and now because of my selfish actions, this might be Paul's last night alive.

"What are we gonna tell him if he wakes up?" Jackson, who is now leaning on the doorframe, looks down at Angel.

"When he wakes up," Christian correct him. I can feel his eyes on me, but I don't dare look up from what Angel is doing.

He has to wake up. I don't think any of us could take it if he didn't. "We'll tell him that he had too much to drink, and then he vomited all over himself before he passed out. Simple," I lie because there isn't anything about this night or this situation that's simple.

Painfully, a slow minute goes by where none of us speak while we watch Angel say a spell under her breath, and glow resonates from her hands. She gets more tired by the second, and all the color in her body is completely gone. I know this is depleting her. I wish I could help, but in this position, I am useless.

I feel so guilty. I pressured her to do this. I had to throw this party, and now someone that I have known since kindergarten is lying on the floor in a pool of his own blood.

"I'm done." Angel stands up, looking weak. She takes two steps before her knees buckle under her. Immediately, Jackson grabs her before she hits the ground, and she gives him a faint smile.

Her knees are covered in Paul's blood, with splashes on her white latex dress, and there are gigantic bags under her green eyes. She's exhausted, and I am surprised she hasn't passed out. I look down at Paul. He's not moving, but his head wound and neck bite are healed. Jordan and Alex carry him out of the bathroom while Paris, Christian, and I scrub the bathroom clean. Neither of us says a word. We just grab rags and try not to think that what we're cleaning up off the floor is actual blood.

Once we're done, I head to my room to shower, trying to get blood stains off my fingertips. The blood runs down to the tub and into the drain, circling like my hopes for his evening. It still baffles me how everything went so wrong so fast. Lately, my life has been more eventful than I would like, and I can't help but wonder if Christian was right. I am not a normal girl, and maybe I shouldn't expect to act like it. What happened tonight is on me, I may not have been the one who attacked Paul, but I was the one who threw this party. I knew deep down that there was a threat, and yet I refused to take this seriously—no more.

After my shower, I put on a pair of sweats and walk down to the living room to see Christian, Devin, and Jackson huddled up in the corner, whispering to each other, being secretive. Jordan has driven Paul home while Angel sleeps in the guest room, and Alex and Paris sit on the couch, their minds miles away from here.

"What are you talking about?" I speak up and look directly at the three boys huddled up in secret. I don't want any more secrets.

Christian looks up. His suit jacket is off, and his sleeves are rolled up, showcasing his forearms. His crown has disappeared, and his hair looks as if it was pulled in different directions. "Alexandra, tonight has been a lot."

"Don't patronize me, Christian. We all just saw Paul lying on the floor to the point of almost dying."

He looks at me, and for a second, I think he's going to argue with me, but then he reads my face, and he can tell that won't be a good idea, so instead, he sits and gestures at Devin. "Just tell her."

Devin nods, and somehow, he has gotten his glasses back, which he pushes off the bridge of his nose. "As you know, werewolves have a keen sense of smell," he says, walking to the center of the living room. "When I was escorting everyone out, I didn't smell a vampire."

"What does that mean?" Alex asks curiously as he sits up at the edge of the couch. "Maybe the vampire sneaked out the window."

Jackson takes a step forward. "No. See, we would have smelt it him in the bathroom. But there was no scent either."

"So it wasn't a vampire?" Paris asks. "It would explain why he didn't finish him off."

I wince at her three words but then shake my head. "No, that bite was a vampire bite. No human or witch can replicate that kind of mark."

"I agree." Jackson nods.

"So what are you thinking?"

"We think that a vampire came in the house, knew that we would be here, so they figured out a way to disguise their smell and attacked Paul," Christian explains, his voice commands all eyes on him as he continues, "Think about it. He follows Paul to the bathroom and turned on the faucets because with that and the music, we wouldn't hear a scream unless we were looking for one. He then attacked Paul and sneak out of the bathroom."

"What I don't understand is why the head wound. He was already drinking his blood. Why not stop there and let him die out?"

"Most likely to knock him out. Probably didn't want Paul to scream."

My phone vibrates in my pocket, and I check it before my brain ingests the information that Christian has put out. I am expecting a text message from my mother checking up on us, but what I see is anything but. My breath hitches as I look at my phone, and my heart skips a beat. I stand, frozen, my eyes skimming over the words that are displayed on the text bubble.

"What is it?" Christian says, walking over to me and then grabbing my phone from my frozen hand when I don't respond immediately.

Unknown

Everyone around you is lying to you. Who are you gonna trust if not them, Queen Alexandra?

PS: I sure know how to pick out Halloween costumes. I knew that dress would fit you like a glove. You're welcome.

Chapter 20

"Wait, the dress you wore tonight?" Paris looks at me after looking at my phone. "That came from…whoever this is?"

"Is that the same person who wrote the letter?" Alex asks.

All these questions go in one ear and out the other. This person was in my house, my room, without anyone knowing. They placed a dress on my bed and got me to wear it. My mind is running a mile a minute, the mysterious person who sent me that letter and painted Christian's car is back, and tonight, they showed that they can come in and out of my house and no one can stop them.

Devin and Jackson come back down from searching my room. "I don't smell anything."

"I told you," Christian says, raking his fingers through the brown curls on his head. "I would have smelled something this morning while I was here or on her dress. There was no scent."

He sounds frustrated, and I know, like me, he is placing the blame on himself.

"Wait, so the person who gave Lexi the dress and the person who attacked Paul both have no scent?" Jackson points out and gives a humorless laugh. "That's too big of a coincidence. They have to be the same person."

"So that means Paul got hurt because of me," I say, coming to the realization. He's right. The coincidence is too big to ignore. Someone is messing with me and now others.

Alex shakes my shoulders, pulling me out of my dark thoughts that clearly are taking over, the anxiety setting in. "Don't do that. This isn't your fault."

"Why not?" I yell back at him, getting out of his grasp. "You all warned me that something might happen, and I didn't listen." I throw my hands in the air in frustration and anger, anger directed at myself. "I was being selfish, and I just thought of myself. Whoever this is came into our house, my room, and we were none the wiser. They got me to wear a dress. Paul could've died because of me. You all were right."

"But he didn't," Christian chimes in, taking a step toward me, his voice trying to calm my hectic mind. "And that's because of you and Angel. You took initiative and did the right thing when we were ready to turn a blind eye."

"He would have never been in that position if I didn't throw this damn party." The words cannot be any more than the truth.

Jordan comes into the house, his silk Indian hair a mess on the top of his head, and he looks as if he aged twenty years in the time it took him to take Paul back home.

Alex walks up to him. "Did he make it home okay?"

Jordan nods, pats Alex on the back, and sits down on the couch with a big huff. "He doesn't remember anything. I told him he threw up and passed out in the bathroom. The only people who remember seeing before even going to the bathroom were Johan and Justin."

"Maybe one of them…," Paris's words start to form a thought, but they don't finish because she must know how crazy it sounds. We have all known Johan since we were kids. We would know he was a vampire. Besides, Johan would never hurt a fly. He's too good of a guy.

As for Justin, he has been on the team with Alex and Jordan for years. They would know if a vampire was among them. No one can hide who they really are for that long. Isn't that what I'm doing, though? What everyone in this room has been doing their whole lives?

"We have to check with Justin tomorrow," I say into the silence that has taken space in the room.

No one wants to believe it can be anyone we know, but that is the most logical thing at the moment. There is no way we can just ignore this anymore. This is a real threat, and we have to take action, not just stand by and wait.

"You really don't think Justin was behind this, do you? Paul is his best friend, and let's not forget that Justin is completely human."

"We don't know that. He could be hiding in plain sight just like we are," I point out.

Justin is Paul's best friend, and I doubt he would do anything like this, but we do have to look at this logically. Johan and Justin were the last people to see him before he was attacked. It's most likely one of them attacked him. I know Johan. He's not a vampire, not even close. So the only other option is Justin.

My mind raced with all the possible scenarios of tonight. Who could have hurt him? Who would want to? If we didn't find him in time, we could have lost him. All this because I wanted to party and live life to the fullest. Christian's words from yesterday in the cafeteria circle in my head. He was right. I am not normal, and to act like I am is obviously not the right thing to do.

The room is overcome by a heavy blanket of silence. No one speaks as we all try to go over tonight's almost-lethal events. I am so overcome by everything in my mind that I barely feel my phone vibrate in my hand again.

Unknown

If you really wanna know who I am, ask Grandma.

The message pops up out of nowhere, and immediately, it confuses me. Why would my grandmother know who was terrorizing me, and more importantly, why wouldn't she tell me?

"I need to find my grandmother."

"It's almost midnight," Jackson points out, looking at his watch.

I shake my head in defiance. I know it's late, but I do not care. I need answers, and right now, she is the one who can give it to me. Right now, at this point in my life, I feel like I am playing a game of cat and mouse. I am getting chased and hunted, looked as if I am a pawn in a game that I don't even know all the elements too. I refuse to be this girl anymore, the one who cowers behind her friends while someone actively threatens her. This mysterious person wants me to play their game, and right now, I will do so with one goal in mind.

"Alexandra, you need to stop and think," Christian says. The lines on his face show worry, and I almost forget that I am upset at him as well. "Whoever this is, is playing with you. They're pushing your buttons, and we have to show them that we are not at their beck and call."

I should ponder his words, take a rest, and figure out my next step instead of running like a bull in a china shop straight to my grandmother. I know that would be the logical thing to do. However, we are past logical. I was secluded from actually living for a month because of their threats, and when I decided to forget it and act like they didn't exist, look at what happened. They want my full focus. They are going to get it.

I put my phone out again, and I dial my grandmother's phone number, and it goes straight to voice mail. Despite everyone's objections, I look up her number with the GPS tracker our parents installed on our phones and see that the address looks familiar.

"She's in the mayor's office."

I try not to think of why my grandmother is at my father's office this late or try to think of all the pointed looks I am getting now. I don't care. I want answers. Tonight was the breaking point. I will no longer be naive, no longer be stagnant. I am meant to be queen, and someone came to my house, got me to wear a dress, and attacked Paul right under my nose. If my grandmother has answers, I refuse to wait until tomorrow to get them. Everyone has kept me in the dark, for ages.

I cross my arms over my chest and look at my friends, which one of them are also keeping secrets from me, omitting the truth to "protect" me. There's a gnawing feeling in my gut, telling me that I am not seeing the whole picture. That there's a lot I am missing.

I push the feeling away because although I can't trust my parents and I am unsure if I can trust Christian at this point, Paris, Angel, Jordan and my brother will never lie to me. We are always honest, even when it hurts.

I feel a small amount of guilt for even letting the thought enter my mind because it's completely ridiculous. Tonight's events and the text messages are making me question everyone, and it's already driving me crazy. I can't control what other people are doing if they are lying or not. So I try to focus on what I can control, and that's getting answers.

Chapter 21

Moments later, I decide to leave and find my grandmother and my answers. Paris, Jackson, Alex, and Christian occupy me while Jordan and Devin stay to clean up and watch over Angel.

"You gonna tell me what's up with you and Christian?" Paris whispers as we settle in the back seat of Alex's Honda Civic. Christian had opened the passenger door of the car for me, but instead, I opened the back seat and settled back there with Paris and Jackson. I know that the move was petty and he's trying to be nice, but I can't bring myself to look him in the eye. He lied after he sat with me all day and heard me talk in great detail about how my parents have been lying to me for years. It hurts to think that he sat there with a secret of his own.

My eyes rise to see the back of Christians head directly in front of me. It's as straight as an arrow, and I know he's listening in, probably wanting to hear my response to Paris's question. But instead, I just shake my head, and we ride the rest of the way in silence.

My brain is far away from this car, and my thoughts are scattered on my parents, Christian, and tonight's events. The past few days have been so eventful and hectic I can't even believe this is actually my life. I don't realize that we have arrived until I hear Jackson open the door.

In front of us is the big white building that my father calls his office. There are no lights on. The building looks almost abandoned. In front, there's a security guard, Robert, who's been working here for as long as I can remember.

Alex is the first to get up the white concrete steps to talk to Robert, and although I try, I can't hear what he tells him because Christian makes it a point to be so close behind me that it distracts me. His smell of pine fills my nostrils, and suddenly, I am enveloped in it earlier this evening when I didn't know the secret he had in his back pocket, just us two in my backyard, happy. How I wish I could go back to that girl, the one who didn't know that she was going to be forced to get married so soon, the one who had no idea what lay behind that bathroom door. It feels impossible to think that I can change in a span of a couple of hours, but I can feel it, the shift of my feelings and priorities.

Before I know it, Robert opens the door to the building, and we are let in. I take a big step away from Christian and put distance between us.

You can barely see the hallway leading to the foyer, and the place looks as if there's not a living soul in at the moment. It's eerie, almost as if its haunted. No sound comes out of the place, and for a second, I think that my phone got the address wrong because there is no way my grandmother is here.

"This doesn't feel creepy at all," Paris says sarcastically.

"Doesn't look like anyone is home?" Alex points out the obvious as we walk around. Paris's heels on the marble floor are practically deafening in comparison to the silence that envelops around us.

Alex uses his flashlight to lead us up the stairs but before we can up them completely Christian's hand shoots up and pulls me back. "Wait."

I turn to immediately find his eyes staring back at me. "What's wrong?" I try to ignore the sparks that come alive where his hand is currently placed. This isn't the time.

"I can smell them." I can't help but raise my eyebrow at him, skeptical. It doesn't look like anyone is here. "Your family. They're this way." He points to the east wing of the building, in the direction of my father's office.

"Lead the way."

He walks us in that direction, our shadows casted all over the floor as we reach the end of the hallway. At the end of the hallway, there are two doors: one leads to my father's office, and the other two to his secretary, Marsha.

Christian waits for a beat and then turns to open the door to my dad's workspace. Walking into the office, and it's completely dark with no evidence him being here for at least a couple of hours. Alex turns on the light next to the door, illuminating the room. In the center of my dad's office, there is his mahogany wood desk and an ugly green couch in the corner where he takes his midday nap. On his desk, there's some paperwork, his laptop, and picture frames full of pictures of my mom, Alex, and me. The office looks the same as it's been all these years.

"I think your nose is broken," Paris says to Christian, and although I don't turn to look at her, I know from years of knowing her that she is rolling her eyes right now. "There's clearly no witches in here, wolf boy."

"My nose is never wrong." His eyes search around the room until they stay fixated on the wall behind my father's desk.

"Maybe you just smelled my father's scent from earlier," Alex pointed out as he looks at the picture frames on my father's desk. "He does spend a lot of time here."

"Christian says he's here, then he's here," Jackson says as he keeps watch at the door. He doesn't even look into the room as he speaks, blindly following and believing Christian above all else.

I stare at Christian, his hands on the wall as if it was the most important thing he has ever studied. His hands roam the wall over and over again until he huffs. I don't agree with Alex and Paris because although I have no way of proving it, I can feel them. Their energy, they are definitely close by.

"We should check the other rooms," I offer up, maybe they are across the hall in Marsha's office of upstairs.

"The scent leads here, Alexandra."

"I understand that, but obviously, there's no one here."

Christian looks at the wall for another second and then turns to look at me as if he just realized something. "Your family practices blood magic, right?"

"Yes," I say, confused and irritated that he's ignoring my previous comment.

"So some of your spells are blood-related, right? Like Paris can't undo it because she is not a part of your bloodline, right?"

"I guess," I say, and my voice is laced with irritation. "What does this have to do with anything, Christian? We're wasting time."

"Just indulge me for a second," he says, putting a finger up, and then he takes a couple of strides toward me. His steps are hesitant like he doesn't know whether to come closer to me or give me space, and if I am being honest, I don't know exactly what I want him to do.

"Trust me."

Those two words, words I have heard my entire life. He breathes into me, and I can hear the meaning behind them. He's not talking about trusting him with this but with everything. He knows he messed up. He knows how much the truth and honestly means to me, especially in the last few weeks. I don't know why. Maybe it's because his brown eyes plead into my own, or the fact that he's so close to ignoring the fact that we are not alone, or maybe it's just because I want to, I nod.

A small smile creeps over his face as he grabs my hand and walks me over to the back of my father's desk. He looks over the wall again until he finds a spot directly at the center of the wall. Christian then leads my hand there and places his palm flat on the surface.

I wait a beat, but nothing happens. "Told you," Paris scoffs. "Your nose is broken, doggy."

Christian ignores Paris's comment and keeps ahold of my hand against the wall for an extra second, and suddenly, my hand starts to warm up. Not like it does whenever we're near, but differently. I take my hand off the wall to see a bright yellow glow emitting from it.

"Well, shit," I hear Alex mumble behind me as I look back at the wall, confused.

The white wall splits in half and reveals a staircase leading down into the darkness. My mouth gapes open for a second. There is a secret room. My heart drops to my ass for the second time tonight. Why in the hell would my father need an extra room in his office that only opens up with blood magic? What is he up to? I have been in this office for years, coming in to bring my father lunch and doing my homework here. I have never even thought that my father would have something like this in here.

Christian taps his nose with his right index finger and gives Paris a sly, mocking smile. "The nose is never wrong."

Paris ignores his comment. "That is some Scooby-Doo shit right there," she points to the cracked open wall in front of us.

I walk closer to the wall and see that the staircase is quite long, leading into a darkness that is just as eerie as when we first came into the building, if not more. The light from my father's office only shows us a couple of stairs, and I guess our imagination is taking all of us for a roller-coaster ride with our minds as we try to assume what's down there.

Paris is right. This is something I would have seen as a child when I was watching Scooby-Doo as a kid on Sundays—a secret passageway in plain sight. I don't even want to think what he's hiding or what else has been in front of me in plain sight.

I try to take a step down the stairs, but Paris immediately grabs hold of me. "You're kidding me, right? You're not actually going down there, are you?" She looks at me like I just grew another head. "This how people get killed."

"Paris, come on," Alex says.

"Hell no." She crosses her arms over her chest, shaking her head frantically. "Are you guys crazy? I have heels on." She points to her heeled boots she changed into after the party. "I can't run in these if we get chased by a monster."

"There is no such thing as monsters," I say, and I know that this situation is serious, but Paris being scared is kind of amusing. She is the adventurous one out of all of us, and she's scared to go downstairs.

"People say that about us, Lexi." Well, she has me there. "I'll keep watch," she says, taking a step away from us and pointing to the door where Jackson is. "He can keep me company."

Jackson looks Paris over and just smirks. "I didn't know you were scared of the dark, pretty girl."

I look at her and her outfit while Alex and I switch to sweats. She's wearing jeans, a T-shirt, and heels—heels she couldn't probably run in. "You sure?"

"Never been more sure of anything in my life. Scream if you need me to call the cops or say a prayer before you enter the gates of heaven."

163

With one last look at Paris, Christian, Alex, and I walk down the large staircase. With each step I take down the stairs, my heartbeat grows louder. The stairs are made of wood—wood that has probably been here for ages from its looks. I try my hardest not to make it creak under my feet, but it's damn near impossible. At the end of the staircase, there's a hallway illuminated by a torch as if we were in the medieval days. Brick covers the walls, and I feel the temperature drop to the point that I am practically shivering. I don't miss the way Christian steps in closer to me so I can feel the heat coming off his body.

There's a light coming out of the room at the end, and I can hear hushed voices coming out of said room.

I motion to Alex and Christian to be quiet as we get closer to the room at the end of the hallway. There's a slit big enough to see the contents of the room and who the voices belong too.

The room is full of candles, and a giant table with a spell book at its center is at the center of the room. It looks almost like a lair. My parents are at the front of the table, facing the door, while my grandma's back is facing me. It looks like they are conducting a spell.

"Rose, you sure you wanna do this?" a man's voice says from the corner if the room I can't see, a familiar voice but not my father's. "This spell seems to be risky."

"I have to," my mother says, her voice laced with determination, but it drops a little when she says, "I have to protect my children."

I look at Alex, who seems to be as confused as me, and mouth the words "protect us" while he just shrugs.

"There might be blowback." Paris's mom comes from the corner of the room, Jordan's parents in tow, and that's when I realize that is why the voice seemed familiar.

What is going on? Why are they all here in my dad's secret cave, so to speak? These are all members of the round table conducting a spell on harvest night—the most powerful night for witches and their powers. It doesn't seem right. Something big is going on, but what exactly?

"You guys are welcome to leave," my dad says, his voice calm with a sharp undertone. "We have to at least try. These are my kids we're talking about."

Jordan's mom, with her beautiful Indian hair, brown skin, and perfectly manicured hand grabs my mother's hands in her own, a small comforting gesture. "We're not leaving. We would do the same for Jordan."

My mom gives her a small smile and looks at my grandmother. "What is the probability of this working, Mother?"

"Not high." She shakes her head. "This has been decades in the making." She points to the spell book. "This spell book from Freya is powerful, and it might work, but I wouldn't hold my breath."

Freya, the witch that made sure Christian and I would get together. What does she have to do with this, and why does my grandmother have her spell book? I have so many questions filling my head that it's starting to give me a headache.

"And if this doesn't work, what then?"

My grandmother shakes her head. Silence is all you can hear for a couple of beats, and then she says in a voice as small as I have ever heard from her, "Then we prepare them for the biggest battle of the century."

"Battle," the word pops out of my mouth before I even register what is going on. Both Christian and Alex turn to look at me, shocked. I cover my mouth as soon as the sound comes out, but it's not the point. The word is already echoing in the air.

"What was that?" my mother asks, and all of them turn to look at the door.

The last thing I see is my father walking toward the door as Christian drags both Alex and me out of there at the speed of lighting.

Chapter 22

I wake up the next morning in my bed. I don't know how I got here until I see Christian sleeping in the same chair I saw him in yesterday morning. Except this time, he has another chair supporting his feet. His arms are crossed over his chest. He still has the clothes he was wearing last night.

Immediately, I recall the events that happened last night: the party, Christian, and my father's secret room. It feels like a lifetime ago and like it just happened. So many questions pop up in my head. I went to find my grandmother to find answers, but instead, I left with more questions than before. What spell were they trying to use, and why all the secrecy? This whole thing feels suspicious and confusing, and I can't help but think that my life is a pawn to something bigger.

I push that thought out of my head and go to the bathroom to shower and get ready for the day. It is 7:00 a.m., and I am kinda mad at myself for sleeping a couple of hours. I head downstairs, making sure I don't wake Christian on the way out.

In the living room, Jackson is knocked out on the couch. Paris, Jordan, Alex, and Angel are nowhere to be seen, so I just assume that they're either in the guest rooms or Alex's room. Devin and Jordan cleaned the house last night, and it almost looks brand new. I invited everyone to stay the night since it was so late when we finally got back to him. I know my mother said not to, but who is she to tell me anything when she has been lying and scheming behind my back?

I'm in the kitchen, making breakfast, when the back door opens, revealing one sweaty Jordan and a barely sweaty Devin. Both are wearing gym shorts and T-shirts.

"What are you doing up so early, love?" Devin asks, his glasses in the bridge of his nose as Jordan walks around me to get a water bottle. He seems out of breath and like he might pass out.

"Couldn't sleep in."

"I hear that," Jordan says, his hands on the counter. "Yesterday was definitely eventful."

I scoff. Eventful is an understatement. I've been trying to forget about last night: Paul lying on ground, my upcoming wedding, and let's not mention what happened with our parents. Last night is stuff you see in books or maybe movies, not my fucked-up life.

I shake my head, unwilling to let my mind wander, and I change the subject. "What's with you? Why are you breathing like you need an inhaler?"

Next to me, Jordan's black hair is covered in sweat and smushed on top of his head. His breathing sounds like he's been getting chased for days on end.

"We decided to go for a race since we were the only tow-up at the time," Devin explains as Jordan swallows the water in two gulps.

"You tried to race a werewolf?" I try not to laugh, but I can't help but envision Jordan trying to keep up with Devin.

Jordan nods. "You know I never back away from a challenge." He then points at Devin and says, "You could have at least taken it easy on me, man. I almost died out there."

Devin just smiles at Jordan. "Mate, I did take it easy on you."

Jordan is silent for a second, his face unreadable as he studies Devin's face. "I hate werewolves."

Perhaps it's the way Jordan said these words, or maybe it's because his face is completely deadpan, but Devin and I just laugh at him, not a giggle but an actual belly laugh that makes me forget about all our problems for a minute.

Devin nods and takes a seat on the stool across the kitchen island. He crosses his hands in front of him and looks at me with a sincere look on his face after just laughing his head off. His soft eyes look into mine.

"I am very sorry about last night. I know that isn't how Christian wanted you to find out."

"It's okay," I say, not sure I want to get into this right now.

I am still trying to piece together what I want to say to Christian and how I want to approach this.

"Find out about what exactly?" Jordan peeps into the conversation. His voice faces with curiosity as he studies us both.

I let out a sigh before I explain, "I'm supposed to be married to Christian on my birthday," I say, even I can hear the bitterness in my voice. Everywhere I turn around, there is someone telling me a new secret about myself. I feel as though my whole life was decided in a meeting, and my invite got lost in the mail. "Some witch named Robin came to the party yesterday to meet me. She thought I knew."

"Wait, so you're supposed to be married and coronated all on your eighteenth birthday?" Jordan says, and when I nod in response, he adds, "Talk about saving money for a party. What, your parents don't like spending money on cakes and streamers?"

I place a strand of hair behind my ear and look at Devin. "You don't have to apologize. I know you were just following orders. It's not your fault that my parents' default talking setting is to just spew lies and withhold the truth."

"Regardless, it was wrong, and I am sorry," Devin says, his voice low and almost shameful.

I really hold no ill will toward Devin or Jackson. It wasn't their place to tell me; it was Christian's. They are his pack. Whatever he says goes, and I can understand that.

"What really pisses me off is that people keep on coming to me telling me all these things about my life, big stuff, stuff that I should have decided. I just don't want to be blindsided again."

"I can't speak for Christian, and of course, I do think you should pull him for a chat, but I know he didn't mean to hurt you. I don't think he wanted to overwhelm you with so many surprises."

"He still should have told me."

Overwhelmed or not, I would have been grateful for the honesty. Yes, I would have freaked, but it's way better hearing it from him than some stranger.

"I understand that," Devin says. "I think he was still dealing with it himself."

I raise my eyebrow and look over at him. "What do you mean?"

"I mean, think about it. He knew his entire life about you. He knew you guys were meant to be together and that he was supposed to marry you, but a part of him didn't really believe it until he met you." He explains, "The only reason I am telling you this is so you'll understand he's point of view. He's not only going to be my alpha, but he's also one of my best mates. I know him, and he's not great with feelings.

"He has lived in denial practically his whole life. Now here you are, and you know nothing about this future you're supposed to have with him. You're still trying to figure out everything in your life, and he's just trying to understand all his feelings for you, and how can someone he's only met a month ago mean so much to him." Devin's words resonate in my mind, speaking to the voice inside me that tells me that I should brush Christian off. "I think you're both confused and in your heads about everything that is going on, as you should be," he adds quickly. "He really just wanted to protect you."

"What you say doesn't change the fact that Christian is a closed book. He can tell you all this but won't even be truthful with me," I say, fed up. I can take lying and being left out of the dark from my parents, but I'd be damn if I am supposed to marry someone the same way. "I won't live this way," I say the words out loud more to myself than to the room.

Marry, the word sounds weird, even in my own thoughts. I can't believe that I am not even eighteen years old, and I am thinking about marrying someone I have known for less than two months. I know that the alliance and my people must come first, whatever that may mean, but I refuse to live my life this way.

"He doesn't tell me, really," Devin says and then adds, "We go on runs together."

"Runs?"

Devin smiles slightly and pushes his glasses off his nose. "Werewolves, when we are in our natural form, we are able to read each other's mind." Jackson comes into the room, his black hair in a tossed-up mess on top of his head. Even waking up from sleeping off a couch, he looks perfectly rested. His tattoos e shine off the light coming from the window. He looks at Devin and takes a sit next to him. "He is going to kill you, you know that, right?"

Devin just grins at him and shrugs as Jordan and I stand here, confused. How did I not know werewolves can read each other's minds? It's a surprising fact as I try to think of having someone who knows all my inner thoughts. It feels invasive.

"So you guys can read each other's minds?" Jordan asks.

He sounds as surprised and astounded as I feel.

"There's more than goes into it," Jackson points out and watches as Jordan and I stare at him, begging him to elaborate. Once he sees we are not going to relent, he sighs and just continues, obviously annoyed, "We can only read our minds in werewolf form. That's how we communicate when we are in patrols or runs, but sometimes, you can read someone's thoughts as if they were telling it to you themselves. We have been trained since kids to control that part of minds, to keep our thoughts hidden if we wanted to."

"But Christian?" I ask, confused. If they were trained to hide it, why didn't he?

"But Christian sometimes lets us in, so instead of talking it out, he just lets us in his mind."

I look at Jackson and Devin, Christian's best friends, and I can't help but feel slightly jealous. There hasn't been a night that I have stayed up just wondering about what goes on in Christian's head and what he thinks. Here they are, and they have a direct line to his deepest thoughts while I have to beg for a little bit of information at a time.

I open my mouth to ask more questions, but I am interrupted by Christian's voice.

"What the hell are you doing?" His eyes are zeroed in on Jackson and Devin, and I watch them visibly shrink. Devin's smile disappears, but Jackson's face stays as deadpan as it did before.

"Mate, we were...," Devin tries to explain but is immediately cut off by Christian's booming voice.

"You were what, telling things I shared in confidence with you to other people?" I see his fist clench by his side, remembering our conversation yesterday, where he told me wolves don't get mad; they go ballistic, and I can see how this is turning out to be.

I feel the need to defend them, protect them from his rage. Yes, they shared some things they probably shouldn't have, but they were doing it for his benefit. "They didn't mean it like that, Christian. They were—"

"Stay out of this, Alexandra," he says, and although he doesn't shout at me like he did to them, I can still feel his anger. "They are my pack."

"Yeah, you won't even let me explain." I roll my eyes at how he's acting. I understand how he feels, but if only he would let them explain or even apologize.

However, he ignores my comment and is committed to his anger. "What possessed you two to wake up this morning and tell her about pack business? Things I shared with you only you two for a reason." His voice is loud and almost cold. Jordan tenses next to me, and I watch as Devin hangs his head. I feel as if I am watching children get yelled at by their parents, and I don't like it.

"We didn't mean to betray your trust, man," Jackson says. "But..." He doesn't finish his sentence, looking at Christian's menacing eyes.

"But what?" His icy glare snaps to Jackson, and I can tell he's trying not to lose his cool by the way his fists remain clenched at his sides and his feet planted on the ground.

"You can't just expect us to sit by while this is all going on. You guys are the future of both of our people. This alliance is supposed to protect all of us, and here we are, arguing about feelings and lies when we should be worried about vampire attacks and whatever battle her parents are so worried about," Jackson snaps back at Christian. I can see the tension on his shoulders. "So if telling her how you feel and why you lied to her is going to help us get over this and focus on what we have been trained for, then I am sorry, man, but Devin and I did what we had to do."

I catch myself holding my breath, not only about what he said but the way Christian just stands there looking at him, unmoving and silent. His eyes don't leave Jackson, and I feel time stretch before us.

The alliance, it's insane how so much rides on Christian and I being together. Not that we have much of a choice. Our destinies were chosen long before us.

I watch as Christian finally unclenches his fist. "Get out." Not even a full second after Christian speaks his last word. Everyone scrambles like roaches out of the room—everyone but me.

I make eye contact with Christian and know exactly what he meant. He wanted everyone to clear the room but us. His feet stay planted while his eyes land on me, and I can feel the anger radiating off him even though I am all the way at the other side of the room.

Neither of us talks for what seems like forever. We just stare at each other. I am still upset about the lie, and I know that he is still upset about what just transpired.

"I would appreciate it if you had any questions about my feelings or my thoughts. You'd come directly to me and not to my pack."

I roll my eyes. I don't tell him that I didn't ask because it doesn't matter. I did want to know, and that is why I let them talk and tell me.

"How I feel is no one's business unless I make it theirs." His voice is almost condescending, and it sparks up my own anger.

"Not even mine."

"That is not what I meant."

"Then enlighten me on what you meant because I am confused. You told me you liked me last night. You even got jealous of Johan. Then I find out I am supposed to be married to you in a matter of months, something you knew you were supposed to tell me, and now you're mad because your friends told me all these confusing feelings that you didn't tell me."

"I tried to apologize for not telling you," he says, his voice automatically softens. "But you have to understand I didn't do it in a malicious way. I tried to do what I thought was best. I will always take control of the situation, and I thought this was the best outcome."

"I am not a situation."

He shakes his head. "I know, and I should have told you. I just didn't want to freak you out. You have so much on your plate."

I nod, not even sure I am mad anymore. It feels so big yet so small compared to everything else. Marriage is a big thing, and I would have liked to have been told prior to this. But if I am being honest, I knew that my parents would have found me a husband. If I didn't find a witch that was powerful enough. However, I didn't think that my marriage would be so soon and destined to be by my ancestors.

"I do like you, Alexandra, and I know that you know that." He takes steps closer to me, and I get to appreciate his looks without anger clouding my judgment. His brown locks are a mess on his head. His eyes are lighter because of the sunlight shining in the room. He still has yesterday's clothes on, a wrinkled dress shirt, and slacks, yet he still looks like Christian. A breathtaking piece of art that has me under a spell I can't quite shake. "My friends were right about me being at a crossroads," he says has he reaches me. I do realize he heard the entire conversation, but I let him continue. "But not about how I feel about you, not about us."

"Then what?" I notice how close he is, his smell filling my ears, and I come to help try to fight myself from getting lost in the smell.

"Everyone expects me to be open, ready and willing. You aren't the only one who got their life decided for them before they were even born," he spoke, his words making me realize that he's completely right.

This whole time, I have been fixated that my life was decided for me, but in reality, it was for both of us. Two kids, whose ancestors used them as pawns, no matter how good, for a reason.

"Before I met you, I felt like I was holding my breath. I was incredibly anxious to meet you. Not because I was excited but because I was terrified. I thought I was going to be stuck in a relationship for the rest of my life, one that was not of my choosing." I know they shouldn't, but his words offend me slightly. I know it's wrong to feel that way because I have had those same thoughts, those same feelings.

"But," he continues, his voice soft as he stares into the deepest parts of me, "when I met you, when I met you, Alexandra, it was like I could breathe again." He takes a step closer to me, and heat radiates off him in waves. He's close enough that I can probably count his full eyelashes individually if I wasn't so preoccupied with his words. "I am at a crossroads, confused and dumbfounded, but not about you but more so about myself. Alexandra..." He doesn't finish his thought, and I can see it on his face, the inner struggle of continuing or letting it go.

Call me selfish, but I need to hear it, hear what's on his mind without prying it out of him. I want him to finish, to give me information willingly, not because I beg for it, not because his friends offer it up, but because he wants to. I don't understand what he means by being at a crossroads with himself, but I really want him to elaborate.

We stand so close to each other, with no words for what seems like an eternity until he gives in. "Alexandra, I don't know how to explain it properly. I am not good with my words, but I need you to know that I feel strongly for you, and if you feel like I am withholding anything from you, it's not because I want to keep you in the dark but more so that I am stuck in my own head. This is all new to me."

The vulnerability behind his words cracks through my armor. He was wrong for not telling me about the wedding, but he knows that, and there is no point in gnawing on that when we have important things to figure out. I appreciate him letting me see little by little what's behind the wall he has. More than that, though, I appreciate that I am not the only one who feels this way. So instead of pushing him to finish his previous thoughts, I nod and decide to be grateful for what I got.

Chapter 23

It is exactly ten o'clock in the morning when I hear my grandmother's voice through the hallways in the house. I have been waiting anxiously for her silently since all my friends and Christian left hours ago. I promised Christian that the moment I got information out of her, I would call him first. That was the only way I could get him to leave and go for a run with his pack. Paris and Angel promised to come over in the morning to hang out, and Jordan and Alex went to the gym. I have been home alone, with just my thoughts and my family's spell book.

So when I hear her voice, I practically run out of my room and try to catch her before she gets to her room.

"Grams, I need to..."

I don't get to finish my sentence because I see her turn around just to find bags under her eyes, a frown on her face, and a look that lets me know she's exhausted.

She gives me a small smile that does not reach her eyes. "Hello, my love."

"Are you okay?"

At the moment, my mind is not worried about the text and any information my grandmother may have. This is the first time I have seen her so beat and so unlike herself. She's wearing the exact clothes she had yesterday, her hair is a mess, and I swear I see what seems like a bruise forming on her neck, almost like something hit her. Most importantly, the sparkle that is always in her eye, the light that I have seen on my darkest days, is gone.

"Grams, did something happen?"

She doesn't even need to answer for me to know the answer. Something is wrong. I know it. Behind me, my mother appears with no bruises but the same clothes as yesterday, and she has a tired look on her face. She looks even more beat than my grandmother.

"Alexandra." Her eyes widen with shock. "I thought you were out."

I shake my head slowly, my eyes still roaming over her, trying to see if she has any visible bruises like Grams. "What happened?"

"Nothing." Her brown eyes avoid my own caramel ones as she lies. I am starting to think that this is her default setting, keeping me in the dark.

In her hands, there is butter and salt, an old remedy for taking care of bruises. She probably came up here to tend to Grandma, not expecting questions.

"She has a bruise on her neck, and you both look like you were up all night and not for a good time. What happened?"

"Alexandra." She shakes her head, annoyed. "This is not the time."

All the frustration that I have felt in the last month takes the form of anger bubbling in me as I watch her try to walk away from me and go into my grandmother's room with Grams in tow. This time, my magic doesn't go out of control. I know exactly what I am doing when I use my powers to slam the door before they try to leave me alone in this hall.

The door slams hard, and I am surprised that it stays on its hinges. They both turn to look at me, anger covering my mother's face while Grandmother is just shocked.

"I will not be ignored anymore," I snap. I am angry, and I have every right to be. They are lying right to my face, evading questions, making me feel like I am a child. With everything that happened over these few days, I refuse to be kept in the dark any longer than I have. "What happened?"

"Who do you think you are?" My mother fumes, stomping over to me. "You will not slam doors in my house and demand answers from me. I am your mother."

I roll my eyes at her mother's comment, a mother who lies and has secret midnight meetings. I look at her furrowed brows, pissed-off expression, and eyes that glare back at me. This isn't the mother I grew up with, the nice woman who swore to always have my back, someone who I can trust.

"I saw you last night, all of you, in Dad's secret passageway."

I see her face drop, and my grandmother just whispers behind her, "I knew I sensed her magic. I told you."

My mother ignored my grandmother's comment. "What did you see?"

"Enough."

Barely anything, but I don't tell her that. I want her to know that she's caught. I want her to fess up what she was doing down there. In the middle of the night with half of the roundtable, on the strongest night for witches.

It's a paused silence, filled with tension from both sides of the hallway. My mother takes a beat, most likely trying to figure out what to say now that she knows that I was there.

"You shouldn't be spying on us," she says softly as she turns back around. "Let's go, Mother."

They both turn around, leaving me to stand in the hallway, frustrated and alone. I should have stopped them from leaving and forced them to tell me what they are obviously hiding. Something happened last night after we left. I can't even say I am angry anymore. I mean, what did I expect to happen? I know my mother, and I know my grandmother. My mom doesn't want me to know, and my grandmother will always follow suit.

I grab my phone from my back pocket to let Christian and Alex know that it was bust, and I'm going to try to figure it out. I should be used to it by now. It's completely frustrating that there is a lack of information in my family, so I grab the doorknob to my room and enter, defeated. However, I don't have time to evaluate my feelings because as soon as I close the door behind me, my back is pinned to the door, and a heavy, muscular hand covers my mouth.

I am about to kick said person in the shin until my hazel eyes make contact with deep brown ones that only belong to one person.

"Don't scream," is the first thing he says as I realize that my body is completely flushed to his. I am sure he can feel my erratic heartbeat pounding against his chest as the hand he has clamped over my mouth sends sparks and goosebumps all over my body.

I am of average height, but being this close to Christian, I feel so tiny as he towers over me so much I have to peek through my eyelashes to look at him.

Christian lets his hand fall off my face, but he doesn't step back. "She's lying. They both are."

"How do you know that?" I say even though I know that myself.

"Their heart rates went over the roof the moment you asked."

"You heard their heartbeats?" I am fully aware that the damn organ in my chest is beating a mile a minute. However, I hope he's not listening to mine too.

He gives me a knowing smirk like he knows why I ask the question, but he doesn't answer.

Being this close to him should be a crime. I can barely focus as I study his flawless skin and full lips. He's so perfect it makes me mad. How can someone like him exist, and why does he have such an effect on me that with one touch, I turn into goo?

I step around him, trying to create some distance before I start to drool. "What are you doing here?"

"I wanted to give you something," he says, and I watch as he pulls out a bouquet of roses from behind his back. Red beautiful roses that make my heart swoon. "They were in my mother's garden, and I asked if I could pick someone to bring to you."

The last sentence comes out of his mouth a little quicker than his usual cadence of sentence. I look at his face, and I see that his cheeks are as red as the roses. He's blushing, so he does get embarrassed. It's such a rare sight that I wish I was an artist so I can make millions of paintings of him in this exact moment. He looks almost like a normal teenage boy if you don't count the muscles and beautiful Greek god–like bone structure.

"I didn't know if you liked red roses. I asked my mom, and she said you would love it, but if you don't like it, you can always throw it away. I won't be offended. I just got them because I wanted to give you something, and they were the first thing that made me think of you. They smell just like you."

His out-of-character rambling makes my heart ache in the best way. The confident Christian gets all nervous for me. I don't even know how to process that, so I don't; instead, I don't hesitate to walk over to him and place my hand on his cheek while accepting the roses in my other hand.

"Thank you. They are stunning. I love them so much."

A huge smile breaks on his face as the words leave my mouth, and God, is he breathtaking. I don't think I have ever seen him smile so big, and now I want to do what I can to make sure he does more often.

"I'm glad. Now I need you to get ready."

I raise my eyebrow. "How come?"

"I am taking you on a date."

I try to ignore the way my heart skips a beat at his words. "You know, usually, a guy asks a girl on a date, he doesn't tell her?"

He shrugs his shoulders and just grins. "Carino, I am an alpha. I don't ask. I tell."

I roll my eyes at his comment, but I can't help but laugh. Bossy Christian is back, and it's like he never left.

"You're not going to tell me where we're going, are you?"

He displays a mischievous grin on his lips. "What's the fun in that?"

Chapter 24

Christian

My whole life, I have felt as though I am the one responsible for the future of my entire species—falling in love with a witch, creating an alliance to ensure the safety not just of the wolves but the witches too. Talk about pressure. Not to mention that my father is so sure that once the alliance is solidified, other packs will want to join ours just to be protected. It's a burden I never asked for, yet I have to carry it.

At least that is what I felt a few weeks ago before I met Alexandra, and she flipped my world upside down. I still remember the feeling of dread in the pit of my stomach that grew with each step I took up to the school on the first day of the semester. I had been in a horrid mood the whole morning, thinking of all the shitty outcomes that could have happened that day. What if she was arrogant and conceited? What if she was a spoiled witch who didn't take her duties seriously? Maybe she would be like any teen our age, focused on the idea of social media likes and how to become famous the easy way. But the thing that really scared me was what if I felt no connection. I know that in life and movies, the girls are the romantic ones, but I would be lying if I didn't say that I would love the idea of finding someone who makes me want to wake up every day. I grew up seeing my father and mother fall deeper in love with each other every day. What if I met her and there was no connection, and I was doomed in a life with someone who doesn't make me feel alive? Regardless of what happened when I stepped into that school, I knew one thing for sure: whether I liked her or not, I would do what was expected of me.

That all changed when I saw her in that crowded hallway. It was like my body knew she was there. The attraction was immediate. The world was black and white until I laid eyes on her, and suddenly, she was the pop of color I didn't know I needed. I knew then and there that she was the reason I had been training my whole life, the reason my mother showed me to cook and clean, and the reason my pack and I moved across states. It felt almost like magic, which I know it played a part in, but there was something more.

Her hazel eyes were the first thing I noticed, so big and breathtaking. Decorating her heart-shaped face, I heard her heartbeat, a slow rhythm that climbed to a whole rock song on its own. Her scent filled my nose, intoxicating with the smell of roses, something sweet and vanilla. I knew everyone was staring at us, and a small part of me didn't care because I knew I could look at her all day. However, I turn away anyway because I don't want to creep her out and mostly because I am feeling things I have never felt before.

Fast-forward to today, we're in my car driving down the road to the bayou, and nothing has really changed. I look at her, and I still feel the same way—an attraction that will knock any man on his feet. But it's more than that; it's her essence, the little things that make her so special. I'm in love with her, and I know it hasn't been long since I have known her, but when I'm with her, I feel it in my bones, coursing through my veins, threatening to make its way out and tell her. But I know I can't do that. After the week she had, it would be selfish to lay it on her. This past week has been beyond overwhelming for her, and I can't add more to the pile, so I suck it up because if I can't tell her, yet I can definitely show her.

"You okay?" I turn to her.

She's been staring out the window and hasn't spoken since we got into the car. I know her mind is millions of miles away. Her head is probably spinning out of control with everything that has happened this weekend.

"Where are you taking me?" She avoids the question as she turns around to look at me.

I can't help but smile because, of course, she's curious. That's her default setting. "Always with the questions, huh?"

"Well, I figured I should ask." She laughs. "You have a habit of putting me in your car and driving me to unknown places."

I smile fondly at the memory of our first date. It's been such a long time since then, and so much has happened. So much stress, so many secrets, and so many things have gone wrong for her.

"Not telling."

She sighs, and her head turns toward the front. "Fine. I don't want to know anyway."

"Of course, you don't," I mock her.

We spend the next couple of seconds in silence, which probably gives her time to come up with her next question.

"What's your middle name?"

The question comes to me as a shock because it's so random and a complete 180 from where we were just at that it takes me a moment to respond.

"Spot."

I wait for her to laugh or to make a joke, but she doesn't. In fact, she doesn't say anything. I turn to look at her, and she's giving me a quizzical look.

"Are you joking?"

I shake my head. "No, unfortunately. My dad, as the alpha, gets to name all the wolves once they transition. He saw me and immediately named me Spot, and as a joke for my fifteenth birthday, he legally changed my name to Spot. My father is practical joker in his spare time, always finding the light in any and every situation. He thinks he's funny. I just can't help but think he's corny. However, that corny streak of his keeps a smile on our pack's face even through the hard times."

"He didn't," she says, and I can see the smile fighting its way to the surface. "Christian Spot Castillo." A burst of laughter escapes her mouth, and finally, she gives in to the joke.

Throughout my younger years, I have always been ashamed of my name. I always felt like the butt of the joke. Whenever I complained to my parents about the name Spot, my father insisted that it taught me to have thick skin and that alphas from our bloodline have never been affected by name-calling of any kind. So I had to learn to ignore all the jokes and dog whistles that came with it and focused on myself.

I hated my name for as long as I remember, but now, watching Alexandra laughing, carefree and young, I'm glad I told her. I'm grateful to my father for sticking me with that name all those years ago. Because now more than ever, the way her laughter fills this car, it feels that all those years of torture and humiliation were completely worth it.

So instead of frowning, as I usually do, I laugh with her—I mean, actually laughed—because when I'm with Alexandra, I am happy. Her happiness is insanely infectious.

After Alexandra somewhat composes herself, she looks at me. "That should qualify as child abuse in some books."

"It isn't that bad." I smile at her. *Not if it makes you smile like that*, I say in my head because I know how corny it would sound coming out of my mouth.

"I guess not."

"It's your time now," I say, "What is your middle name?"

"Oh, simple, Rosie. My grandmother is Rosa, my mom Rose, and since they wanted to name me after my father, they decided I should have the name somewhere in there." She points out, "My family is really big on tradition."

I nod as the car turns right on the dirt road. We're close, and for some reason, I am nervous. In hindsight, I probably should have warned her about where we're going, but in all honestly, I didn't know how she would react. So I stayed quiet, and now I am thinking that was a mistake. There's no going back now.

At the end of the dirt road is the house, beige color with a large porch like most houses in New Orleans. The outside of the house is surrounded by about a dozen of people, all having a good time. listening to music, grilling food on the barbecue, and children playing with a red kickball.

"Did you bring me to a cookout?" she asks as we drive up the driveway.

Every pair of eyes is on my car as it comes to a stop. I see Devin and Jackson walking toward us, both of them with giant smiles on their faces.

"What are they doing here?" Alexandra asks, her eyes looking around, probably confused as to what is going on. She studies everything, from the people, the food, and the house. I think the puzzle pieces are starting to piece up in her mind.

"Christian, where did you bring me?"

Her brown eyes make eye contact with my own, and I see the slight flicker of panic reflect off them.

"My house."

Chapter 25

Alexandra

Did I just hallucinate, or did he just say his house? No, there's no way. There's no way that Christian brought me to his house with no warning, no heads-up. I could have changed out of jeans and a plain white T-shirt. I could have brushed my hair out of the messy bun I have slapped on the top of my head, and most importantly, I could have mentally prepared for this.

All this, I practically yell at him as I freak out in his passenger seat. "Are you crazy?"

"Are you?" He laughs as if this is actually funny. BTW, it is not. "I have never seen you like this, so nervous."

"What did you expect me to be? Calm, cool, and collected? I'm meeting your family, Christian."

Again, he laughs and throws me a winning smile. "I met your dad."

I scoff. "Through passing, that is not the same thing, and you know it."

"I'm sorry. By the time I thought I should have warned you, we were on our way here."

"Christian, I can't meet your parents looking like this."

"What is wrong with what you are wearing?"

I look at him and roll my eyes. He's being purposely obtuse. "I look homeless, my hair is a mess, and—"

"I think you look beautiful," he says very bluntly and too quickly, as if he's been thinking about it for a while.

I look at him, and my cheeks are burning up. Fuck, why does he do that? Just say stuff like that, as if he didn't know how he affects me.

"My parents have been hounding me about meeting you, and besides, I thought a cookout would be a nice distraction." His eyes bear into mine, and I appreciate the thought. I appreciate that he thinks about me and cares for me enough to just get out of my own space and just be.

The problem with that is that now I have to just be here, in his space, with his family that I have never met. What if they don't like me? What if they think I am unworthy of their son and their alpha? I've read enough about wolf heritage to know that their alpha is their protector, and his pack protects him. What if they assume what I already know? That the environment that surrounds me and my community is too dangerous for Christian.

As I ponder this in my head, Christian reaches over to grab my hand. A small gesture that practically sets my body on fire. "We can leave if you want. They can meet you another time. It's whatever you want to do, Alexandra." He gives my hand a quick reassuring squeeze. "We'll go."

"No." I can't just leave. They are all staring at us, waiting for me to come out, waiting to meet me. Leaving now will just be a slap in their face and show them how much of a coward I really am.

"Let's stay," I say, my voice barely above a whisper.

"You sure?"

I nod, and with another squeeze, he lets my hand go as we get out of the car.

The weather outside is fairly warm but not warm enough for how I am feeling. I'm practically sweating by the time I get to Devin and Jackson, who meet us about twenty feet from the car. Around us, people stare at us, people who I assume are Christian's pack. There are men, women, and children all over the property, grilling, talking, and playing games. Their eyes wander to us, probably curious as to who their future alpha has been spending all his time up.

"Hey, don't be nervous?" Devin says as soon as I walk up to him.

Is it that obvious that I am practically shaking in my boots?

"Yeah, your hair doesn't look that bad?" Jackson says with a grin plaster on his handsome face.

I look at him, confused. How could he have possibly known that I was insecure about my hair? I only just told Christian in the car, and there's no way he heard me unless…

"You spied on our conversation."

Jackson's grin grows in size as he nods his guilty little head. "You're around werewolves, darling. What did you think was gonna happen?"

Christian hits him on the side of the head. "Leave her alone."

Jackson puts his hand up and just laughs. "Alright, just having some fun with the princess."

"Your parents are waiting," Devin says on a more serious note, and although I know he probably listened to our conversation as well, he doesn't comment. That is why Devin is my favorite, sweet and complete gentleman.

I look behind them on the porch. There are two adults standing by at the porch. It must be his parents because even from over here, I can see the way they smile at us, especially at Christian.

"Ready?' Christian says, and he grabs my hand and leads me to them.

My heartbeat races at about a hundred miles a minute with every step I take to the porch. There's a huge man about the size of Christian but about a couple of inches taller. His skin is as tan and brown as Christian's, but his eyes are more on the hazel side. The haircut he has on his head is recent, I can tell, and it's quite short, unlike Christian's locks of curls. He has a full-mouth smile plaster on his face while he's dressed in a plaid button-down shirt and jeans.

Next to him is a petite woman, and when I say petite, I mean she can't be any taller than five feet, and that is stretching it. She's slim, with light brown skin and curls that lead all the way down her back. She, as the man next to her, has a plaid shirt on, but her jeans are small cutoff that show off her perfect chocolate legs. She has a couple of wrinkles in her face, but something tells me it's from smiling because the wrinkles surround her beautiful brown eyes—those that I have seen many times before in the face of her son.

As soon as we make our way to them, Christian's mother envelopes me in the warmest hug known to all mankind.

187

"Alexandra." Her voice tickles my ear. "It's so great to finally meet you."

She smells like pinewood and fresh grass with a hint of honey. It's nice, and it feels so familiar that can't help but hug her back with the same passion she gives me.

When the hug finally breaks, I smile at her. "It's so nice to meet you, Mrs. Castillo."

"Oh, honey, no, please call me Tanya." She swats her hand in the air as a sign of dismissal. "Mrs. never really suited me."

"Tanya," I correct myself. It feels weird calling an adult by their name when my family has always taught differently. But if that is what she wants, then who am I to object?

"Same goes for me. I'm not a missus either," Christian's father jokes, and it makes Tanya and myself laugh.

"Dad." Christian groans as though he's embarrassed, but I think his parents are adorable.

He puts his hand out for me to shake. "Call me Robert."

I shake his giant hand in return. "It's nice to meet you, Robert."

All of a sudden, the nerves that we were overflowing my body earlier leave me alone, and I actually do feel calm. Surrounded by nature and good people, I really do forget my problems. For the next hour, I spend time with Christian's parents, and I also meet his sister Santana. She's an exact replica of her mother, except she is about my height, sixteen years old, and practically annoys Christian every chance she gets. Tanya shows me her rose garden and even brags about how Christian picked and dethorn the roses he gave to me.

I've met Jackson's grandmother and Devin's mother, both sweet women, although Devin's mother seems quite protective of Devin, fixing his hair, straightening up his shirt, and asking him who is texting him every time his phone gets a notification.

I also get to see another side of Christian that I didn't know even existed. Here, around his friends and family, he's happy and more relaxed. A carefree Christian. He jokes around with his parents and the boys. He even tortures his little sister when he gets the chance. I watch as he grills next to his father, which you can tell he idolizes. How he always smiles at his mother when she's telling a story. Even how he winks at me every time he catches me staring at him and kissed me on the cheek twice when he thought no one was looking. He's sweet, charming, and attentive. It's almost too much for my heart to take.

Once we eat a dinner of steak and grilled vegetables, I sit on the steps on the porch with Santana, who just finished telling me about how she's getting used to her new school.

"I just joined the cheerleading squad, and this cute basketball player Tony says I have great moves." She gushes as we watch the boys play football.

Talking to Santana makes me jealous. Don't get me wrong. I love Alexander probably more than anyone on this earth, but I have always wanted a little sister. She's sweet and young. The problems in her life are boys and mean girls. Nothing I wouldn't be able to give her advice on.

"I'm a cheerleader too," I point out, and her eyes light up like the Fourth of July.

"No way," she shrieks, and it causes her parents and a couple of pack members to look over at us.

"We were meant to be sisters," Santana wraps me in her arms and gives me a side hug so tight I am afraid my eyes are going to pop out.

I smile at her as she lets me go, and we return our attention to the group of handsome men in front of us playing football, and although all the men are big, the only one I really pay attention to is Christian. You can tell Christian was meant to be an alpha even if you didn't know him. His presence on the field portrays he's a mature leader. He's quick on his feet and his reflexes, dodging the other team with a speed of lighting. If you were to blink too fast, you would miss him on the field. It's fascinating. His team consists of Jackson, Devin, and one of the other pack members I met earlier, Sam. The other team doesn't stand a chance as they race around their makeshift field.

Christian's smile never leaves his face. Even on the rare occasions that the other team scores a touchdown, he's still happy. It makes my heart warm up like the sun in the Sahara Desert. The game is 40–28 in Christian's favor when a blonde-haired beauty with cutoff shorts walks up in the middle of the field and interrupts the game.

The girl has a full head of golden locks and a tan that you can only get from lying in the sun all day. I can't quite decipher her face from here, but she walks up to the boys with a sass in her walk as though she owns the whole probably. They all stop and look at her.

"Who's that?" Curiosity gets the best of me, and I ask Santana.

Santana rolls her eyes. "That right there is the devil incarnate, Jules," she says, and the sound of distaste is so evident in her voice that I know she is not a fan.

I look over at Jules. She smiles at the boys as she walks like a woman on a mission all the way toward Christian.

I try not to freak out at the show-stopping girl with gorgeous hair and a banging body just walks up to my Christian. Confident walks, flips her hair, and just smiles. I can't hear her, but I can tell I already don't like what she's saying.

"She's flirting," Santana says in my ear. "She always does."

I turn to look at her, trying to contain myself. As much as I hate it, I am a jealous person. It's one of my biggest flaws, right next to overthinking and insecurity. "Can you hear her?" I know it's wrong, but I want to know what she's saying to him.

Santana bites her lip reluctantly, probably questioning if she should. She then sees my pleading eyes and must feel bad for me because she gives in.

"She just told Christian that he looks good out there."

I look at them. That's not too bad, right? Hell, I've said that before to my own brother. It doesn't mean she's flirting. Besides, it's not like Christian is reacting to it.

"He just told her thanks." Santana narrates their conversation.

Thanks! Why is he thanking her? I take a deep breath and try to control the raging urges that tell me to go over there and stick my throat down his throat. Possessive, maybe. I don't even know if I have the right to be possessive. Christian and I never talked about what we actually are, so can I really be mad?

"Jules just told him she missed him over the last couple of days."

Maybe I don't have the right to be pissed, but I am real fucking pissed. Breathe, I tell myself, there's no need to be angry, no reason for my magic to take over. Not in front of all these people, I can hurt someone.

190

"And...," Santana says, and her voice lowers and comes to an abrupt stop. I turn to look at her. She doesn't want to tell me what was said. Is it that bad?

"What?" I look at Santana's brown eyes as she looks at mine. A beat goes by, and she doesn't say anything. "What did she say?"

"She asked what she would have to do to get tackled by him,"

When I was nine, Anitta took one of my Bratz dolls when we were on recess in the playground. At first, I tried to make it seem as if it didn't bother me. Maybe then she would realize that I wasn't going to play her game. So for the next ten minutes, I watched her play with my doll, I watched her brush her hair, and I even watched her go down the slide with it. The more I tried to convince myself I didn't care, the more I tried to calm myself down, but it had the opposite effect. I couldn't calm myself down. I couldn't act like I didn't care because I did care. So as I watched her play with my doll, I just got furious to the point that I marched right up to her and punched her in the face.

That is exactly how I feel right at this moment. The more I try to look away from Jules flirting away from Christian, the more I notice her presence. She subtly touches him. She compliments him. She even joins their game of football. What makes me even more pissed is the fact that Christian lets her. Santana says that she knows for a fact that her brother doesn't see anything in Jules, that although Jules has had a crush on Christian since they were kids, he doesn't really acknowledge it because, according to Santana, he wouldn't know someone was flirting with him even if that person had a T-shirt on their body saying, "Hey, I want you." But if I am being completely honest, I think that is some complete and utter bullshit. How can he not tell that she's flirting with him? She follows him around the whole field. She even winked at him once. She's all over him.

It's frustrating how he just lets it happen. It's frustrating just watching her smile, and she just goofs around with him right in front of me. I talk myself down every time I want to walk over there and give them both a piece of my mind. I keep on telling myself that I am not a crazy person, that if I went over there, I would be acting a fool. He hasn't even said if he's my boyfriend. We haven't even had that talk, so why am I tripping over it? Why am I getting up from off the porch and marching over to their game, just like I did in the third grade? Because you're crazy. My inner voice screams at me, but I swat it away with a swish of my hand. This has gone way too far. Why would Christian invite me here just to have another girl flirt with him all in front of me?

Santana walks up behind me, whispering, "Please don't kill them. Christian is just an idiot, and Jules, well, Jules just wants attention."

"Well, she's gonna get it," I say as I stalk about between their game.

"Oh god."

In complete honesty, I don't know what I am going to say or even what I am going to do, but I do know that this has gone on for way too much, and if I don't do something about it, I might just go insane. I walk up to the middle of the lineup, aware that I am ruining their game but not interested in the slightest. I hear mumbles coming from the other team saying stuff like, "What is she doing," and I am pretty sure I hear Jackson say, "Christian is in trouble."

Christian is the quarterback, and right next to him is Jules, a little too close for my liking. All heads turn to me as I stop in front of them.

He looks up at me perplexed, sweat covering almost every inch of his body as he straightens up.

I know I must look weird coming into the middle of their game with Santana hot on my tail, and now that I am here, I don't know exactly what to say, so I just say, "Hey."

"What's up?" Christian smiles at me, and I almost forget that I am mad at him, almost.

"Christian," Jules pipes up from right beside him, "who's this?"

I look at Jules. She really is a blonde goddess with sun-kissed freckles on her skin and hazel eyes that fit just right on her face. She really is beautiful, and I probably would have told her that if it wasn't for the look of disgust she has when she looks over at me.

"This is Alexandra," Christian says, and his smile grows. He's trying to be cute. Can he not tell that I am mad, or is he really that dense?

"Oh, that's right," Jules says, and again, the look of disgust is evident on her face as she gives me a once over. "You're the witch. I've heard so much about you. I thought you might be, I don't know, taller." She smirks.

I am not that short. I'm average height, so I know for a fact that the comment was meant to be a dig because compared to the Amazonian, probably a five-foot-eight woman, I am short.

"That's weird. I haven't heard about you at all," I say the first thing that pops out of my mind, and I don't care if it's rude. She started it.

Behind me, I hear Santana snicker, and Sam say, "World star."

Jules narrows her eyes at me, but before she can say anything, Christian intervenes. "Alexandra," he says, and once I look into his eyes, I know that he wants to ask me what's wrong, but he doesn't.

"I would invite you to play, but I know how you witches feel about getting down dirty," Jules says, and again, it's another dig.

"Wait, guys," Christian says, and I think he's starting to figure out that this right here isn't a friendly chitchat, but a war between me and the girl who has made it very evident she wants him.

"I know you princess types," she continues, and I can feel my blood starting to boil. I'm trying my best not to erupt in a fit of magic, but she is testing me. "You're gonna try to take Christian away from here and change him from an alpha wolf to your little servant dog."

"You sound jealous," I bite out.

She rolls her eyes and laughs. At this point, people from around the house are watching us, and with their heightened hearing, they can probably hear us as well. The sun is coming down, and they are in for the show.

"You should like a spoiled princess."

"Better than sounding like a bitch." As soon as the words leave my mouth, I know that they are wrong, but I feel too angry, too disrespected to even care.

I see her charging for me, but I charged for her as well. I don't care how big she is. I know that I can put up a fight. But before we can lay our hands on each other, we are both lifted off the air. I look behind me, and I see Christian, quicker than ever, with his arms wrapped around me.

193

Devin is holding up Jules as she tries to escape. "Let me go. I am going to kill her.'

"I'd like to see you try," I spit out as I struggle to get out of Christian's firm grip.

"Who the fuck do you think you are?"

"I'm his girlfriend, that's who," I say as Christian is practically dragging me off the field and into the banks of trees. I see Jules's face drop as I say I'm Christian's girlfriend, and I wish I can take a picture of it and frame it on my wall.

But then it hits me. I said I'm his girlfriend, and as Christian drags me into the forest, I can't help but feel a ping of embarrassment. How dare I say that without even discussing it with him first? What if he doesn't want a girlfriend, or what if he doesn't see me exactly in that way? We haven't even kissed.

Christian finally drops me to my feet after much pleading and slaps to his forearms when we are far enough that I can't really see the pack anymore.

"What was that about?" Christian asks as soon as my feet hit the ground. His eyes are studying my face, and I can see how he's trying to figure out what got me all riled up.

I roll my eyes at him. "Don't act as though you don't know." I refuse to think Christian is so dense that he doesn't see what is right in front of him.

"Don't know what?"

I look over at him, and he truly looks conflicted, as if he had no idea how today's event transpired. He looks innocent in his gym shorts and a cutoff T-shirt that shows off his huge, glorious arms. He's sweating but in the best possible way, making his muscles glisten and my insides clench. I want him to hug me. Even though I know I am being irrational, I want him to just hold me. But I can't quite let go of my anger.

"She was flirting with you, Christian. From the moment she stepped onto that field, she has been flirting with you."

"Jules?" he says, his voice actually sounding perplexed as if that is the last thing that can ever happen in the world. "She's always been friendly."

"Friendly," is that what we're calling it now? Does he really expect me to believe that? "That is not friendly. That is a woman trying to get in your pants, and if you cannot see that, you need to go get your eyes checked."

"Alexandra, I didn't…" His eyes search mine, concern and confusion all over his.

"Just shut up and leave me alone," I snap at him. I'm actually livid.

He let her flirt with him right in front of me. Christian let that goddess of fucking bitch all in his face, smiling and winking as if it was no big deal. I hate it, and I hate that it affected me so much. I don't want to be this girl, especially when I don't even know what we are.

Christian takes a step closer to me. "Alexandra, you're overreacting. Jules is a friend, and she was…"

I don't know what possesses me, maybe the anger or the annoyance from Christian not listening and trying to say I am overreacting, but the spell just comes out.

"Claude os tuum." The words come out of my mouth. And just like that, Christian's mouth is shut midsentence. His eyes widen as he looks at me, confused. He tries to open his mouth, but it won't work. I spelled it shut—a spell my mom would use on Alex and me when we wouldn't shut up and listen. I would hate when my mom would use that spell on me. It was almost as if your mouth was sowed shut, and there was nothing you can do about it. All the words you want to say are locked behind your lips, and the witch that cast the spell has the key. In this case, I am that witch, and I refuse to let him talk until I feel like it.

"Don't say I am overreacting. I know what I saw."

Christian points to his mouth and then raises his perfectly sculpted eyebrow as if to say, "Really?"

I shrug my shoulders as I look out into the distance. "I told you to shut up."

I don't look at him, but I know he's rolling his eyes. He walks closer to me, but I take a step back, not wanting him to come any closer. I know if he touches me or even gets close enough for me to be wrapped in the warmth and scent that is him, I'll cave. I don't want to do that. I want to simmer in my anger. I hate that I am in this position, and I hate it more that he put me here.

"You brought me here just so I can see another girl flaunt herself around you." This time, my voice doesn't sound mad but instead hurt. Because at the end of the day, that is exactly how I feel: hurt and betrayed. "If there's a part of you that wants her, you could have just left me alone."

Christian looks at me, his eyes sympathetic, and I want to cry—cry because I'm embarrassed at how I acted out, cry because I let this get to me, and cry because Christian can't see how much I care for him and how far I really am willing to go to prove it. It's frustrating.

Before I can stop him, he takes slow steps toward me. He wraps his arms around me while mine just dangle at my sides. I know how I acted was immature, but I was upset—extremely upset. We stand like this for a good minute, and then he just holds. His warmth envelops me, and he holds me tight. The anger slowly melts out of my body, and I just let him hold me. I'm ashamed and envious that this girl who is in his pack and looks like that wants him. How am I supposed to compete with that?

"Aperiam os tuum," I say the spell to open Christian's mouth and just hold him back.

"I'm sorry," Christian whispers in my ear. "I should have put a stop to it. I just didn't realize what was going on." One of his hands finds its way into my hair. "She is just a childhood friend. Nothing more, nothing less. I want you, just you." I feel his words being spoken into my hair. "I'm sorry I didn't act like it."

His words just float in the air for a couple of more beats before my heart overrides my mind, and I wrap my hands around his large body even tighter. The sun is down. It's dark enough that I can only see a couple of feet in front of me. And the lights in the far distance that are the house and its occupants.

"But she looks like that, and you look like you. I know that you have a duty to me, but I don't want to get in the way." I start to ramble but immediately get interrupted by his lips.

Soft, demanding, and eager are what I would use to describe Christian's kiss. His lips taste just like I imagined, sweet and mine.

He forces his hand in my hair, angling my neck so he can deepen the kiss, and the act alone makes my knees buck.

I have kissed people before, but I have never been kissed like this, like I am being claimed and devoured all at once. His tongue explores my mouth, and I can't help but wrap my arms around his neck and pull him in closer. I can't get enough. It's like I was starved, and now suddenly, I now know I will never be satiated, and I don't care.

I bite his lip, and I hear an actual growl come out of him before he pulls me in and practically pushes me up against the tree. I am stuck in between Christian and the tree trunk, yet my mind is racing. This is what it feels like to be kissed—to be kissed by someone like Christian, powerful and with a sense of need.

His fingers get lost in my hair while mine roam through the hard planes of his back. His lips are awakening feelings in me that I didn't even know I could possess. He bites and licks, taking no prisoners in the way his lips take a claim on my own. I could stay here forever, but after what seems like too short of a time, I feel Christian pull away from me.

Christian's lips are swollen from kissing, and his eyes are darker brown than they were before, and I can see by the tent in his pants that he is aroused.

He doesn't pull away when he speaks into my lips in a possessive tone that makes my insides.

"Are you blind? I don't want Jules. I want you. Not out of duty. I don't know how many times I need to prove that or say it so you can believe it."

I don't say anything because I can speak with how seriously his eyes stare into mine, almost like he wants to imprint what he just said into my mind.

"You're mine. I am yours. If you knew how I felt, you wouldn't question that ever again."

I nod before a small grin appears on his lips. "Besides, like you said, you're my girlfriend."

My cheeks immediately heat up, and I bury my head in his chest from embarrassment. "Yeah, I was hoping we could just not talk about that. Call it a crime in passion." I still can't believe I screamed that at the top of my lungs.

"Well, it's settled. You are my girl." He raises an eyebrow.

"Maybe." I smile. My jealous mood seems like a bad memory as I stay in his arms.

"I think we can change that to a yes," he says, and then he leans in to kiss me once more.

The kiss isn't like the first one, but it has the same effect on me. It starts slow, at a smooth rhythm. It's almost sensual, and it gives me chills all over my body. He bites my lower lip, and when I gasp, he takes full advantage to have his tongue explore my mouth. The kiss is passionate and breathtaking, a kiss you only read in books or imagine in your dirtiest dreams—a kiss that will have me fighting every girl in a mile radius if they dared look at him.

When the kiss breaks, my lips immediately pout, and I feel Christian's warm calloused hand rub against my cheek. "So is that a yes?"

"It's a hell yes."

He chuckles and leans in to kiss me but stops about an inch away. "Were you really gonna fight a wolf?" he teases, and it annoys me that he finds this funny.

I roll my eyes, but I say proudly, "She could have been a giant, and I'd still square up."

"Well, just so you know"—Christian laughs as he leans in closer to me—"you jealous does things to me."

His grip tightens around my waist, and his words make me heat up, but the way his eyes turn more gold than brown, they stare back at me, filled with hunger. "What does that mean?" my voice barely squeaks out.

"You know what I mean, Alexandra," he says, and he leans in closer to where his lips almost touch my own. "It's sexy as hell," and then his lips crash into my own once more.

Chapter 26

Once I get to school the next morning, I have one mission in mind. No matter how much I want to daydream about Christian's kisses, I can't. Paul was attacked days ago, and I need to figure out what exactly is going on and how I can stop it. Paul only remembers two people seeing him before he passed out: Johan and Justin. The boys checked with Justin, and he doesn't remember seeing anyone suspicious, so next up is Johan. Maybe he saw something, and maybe that can help because, at the moment, this is the only lead I have to figure out who's coming after me.

I try to reach him in the first period, but by the time I get to the classroom, the lesson has already started, and I am too late to ask Johan, who is now sitting in his usual seat. He smiles at me as I sit down, but that is the only interaction we have until the bell rings, signaling the end of the first period.

The classroom starts to file out while, in the back of the classroom, I ask Johan to stay back.

"What's up?"

"How was your weekend?" I ask, trying to make conversation before I ask what I really want to know.

"Pretty chill. Anita and I went camping." He smiles proudly, and his eyes glisten. I don't know if it's excitement or just because of the mention of his girlfriend's name or if it's something else, but I don't have time to dissect that now.

"How about you?"

I nod. "Pretty uneventful," I lie, "other than the party, of course. Pretty wild night."

His smile grows. "Do you want to ask me something?"

"Why do you ask?"

"I know you, Alexandra." He laughs as he grabs his bag and places it over his shoulder. "I know when something is on your mind. Does this have to do Anita?"

"Of course not." I shake my head, and I say it louder than I wanted to, making Johan frown. "Sorry, it's just that one of my dad's watches went missing." I come up with a lie quickly. I have spent the last ten years of my life keeping Johan from this side of my life. I can't have him snooping around. "I was just wondering if you saw anything or anyone weird at the party."

Johan waits a beat and searches my eyes as if he doesn't quite believe me, but he just shakes his head and says, "Sorry, I didn't see anything."

Shit, now we're back at square one and even more confused than ever. How can a vampire sneak into my house undetected with no smell and no one saw him? It just doesn't make sense.

We walk out of the classroom, and right as I suspected, Christian is there standing, waiting for me. Johan stops in his tracks as he sees Christian and looks at me. "I can walk you to your next class. I'm going that way anyway."

"That won't be necessary," Christian says as he casually wraps an arm around my shoulder. Immediately, my cheek heats up, and I have never wanted to thank God more for making me black because I'm sure if I wasn't, I would be beet red. It's like a dog marking his territory in a not-subtle way. "I think I can walk my own girlfriend to class." He emphasizes the word *girlfriend*, and I watch as Johan's face drops.

Johan's face is unreadable, but I can swear I see him squeeze the strap of his bag. "I'll see you later, okay?"

He looks at Christian and then at me again, nods, and without a word, he just walks away. As soon as he's far from earshot, I turn to Christian. "You didn't have to do that."

"Yes, I did, Alexandra." He looks at me. "I know he wants you. I can sense it. You're lucky that I didn't just punch him because of the eyes he gave you."

"That wouldn't be a fair fight, and you know it." I roll my eyes. I know that wolves are territorial, but this is crazy.

"I won't lay a finger on him. I know you care about him."

"Thanks. Now walk me to class before I'm late again because my boyfriend's only setting is being irrational."

He laughs at me and makes sure I get to class, which surely I am late to.

Chapter 27

The weeks go by with no new information and no more clues. No notes have appeared in my house, my locker, or anywhere else. If I hadn't been through this before, I would have just assumed that whoever my terrorizer is has decided to leave me alone, but I am not that naive anymore.

The time goes by pretty quickly. Christian and I spend so much time together, but it isn't like before when he protected me and stayed distant. Now we're in a relationship, and I cherish every second I get to spend with him. The wolves spend most of their time in the bayou, training and getting ready for any danger. Christian stays focused on his training most days, which is great because it leaves me to stay home and practice my magic. Alex and I practice our craft every day after school and on Saturdays and Sundays with Mom. It's physically draining, but I am showing progress.

The relationship between my parents and I has become quite strained, mostly because they spend most of their time out of the house, doing God knows what. I never again brought up the secret room in my dad's office because, frankly, I knew that all I would get in that conversation are a whole bunch of lies. We barely talk, and if we do, it's only small talk. No one brings up my upcoming coronation. No one mentions the looming danger that lives over our heads. It's almost as if my parents decided to keep Alex and me in a bubble, protecting us from everything, even the truth. My mom gradually progresses our training, adding new elements almost every weekend. It's almost like she is actually getting us ready for battle but tells us nothing about the enemy.

Christian has been my peace through all this. Even though our schedules are hectic these days, we still find time for each other, whether it's dates, car rides, or having him sneak into my room at night so he can cuddle me to sleep. I feel myself falling deeper and deeper for him with each passing day.

By the time Christmas Eve comes up, my brain and body are in dire need of a break. Tonight is my family's Christmas ball at my family's house. My parents throw this party every year, and every year, it's the same people, the same music, and the same rule: absolutely no magic. We open presents in the morning and then invite the entire half the town to come and celebrate. This year, my parents allowed me to extend an invitation to Christian and his pack. I figured Christian and I have been dating for a while now. It's about time he meets my family officially. Since he sprung his family on me on our second date with no warning, I think having him attend a ball with my parents, watching our every move, is only fair.

I get ready in my room at around seven. Smooth jazz plays downstairs by the band that my mom surely hired. I look at the dress options laid on my bed: a red dress, a white dress, and a silver one, all of which I picked out and bought myself, not needing a repeat of what happened the last time I wore a dress.

After what feels like forever, I decide on the white dress and go put it on. The dress is a tight white dress that falls to my feet. It's all silk, with a sweetheart neckline and an open back that stops right at my backside. The dress may be a little risqué for a Christmas ball, but it makes me feel confident and beautiful. My curly hair is all out, and it almost looks perfect. I have diamond earrings that are shaped like small hearts and, finally, white toe-pointed heels.

I look at myself at the full-length-size mirror in my room. Somehow, I look older and more mature. I guess you grow up faster when there's danger all around you. I try to think back to the beginning of the school year. I was in this exact position, looking in the mirror, scared about the future. Somehow, this feels different. I have no idea what's yet to come, and I can't help but always expect the other shoe to drop, but I am no longer the witch I was all those months ago. I am no longer afraid of my powers or what they might do to those around me. I have worked nonstop, learning how to control my emotions and my powers. I have read every spell in my family's spell book. I read up on werewolves and vampires.

A knock on my door brings me out of my thoughts, and just in time to see it open and reveal Alex in a black tux, bow tie, and white button-up underneath. He looks handsome as always, with his hair cut short and a small smile on his face. His eyes go wide as soon as his eyes lay on me.

"Wow, you do you have a death wish."

I roll my eyes. "Thank you, Alex. You look good too."

"I'm sorry," he apologizes as he takes a step back and lets me close my bedroom door behind me. "You look beautiful, but don't you think the parents are going to be a tad bit upset when they see what you have on?"

"Mom gave me money to buy any dress I wanted," I simply explain as we make it down the stairs.

"I am not sure that is what she meant when she gave you the cash."

"Well, too bad."

If my mother has a problem with the dress, she will have to take it up with me when she sees me, but knowing her, she won't bring it up until after the ball. She wouldn't want to make a scene in front of anyone.

Tonight, our house is practically indescribable. The foyer is decorated with white roses, the chandelier on the ceiling has been cleaned, and the marble floors have been waxed. Once we get downstairs, there is a group of older folks entering the house, most of whom give me a dirty look or more of a surprised look. I ignore them.

We enter the living room, and the couches are all cleared out of the way, making the room look almost double its size. On a good day, our living room can fit almost twenty people now. It would be close to fifty. There's a smooth jazz band playing in the corner of the room and a bar set up at the other end. No doubt my mother hired both of them. There are plenty of people already here: politicians, lawyers, judges, and most importantly, witches.

People double take when Alex and I walk by, the mayor's kids, what a commodity we are—the star quarterback and the future priestess. I know that is what people see when they look at us, at least the people who know. We are meant to be the perfect children in the perfect family. If they only knew how fucked we really are.

Alex and I get a couple of glasses of water from the bar. I search around the room. My parents are nowhere to be found. Mother probably wants to make an entrance.

"So," Alex brings me back to reality, "is Christian coming tonight?"

"Yeah, his parents and some of his pack," I say, and just the sound of his name brings goose bumps to my skin.

Over the last couple of weeks, the feelings I had for Christian only intensified. It's like he's a magnet, and every day, he pulls in further than the day before. It's addicting getting to be around him. I know I love him. That is the only explanation of how I feel, the butterflies I get when I am around him. The way my skin ignites when he touches me is almost torture. I need to tell him how I feel, or else, I will go crazy keeping it in, but I haven't found the right time or place.

"How about you?" I ask my brother, trying to avoid my thoughts and be more present.

He raises his eyebrow, skepticism written on his face. "What do you mean?"

"Did you invite a girl?"

Alex has changed since last year, and I can't believe it took me this long to notice. He has never been a player, but there has never been a shortage of girls chasing after him, trying to get close. Junior year, Alex would always invite girls out to dates, dinner, or even our family's ball. He hasn't been with a girl since last year's prom, where Stephanie, a senior, and he was dating at the time.

He shakes his head. "Nah, Jordan is my date."

"Jordan has been your date for everything this year."

"Is that wrong?" he says, his eyes refusing to make eye contact with me as he takes a swig of his water.

"Not really," I examine him closely. He's acting almost nervous. "I mean, you used to have girls coming in and out of the house last year, and then Stephanie. I don't know. It's just weird."

"Last year, I was just a boy trying to satisfy a need," he says bluntly.

"What about Stephanie?"

My brother's ex is the one girl he's brought home that I actually like. She was sweet, kind, smart, and a witch. She was the perfect package, with her long tan legs and short auburn hair. Stephanie moved to New York for college. Alex and she broke it off because of the distance, but I know he still has feelings for her. That must be why he hasn't moved on. Stephanie loved him, and he loved her just as much.

"What about Stephanie?"

"She wasn't just you satisfying a need, and you know it."

Alex stares off at the people all around us, refusing to look at me. I know he would rather drink gasoline than have this conversation, but he's my brother, my best friend. I should make him have the hard conversations.

"It's okay to miss her," I say softly.

He shakes his head. "Stephanie and I are over. We have been for a while," is all he says, and something about his tone is telling me not to push him further, but I don't listen.

"You loved her, Alex. It's okay to admit that you haven't moved on."

"Believe me, Lexi, you don't know half of it." He turns to me, his eyes burning into mine. "I have moved on."

I don't know if it's what he says or the fact that this is the first time that he has actually given me eye contact while having this conversation. However, he looks serious, as if there is something that I don't know, which is impossible because Alex and I share everything. We don't lie or hold anything against each other, especially after learning that our parents have been doing it forever.

I want to ask him to elaborate, but right as I open my mouth, Jordan comes in between us.

"Jesus, Lexi." He looks me up and down. If it was anyone other Jordan, I'd probably feel creeped out, but Jordan is like a brother with eyes for everyone. "You look hot."

I table the conversation Alex and I were having and smile at Jordan, who is dressed in a red tux with satin black lapels and a matching bow tie. "Ditto." I smile.

"How's everything?" he asks, and I try to fill him in about all the spells I have mastered and how my magic is progressing.

After I'm done giving him the cliff notes version of my work in the last couple of weeks, he just smiles down at me, a warm smile, not an "I'm checking you out" smile or an "I just said a joke" smile, but one that I haven't seen on his face.

"What?" I say after noticing how he stares at me.

"I'm not a dork." He shakes his head. "But I am so proud of you."

The compliment comes out of left field, surprising me, but it melts my heart either way. Jordan is Alex's best friend, always has been, and we haven't been the closest of friends ourselves. But hearing him say that makes me feel happy. There's so much more to Jordan than the cocky playboy, and I'm lucky that I am one of the few people who gets to see it.

"Thank you."

"So." He looks at the bartender behind us, a pretty girl with green eyes and black hair, who practically melts when he looks at her. "What do I have to do to get my friends and me a couple of shots?"

She blushes and looks around. "I am not allowed to give out alcohol to anyone underage," she says, and it's evident that she's about our age too, maybe a year older. Regardless, nothing is going to stop Jordan from charming the pants off her and getting what he wants.

"I won't tell if you don't."

Again, her pale cheeks turn red as she reluctantly looks around and gives in to serving three shots of tequila.

I know I probably shouldn't drink, considering that my parents and almost every adult that they know are in my house. However, I don't care. I throw back the drink, ignoring the slight burn it leaves behind.

"One more." Jordan notions to Alex and me, and before we know it, we are three shots deep by the time Angel and Paris join us.

Angel is in a floor-length gown, light blue in color, with a halter top design that makes her look like Vanna White from *Wheel of Fortune*. Her hair is in a slick bun, and she has a slight makeup, highlighting her already God-given beauty. Paris is in a black gown with a slit along her right leg and a sweetheart cut up the top that shows her breasts slightly. Her red hair frames her face and her signature red lipstick. They both look gorgeous, as always.

We talk and make comments about the people around us like any teenagers do when attending an event that their parents force them to come. It almost feels normal, sneaking drinks behind our parents' back, talking shit, and just enjoying each other's company. The alcohol warms up my body, and I feel careless and free.

I feel a familiar hand on my lower back, an hour into the party, sending chills through my entire body, Christian.

"Well, hello there." His voice is low and deep in my ear as he presses his chest closer to my back.

I haven't even looked at him, and the storm of butterflies has taken over my stomach, and my heart becomes a marching band all on its own.

A smile creeps on my face as I turn around to look at the work of art, which is the man who stands before me. Every day, I see him, and every day, I am astounded by his beauty, his deep brown eyes, curly hair, and a devilish smile that makes my knees buck. He's dressed in all black—a black tux that fits him like a glove, a black shirt that I am sure hugs all the right muscles, and a black tie. He looks breathtaking—correction, he is breathtaking.

"Hey." I smile up at him, and before I can say anything else, his lips cover my own. His tongue takes my mouth as if he knows it's all his to explore whenever he wants. His hand cups the back of my neck, holding me in place as his mouth continues with its sweet torture.

Something about him drives me insane. It pulls me to him in the most epic way. Everything about this man makes me dizzy and steady all at once, just his touch can break me and bring me to my knees.

Christian pulls away after what feels like such a brief time and looks down at me with hooded eyes. "Sorry, I couldn't help myself," he whispers, his voice husky and breathless.

"I don't mind."

"Well, I do," Jackson says from behind Christian, Devin right by his side. "Next time, warn me first." He fake gags and rolls his eyes.

"I agree." Paris scoffs and takes a swig of her "soda."

I can't help but giggle because I could care less. My cheeks feel hot, and I can't tell if it's the alcohol or the fact that Christian has his arm around me, or maybe both, but I like the feeling.

"Have you been drinking?" Christian asks, ignoring our friends.

"A little." I wrap my arms around his neck, pretending not to notice all the eyes that stare at us.

His brown eyes look down at my own, his voice low as he whispers in my ear, "You're driving me crazy with this dress."

His fingers caress the small of my back, leaving goose bumps in their wake as his eyes stare fiercely into my own. It doesn't matter how many times he touches me and how many times he looks at me that way. It will always feel like the first time.

"You like it."

"I'd like it better off," he says, and a devilish smile appears on his face, making my inside turn into butter.

Maybe it's the alcohol in my system or the fact that when Christian looks at me, I'm brave, but I just smile and say, "You should take it off."

He raises his eyebrow, and his smile grows bigger as he pulls me closer. "I've been a perfect gentleman lately. Don't tempt me, princess."

Oh my. His words speak directly to me down there. How can he make simple words sound so sexy and mouthwatering?

"Maybe you need a little tempting." Christian is right. He has been a perfect gentleman, never pressuring me for always being there for me. In fact, this is the first time he even mentions a comment like this.

"Are you sure?" he asks. It's not like I'm a virgin, and although we've waited, I do want him. I want him more than he may ever know in every kind of way.

I bite my lip, nervous for the first time tonight. I know what he's asking. Am I ready to take this next step with him? Am I ready to give him all of me? If I'm being honest, I have been ready since the moment I saw him in that hallway on the first day of school. I love him.

I smile up at him. "I am more sure about this than I have ever about anything in my life."

Chapter 28

Christian

"I am more sure about this than I have ever been about anything in my life."

Alexandra's words have been echoing in my head for the past hour. She wants to have sex with me. I try not to get too excited, but I am a man. A man incredibly in love with this woman that every time I see her, I want to fall and worship her at her feet.

For the past hour, my body has been buzzing, alert to every touch, every look she gives me, every single thing. It's almost a game. She knows what she's doing, building my anticipation up as she walks across the floor, talking to people but always looking up at me.

Even when she introduced me to her parents, all I could think about was the moment I would be able to kiss her again. To feel her soft lips crush against my own. Her silk skin in my hands, she's walking temptation, and now that she's given me the green light, I'm like a dog in heat. No pun intended. Everything she does makes me hard, and it's getting more difficult to control myself.

The party is in full swing, and everyone is dancing, talking, and enjoying themselves when I hear it. The sound of glass breaking; it's faint. I look around the room. Nothing seems broken, and no one looks as if they dropped anything. But I hear it again. This time, I also hear a thud, almost as if something or someone fell. It came from upstairs. Immediately, my eyes go to Alexandra, who is talking to some girl from school across the room.

The breath I didn't know I was holding releases as Devin and Jackson come up next to me. "Did you hear that?"

I nod. "Watch everyone down here," I tell Devin. "Jackson and I are going to check it out."

Devin just nods and follows my order as Jackson and I head upstairs, quietly trying now to make a scene. It's probably nothing, but I know if I don't check, I know it will bother me all night.

"Be careful," my mom whispers to me as I walk past her to go up the stairs.

The one thing I have always loved about my mother and father is although they have been training me to fend for myself since I could walk, they still worry. They have always worried, knowing that I can very much take care of myself and those around me.

Jackson reaches the second floor, and immediately, as my feet meet the floor, I can smell it—the smell of the bloodsucker malicious creature.

"Is that?"

"Vampire," I finish Jackson's sentence, and immediately, I am on the defense, my fist curled up in a ball at my sides. I haven't come across many vampires, but I will never forget what a vampire smells like. It's a mix of blood and darkness.

"It's coming from Lexi's room," Jackson points out, but I am already an ice in step ahead of him, making my way to the room and opening the door. The room is dark, and all you can really see is the light from the moon outside from the window, but the smell of vampires is so strong it's almost nauseating.

Alexandra's window is broken, shards all over the floor, crunching under my feet as I look around. There's no one here, not in the closet, not under the bed, nowhere.

"What's that?"

I turn in the direction of Jackson's voice and a rock under Alexandra's desk. This is what must have broken the window. A giant-sized rock with a note wrapped around it. As soon as I pick it up, I smell the stench of vampire all over it. The vampire didn't come in. He or she threw the rock.

"Hey!" Alexandra comes up behind me. "This is where you sneaked off to." She smiles at me when I turn to look at her, but that smile drops as soon as she sees the rock in my hand.

"What's that?"

"Someone threw this at your window."

She doesn't grab the rock at first. Instead, she just looks at it, hesitant, as if she's debating what to do with it. I can't read her face in the dark, and I almost turn on the light to see her more clearly when she grabs the rock out of my hand. She places the rock in one of the drawers on her desk and just closes it. She doesn't look at the note. It doesn't say anything just closes the drawer and smiles at me.

"There was a note on that," I point out, but she ignores it.

"We can deal with that in the morning." She looks up at me and places a small kiss on my lips. "Nothing is going to ruin my night. I won't let it," she says to my perplexed face.

I just nod, looking at her. I can't tell if she's deflecting the problem, or she really is refusing to have this ruin her night. Either way, she seems calm and content. I wouldn't dare spoil her mood if it could wait.

"Well, in that case"—Jackson claps his hands, and a smile creeps on his face—"I am going downstairs to hit on a pretty girl and hopefully take her home with me."

He closes the door behind him and leaves Alexandra and me to ourselves. The realization hits me, and again, my body is alert, buzzing with the need to touch her. The tension in the air is palpable and louder than any music that can be playing downstairs.

Alexandra bites her bottom lip, and immediately, my eyes go to her mouth. I can hear her hear beat. It's mirroring my own, loud and thunderous. Both of us just stare at each other in the darkness, which is her room. I can feel it in my blood the need to be with her. To have her in my arms is more powerful than any magic in any universe. Her eyes look up at me, innocent and dangerous at the same time, almost daring me to kiss her, to claim her because she's all mine.

Just like that, all self-control I had left crumbles in between us as I crash my lips onto hers. Immediately, I take her mouth with my tongue, not wasting any time, needing to taste her. She moans softly. The sound is like music to my ears and the key that releases the inner animal in me. My hands grab her hair and give it a small yank, making her open her mouth more so I can explore every inch of it.

Mine, I want to say. *She's all mine.* Her sounds, her lips, and her body, I want it all.

I feel her hands in between our bodies as she grabs the jacket from my suit and starts to take it off, eager as I am. My body reacts to her small moans and the flick of her tongue against mine that I'm as hard as a stone. It's almost painful. Before I know it, I am guiding her toward the wall, and I start to kiss her neck, biting and sucking wherever my lips lead me.

"Christian," she moans my name out, and I swear it's fucking heaven on her lips. I bite down harder, unable to control myself, unable to stop.

I wrap one of her legs around my waist, needing her close, as I kiss her more. Our hands are a tangled mess as she grabs my hair and pulls me closer to her, and my hands grab onto one of her breasts, and it feels amazing even through the silk. I can feel the peak through the fabric, and god, does that make me want her even more. To feel her body react this way to me and my mouth, it's fucking hot. Nothing can make me want this girl more in this moment.

"I love you," the words come out in between kisses before I can stop them.

Her beautiful hazel eyes go wide as the reflection of the moon highlights her face. I don't need her to say it back or even acknowledge what I just said, but I do know that I couldn't keep it in any longer. Looking at her, amazed by her beauty and strength, I can't help but adore her.

I cup her face and look into her eyes. "I love you, Alexandra. More than you or even will ever fully comprehend. You consume me to the point that I think I am going crazy when I am not with you."

"Christian." Her voice is small.

She searches my face. I don't know for what, but frankly, I don't care. I don't need her to say it back. I know she loves me. I know she feels as strongly as I do. My intention isn't to rush her but to let her know. I would do anything in my power to show her that she's mine and I am all hers.

She leans in and kisses me, not as eager as before, but instead, these are sweet and longer. Her hands make their way to my hair, pulling slightly.

"Christian." She wraps her hands around my neck, pulling me close enough that I can feel her breath on my cheek. She looks at me, and I already know what she is going to say before it comes out of her mouth. Her heartbeat quickens under my touch, and the anticipation is killing me. Her finger caresses my cheek slightly, but her eyes never make contact with my own as she whispers the best words she can tell me.

"I love you."

"I know, *princesa.*"

Alexandra

I feel as if I'm walking on air as Christian and I join the party. My hair is fixed. My dress is straightened out, but my mind is all over the place in the best way possible. Christian gave me a mind-blowing orgasm and told me in loved me in the span of thirty minutes, and I can't help but feel giddy all over. I'm glad I didn't look at that letter that was on the rock. I made the right choice of ignoring it for now. My life for the last couple of months has revolved around threats and witchcraft, and I am so happy that I finally get to spend some time away from that.

Christian and I join our friends, but no one mentions our absence, and for that, I am grateful. We all talk, laugh, and enjoy our first unproblematic night in a while.

I feel my mother's eyes on me through the night—probably wants to rip my head off for wearing this dress. A small part of me relishes in the idea that she's painfully angry because that is how it's been for the last couple of weeks for me. I have been so mad at her and my father for keeping all this from me that I have barely said anything to them. My anger has been boiling up in me. I'm scared that one day, I'll explode without warning.

The boys leave to get something to drink while Paris, Angel, Santana, and I stand in the corner of the room.

"So are all wolves hot?" Paris asks Santana as she stares at some of Christian's pack who's dancing.

"I wouldn't say that, but we all work out, so it's probably why you find them attractive."

"I want all of them."

Santana just laughs at Paris's insanity, and Johan and Anitta come into the house.

The mood immediately shifts as my eyes make contact with Johan's blue ones. Ever since he came back to school, the light in his eye has been misplaced and something that brews underneath is something similar to pain. Johan and I haven't talked in what seems like forever. I even forgot that his parents get an invitation to this every year. He's in a black tux. His blond hair is groomed. He looks nice and clean—not a hair out of place. Anitta stands beside him in a dress that I never would have thought she would wear, but it's beautiful nonetheless. A purple dress adorns her body long sleeved, and it starts from the beginning of her neck to the end of her toes. You can't see any skin other than her face and hands. Completely unlike Anitta, if anything, you would have to fight her on keeping clothes on. Her sleek black hair reaches to her backside, and her face looks emotionless. Not bitchy, not happy, just stale.

Johan whispers something in Anita's ear, and for a second, she frowns but just walks away. Johan, however, stands in the foyer, his eyes surveying myself and the girls. He doesn't smile but just stares for a beat before moving his legs and walking over.

Paris seems to notice because I hear her mumble in her cup, "Mayday! Mayday!"

"Ladies," he says to the girls, and then his eyes end on me. "Lexi, you look beautiful."

I don't miss the way he glances up and down my body before landing back on my face.

"So fuck us, huh?" Paris says, and I can tell by her tone it's supposed to be a joke, but the energy has shifted. We have all but cut Johan out of our lives. None of us talk to him. It doesn't mean we don't care for him. He doesn't belong in our world. It was a matter of time before it happened, and with everything going on, a small part of me is glad that it's sooner than later.

He smiles, but it doesn't reach his eyes as he looks at my friends. "You all look beautiful."

"Who are you?" Santana says, and I almost forgot she was there.

She purses her lips at him as she glares at him. Clearly, she's Christian's sister.

"Santana, this is Johan," I say, and I don't elaborate anymore because I don't know how to classify him. I don't want to call him my ex because it seems mean, and if I call him my friend, that wouldn't be the complete truth.

"I'm her ex-boyfriend." Johan looks at Santana, giving her the once-over. He looks annoyed, like he can tell who she's related to. "Who are you?" His tone is sharp.

Santana's voice is cold as she snaps at Johan. "I'm her boyfriend's sister." A fake tight smile decorates her lips as she sizes him up.

I see how the word the boyfriend hits Johan. His face drops, but he recovers quickly, and she turns to me. "You two still a thing?"

I look into his eyes, and I can't help but feel bad. This sucks, but on the other hand, he moved on as well. He's with Anitta. I want him to be happy, and I would wish he wanted me to have the same.

"Yes." I don't mention the fact that he knows very well that Christian and I are at thing. I see him stare at us when he thinks I'm not looking.

Johan nods slowly. "Understood." The muscles in his face clench slightly.

"You look really nice," Angel says, trying to lighten the mood.

Johan ignores Angel completely and keeps his eyes fixated on me. "So what, we can't be friends anymore?"

"Johan." I shake my head. I knew this was coming. This is not the time or place to be having this conversation.

"No, Lexi. I didn't realize that when we broke up, you would take all our friends with you. That I would be left alone," he adds the last part, and I can hear the sadness that breaks through his voice.

"Johan, I didn't mean for that to happen."

"I didn't mean to be in love with you, but here we are."

Ouch, that stung. If I thought the energy before was weird, now it's just uncomfortable. Johan just said he's in love with me. As in the present tense, in front of my friends, in front of Christian's sister. He just said it as if his proclamation of love wasn't a big deal, as if his girlfriend wasn't in this house. I'm left speechless.

216

"I think I want a drink." Angel clears her throat, and her green eyes are filled with sympathy as she walks away. Paris follows suit after giving me a reassuring squeeze on the shoulder.

"Can we talk? Alone, please," Johan says, and his voice is vulnerable.

I know I should say no, that I should push him way, but the way he's looking at me breaks my heart. He gives Santana a pointed look, but she doesn't budge under his gaze.

"I'm going to see if I can find my brother," Santana says after what seems like a second. She rolls her eyes in disgust at Johan.

I nod, and the next thing I know, Johan is leading me out of the room. I make a quick glance to see Christian, but he's nowhere to be found in the sea of people that occupy my living room.

Johan leads me outside to the front porch. No one is out here, and it's quiet. An eerie silence fills the void between us as we step out. The air is chilly, not exactly freezing, but enough to make me shiver. The feeling of dread fills my body as I look at Johan's unblinking face. I haven't felt this way since last year on prom night when I ended it between us.

"Lexi," he says as he looks me over, "you really look beautiful."

"Johan, you said you're in love with me," I point to the obvious. We can't just tiptoe around the fact that he said that. He can't feel that way about me, not again. "You can't be in love with me."

"Lexi, you think that I haven't tried to forget you. I can't!" he shouts, and it makes me take a step back. He has never raised his voice at me. I didn't think he was capable of such a booming tone.

"What about Anitta?" *What about Christian*? I scream in my head. *I love him.* But I know admitting that in front of him would be cruel.

"I've tried, okay? I really have," he says and steps closer to me. "She isn't you."

"I'm with Christian," is all I can say. My mind is racing at his confession.

I see anger flare in Johan's eyes. It's slight, but I don't miss it. He runs his fingers through his hair in frustration. What did he expect to happen? That he would confess his feelings, and I would just take him back.

"Johan…I don't feel the same way," I add, and I bite my lip, fighting the need to ramble. Even though we are outside, I am feeling extremely claustrophobic.

"That's a lie." He shakes his head and takes another step closer to me. I mirror his actions, taking a step back until I am leaning on the porch rail.

"I'm not lying, Johan." I immediately regret coming out here. It was a bad idea.

Johan shakes his head. "You're confused." He looks hurt more than I have ever seen him. The pain in his face, I put it there, may have been an accident, but regardless, the damage is done.

"I'm not."

"I miss you," he says, his voice soft and persistent as he closes the distance between us. His eyes search my face, and I know he must see how panicked I am, but he ignores it.

That feeling of dread that filled my body earlier has now tripled. I want to go back inside to avoid this conversation and him. He's too close, suffocating me with his presence. I want him to leave, to stop freaking me out.

"I missed your lips," he adds, and I watch as his hand comes up to touch my lips.

I maneuver my head to the side, avoiding his touch. This isn't the Johan I know. The Johan I know wouldn't invade my personal space. He wouldn't have tried to touch me when he could visibly see I was extremely uncomfortable.

"Johan," I try to move around him, but he's blocking my way. "Back up, Johan."

He grips my arm, and it's so tight that I know it's going to leave a mark. "You had the softest lips."

I look at his eyes, and I can see the intention behind them as clear as day. He's going to try to kiss me. "Johan, don't."

"You used to say I was a good kisser." He leans in, and I can't believe what's going on. This isn't the sweet Johan I know. He would never do this. He grips my hip with his other hand to hold me still, and it's so hard it's painful.

I push his chest, but he doesn't budge. He's like a brick house. I don't remember him being this strong. I push again and again, but he keeps leaning in as if it doesn't bother him. I wiggle my face around, but it doesn't work.

Christian is my first thought. *Christian*! I scream in my brain even though he can't hear me. I don't know what to do. I should use my magic to push him off me, but regardless of what's happening, I don't want to hurt him. If I use my magic right now, with my heightened emotions, God knows what I would do to him.

I wiggle my body, trying to get out of his grip, but it's useless. It doesn't affect him in the slightest. "Johan, stop it."

"Don't resist me," he says as he holds me in place, and he leans in and kisses me.

His lips barely touch my own when he's ripped away from me and tossed on the grass in front of the house. I look up to see an angry, seething Christian. "Get your hands off her!"

His eyes are a flame under the porch light, and I watch as he leaps over the porch steps and onto Johan. I hear the first blow better than I can see it. However, Christian doesn't stop there. He punches him again and again to the point where I see blood.

"Christian, stop it!" I say because I'm starting to see blood fly out. He's going to kill him. No matter what I feel about Johan at the moment, I can't let Christian do this. He'll hurt him. I try pulling Christian off him, but he doesn't budge.

"I told you not to touch her!" Christian shouts as Johan lies on the grass, covering his face. "I'm going to kill you," he says, his tone as menacing as he can be.

"Christian, let him go." I pull at his shoulder and his arms—nothing.

Christian holds Johan by the collar of his shirt and delivers another blow and another. I swear I see blood coming out of his mouth and the bones on his nose break.

Behind me, Jackson and Devin come up and help drag Christian off Johan. They hold him back, but Christian is out for blood. He tries to get out of their grip, but they hold him out, barely containing him.

"What the hell is going on?" Alex appears on the lawn, taking one look at Johan and pulling him to his feet. I was right. His nose is broken, blood rushes out of it, and I see bruises start to form.

"He was kissing her," Christian spews out and tries to lunge at Johan again.

"Oh well, in that case," Jackson says, raising his eyebrow as he lets Christian go.

"No," I screech as I myself in between the boys, but my eyes lock on Christian. "Don't do this. You already hit him. Just stop," I say, searching his face. I know he's mad. Hell, I would be too. But this isn't a fair fight, and he knows it. No matter how enraged I am at Johan, I don't want to see him get hurt.

I don't know how I wasn't turned to Christian for too long, but before I know it, Johan runs up behind me, pushing me out of his way. He has something in his hand, and in no time, he smashes it on Christian's face. Christian stumbles back, not enough to fall but enough to know that whatever Johan hit him with made him bleed. The object tumble to the ground as Alex and Devin pull Johan back.

"Christian." I hurry to Christian, grabbing his face in my hand. He's bleeding. I look at the ground and see that Johan hit him with a brick from my mother's rose garden.

I want to shout; in fact, I want to hit him, not for kissing me but for hurting Christian. I know I shouldn't, that I need to be the voice of reason and calm because if I'm not, no one will be. So I suppress my feelings as I search Christian's enraged eyes.

"Move, Alexandra." His voice is menacing, scarier than I have ever heard it. I'm blocking his way toward Johan, but I know Christian. No matter how angry he is, he won't push me out of the way. He needs me to move to get to him, and I won't let it happen.

"Let it go."

Christian looks at me, his face angry and his breathing heavy. He points in Johan's direction. "He forced himself on you, pushed you, and now you want me to just let that go." He gives me a humorless laugh.

"You did what?" I hear Alex shout behind me, and when I turn around, I see Johan crouched on his knees. Alex just punched him in the gut. "How dare you?" His voice is booming. I have never seen Alex this angry, and I hate that it's because of me.

All this because I didn't stop Johan. I should have been more direct, more stern, when I knew he still had feelings for me; but instead, I didn't. I was a coward and wanted to have my friend, and now look at what has happened.

The doors to the house open, and suddenly, there are people filing out. My parents, Christian's parents, my friends, Anitta, and much more all have come to see the show that is this spectacle.

"What's going on here?" my dad asks as he looks us up and down, stopping when he sees Johan on the ground and the rest of us around him.

"Christian." Tanya comes up to his face, the worry evident in her voice. "Are you okay, mijo?"

He nods, but he doesn't stop staring at Johan. "You touch her, and I swear I'll kill you." The threat in his voice is apparent. He's not kidding, and although I don't want Johan to die, I will say a part of me feels the same again.

He turns around and looks at me as Anitta rushes to Johan's side. Everyone around us just stares, murmuring what they think happened here. Angel and the girls come up to me, and they all ask what happened and if I'm okay, but I can't take my eyes off Christian. He's staring back at me, cuts and bruises on his face. He looks hurt.

I walk up to him. "Are you okay?"

He just nods, and I know that he's too mad to talk.

"You want to leave?" Another nod. "Get in the car. I'll be there in a second," I tell him, and with one final look, he walks away.

I watch as he climbs in the car and doesn't say anything to anyone. I turn to look at the crowd, all who expect an explanation, all who will not get one. My parents look at me as I walk past them to go inside the house.

My mother grabs my hand. "Where are you going?"

"With Christian."

"You care to explain what happened here, young lady."

She frowns as she looks Johan, who is using his jacket to wipe the blood off his face. My father stands right next to her, and I realize how bad this must look, especially for the mayor and the high priest-ess. It's evident a fight broke out, even if no one knew why, and it looks bad on them that it was at their party in front of their house.

"I'll tell you everything tomorrow morning." I let out a sigh, suddenly tired and filled with the overwhelming need to leave. My mother and I have barely spoken a real conversation in weeks. Just pleasantries in passing, both of us tiptoeing over each other. I know she's lying and hiding something from me, and she knows I know it. I am not in the mood to keep up the charade tonight. "I'm going with Christian."

"You will not be staying the night in a boy's house. I forbid it."

I look my mother right in the eye. I know she's serious. However, I don't care. I don't care how she feels and what she tells me because she hasn't cared for me at all.

"I won't stay with Christian on one condition," I say, and when my father and her look at me, I add, "You tell me about what you were doing in Dad's secret lair."

"What did you just say?" my father says, and I can tell by his face he's shocked.

My mother, on the other hand, is silent, and she looks every-where but my face. Stern face as always. They don't say anything, just stare out to space as if I didn't just say something.

I shake my head. Even when I confront them about it, they won't tell me the truth. I'm tired of this. I'm tired of them.

My mother lets go of my hand, and I take that as my cue to leave. I turn around and head to the house. My phone is in the living room. I grab my phone and just head back out. People are still in the yard, talking, and some are even leaving.

"Alexandra," my mother calls out for me, but I don't turn around. I walk straight into Christian's car without looking back, ignoring her like she has me. I know she won't follow me. It will make a scene, and that's the last thing she'll want.

Twenty minutes go by before we make it to Christian's house in the bayou. We didn't speak the whole car ride. I know he's mad, so I don't push any conversation. I just let him drive us in silence. He needs to clear his head.

Once we get inside the house, he leads me up the stairs to the room at the top of the stairs. He opens the door, and at first, it's all darkness, but once he turns on the lights, I realize that this is his bedroom.

I've been to Christian's house a couple of times since the cookout, but not once have I come up to his room. The room is covered with white walls that have bookshelves in almost each corner, a full-size bed at the center, and a television with video games across it. He has a black desk filled with papers, a laptop, and more books. It's a typical boy's room, minus the mess and smell of BO.

My feet carry me to one of the bookshelves. "I didn't know you read," I say more to myself than Christian.

I can read through the books *Romeo and Juliet*, *Macbeth*, *To Kill a Mockingbird*, and *The Count of Monte Cristo*. There's a whole other side of Christian that I didn't know. I look at the video games and even some of the pictures he has on his desk, pictures of his pack and his family.

It feels like forever that I spend checking out his room, getting insight into what is his. A look into his life that I didn't have before. It's amazing. I turn to look at Christian, who is just leaning on the doorframe, his eyes watching my every move.

His hair is a mess, and there's dried blood coming from his lip and a cut on his cheek. His suit is wrinkled, his white shirt has specks of Johan's blood on it, and his pants have grass stains on the knees.

"Where's your bathroom?" I ask, and he points to a door next to his closet.

I grab a wet washcloth from the bathroom and come back to lead him to sit on the bed. He looks up at me as I stand in between his legs and go to wipe the blood from his face.

"That's not necessary," he mumbles, but I don't stop.

The cut on his cheek and the split on his lip has already healed due to his wolf side. But I can't help but feel guilty. If it wasn't for me, he wouldn't be out in this position.

"Are you okay?" His eyes stay on my face as I try hard to concentrate on what I'm doing.

I nod. I don't want to relive what just happened tonight. I'm still not sure, and I don't believe it even happened. The Johan that showed up tonight is not the sweet kid I grew up with.

Once I'm done cleaning the blood from his face, I raise my hand to push the strands of his hair off his forehead, but he stops my hand midway in the air.

He turns my hand so it's palm up, and he examines my wrist. There on my wrist is a mark from where Johan grabbed me. I knew he had held on to me tight—so tight that a bruise was starting to form.

Christian's eyes close, and I know he's trying not to lose his temper. "I'll kill him." His voice sounds almost strangulated as he caresses the bruise with his thumb.

"Hey." I grab onto his face with both of my hands. I squeeze slightly so he opens his eyes. "I'm okay."

"I didn't mean to scare you," Christian says. His voice is so small that I almost don't hear it. "When I saw his lips on yours, I lost it." He shakes his head like the thought is unbearable.

"You didn't scare me. You were defending me."

"I'm selfish."

I look at him, confused, because what he did was probably the least selfish thing he could have done. I don't understand why he's so hard on himself.

"You're not selfish."

Christian takes hold of my hips and holds me steady as his eyes search my face. I can see the complicated mix of emotions flicker in his eyes.

"I am. When I saw him, yes, I was angry that he forced himself on you, but I was even more enraged that he kissed you." His tone is icy as he relieves tonight's event. "I hate that he kissed you, that he even touched you." His grip tightens up around my hips as his eyes burn into my own. "I don't want anyone to ever be able to touch you."

His eyes are hooded as he caresses my bottom lip with his thumb. "I want to be the only one who gets to steal your kisses, the only one to touch you." He pulls me closer into his chest as if he can't get me closer, which makes my insides curl with anticipation. "You're mine, Alexandra, all mine. I don't want to share. I can't share you."

Without thinking, I move my dress to the side and cradle his lap. We were close before, but for some reason, it didn't feel like enough. With Christian, I always want more, more of him especially.

I place a peck on his lips and then another, before he continues, "That is why I'm selfish, cariño." His voice is husky and laced with a bit of danger. It speaks to me down there.

Cariño, I looked up that word before when he said it the first time, and it means dear in Spanish. Yet that word should be illegal coming out of his mouth, such an innocent word, but he makes it sound so hot.

"Then I'm selfish too," I say as I wrap my arms around his neck, pulling him closer to me.

"Why is that?" He kisses my neck, leaving a trail of sweet feather-like kisses. It's distracting, and it makes me forget about everyone and anything outside of this room. It makes me want to lock the door and throw away the key.

"Because you're mine too."

"Say it again," Christian says in between kisses.

"You're mine."

"Mmm." He hums into my neck before he leans his forehead against my own. "Alexandra, I have been yours since the moment I saw you in that hallway."

I don't question his words because I know there's truth to them, especially since I have been his that first day in the hallway as well.

"Alexandra, I lied to you tonight."

"About?"

He moves his head so he's looking into my eyes. "I shouldn't have said I love you." As soon as those words leave his mouth, I feel my heart start to drop. He must realize what he said because he continues letting his words fall out of his mouth quickly.

"That doesn't feel right to say because it's more than love when I am with you. You're the bright light in the red that is my anger. You're the only one I can open up to without feeling invaded, the only one who makes me believe in destiny.

"I don't think I'd be able to function without you, cariño, and I hate that. I hate that when I'm not with you, I can't stop thinking about you. I hate that when I am with you, I feel weaker than I ever have been and stronger than I can ever be."

His words leave me breathless and lightheaded as I take in exactly what he says. It's almost like he has read into my mind and spoken all my feelings back to me. I can't be without him, yet I hate myself for being so in need and fixated on his energy, to be so obsessed with someone that it feels like I can't breathe when they are not around. I didn't know love could feel this way, and out of all the things I expected for this past couple of months, Christian and the feelings he provoked in me were not one of them.

In the past couple of months, Christian has not only opened my eyes to my life and helped me accept what and who I will be, but he also has given me the courage to believe that the girl I am is just as powerful—something that I have struggled with my entire life.

"I was taught to never need anyone, but I can't help it because I know deep down, I am in need of you. I need your soul"—he places a kiss on my forehead—"your body"—another kiss on my lip—"and most importantly, your heart." He kisses my collarbone, leaving shivers in its wake.,

Christian's words speak to the romantic in me, but he doesn't let me respond because he continues, "And that scares me. I need you like I need air. You keep me sane. You keep me alive. My whole life, I have been training to be the hero in your story, but after tonight, I know for certain."

His words, his eyes, his presence it's all too much and yet not enough. I don't know how to react to what he's saying or even how he's saying it because no one has ever made me feel this important, this needed, this wanted. It's intoxicating, and now that I found this feeling in Christian, I don't think I can let it go. I am in need of him too.

"You know what for certain," the words barely make it past the lump in my throat. Tonight has been a lot, but I did not expect this, this declaration, this outpour of emotions. Christian, the boy whom I had to practically beg to tell me his last name, now is confessing his feelings to me willingly, and I am the happiest girl on this planet.

Christian's eyes stare deeply into mine. "I know that if it came down to it, I would be the villain if it meant I get to keep you."

Chapter 29

The next morning, I am still shaken up by Christian's confession. My head can't ponder why someone like him would feel so strongly for someone like me, so insecure and naïve, but my heart can't seem to care. He's perfect, and he's mine.

I stayed the night despite my mother's wishes, and I know I am going to get an earful when I get home, but I can't bring myself to care. It's Christmas morning, and I am with Christian.

This is the first night we made love, and it was completely incredible. He touched me so tender and passionate, yet I can see the hunger in his eyes that I am sure mirrored my very own. I can still feel his muscles under my fingers and the way he kissed every inch of my body, making me feel worshipped. I still have bite marks from when he teased me and hickeys that decorate my collarbones. The whole night with him was fantastic and very much needed after everything these past few months.

Now tall trees surround us, enveloping us in the color green from the forest that is around his house. This morning, Christian woke me up to tell me he had a Christmas gift for me but that I would have to open it out here in the forest.

"Can you at least tell me what it is?" I say as he practically drags me to the middle of the forest.

Christian just gives me a small grin and a shake of his head. "Now you know that isn't going to happen."

"But why?"

As soon as the words come out, I realize that I sound like a spoiled little girl whose parents just told her no.

We don't speak for the rest of the walk, and I get time to take in my surroundings. I have never been this deep into the woods if I wasn't at the playhouse. The sun shines through the trees, and even though it's winter and there is a breeze in the air, it still looks beautiful and calm.

Before I know it, Christian stops right at the center of the forest, letting go of the hand he was holding as he led the way.

I look around, searching for something, anything to indicate the surprise, but I don't see anything that stands out.

"What are we doing here?"

"I want to show you something," he says, looking around at anything that isn't me. His stance is uneasy as he stands a couple of feet before me, and I can't help but think as though he's nervous.

"What is it?" I try to take a couple of steps toward him, but he just shakes his head and takes a couple of more steps away from me.

"I need you to give me some space."

I can't help but feel slightly rejected. This is a complete 180 from the man I was with last night, and I know that he's nervous. That his nerve is why he's acting this way; however, it stings.

I watch as he takes off his shoes first and then goes to reach for his gym shorts.

"You brought me into the forest to show me your dick," I mock him as he strips out of his gym shorts and stands before me in his black Calvin Klein underwear.

The sight is truly one to behold. The moonlight did not do his body justice last night. His tan, brown skin shines under the sun to the point where he's practically glowing. His abs and pecs look as if they've been sculpted out of clay while his huge legs hold him up. I want to lick him, each and every part of him until my mouth is run dry. I stare from his broad and wide shoulder all the way down to that bulge in his pants.

"Eyes up here, cariño." Christian's voice snaps me out of my dirty thoughts. My eyes flick up to his, and although his tone is filled with humor, his eyes speak a different story, one filled with hunger, while his lips are spread into a knowing smirk. "Don't look at me like that, Alexandra, or I'll fuck you up a tree," he says so nonchalantly that my thighs clench on instinct.

A lump in my throat forms, making it hard to swallow, and my mouth is bone dry. Images of Christian pushing up a tree shouldn't make me so hot and bothered, but it does.

He smiles at me wickedly, like he can read my mindset. He doesn't comment on it. "I don't want to scare you, Alexandra. We can leave at any time." His smile has dropped, and his eyes are avoiding my own once again.

I shake my head in confusion. "Christian, what is going on?" My heart races underneath the clothes that Christian gave me this morning. I still don't understand why he's practically naked in front of me.

I'm not scared, not of him, but of his tone. The way he searches my face, I know that he is.

"I need you to promise if this is too much for you, you'll tell me, and I'll take you."

I don't know why. Maybe it is the urgency in his voice or the fact that I trust him impeccably that makes me just stand in silence and nod at him. I don't know what has him so on edge, so unlike himself, but I watch as he takes a couple of steps back and creates a bigger distance between us. He glances one more time my way before he looks down at his feet and takes a deep breath. Each one is getting bigger than the one before it.

In just a second, Christian jumps a good ten feet above the ground. My eyes follow him, but the glare from the sun blocks him from my view. I lose him in for a second before he comes down just as quickly as he came up. My heart drops into my stomach because this isn't the Christian who went up in the sky a mere second ago; instead, it's the wolf Christian.

I haven't seen a wolf in real life, and I've only seen Christian's wolf side in my dreams. The same colored fur as in my dreams, midnight black. His brown eyes look at me as he stands on all fours in front of me.

I walk slowly as I circle around him, taking him in. I know I should probably be freaked out, but he's so beautiful I can't think of anything else. Christian doesn't move, and it almost looks like he isn't breathing as he lets me get close. He's huge, about six feet tall, and almost ten feet long. His black fur is soft in between my fingers, softer than his silk-like human hair. He has long black claws that tear into the ground and a tail that's almost three feet, with a white spot at the end of it. That's why his dad calls him Spot. I can't help the grin that covers my face as I unlock the mystery.

I walk back toward his face, and I look into his deep brown eyes. The same eyes I fell in love with, except they're larger, and the gold specks that usually surround his pupils are darker now. Almost yellow. They follow me as a pet on top of his nose, relishing how he scrunches it lightly. He's an actual wolf. He looks just like the animal, except larger.

Now I know why he wanted to make sure I knew I could leave if I wanted to. To anyone else, this creature in front of me would be terrifying. The razor-sharp teeth poking out his mouth, the long claws that can probably rip a person in half. He's huge, bigger than any animal I have ever seen. However, when I look at him, I don't see those things. Instead, I just see my Christian and another layer of himself that he decided to peel back for me.

"You're beautiful, Spot." I smile up at him, breaking the silence it took me to admire him fully.

I see him roll his eyes and then watch as he nuzzles up closer to me.

"Can you hear me?" His voice infiltrates my thoughts. I look at his unmoving mouth just to make sure I'm not imagining it, but no, he's actually in my head, just like in my dream.

I nod. "How?" I say the words aloud.

I recall Devin mentioning that when in wolf form, they can communicate telephonically, but last I checked, I am not a wolf.

"I don't know how. I've only ever been able to communicate like this with my pack, but last night, I heard your voice in my head, screaming my name. I wanted to see if this would work."

I try to think back to the moment he is talking about. Right when Johan was going to kiss me, I screamed out Christian's name in my head, wishing he would come and find me. It's weird. I didn't do a spell or even try to communicate with him; it just happened.

The whole thing is very strange, but before I can ask any more questions, Christian lies down on the ground, his body flat while his head is held high.

"Climb on."

I look at him dumbfounded. He wants me to climb on him. "For what?"

"We were going on a run."

I gape my mouth at him and can't help but look around the forest. He must be talking to someone else because there's no way I'm going to get on his back for him to super speed.

"Hell no."

"Why not?" His tone is offended as his brown eyes narrow at me.

"I can fall. There's no saddle. I'm way too heavy for you to be running through the forest." I cross my hands over my chest as he gives me a look that says that they are all the dumbest reasons not to climb on.

In case he hasn't noticed, he's six feet above the ground. A fall at the speed he runs will definitely fuck me up for life.

"Stop being chicken," he speaks, and his face breaks into a smirk. The space above his eye where his eyebrow should be raised, almost taunting me. I know what he's doing, baiting me. He thinks mocking me will get him what he wants, and I hate that he's right.

I roll my eyes at his childish comment and take a deep breath as I climb up on top of him. I used to ride hours when I was a child before I fell and dislocated my ankle. Being on top of Christian while he's in his wolf form feels just like this: like I'm on a horse, a horse with a ton of fur and sharp teeth, but a horse, nonetheless.

I can do this, I tell myself as Christian starts to stand. But as soon as he reaches his full height, I start to doubt myself. I'm up high, way too high. God, why is he so fucking tall?

"Hold on to my fur. We're already late."

"Late to what?" I look at anywhere but the ground. I have never been scared of heights, but right here in this moment, I feel like I am.

"Stop asking questions and pull, cariño."

"I don't want to pull on your hair. I don't want to hurt you."

"You didn't seem to mind last night." And although I can't see his face, I know that he's smirking. The comments make my face heat up, and I silently curse myself for that. I did pull his hair plenty when we were in bed, but I did not expect him to bring that up.

My fist wraps around his long fur, and I yank it hard to teach him a lesson. I don't think he notices because he starts walking. Long strides, but they're not fast, almost like he's letting me get used to being on top of his moving form.

After a couple of steps, I try to speak to him using my mind. "Where are we going?"

"It's one of your presents," he speaks.

"Are you ready?" I can hear the mischief in his voice, almost like he's up to no good.

"Ready for what?" I raise my eyebrow, looking around the trees. There's nothing out of the ordinary—nothing I can point out anyway.

"Just hold on tight, *cariño*."

I raise my eyebrow at his comment, and as soon as my grip tightens around his fur, Christian takes off.

The slow stroll he had before has turned into a full-on sprint. Christian moves so fast I can't make out our surroundings, just shades of green and brown in my peripheral vision. He moves within between the trees with such grace, almost like he's not going one hundred miles per hour. I've heard wolves are fast, but I never could have imagined this. It's almost like he's flying, speeding through the trees, not stumbling once. It's astounding.

There's a tree ahead of us. This one is different from the others. It's taller and bigger than any other tree, and it almost has a luminescent glow to it. The closer we get, the brighter the glow becomes. I have never seen anything like it before. Christian speeds up a tad bit and races toward the tree.

"Christian," I say, my voice barely above a whisper. He's going to crash if he doesn't slow down.

"Christian," I say again when he doesn't slow down or even acknowledge me, "the tree."

Again, he doesn't respond and instead continues to head straight to the tree. It's almost ten feet away.

"Christian," I scream as he races into the tree. I close my eyes and just wait for the impact that I am sure is coming. At the speed Christian was going, I am sure it's going to hurt, but as I squeeze, my eyes shut and wait for the pain to envelop me, but nothing happens.

Under me, I feel Christian has slowed down, and he speaks into my mind, "Open your eyes. We're here."

Reluctantly, I open my eyes, and I am a loss for words. Earlier, we were in the woods, but now we're in a field with green grass, some daises, and a glowing sun. It reminds me of a scene from a movie, an alternate universe almost—completely stunning.

"The tree is a portal, Alexandra, a gift from the witches a long time ago. It gives us a place to run as a pack, away from the humans."

I look around, astounded, as Christian takes us further down the field, where there are about twenty or twenty-five other wolves waiting. I feel as though he just brought me to a sacred place of his pack, and I am eternally grateful, not to mention nervous.

As we walk to the pack, I notice that they all part to let Christian walk through. The wolves of the pack are many, and they all look big and strong, but none of them compare to the way Christian walks among them, just like the alpha he is meant to be.

Suddenly, my brain is filled with voices, a jumble of different words, and that I can't quite make out, and it's almost too much. It's almost as if I can hear the pack through Christian's brain, all speaking. I don't know how he does it.

Christian's voice goes above all others. "You'll able to hear what I hear since we're connected. Don't worry, I can usually focus on one voice at time, but I was nervous," he tells me, reading my mind as always. I want to ask him why he's nervous, but before I do, the voices go away. As he struts through the pack, he make his way to the end of the group to find three other wolves at the front.

A huge black one stands taller than all others, which I assume is Christan's father, and right next to him is a beautiful white wolf, a little shorter but with her head held high, Tanya. Christian walks up to them slowly and lowers himself almost as if he was bowing. So I bow my head in solidarity and respect. After a couple of seconds of this, Christian steps back up and takes his place next to who I am guessing is his sister Santana, white wolf like her mother but with a black spot around her right eye. She looks younger than a lot of the other wolves, but she holds her own.

As Christian stops, I can't help but look at the crowd in front of me. All the wolves stare back. The power that radiates in this place from their presence is almost intimidating. All majestic creatures, beautiful in their own way. It's a sight to behold. In one of the front rows, I see two wolves that stand out to me—one with a devilish smile and brown fur as he stands tall, and another one with light gray fur whose blue eyes I recognize, Jackson and Devin.

"Welcome to the run," the alpha's voice booms in my mind, and I turn to look at him. He stands in front of the crowd of his subjects, tall and alert. "Each year, we celebrate holidays with our families and then spend the next day with our pack running on this field to solidify the bond that is one's pack."

"The werewolf species has always been close, and that is why these runs are important, not only to get back in touch with our wolves' sides but also with each other," Tanya adds behind her husband.

"We have a guest with us today, the next high priestess of the witches of New Orleans. Let's welcome her with open arms and show her what it means to be a werewolf."

As soon as the wolves hear this, they all howl loudly, including Christian. The sound is almost deafening, but I am overcome with the feeling of love that surrounds me. They all seem excited to be here, to be with their alpha, and enjoy the day. A small part of me is envious because no matter how much I pride myself on being a witch, I have never felt this type of love or respect from my coven.

Once the howling has ended, the pack starts to run, and when I say run, I mean really run, speeding past each other, racing through the field without a care in the world.

Christian stays put with Santana by his side as Devin and Jackson make their way to us.

"You think you can keep up, Spot. I know you have some precious cargo," Jackson's voice speaks through Christian's mind.

"If I remember correctly, I beat you by a landslide with a broken leg, Jax."

"Whatever you say. I'm feeling lucky today. I know you won't go at your usual reckless speed and maneuvers because you got your girl riding you."

"He's going to win," I say out loud proudly because I believe not only in my man but the future alpha of this pack.

"Don't antagonize him," Devin warns Jackson. "Last time you did that, you almost shed a tear as he passed you up."

The boys keep on talking, but I can't help but feel like we're being watched, specifically me. About one hundred feet from us, there's a wolf, standing alone. Without needing to be told her name, I already know who it is. With her light brownish fur that the sun bounces off perfectly, I already know that it's Jules. She is as gorgeous in her wolf form just as she is in her human form. She stares me down with narrowed eyes, and I swear she makes a point to show me her sharp teeth, but just like that day at the cookout, I am not afraid of her, not in the slightest.

"Ready," Christians speaks in my mind, snapping me back to him. "We're going to run. If it gets too much for you, just let me know. I will slow down."

I watch as he positions us right in between Devin and Jackson, with Santana on the other side of Jackson.

"Just tell him to slow down now to save yourselves the heart-ache. We all know I'm going to win," Jackson says, confident.

"Oh, brother," Santana says, and even though I can't see her face, I know she's rolling her eyes.

"There's no shame, Lexi. I mean, if you can't handle the speed."

"Leave her alone," Devin says, and it makes me smile at how he defends me. He doesn't have to, but Devin always seems to have my back.

I grab onto Christian's fur tight enough that I don't feel like I'm going to fall but not too tight to cause Christian pain. "Let's win this, baby," I speak into Christian mind, and as a response, he howls.

"Thirty miles, no dirty racing," Santana says as they all get in position to go. The field ahead of us looks endless, and I feel my heart as I feel Christian under me.

"Ready," Devin says.

"Set," Jackson follows.

As I feel Christian under me position himself for a race, I hear him say, "Go."

And just like that, all four of them take off racing through the field as if it's nothing. Jackson takes the lead with Christian and I right behind him while Devin and Santana fight it out for third place. The wind goes through my hair, and I know it's probably a mess, but I don't care. I feel so happy and free at the moment that nothing can ruin my mood.

Out of the corner of my eye, I see Santana jump over Devin and beat him for third place. It was almost as if she was flying as a figure goes in the air and gets to about twenty feet from us. Devin doesn't seem to mind to be last, and I think it's because like me he's having fun.

Christian doesn't let Santana pass him, no matter how many times she tries. But I can't help but feel like he's holding back because of me.

"Christian, you're letting him win."

"He was right. I can't put you in danger. If I go too fast, you can fall."

"I won't."

"It's not worth the risk."

"You won't let anything happen to me."

"The finish line is so close. Can you taste my dust yet, Castillo?" Jackson brags from his spot in first place.

"You know what," Christians says, "hold on tighter, cariño."

I can't help but grin as I watch Christian go faster than he did before and meet up with Jackson. They're neck to neck, and if I'm being honest, it's impressive how fast they both are. I can see the competitiveness in both of them as they get closer and closer to the finish line.

Next thing I know, Christian takes the lead while Jackson is a few feet behind. "Who's tasting dust now?" Christian says, and it's clear there's a smile in his voice. He's happy, and it makes my heart swell just thinking about it. Happy Christian is my favorite Christian.

Right before we hit the finish line, I can hear a female voice in my head with a menacing tone, "Kill her."

Right off our left flank comes Jules charging toward us, getting ready to attack. I know she's after me by the way her eyes stay fixated on Christian and me. He speeds up just in time that her leap falls short, where she doesn't pounce on Christian, but she scratches me in the process.

"Ahh," I yelp in pain as I see the tear in my right shoulder, blood coming out of it. To think this is just a large scratch from her claw, but it's incredibly painful. I don't want to see what else she can do. I turn around to see her charging toward us again. Determination and anger fills her eyes.

The atmosphere has now shifted from fun and friendly competition to now escaping a murder attempt.

Jackson tries to get Jules, but she's quicker and dodges him in no time. Santana and Devin chase behind her, but like Christian, her speed is too great.

Jules gains momentum quickly and charges toward us again. This time, Christian invades her completely by turning to the right to turn around and runs toward the others. Jules recovers quickly and is right behind us before we know it.

Jackson jumps up at the exact moment that Jules does and knocks her down. I see them scramble on the ground with one thing that's evident. Jackson is just trying to stop her, not hurt her, but she is out for blood. She bites down at his neck hard, and Jackson howls in pain.

My heart breaks at the sound of it. Jackson may be a lot of things cocky and arrogant, being his best qualities, but looking at him on the ground as Jules's mouth stays attached to his neck makes me almost angry.

Another werewolf comes in, with golden fur, just like Jules, and jumps on Devin as he tries to make his way toward Jackson. He pounces on Devin, but Devin recovers quickly and knocks him off.

"Santana!" Christians yells to his sister, who rushes to him. "Climb up on her," he orders me.

"No." I know it's selfish, but I don't want him to be out there with them, with her. She seems hell-bent on hurting someone, and I'd be damn if I just offer Christian up on a silver platter for her.

"Alexandra," he warns, and I know I don't have a choice in the matter. So I try to do as quickly as possible even though my arm is killing me.

As soon as I'm off from Christian, he runs back to his friends. A long howl escapes his mouth.

Santana turns to leave, most likely to get me safety, but I refuse to leave here.

"We have to make sure he doesn't get hurt."

I look at Christian as he pounces on Jules, knocking her off Jackson. They roll around for a couple of seconds before she pushes him off her. Devin, who is fighting with the unknown wolf, gets bitten as the wolf jumps on his back. He tries to swing him off, but the wolf doesn't budge. His teeth are sunk into his neck as he doesn't let go.

I can hear Christian in my thoughts screaming at Jules, "I don't want to hurt you. Stand down," he demands.

"You're not alpha yet," she spits out at him as she slowly circles around him. "You choose a witch over your own kind, and then you bring her here. Showing her off as if she isn't New Orleans trash. How dare you."

"Stand down, Jules." Christian's stance is unwavering, but he follows her movements with his eyes. "You hurt one of your kind and attacked the future queen. I won't hesitate to put you and Jason down."

Jason must be the other wolf that has Devin in a chokehold, and by the looks of how their furs match one another, I would say they're related, her brother, maybe.

"You don't have it in you," she says as she lunges toward Christian, who is obviously stronger and faster than her.

He evades her quickly. But at closer inspection, you see that Jules wasn't actually after Christian but the wolf behind him, Jackson. He hasn't moved since her teeth have been pushed off him.

Jules hovers over Jackson, her teeth inches away from his neck, a silent threat. "That looks like it hurts."

"Get away from him," Christian snarls, his teeth poking out. He starts to make slow steps toward Jules, but she growls in response, making him freeze in place.

Meanwhile, Devin and Jason are fighting, rolling around on the field, as Devin tries to get to Jackson, but Jason won't let him. Just like Jackson's fight with Jules, Devin isn't trying to hurt Jason, just trying to move past him.

"You may not be able to kill for your kind, but I will," Jules says into Christian's mind. "You could have had me to lead beside you. I would have been perfect." She places a paw on Jackson's neck where her bite marks are still evident, and you can hear a small whimper come out his mouth.

"She can't possibly love your pack as much as I can, as much as you do." She throws a look of disgust over at me.

There are flaws in her logic. How can she stand there and tell Christian that no one can love the pack like her while she's actively attacking its members? All this because she wants to be with Christian, to lead beside him.

I glance over at Christian. He doesn't look scared or even threatened by her. However, I know him, and I know how much Jackson means to him. He can't possibly lose him, not even for me.

"So you have three options." Jules's obnoxious voice brings my attention back to her. "Take that witch back from where she came from and choose me as your queen."

"That's not going to happen," Christian responds quickly, not even thinking it over. It's not an option for him.

The rejection angers Jules even more, and she places more pressure on Jackson's neck, trying to make a point. "Option two, I kill your best friend," she threatens, and immediately, the air is thick with dread.

My heart drops as soon as she says those words, and it's clear I am not the only one.

Santana growls from under and starts stalking closer to Christian. Jason stops fighting Devin, and he also wasn't prepared for what she said.

Christian once told me that killing another werewolf was forbidden and that no one ever does such a thing because the loyalty in the pack grows strong. I know that all the other wolves, including Christian, are astounded by what she just threatened to do to one of her own.

"What's the third option?"

"You're going to have to kill me." She actually smiles. Her teeth are full-on shining as she looks over at Christian.

Jules knows that this is an impossible choice. Christian would never kill her. She knows this. Jules gave Christian three options, but only one was a clear choice. He can't kill one of his own, and he won't let anything happen to Jackson, so he has to let me go. That is what she wants. She wants Christian to choose her and kick me to the curb. All this because I am not a werewolf.

If this was a movie, this would be the part where the girl tells the guy to give her up for the sake of his pack. Even though she loves him, she can't let him lose his friend. I have always hated that girl in the movie, hated how she couldn't find a solution, but now I finally understand her. The need to make sure Christian's heart doesn't break because if she does go through with it, Christian will never be the same again.

However, I refuse to let him go. Call me selfish, but I know that us being together is what is best for both his pack and my coven.

"Ventus," I say the spell. I know I shouldn't be doing magic right now, especially since my arm is still bleeding out and I am weakened, but I can't let anything happen to Christian or Jackson.

Abruptly, a huge gust of wind pushes Jules off Jackson and down on the ground.

"Witch!" I hear her shout as she slams into the ground.

Jason turns around, looks at me, and starts to charge over. "Ventus." I raise my hand and hit him with another gust of wind, this one pushing off further back to the side.

I jump off Santana and watch as Christian looks at me, studying my face. Devin and Santana run toward Jackson to make sure he's okay, but me, I have plans for Jules. She almost killed Jackson, gave Christian an ultimatum and hurt me. I am done playing nice with her.

Jules stands up and looks as if she's going to kill me. Before she can move, I yell, "Radices," and up from the ground, roots start to grow, long and thick, I move my hands, and the roots mirror my actions, moving and enveloping around her legs, keeping her still.

"What are you doing!" she yells.

She tries to budge, but she doesn't move. The roots have her tied to the ground.

I know I can keep her like this, and that would be punishment enough, but somehow, it doesn't feel right. She ruined a perfect day. She tried to kill me and Jackson, and I can't let it slide. Anger consumes me, and I want her to feel pain.

"Dolor!" I scream, and Jules yelps as she crunches down in pain. At this point, I am shaking, the magic vibrating inside me, but I can feel it wearing my own. Or is it the loss of blood?

"Christian is mine, whether you like it or not." I raise my hand again to cause her more pain, doing just as if I were her alpha, looking for the weakest point she has and exploiting it.

"Ahh!" she yelps, and the sound echoes around us. I have tunnel vision, and the only I see is her. I don't that she's hurting. She did this to herself when she attacked me first.

I am so tired of people pushing around, thinking I will not fight back. I am going to be queen, whether she likes it or not, and it's about time I show her I am not just a figurehead but a witch with actual power who she should fear.

"Alexandra!" Christian's voice screams into my head, yet I am so far gone it might as well be a whisper.

I take steps closer to Jules. My brain is in autopilot mode, and my body is doing what it wants. I squeeze my hand into a fist to puppet me, squeezing her. Her head bows down, and she yelps again and again. Her sounds of misery fill up my ears until it's the only thing I can hear.

Jules's eyes find mine, and I watch as she looks at me with such hate. If the roots weren't holding her in place, she would charge toward me. I know it, and just for that, I squeeze again.

"Stop it, Alexandra!" Christian is off to the side of us, reluctantly making strides toward me, but my eyes stay fixated on Jules.

"You're defending her. She almost killed Jackson. She tried to kill me!" I shout, pissed that he is choosing her.

"I don't care about her. I care about you. You're going to hurt yourself." His voice is almost pleading as he makes toward me.

I know he's right, and I know I should stop, but every time I look at her, I get more and more upset. She ruined a perfect day, and that irks my soul. I hate her. I hate that Christian and I can never have a moment to ourselves without it being tainted by what we are or those around us.

It's not all Jules's fault, I know that, but my heart just comprehends the feeling of hurt, and right now, she is the one person I can take it out on. Before I can hit her with another wave of magic, Christian's father shows up with his queen right by his side.

"What's going on?"

"Jules attacked Lexi, Daddy." I hear Santana's voice in my head, but I don't turn to look at anyone but Jules. "Then she threatened to kill Jackson if Christian didn't give in to her."

"You attacked two of your own." His voice is directed to Jules as he makes his way over to her. I don't miss the way he considers me one of his own, and if the situation was different, I probably would have smiled.

Jules is still tied to the grown by the roots I placed her in. I make the roots go tighter without even thinking about it, and she yelps in pain.

"Alexandra, stop it!"

I make the roots tighter, her howls making their way into the guilty conscience of my soul. I shouldn't have done this, I know. Her pain won't make me feel better. If I continue with this torture, I am no better than she is and no more better than what she thinks of me.

Slowly, I let go of my anger and release her from the roots. Jules takes a deep breath but continues to stare daggers at me. She doesn't move, though, most likely realizing she's been caught.

All eyes of everyone on the field are on me. Some have curious looks on their faces; other, worried. It's evident that what I did left an impression on them. The question is, Is it a good or bad one?

"Jules, what prompted this attack?" The alpha slowly makes his way over. His stance isn't threatening, but his figure is humongous. Anything can be considered such.

Jules ignores everyone else, the alpha, Christian, and the other wolves who have started to gather around us. Her stare is trained on me, a slightly evil grin appearing on her face.

"She's coming for you."

Chapter 30

Two hours later, after that incident in the field, I am in my living room, getting healed by Angel while all my friends look at me as if I am a wounded deer.

"So she just wanted Christian to herself basically," Paris said as she sat next to me on the white leather couch.

"Basically." I sigh as Angel finishes. My arm looks good as new, with no blood spewing out, the cut completely gone, almost as if it never happened, except for the dried-up blood. "Jules just came out of nowhere and decided to attack. Jackson tried to stop her, and that's when she bit into his neck and wouldn't let go. She lost it and wanted to kill him."

"Thank you, Angel." I smile at her as she goes to clean her hands.

Before Angel healed me, she stopped by Christian's to heal Jackson. He heals up, but he is still unconscious. Angel said it should take a while longer because even though wolves do heal quicker. Normally, that rule goes out the window when it's a wound from one of their own. Christian and Devin stay with him, and Christian promises to call as soon as he wakes up.

"What's going to happen to her?" Alex asks as he brings me a cup of water. His eyes had bags under them, almost as if he hadn't slept at all last night. "I thought hurting another werewolf was against wolf law."

"It is, but I don't know."

I left as soon as angel finished with Jackson. I couldn't stand to be there after what just happened. I needed to leave.

Jules last words still echo in my mind, "She's coming for you." I have no idea who she was referring to, but I know she was talking to me.

Christian and his father tried to get her to talk and figure who was this she that Jules mentioned, but it was no use. She stayed silent throughout the whole questioning, refusing to speak, but she made sure to keep her eyes on me the whole time, as if I am the threat and not her.

Christian stayed behind to try to get information out of her, assuming that if I was gone, she might be more prone to giving up whatever she must know.

"Well, I am glad you defended yourself." Angel nods. "That girl had it coming. Poor Jackson too. I know that he probably feels betrayed."

"I do."

We all turn to the sound of Jackson's voice, and there he is with Christian and Devin by his side as they stand at the archway leading to the living room. "But you lose a friend, and you gain a friend." He smiles at me, not his charming cocky one but a more modest shy one.

I know that they all grew up with Jules, that they trained together and hung out together. I couldn't imagine the feeling of having someone so close to you betray you in that way.

"Thank you. The guys told me how you defended me. I hope you know that I will do the same regardless. This morning, I defended you out of duty, but from now on, I will defend you because you're my friend."

I nodded at him, and I couldn't help but smile. Who knew that Jackson was a softie underneath all those muscles and tattoos? I appreciated the gesture, and in the last couple of months, I have considered both Devin and Jackson as friends, and I am insanely glad that they felt the same way.

"How you doing?" Christian comes up to me, no smile and no affection.

I know what Jules said spooked him. I saw the way his eyes completely changed when she mentioned there was someone else.

The truth is, we all changed.

The stack against is getting higher by the minute, and we don't even know all the players.

"Better now," I lie.

"Jules won't talk," he says, describing what I already know.

She knows what she is doing. She doesn't get what she wants today, but at least she creates a sense of fear and doubt. She must know that there are people out there who don't want me to rise to power. She's one of them. By dropping that minuscule bomb, she opened up a can of worms that can never be closed.

Alex sits across me, but his eyes are trained on Christian. "Do you think she knows who has been sending threats and breaking into our house?"

"If she does, she's not telling us." Christian runs his long fingers through his hair, exasperated.

"I think she does," Devin says, and I can see tiger wheels in his head turning. "I mean, think about it. This person knows your grandma, according to the text you were sent. Most likely a witch, right?" He says as if he is figuring out the pieces to a puzzle, "then there's the attack on Paul, clearly a vampire, and finally, Jules attacks us in the one place only werewolves can go."

"Jules doesn't know any witches or vampires."

"That we know of." Devin throws his hands up in the air. "Lexi said that on multiple occasions, she saw a figure watching her. What if the day you brought to the cookout, she was being watched then?"

I shake my head, confused on the point he is trying to make. "What does that have to do with anything?"

Devin's blue eyes turn to me, and I can see the fire behind them, almost like his Sherlock Holmes, and he cracked the case. "If you were being watched, they could have seen you and Jules not get along. Could have seen that she had feelings for Christian and that, clearly, she wanted him. They could have targeted her, tell her she was doing right by making sure you and Christian don't end up together."

"The wolves wouldn't betray us like that," Christian says, so sure of himself.

"They wouldn't, but Jules"—Jackson shakes his head, almost like he doesn't want to believe what he's saying—"she would."

It seems like every step we take forward, we get pushed three back.

There were no threats since Halloween, no figures, no breaking in.

Now, for some reason, it feels like my life has been turned upside down, and my room is just a visual representation of just that.

Christian and I headed up to my room after Devin dropped his theory on us like a bomb. All of us are shocked and confused, but there is truth to what he said. It makes sense whether we want to believe it or not.

My room is destroyed, my bed is tousled, and my full-length mirror is shattered to pieces on the floor and my desk is flipped over with its drawers flung open and thrown on the ground.

"What the hell," I whisper as I look at the mess that is my life.

Christian walks in after me, and his eyes are as wide as my own, looking at the damage in my room. Just yesterday, my room was okay, clean and organized. The only damage there is from the window due to the rock that is thrown in. My room is thrashed, almost as if the person who destroyed is angry. This must have happened after I left for the night.

On the center of my bed is the rock that was thrown to my window just last night. I remember putting it in the drawer of my desk. Whoever did this is obviously distraught at the way I just ignored the message and decided to prove a point.

"Be careful," I tell Christian as I try to maneuver over the mess that is my floor to get to the rock. "There's glass all over."

I feel Christian's arm wrap around my waist and pulls me back, so I am now standing against his chest "Cariño, I'm not the one who's barefoot."

I look down at my black-painted toenails and frown. I can't walk through this, at least not without shoes. Glancing down at the mess, I know I should feel panicked, maybe even frightened, but I don't—just tired and annoyed. This is the work of my stalker. I am sure of it.

"Can you smell anything?"

"Just you," Christian whispers as he looks around, maybe looking for a clue.

Christian walks to the bed and retrieves the rock without looking at the note, allowing me to be the first to examine it.

Sticks and stones may break bones, but when
I get ahold of you, I promise I'll do way worse.

My breath gets caught in my throat, and it's almost as if I can't breathe. This is a threat, an actual threat to harm me. Clear as day, and now I can't help but think back to my room and think that was just a taste of what's coming from me.

"Give me this." Christian yanks the rock out of hand and tosses it to the floor.

He grabs my face with his warm hands and urges me to look him in the eyes.

"I will protect you, Alexandra. I will always protect you." He squeezes my cheeks.

My gaze falls back at the rock, and without thinking about it, my heavy breathing almost makes me pass out. I can't breathe. I can't think. The last time I felt this scared was the night of our first date when I had the first inkling that this threat might actually be real.

Here I am, months later, my heart beating so fast it might come out of my chest, and I feel no better. Not after all the training, all the confidence I have found in my magic. No, I am still that scared girl I was months ago because I know that I can't do anything against a threat. I don't even know when or how it is coming.

"Don't do this," he whispers, his eyes urging me to look at him, but I can't. I am frozen in thought, frozen with the idea of fear, as I look at the ground and see the rock.

I was right not to look at the rock yesterday because if I did, I would be just like I am now, paralyzed with fear. I wouldn't have been able to enjoy myself.

"Cariño," Christian's voice infiltrates my mind, attempting to break through the thoughts of fear. "Look at me, please." His voice is so smooth and calm, and maybe because I crave calmness, I look over at him and lock eyes with his brown ones.

His thumb caresses my cheek in a loving matter in an attempt to soothe me, and it works slightly.

"Christian, what if Devin is right? What if it's more than one person?"

Christian doesn't think, but he says so surely, "Then we will handle it."

I shake my head. "We?" I am not fighter. Who was I kidding? Yes, I can be powerful, but under a threat, I would do nothing. Look at me know, having my fear paralyze me to the point of almost losing control. I can't save myself, and what hurts more is that I know if it really came down to it, I probably wouldn't be able to save Christian.

Coward, that is what I am. I have known it for years, but now whoever is terrorizing me seems to know it too.

"Don't do that." Christian tilts my head so I can look nowhere else but directly at him. "Don't get in your head. I know you. You can't doubt yourself."

"I am not my mother. I can't handle this."

"But you have been handling it." His hand moves to cup my cheek. "You are not your mother, but I have seen what you can do when you don't even try. You make the world break open, and roots appear from its cracks. You make lights explode and glass break just by breathing. You are so powerful, Alexandra, but more than that, you're smart and strong and resilient. I have seen what you've been through the last couple of months, the threats, the attacks, and all the lies. I see how you preserve, and you don't let it break you."

His words are dripping with admiration. "This"—he gestures at the rock and my room—"this won't break you."

I want to believe his words so fiercely—to see myself how he sees me and never forget it. But I can't. All those things he mentioned were things I didn't control—things that went haywire because of my emotions. I can't control this newfound power in me. The strength of it wears me down daily.

"I want to believe, but—"

"Then do."

"Christian, it's not that easy." I break out of his hold and turn to the door. I can't look at him right now. I can't let him see the fear that is crowding my tearful eyes. "I don't even know who I am really. Everything in my life has been either decided from me or kept as a secret so locked up that not a single person will tell me."

"Alexandra, make them tell you." He walks over to me. "Make your family tell you about the prophecy. Make then tell you what was going on that night of Halloween about the text. Make sure you have all the pieces, and then when you do, we will figure out what to do."

"I have tried!" I scream at him in desperation. "I have tried to talk to my family. I have tried to ask them for answers. They refuse every time."

"Try harder. You are not a victim!" Christian screams back at me, and I can tell he's getting upset, angry that I am not seeing what he sees in me. "And I will not let you feel that way. You're a fighter. I have known it since that day you walked up to me in the cafeteria and every day since. So you do what fighters do, and you fight, Alexandra."

As if right on cue, my grandmother's voice speaks from downstairs, wishing us all a Merry Christmas as she enters the house.

"I just got you," Christian's voice softens, and for the first time, I see fear in his deep brown pools. "I won't lose you."

Without thinking, I grab the rock from the floor and race down the stairs. I need answers, and now that the three of them are here, I am going to get them.

I hear Christian behind me as I carry the rock with me. My grandmother is surrounded by my parents, my brother, and our friends.

Her face lights up when she sees me, but I ignore it. I ignore it all and stomp my way to her. A woman on a mission

"You're all going to tell me what's going on, and you're going to tell me now."

Everyone turns to look at me, mouths open and eyes wide, but I don't care. I know I am being rude. I know that it's Christmas, but I am fucking done with being in the dark. I'm done with secrets and lies.

Christian is right. How can I fight without having all the pieces? The pieces they are withholding from me.

"Alexandra," my mother says, but before she can finish, I shove the rock that destroyed my window in her hands.

My parents study the rock, and I swear I can see the color leave their faces. "I have a destroyed bedroom to match, and this isn't the first threat, and I doubt it will be the last. So someone needs to tell me what's going on, or I am going to flip."

My father and grandmother exchange a look while my mother avoids eye contact with me. "They're coming for her," she mumbles, and if the house wasn't so quiet, I probably wouldn't have heard it.

"Who is?" I ask, getting irritated that they aren't telling me the whole story.

My grandmother looks at me, then at Alex, and finally, my mother, her hazel eyes filled with sadness. "We need to tell them Rose," she tells my mother, and right when I think she's going to say no, my mother simply nods with a single tear leaving her eye.

Chapter 31

Ten minutes later, we are all in the living room, us kids on the couches while my parents and grandmother are on the other side of the room, all of which have a glass of wine in their hand.

"You need to know what I am about to tell you isn't easy for any of us to share," my grandmother starts off, her voice soft, filled with something like hurt or regret. "You all know the story of the witch Freya and the war that happened for the amulet way before you all were born. Well, what you don't know is that that amulet had the power to make vampires immortal. That is why it was so important back then. They would be able to live forever if they could get their hands on the amulet and keep it safe. The witches couldn't let that. It's unnatural for something with that much power to live that long. So they were planning to destroy it. The vampires wouldn't let that happen, so the war started, and the werewolves intervened."

I already heard this story before, and I don't know why she's repeating, but I let her finish.

"It was destroyed, and with it, so many of our people slaughtered. We decided to combine forces. In comes Freya."

"I know this story. She foretold that the strongest time to make an alliance would be when a boy with a crescent moon birthmark was born, and a witch a twin was born, only then will it work." I motion to Christian and me.

"Yes." She rolls her eyes at my interruption. "That is true, but she also foretold of a prophecy, just like something like a vampire can't live forever. A strong alliance like yours must be tested. The birth of fire and ice will set the clock in motion. A devil is made of blood of one's own. Death will be immediate. Betrayal and lies will succumb the queen, and only then will rose and pine, fire and ice will fight the final battle," she recites the prophecy as if she has it ingrained in her memory, and I am sure she does.

I try to think over what she just said, but it doesn't make sense. It's just a riddle that confuses me the more I think of it.

"Everyone was so confused about it, but no one even thought to look into it. Many years later, your mother discovered she was pregnant. She was so excited. I just remember the grin on her face when she told me." My grandma has a small smile on her face as she remembers the memory fondly, but then the smile fades as fast as it appears.

"She went to the doctor and found out she was having twins, and just a week before, we heard of the wolf with the crescent moon. It was such a joyous time for all our people, wolves and witches combined. We knew it was our time for a great power to be brought into the light. A time for witches and wolves to become one against the evil that has plagued us for years."

"But then we remembered the prophecy. Death will be immediate." She repeats, and I don't miss how my mother has yet to raise her head this entire conversation.

My mother's eyes stay trained to the ground, and I believe this is the first time I have seen my mother look so small—fragile even.

"Your parents and I were so nervous. All we wanted to do was protect you both, so we sought out a seer to see if she could tell us about the prophecy and what it meant."

"What did she say?" I ask, and even though I need to know the answer, a part of me is terrified to find out.

My grandmother shakes her head slightly. "She said that only thing she can see was that the person that would do you guys harm would be your cousin."

The word cousin hangs in the air for about five seconds before protests and confusion start pouring out of Alex's and my mouths.

"Cousin? We don't have a cousin."

"You told us mother was an only child," Alex points out.

"Your mother had a sister." My father mentions, his eyes never leaving my mother's figure.

My mother lets out a sob, and my grandmother just shakes her head again and again. A feeling takes over the room, one I can in describe as guilt—guilt all over them, guilt from keeping her a secret. I try not to feel disgusted knowing that everyone has their reason, but there is a lot. I think back to the spell book my mother left in my room. How in its pages of gifts, there were two names crossed out. It's all starting to make sense. But why aren't they here? Why haven't I met them?

"I did have a younger daughter. Her name was Rosalie."

"Was?" I ask, confused.

"You guys have to understand once your mother found out about the prophecy, all she could do was think about you two and how to keep you safe," my father says as if that is a response to my question.

"Where are they?" this time, my voice comes out sterner. Something is wrong. There's something else they are not saying.

Grandma just lets out a deep breath. "Rosalie had a family. A husband and a daughter. And according to the prophecy, Rosalie's daughter would be a danger to you and Christian in the future."

I steal a glance at Christian, whom I was expecting to see staring forward. However, he's sitting right next to me on the white couch with his eyes trained on me, almost like he's waiting to see how I react, to either calm me down or be a shoulder to lean on.

"One night, your mother went over to Rosalie's house to beg her to bind her daughters' powers," she continues. "She explained the situation and how you guys were the future for our people, but she didn't want to hear it. She got so upset. She yelled at your mother and called her selfish and asked her how dare she ask her to do such a thing. Not only was Rosalie not the queen, but now she wanted her daughter to be human to protect you guys. It was too much."

That's understandable. I know my mother would have felt the same way if the situation was in reverse.

"And?" I have a weird feeling in my gut. The worst is yet to come. "What happened? You guys just left?" I ask my mother, wanting her to at least contribute to the conversation, but instead, my father speaks up, stepping in front of her, almost shielding her from the rest of us.

"Your mother was pregnant and high off emotion. She didn't just have one set of powers in her, but three. It was so hard to control. Her emotions ran so high that night, and one thing led to the, and a fire started."

Tears start to gather in my mother and grandmother's eyes, and no one speaks as we watch the emotional scene unfold. My father holds on to my mother, who again has not looked up once as she stares at the floor. I can feel it in the room, what they are not saying, the missing piece of the puzzle. The reason no one said anything about this before.

All the secrets, all the lies, they're starting to make sense. They didn't keep us in the dark to protect us, no. They kept us in the dark because the truth of what happened was way worse.

"They died," I say, and right as words leave my mouth, I know they are true.

That is why my mother is always in control all the time and why she wishes for us to do the same. The one time she wasn't, she unintentionally killed three people.

My father nods. "It was a terrible accident. I barely got your mother out in time, and when I went back to check the house, the flames had already overcome it."

"Shit," I hear Jordan mutter under his breath from the other side of the room.

Christian places a hand on my thigh and gives it a slight squeeze, but the touch is so distracting and comforting that I know that if I stay put, I won't get more answers, so I stand up away from him and everyone.

This is too much, but I know there is more.

"So if it isn't my cousin coming after me, then who is?"

I know that this is insensitive. To keep asking questions when clearly they're distraught. I also know I should process the bomb that just got dropped, but I can't. There's more.

"We don't know. About a year ago, we heard that there was a witch in Lake Charles who was gathering rogue witches, vampires, and even werewolves for a rebellion."

Devin and Christian exchange a look. He was right. There was always more than one person.

I stop my pacing and look at my parents in even more shock, surprised at what else they've been hiding."

"You knew about this a year ago, and now you're telling me?"

"Alexandra." My mother finally raises her head up, and I see her red eyes.

"No, Mom. You let me sit as a naive little girl when I was in danger this whole time. You kept a whole prophecy, a marriage, and the fact that I was destined a secret for way too long."

"We thought we could protect you."

"By lying to me?" I roll my eyes in anger. "No, you wanted to protect your secret at the expense of my life."

"Alexandra." I watch as my mother takes a step back, almost like my words were a slap to the face. "Don't speak like that."

I shake my head violently, trying to push off her words. "Lie after lie. You don't get to tell me how I get to speak. You don't get to dictate how I react to this."

As soon as the words leave my mouth, my phone dings, notifying me that I have a message.

I grab my phone out of my pocket. I need a distraction, even if it's a stupid email or status update from someone I know. But all I see is a message and two photos. They aren't the only ones lying. The first picture is so shocking I don't even scroll to the second. Right before my eyes, I see a picture of Angel, my best friend, and Alex, my brother, in the park kissing in pure daylight. My head snaps up, and I see Alex at the end of the couch, right next to Angel.

"You're dating Angel."

Alex and Angel's eyes widen as I turn my phone around and show them the picture.

"It's not what it seems like," Angel is the first to speak. Her words come out of her mouth faster than lighting.

"So you're not dating my brother?" I ask, and her mouth turns into a straight line.

It all makes sense why she wasn't acting normal and why Alex said that he had already moved on. He moved on with her. All the signs were there.

How many more people need to lie to me for me to get that no one can be trusted?

Alex steps forward between Angel and me, almost shielding her from my wrath. "If you're going to be mad at anyone, be mad at me. She wanted to tell you. I told her it wasn't a good idea."

DAISHA ALICEA

I shake my head in anger. "You date my best friend and lie to me for God knows how long. You knew how badly I felt after finding out Mom and Dad have been lying since day one, and you go and do this."

"You don't get to do that!" he shouts back at me, and I take a step back, surprised at the anger being directed my way. "I have been there for you every step of the way. We were just protecting you from the truth."

If someone else tells me they're "just protecting me from the truth," I'm going to scream. I am not a fragile little girl. I can handle honesty. Why does no one seem to believe that?

A humorless laugh escapes my mouth. "You sound just like them." I point to our parents who are watching this scene unfold. Both have gaped mouths and frozen stances, almost like they can't believe what is happening right now.

"Lexi, that's not fair," Paris intervenes. "Don't compare the two."

I turn to look at her, and I see how she avoids eye contact with me—something she has never done.

"Did you know?" The question leaves my mouth before I can even think.

Her brown eyes widen, and she takes a moment to respond. "Not at first."

I feel as if I have been slapped in the face. Around every corner, there's a new secret coming out. A new lie that I didn't see. I can't trust anyone. No one in this house has been honest with me, and yet I'm supposed to just be okay with it.

I turn to Jordan, who is still sitting on the couch watching all this, and for once, he's been uncharacteristically quiet. "Did you?"

He immediately raises his hands in surrender. "I swear to God I didn't even have a clue."

"Anyone else have any secrets they want to tell me, or do you guys want to keep lying to me for eternity?"

"You're being dramatic." Alex rolls his eyes at me. The fact that he doesn't get it pisses me off, and I want to tell him off, but he continues, "No one tells you anything because this is how you react, like a child. So what I like Angel? She makes me happy, and surprise, not everything is about you!" he yells, his tone very pointed. "Mom and Dad lied to protect us and make sure we didn't live the weight

256

of their mistakes. But do you see that? No. You just see that you're being left in the dark, and everyone is betraying you. The world isn't so black and white, and you need to understand that."

I look at him, surprised that he would even speak to me like this. Alex never gets mad at me, not like this. His words register in my head, but it doesn't change how I feel—left out.

"How about we separate for a second?"

Christian stands up and tries to pull me away, but I won't let him. No, I'm too angry to walk away.

"I am about to be queen. You don't think I should know what's going on?"

"Oh, now you want to act like a queen?"

"What the hell is that supposed to mean?"

"Okay, stop it." My mother gets in between us. "This is what they want. They want all of us divided because that way, we're weaker."

"Don't do this, guys," my father says, backing up my mom, but it's like I don't even hear them because right now I am in a staring war with my twin brother.

There's obviously something he wants to say.

"What did you mean by that?" I ask, my eyes narrowing at him.

"Alex, stop it," Angel speaks up, but he ignores her pleas.

"I mean that up until a couple of months ago, you weren't taking this seriously. Always complaining about having to take over, not having initiative, and you have the nerve to say you're unprepared because of our parents. You don't bother to try to discover your gift, and for years, I have heard you complain about having to be queen. You don't know how lucky you are to be able to do something with your magic. No, of course not, because you're an ungrateful spoiled brat," he rants, his voice booming louder with the words that escape his mouth. "Wake the fuck up, Lexi. You're unprepared because of no one but yourself. Don't blame us for your shortcomings."

Ouch. If there were ever a couple of sentences that could break my heart, it was that right there. And much worse, it came from the person I considered my other half.

I'm no longer angry anymore. I no longer care about anything. They can sit here and say what they want. They can lie and say it's to protect me. He can bash me for what he thinks of me. It's irrelevant. I'm done. I just turn around and try to head to my room. Christian tried to grab ahold of my hand, but I pushed him away. I want to be alone and simmer in everything I learned tonight and, mostly importantly, what my older brother thinks of me.

I get to my room, shut the door, and sit on the bed. This day has been insane, and it's not even nightfall. Worst Christmas ever.

I look at the mess in my room, and I can't help but let out a humorless laugh. The mess in my room, the one that had me panicking earlier, is nothing compared to the mess that is my life.

I try to think of everything that was said tonight. Can I even be mad? I understand Why my parents kept the secret, although I wish they told me, I understand. I understand why Alex kept Angel a secret as well.

The logic makes sense to me. But my heart can't seem to comprehend how everyone I have ever loved has been lying to me right under my nose, and I was none wiser.

Alex was right. I didn't really take my magic seriously until this year. It wasn't because I didn't care or that I was ungrateful. I was terrified. I know that if it came down to it, I wouldn't be enough for the witches and now the werewolves. If he really doesn't think I'm good at it, then I should give the throne to someone else.

My phone beeps again, this time as a reminder that I haven't looked at the other picture I got sent.

This one is a picture of a woman, a man, and someone whom I assume is their daughter. They look happy, as happy as a family can be, with bright smiles and lit-up eyes. The woman reminds me of my mother, with the same hair texture and brown eyes but a bigger smile than I have ever seen on my mother's face. The man to her right with his gray eyes and pale complexion, and finally, the little girl in front. She can't be any older than three in this picture. She has beautiful long black hair and a sweet smile that adorns her face. Her brown eyes stare back at me and, for some reason, feel familiar—not because they remind me of my mother's eyes, but something more. Almost as if I have met her.

Then it hits me like a tidal wave. This is my aunt Rosalie, her husband, and their daughter. The reason the little girl looks so familiar isn't because we are related, but because I have met her before. Rosalie's daughter isn't dead. She's very much alive, and she's been in this house. I have talked to her, and I have shaken her hand.

"Robin," the word escaped my mouth as I turned to leave my room and tell my parents. The threat has been here all along.

As soon as I turn around, and almost as if I conjured her up, she stands in front of me with a devilish smile and evil eyes. Her black hair frames her face, so all you see is half her face. She's in all black and stands over me with her slender figure.

"Hello, cousin."

The side of her mouth tips up, and suddenly, a chill runs up my spine. I have a feeling this day is going to get worse.

Chapter 32

I can't believe that Robin was the one behind all this. I met her once, and yet I didn't even know we were related. I should have looked into her after we met. I remember thinking she felt familiar and the way the surge of magic happened when we touched hands—her obvious disdain for Christian and werewolves in general. The pieces were there. I just didn't put them together.

Now I am paying the price for my ignorance. After Robin appeared in my room, she told me if I screamed, she'd light the house on fire just like my parents did to hers once upon a time, but that she'd make sure everyone in the house died if I didn't go with her quietly. She then took me from the house and threw me in a big white van, where she and a big bald-headed vampire drove me here to an abandoned building in the middle of the forest with no phone and no shoes.

I wasn't even able to get a good view of the huge old building before getting dragged up the cement stairs and into a room. Once in the room, the vampire forces a potion down my throat, forcing me to take in every single drop. The taste is vile, and it makes me gag. I have made this potion before, with my mother. It's made to make witches dampen their powers for a couple of hours.

My body moves on autopilot for the next thirty minutes. Robin leaves me alone with Baldy and another vampire, female about my age with brown hair and a snarky attitude. She orders me to strip down to my underwear and put on a white flowy dress. It fits me perfectly, but somehow, that doesn't surprise me.

The whole time while this is happening, I am numb. I don't cry. I don't beg. I just let my mind wander. The last conversation I had with my family ended in an argument, and I will never be able to change that. I didn't get a chance to hug Angel and make sure she knew that I'm glad she found a man worthy of her. I didn't get a chance to tell Alex how much I loved him and how I understood where he was coming from. I didn't even get a chance to hug my parents one last time. And even Christian, we will never see where we could go. How can we lead together? How much I wanted to be with him. It's all gone because regardless of what happens tonight, I seriously doubt I will be leaving here alive.

The vampire girl snarls as she looks at me in disgust. "You witches really are fragile creatures, huh?"

I ignore her comment and look forward to a brick wall standing before me in this empty room. There are no seats, nothing in this room, just Baldy and the coldness.

"Where is she?" a familiar female voice appears behind me, and I turn to welcome it.

Jules, in her golden-haired glory, stares back at me, a smile on her face. "You know, when Robin told me she was going to bring you in today, I could almost taste my revenge for your little stunt this morning."

"How could you?" I start to ask her how she could betray her pack when, suddenly, I am welcomed by a hard slap that brings me to my knees and makes blood appear from my mouth.

I don't fight back. I don't need to give Robin a reason to attack my family. So I take it even though every bone in me wants to hit her back.

Jules crouches in front of me and pulls me by the hair as she stares down at me. I don't give her the satisfaction of yelping in pain. I just stare hard at her, hoping that she can see the hate that I hold for her in my eyes.

"You are so pathetic." She then pulls me by my hair so I'm standing next to her and basically drags me out of the room.

I want to go home and be in my bed. I want to go back to being the girl I was six months ago, but I know that's impossible, and there's no point in wishing that, so I push that thought out of my head and try to focus on what's in front of me.

She leads me past a corridor until we reach what I saw would be the cafeteria of whatever this building used to be. Unlike the entire building, this room is actually decorated. The walls are covered in curtains. For some reason, there's a wooden stanchion about eight feet tall in the middle of the room, and right across it is an actual throne, where Robin happens to be sitting.

Her eyes follow my every movement as Jules drags me across the room and throws me at her feet as if I was a peasant and she was my queen.

I look at Robin, and she looks so differently from the girl I met months ago. The girl I met months ago was kind and had beautiful eyes, but the woman I see in front of me now, I can sense the evil coming off in waves, threatening to knock me over.

"Hello, cousin." She smiles at me, the type of smile where you know it's fake.

I won't dignify her sentence with a response. We may be blood, but she's not my family.

"You have nothing to say, like mother and daughter. You guys always think you're above the rest of us. Born to be queens, but did you really earn it?"

"I have been watching you studying your movements for the last couple of months, and I have been extremely underwhelmed." She grins. "You have every right to be insecure. I mean, I would be too. If I knew the only reason I was meant to be queen was because I came out of the right uterus."

I hear it in her voice, a slight ping of jealousy. Almost like she wished the rules were reversed and that she was the next high priestess and not me.

"You know, when I was a little girl, your mother used to come visit me all the time. She was my favorite person until, of course, she killed my family," Robin says. Her smile is now in a firm line as she gets up and circles around me like a shark right before it pounces on its prey.

"I heard Grandmother and your parents explain their version of the story." She stops right in front of me, her body casting a shadow over my own. "I have been waiting for months for them to tell you, to admit what they did, and they just brush it off as some mistake." Robin crouches down so she's looking directly into my eyes. "Your mother came into the house with one mission: to make sure her precious daughter would never have to face any adversity when it came to the crown, so she killed her own sister."

Her words sting. I know what she is saying has some truth to it, but my mother would never intentionally kill anyone, especially her own blood.

"Did she know she was making you soft and weak? A queen needs to be strong and powerful enough to crush your enemies without a doubt in her mind." She pulls my hair back, and pain shoots from my scalp, and I look at her upside down. "You aren't worthy, and no wonder it was my destiny to rip you away from the throne before you let us witches into an era. We have to depend on mutts to do us bidding."

I let her insult me, not that there's nothing I can do about it. She thinks I'm weak. She thinks she should be the next high priestess, and I know enough about history to know that means she has to get rid of me for that to happen.

I try not to dwell on that fact, and it's almost like I'm numb. As long as my family and friends are safe, she can have me.

"You don't deserve it," she says through gritted teeth before she pushes me toward where I am landing on my face. I can feel Jules and Baldy watching me, and I know they are rivaling in it. A vampire and a werewolf watching a witch on her knees getting thrown down like a rag doll.

"What are you going to do to me?"

"Oh, she talks," Robin says as I sit upright to look at her. She looks at me as if I'm something she scraped off the bottom of her boot as if I'm beneath her, and I'm sure she believes that I am.

"Don't worry about that yet. Just know that you'll be fine before you can hear the final screams from your family."

This gets my attention and I glare at her. "You said you would spare them if I left with you."

"I lied." She smiles. "Did you really think I would spare your family after all the heartache they caused mine? They have to pay for that in blood."

I feel like I'm going to be sick. I played into her hands. She got me alone. She got me to take that potion that sedated my powers for good knows how long, and now I left my family even more vulnerable.

They're going to come find me, and when they do, she's going to kill them. That is why she hasn't killed me yet and why he has taken her time with me. She set the trap, and now I'm the bait.

"You can't kill them. I won't let you."

"Alexandra, what are you going to do? You don't have your powers, and even if you did, you're no match for me." She walks back and takes a seat on her handmade throne.

She's right. Everything I have has been given to me, unlike her, including the right to become queen in the power that comes with it, and I could see it in her eyes that she hates it.

"Is that why you sedated me? Or is it because perhaps you think I can actually take you? It's the only logical reason why you would take the weakest link and sedate them if you really felt like they were not a threat."

She's trying to make me feel less than her, hence the throne and me kneeling on her feet. She knows that I'm insecure about my powers. She's been watching me for months. That's why she's poking at it. Does she know all that was left out the window the moment she threatened my family?

"Don't get cocky," she warns.

"How could I? You're cocky enough for the both of us cousin."

And this time, I gave her a smirk, the same one she gave me once I entered the room.

I expect her to be mad, so I don't react when she marches toward me and places her foot on my chest and kicks me back to where I hit my head. I expect that.

What I don't expect is how much it hurts or how I feel the wind knock out of me. And I definitely don't expect a large black wolf to jump over me to growl at her.

Christian is here quicker than I thought he would, but I knew he'd come. Where I go, he follows, especially if I'm in danger.

"Took you long enough." Robin smiles as she looks at Christian in his wolf form. Just like me, she probably expected it. Christian just responds with a growl while he speaks into my thoughts.

"When I tell you to, you fucking run."

"What about you?" I speak back in his mind.

"I'll be right behind you."

Suddenly, Jackson and Devin come in also in their wolf forms, and this makes Robin's smile grow larger, and her eyes light up with mischief. She's enjoying this.

"Now we have a party, guys."

Jackson doesn't hesitate once he sees Jules in the corner. He doesn't even give her a chance to transform. He goes after her. The buzz cut whistles, and three more vampires come out of nowhere. Devin lunges to them, and when he does, Christian yells in my thoughts with an urgency I never thought I'd hear from him, "Run!"

Chapter 33

I run down the stone stairs barefooted and into the bank of tress, trying to escape what waits behind me. It's already dusks, and the sky above me is an ominous gray. I try to run through the trees, knowing that Christian, and his wolves can only hold off the vampires so long.

I need to move fast. My heart is pounding so hard that it threatens to escape out of my chest. The crunching of leaves under my feet and the sound of my breathing is the playlist of the night. I don't know where I am or where I am going, but I do know that I can't get caught by Robin and her goons.

"Alexandra, run faster," Christian's voice filters through my brain. "I can still smell you."

"I'm trying."

As soon as I speak into my thoughts, I hear movement behind me. Something is chasing me, gaining up on me like I am prey, and they are ready to pounce. I can feel it in the air, the tension. I won't let them catch me. I cannot. There is too much riding on Robin getting ahold of me again. I have to get away. I try to run faster, hoping the direction I am going will lead me to some places of solace. All I see ahead of me are tress and a hill that goes down, so I take the hill, hoping it will lead me somewhere.

"Run, Alexandra," Christian says again, and this time, he distracts me as I go down the hill. I trip over my feet, and I end up rolling down the hill, getting soaked in wet ground, and leaves stick to me.

Once I get to the bottom of the hill, I hit my head with a rock, making me yelp in pain.

My body lays at the end of the steep hill, pain shoots through all the nerves in my body as I try to catch my breath. I have to move. If I stay here, I will get caught. However, I don't even know if I am going to be able to get up. It hurts to even think. My head feels woozy, and I feel liquid come off the top. I touch it and see that it's blood.

Run! I silently yell at myself. The vampires are going to get a hold of me just by the scent of my blood. I get up as fast as I can. Despite the dizziness that I feel, I try to run as fast as I can. I tell myself that I will stop and rest when I am safe, but that thought seems like a foreign dream, like seeing a unicorn or becoming a billionaire.

Practically impossible. Regardless, I try to let my legs carry me away, but deep down, I know I won't make it. My vision is starting to get blurry, and nausea creeps its way in my throat.

I stumble around trees until I can't anymore, but it doesn't matter. I can feel eyes on me. Someone is out there watching me as if this is just a game. They're hunting me down, as if I'm the weak deer, and whoever is watching me through the bank of trees is the one with the gun. I lean on a giant tree; little droplets of rain start to fall from the sky.

"Christian," I whisper in my thoughts, hoping he can come and get me.

I slump down onto the damp ground, mud immediately drenching this dreaded white dress. I feel defeated. I have worked so hard and tried so hard just to fail at the end. I can't believe that this is how it will end. Robin will win, and the witches of New Orleans and the wolves will be left weak all because I didn't see what was right in front of me. How could I continue to be so dense after everything that has happened? Robin was right. How could I even dream of being queen when I don't see when there's evil right in front of me?

In the corner of my eye, I see something move from the trees surrounding me. I strain my eyes even though it hurts. I see a familiar figure coming through the banks. The leaves under him don't crunch under his weight, almost like he's floating over the ground. When he comes within ten feet of me, that is when I recognize his face. It's Johan. He smiles when he sees me, a smile that makes my skin crawl, but I don't over think it.

It's at this moment that I realize that this is my dream, the dream that I have been having since I met Christian. The running, Christian's voice, the falling, and now Johan. It's too similar. It's all coming true, and if I remember correctly, Christian will show up soon. I just have to wait it out.

Johan walks closer until he can crouch down in front of me. His eyes darken as he looks at the blood dripping off the wound on my head.

He doesn't bother to look into my eyes as he examines the wound as if it were the most interesting thing in the world.

"Johan, help me," I say, and as the words come out of my mouth, I realize how stupid they sound. Johan is human. What can he possibly do? If anything, I should be telling him to run off before the vampires arrive. One look at him, and they will eat him alive. I can't risk it, but before I can warn him or tell him to hide, he touches a drop of blood and watches it from his finger.

"I wish I can."

He almost sounds regretful when he says the words.

He doesn't ask what happened or how I got here. I don't even know what he's doing in the woods. He just keeps staring at my wound, almost like he's thirsting for it.

"Johan." I start to talk, but suddenly, Christian appears in his wolf form in front of us. His black fur is wet from the rain as he stares at us in anger.

I let out a sigh of relief as I see him, but it's immediately short-lived as I watch his brown eyes glare at Johan as if he's a threat. His stance is threatening, and the growl that comes out of his mouth is menacing. Johan doesn't act the least bit surprised as he stares back at Christian. If anything, his mouth is turned down in disgust. He looks at Christian as if he's the scum of the earth while Christian looks as if he wants to pounce. I don't know what to do. I feel like I am missing a piece of the puzzle. What is going on?

"Christian," I say in my thoughts, urging him to look at me, but he refuses to look anywhere else but at Johan.

Johan's sneer just turns into a malicious smile. "I guess the secret's out. I was wondering when you would find out."

I look in between them, perplexed as to what is going on. An uneasy feeling fills my stomach. This doesn't feel right.

Christian growls at him, showing off his fangs in a threat.

"Oh, don't be that way, wolfie," Johan says, his voice has a playful edge about it. I don't understand why he's not terrified of Christian.

Up until now, Johan didn't even know that werewolves existed. How is he not running for the hill in terror?

Christian takes a slow step toward Johan and me, and before he can fully come over to me, I am snatched to my feet by Johan at lightning speed. I don't even see it happen. One second, I am on the ground bleeding, and the next, I raised up with Johan's hand around my neck, keeping me flush to him.

When did Johan get so fast? Faster than Christian.

"I wouldn't come close if I were you unless you want me to use my fangs as well." Johan's voice brushes my ear, sending goose bumps of fear down my neck. His tone is threatening, and I don't quite understand what he means by fangs.

I turn my head to look over at Johan, and suddenly, my heart drops. Right there in his once-boyish smile are two fangs, vampire fangs, if I am being technical. He shows them off as if they are new toys he can't wait to play with. Immediately, I try to wretch myself out if his grip, but there's no use. It's iron-tight, and I am not at my strongest. My eyes widen as I look over at Christian. My feelings are everywhere, from physical pain to confusion and lastly to one I would never have thought I would associate Johan with, fear.

"How stupid do you feel, Alexandra?" He whispers in my ear. "I was the one behind it, those attacks. The note in your locker, Christian's, car, Paul. All of it," he brags. "I watched you for months, and you were none the wiser. You had no idea I got turned into a vampire. Sorry, I had to keep it from you." His voice caresses my cheek in the worst way as he moves in closer to me. "However, I would call us even. After all, you have lied to me for years about being a filthy witch."

As the last words leave his mouth, he tightens his grip on my neck, almost like he's angry. It's so tight I'm surprised I can even breathe. Christian advances closer, slowly with another growl leaving his lips. Johan puts his hand up to stop him. "Make another step, and I will break her neck before you even get a chance to attack."

My blood runs cold after hearing those words come out of Johan's mouth. He just threatened to kill me without even thinking. This isn't the Johan I know. I try to think about the past couple of months, and he's right. I didn't notice how he was right in front of me. I could see the signs of him changing, the light in his eye disappearing, and his actions being unlike himself, but I never assumed it was because of this. I never would have guessed it.

Christian stops in his tracks, his eyes translating threats that even though Johan can't hear him he can sure convey what he means.

Touch her, and you die.

"Johan, please," I say, trying to wiggle out of his hold. I still feel lightheaded, but I need to get away from him and to Christian.

"Johan, please," he mocks me as if the sound of my voice aggravates him.

He forces my head to turn to him, and his once-blue eyes are darker than I have ever seen them. "This is what you wanted. I gave you your chance, and you chose him, a mutt." He spits out at Christian. "Now you want to beg." His lips turn up a sinister grin. "Beg for him."

I don't get a chance to figure out his words because as soon as they leave his mouth, vampires come in from the shadows and the bank or trees, almost twenty of them surrounding us. Fangs out as they snarl at the center of the bank, at Christian.

Immediately, I know what Johan is going to have them do: attack him right in front of me. I thought my blood was cold before, but now it's arctic as I stand frozen in fear. Christian, my Christian. He won't stand a chance against all of them. I make eye contact with Christian. Although he is completely surrounded by blood thirsty animals, his eyes are locked on mine.

I see no sense of fear in his brown orbits, just anger, and it's all directed toward Johan and the hand he has around my neck.

Christian might not be scared, but I am. The thought of him getting hurt because of me makes me sick, and I have no choice but to do what Johan said.

"Please don't, Johan. Don't hurt him." Desperation coats my voice.

"Oh, honey, hurt him?" He repeats my words as if they are a question. "I don't want them to hurt them. I want them to kill him."

My heart drops and breaks at the same time as those words leave his mouth. How could he say that so carelessly?

"Johan," I plead at him, "please don't. I will do anything. I will go back with you." The words come out pop my mouth before I can process what I said.

"No!" Christian screams in my thoughts, but I ignore him. I refuse to let him die, even if that means I will be placed at Robin's feet to do what she pleases.

"Willingly." Johan's eyebrow raises.

Christian objects, "Alexandra, no. I can handle them. Don't risk your life for me. Your people need you."

I don't even hesitate when I ignore Christian again and nod at Johan. I know my people need me, and I may be thinking selfishly, but if I can stop Christian from being hurt, I will, no matter the cost. My people will be fine. They're fighters, and Alex can take my place and lead them. They will be okay. However, if I lose Christian, knowing I could have prevented it, I will never be okay again.

"Take me to Robin."

And although I am dizzy, I try to stand straight to show I mean business.

"Alexandra, I said no."

Johan studies my face to see if I am bluffing, but he must know that I am not, not when it comes to Christian. Not when it comes to the man I love.

"You're an idiot," Johan says with a smile on his face, like I am somehow missing the joke. He bends over, laughing as he still has a hold of my neck—a real laugh too, one that makes you question his sanity because who can laugh at a moment like this?

Johan looks into my puzzled face. "She really is always two steps ahead, isn't she?"

I raise my eyebrow, but that only makes him laugh more. "You were going back regardless of what happens right here. This was a trap," he says, and all the blood flushes from my face.

A trap? What does he mean by that?

"Robin let you go because she knew that Christian would do anything to protect you, even if that meant leaving his own to fend for themselves. She let you leave. She let Christian get close enough to follow you, and then she sent me to retrieve you when she knew for sure."

"Knew for sure what?" I ask, still not understanding why and how Robin planned this out. She couldn't have possibly known all of this, could she?

Johan just smiles, not answering my question. I turn to Christian. Dozens of vampires are surrounding him, and he still stares at me with those brown eyes that allow me to get lost in them. He looks at Johan, then back at me, thinking, and then I watch as the snarl on his face drops.

"That you would risk your throne and people for me," Christian speaks into my thoughts, and suddenly, I feel even more nauseous.

That bitch, she played me right into her hand, and I was none the wiser. She has always been one step ahead of me, and now she knows my deepest weakness: Christian. She knows that if it ever came to Christian and staying queen to my people, I would choose him every time. Even if it meant I wouldn't fulfill the prophecy. I should have known I wouldn't be able to escape her, that what Robin really wants is my submission, and without it, she won't stop. Now she knows how to get it.

"Let's go back to the party," Johan says, knocking me out of my thoughts, and suddenly, the vampires storm Christian in a heartbeat, jumping on him, trying to get him down. It almost looks like they're trying to get him to heel, just like a dog, and that infuriates me. I hear him yelp and whine as they bite and pull him in all directions.

"Christian!" I scream, and I try to wretch myself again from Johan, but it's no use. He just stands there, enjoying the show like a psycho.

"Christian!" I scream again as I watch him try to defend himself. He gets a couple of them off him, but they are too many. He needs help. I try to do a spell, but I'm weak, too weak, but if I don't try harder, he will die.

Tears fill my eyes as I scream his name again, trying to use emotions like he taught me to get the vampires to stop, but with all the straining, black dots in my vision start to take over, and suddenly, I am fainting in Johan's arms.

The last thing I hear is Johan mutter, "You're an idiot."

At the same time, Christian's voice invades my thoughts. "I love you, Alexandra."

"Wake up."

Cold water flashes on my face jostling me awake. I open my eyes and try to gather my surroundings. I'm no longer in the woods. I'm in a cold, damp basement, and I'm not alone. On my left, there's Alex, my right, Paris, and directly across us, sitting against the wall, are Angel and Jordan.

They are all shackled to the walls like prisoners, and when I look down, I, too, am accessorized with the same iron shackles.

"How did you guys get here?" I turn to Alex.

The last time I saw them was after our fight. I prayed that they stayed away from this—hoped that they would not be taken.

Alex opens his mouth to respond but is immediately interrupted, "That would be me." Johan, whom I didn't see standing in the corner with a bucket, moves into the center of the room. "I just came to Alex, telling him that I saw someone take you, and next thing you know, the whole gang is hopping in the car, ready to save you like the hopeless princess you are," he speaks in a voice that is unrecognizable to the one I grew up hearing. "I was quite convincing. I should try acting when this is all over," he jokes, but no one laughs.

This Johan, the one in front of me, is evil, petty, and mean-spirited.

From threatening Christian, and I, to—

"Christian," I speak out loud as the memories of what happened before I passed out cross through my mind. The last thing I remember is him getting attacked by vampires before I tried a spell that didn't work.

"What did you do to Christian?" I ask Johan.

His dark blue eyes find mine, and I see mischief and something like playfulness in them. He's enjoying this.

"Don't worry. Your lover isn't dead...yet," he sneers.

The breath I didn't know I was holding escapes my lungs. That's a relief. Now I pray he isn't badly hurt.

I look Johan over; his hair is a tossed-up mess, and it almost looks like he's been pulling it out. His once-kind blue eyes are now dark and covered with hatred as they glare back at me. This isn't the Johan I know, and I can't believe I missed the signs. I try to think back on the last couple of months. I remember seeing the light slowly disappear out of his eyes over the weeks. However, I assumed that was because of the breakup and Christian. I remember how that night in my parents' yard, he was so aggressive, which is so unlike him—differences that I should have noticed before, but now it's all coming together. How could I have been so incredibly dense? Paul said that Justin and Johan are the last two people he remembers seeing after he got attacked. I just assumed Justin had something to do with it or that an outsider came in. The signs were right there.

"How could you do all this? How could you be a part of this?"

"How could I?" he shouts at me, making me pull on my restraints.

His eyes are menacing as they look Alex and me over. He walks up to Alex, whose arctic glare stares him down. I watch as he clenches his fist as Johan walks over and crouches down in front of him.

"You were supposed to be my friend. How long have we known each other?"

"Twelve years," Johan answers his own question, and the atmosphere in the room gets tense.

I keep thinking of Christian and where he's at. I need to get to him and make sure he's okay, but these restraints won't let me do magic.

They have an X marking with a line across, signaling that they're cursed. Whoever wears them will not be able to do magic.

"In those twelve years, I told you everything. I told you about my family and school, even when I knew I loved your sister," he continues. His tone is calm, too calm compared to the shout he had a minute ago. "We were so close, at least that is what I thought," he says. "You've been to my house. I've been to yours. We played football together and told each other secrets. We were more than friends. We were brothers."

Alex stays silent, letting his eyes convey the anger that he feels.

"How could you lie to your brother like that?"

When Johan realizes that Alex isn't going to entertain his conversation, he turns his focus to me, his eyes staring daggers into my soul. "You were the worst part of this. You made me fall in love with you. You dumped me, and then you parade your dog around me." He rolls his eyes in disgust. "You could have had me, told me the truth, and I would have kept your secret. I would have fought for you, Lexi. You didn't give me a chance. You just let me suffer, thinking I was the problem while you opened your legs to a fucking fleabag." He spits the words at me, and I would be lying if I didn't say they stung as they came out of his mouth. He's right, not about the Christian part but about the fact that I didn't tell him the truth. I gave him a lame excuse, and he saw right through me.

"You're nothing but a slut," he says directly into my eyes as he pulls back to stand, almost like being around me repulses him. "You disgust me."

"Watch your mouth," Alex speaks through gritted teeth.

Johan just laughs him off. "What are you going to do if I don't? You are bound by this stupid cuff. You have no powers. You're weak," he mocks as he opens his arms, the bucket still in his hands, and spins around the room. "I, on the other hand, have the strength of ten men and the speed of a goddamn cheetah. I am unstoppable," he says the last three words with pride.

I can't help but feel baffled by the display that Johan is making in front of us. This cocky, evil man isn't the Johan that we know. I created this monster, and now I have to live with it.

"You're a blood-sucking demon. That's nothing to brag about," Jordan speaks up from the corner of the room. He looks at Johan almost with pity in his eyes, seeing the boy who has tricked himself into believing that being a vampire is something to boast about.

Johan's eyes darken, and his smile drops as he turns to Jordan. "Blood-sucking demon," the words come out of his mouth as if he's trying to see how they taste coming from him. He leans his head to the left, and in a blink of an eye, he crouches down, grabs Paris from where she sits, ripping the shackles from the wall, and holds her against his body, facing the rest of us.

Johan makes it a point to pull Paris's hair so her neck is exposed, causing her to yelp in pain. His eyes survey the rest of us in the room as he shows us his fangs in a silent threat. He's going to bite her, actually, put his fangs in her neck, and drink her blood.

"Johan, let her go."

For the second time tonight, after being kidnapped, trapped, and locked in a room without my powers, I am terrified, not for my life but for Paris's, my best friend who has fear written all over her face as she squeezes her eyes shut in anticipation for the worse to come.

"Please." The word is barely audible, coming out of her mouth. "Don't do this."

"Let her go. Think about this."

I try to look around at anything I can grab to throw at Johan or maybe attack him. I refuse to let him hurt her, but when I look around, I don't find anything. The room has been stripped bare, and we are powerless. Johan was right. Without our powers, we are weak compared to him.

The feeling of helplessness takes over me as I think of all the things I can do in my current position, but I come up blank. In the center of the room, Johan holds Paris, and at any minute, he's going to sink his teeth into her. I watch as Angel's green eyes widen as saucers as she stares at what is taking place in front of us, Jordan right next to her, telling Johan to let Paris go, and Alex right next to me, who has anger radiating off him in waves. My friends and my family are stuck in a room where we have no options. Not to mention that Christian is tucked away at God knows where—probably hurting almost because of me.

I should have seen the signs. I should have seen what was right in front of me, but I didn't, and now I am not the one paying the price—my friends and family are.

"Let her go!" I scream at Johan, anger bubbling under my skin.

I have never felt so helpless in my life, not when I was a little girl, and Alex got his gift before I did, not when I saw Paul in a pool of his own blood, not even when threats kept on coming my way. But tonight has been a series of helpless events, starting with Robin taking me, Johan, and his vampires attacking Christian, and now Paris. It infuriates me that people keep getting the better of me, but not anymore.

I look at the shackles that are preventing me from moving or using magic. I will it in my mind—to shatter off me so I can save my friend. Paris will not die in front of me, not today. I yell to myself in my mind. Nothing happens, though. My brain freezes as Christian's words echo in my ear. "You are not a victim. You're a fighter."

I try again, this time, digging deep past my inner demons to the powerful magic that lies dormant inside me. I stare at the shackles and imagine them breaking in my mind over and over again. Until suddenly, a spark inside me lights up, awakening the magic deep in my gut and allowing these shackles to fall off my hands like cheap handcuffs.

I look at them in awe, and although I can't quite understand how I broke a cursed object, I don't dwell on it, not while Johan has Paris in his clutches.

With tired and bruised feet, I rise from the ground, no longer in fear.

"Let her go," my stern voice directs Johan to look at me, and the grin on his face slips as he sees that I am no longer powerless.

"How did you—" He doesn't finish his sentence because with a whisk of my hand, he is slammed against the brick wall like a rag doll.

Paris clutches to her neck, with her still shackled hands as if she can't believe it's still there. "Oh my god, I love you," she says breathlessly.

I give her a small smile, and with another flick of my hand, all their shackles are off too. It doesn't take me imagining them to break off. It just happens.

"How did you do that?" Alex jumps up to my side.

I don't know how to answer his question. I just feel it in my bones.

Christian, my mom, Grandma, they were all right. I am strong. I am powerful. There's a reason I am meant to be queen, and that same reason is circulating through me. Not like before, like electricity zapping through me, but more like flowing in me like a power line.

For the first time, I have full control of my powers, and the reins in my hands feel just right.

I loom over to where Johan is lying, trying to get up, but with my magic, I will let him stay put.

"Let go of me, you bitch."

"Where is Christian?" I ignored his pleas and insults. I would feel guilty if this was the Johan I cared for all these years, but this hollow version of the man he once was attacked my boyfriend, kidnapped my friends, and terrorized me for months. He gets no sympathy from me. Not anymore.

"Like I will tell you." He rolls his eyes.

"You're going to tell her," Jordan states, but his eyes are focused on Paris and how she still seems to be shaking and rubbing her neck.

"Who is going to make me?" Johan says, and then his eyes find mine. "You wouldn't hurt me. You wouldn't hurt a fly."

Before I can even speak, Alex comes from beside me. "She wouldn't, but I would." And with that, his left hand raises. "Confractus." And on cue, the bone in Johan's left hand breaks. The sound echoes through the room right before a scream lets out of his mouth.

"You can still feel pain just like the rest of us."

"Let me." Paris steps up and breaks Johan's other hand in retaliation.

"Where's Christian?" I ask again. This time, ignoring his screams, I won't lie and say it doesn't hurt me to hear them, but right now, all I care about is Christian.

Sweat and tears cover Johan's face as he searches all our faces. I don't know what he sees, the faces of the people he betrayed, memories of what once was, or the fact that now, not one person in this group will ever care for him like we once did. Whatever he sees makes his eyes gloss over with fear as he tells us that Christian is being held in the throne rooms.

Chapter 34

We made it to the throne room, and I don't know what I expected, but it wasn't this. The wooden stanchion that was in the center is now occupied by Christian. He's tied to the stanchion with cuts and bruises covering his entire body.

He's tied up by his hands, but there's also rope around his neck that is decorated with wolfsbane. I try not to let my eyes fill with tears as I watch what's in front of me.

I ran toward him, not even bothering to search the room. Suddenly, I get zapped by a bolt of electricity.

It knocks me down to the floor, but it's not enough to knock me out.

However, I will definitely feel that tomorrow if we make it out of here. I raise my head to see Robin right next to the throne with a giant smile on her face.

"See, cousin, I have a gift just like everyone else in the family," she speaks of the bolt of electricity that came out of her hand. "Well, almost everyone." She smiles.

I notice in her hand there's a dagger, completely black, but when reflected by the light, it almost looks red. And she stands proud in front of us like this is what she's been waiting for. Although I don't have my gift, Alex does. So he goes to attack her, but she's too quick. She zaps him. I watch as Alex's body drops to the ground.

Angel runs immediately to check on him, not even watching her back. However, she's not Robin's next target. She zaps Paris and Jordan, and they both end up on the ground. Unlike when Alex and I fell, Paris and Jordan are on the ground shaking, almost as if they're having a seizure.

"What did you do to them?"

"A higher voltage." She walks away from the throne, the dagger still in her hand, and she plays with it. "This is a family affair. Can't have your friends getting in it be ruining all my fun."

I watch Paris and Jordan shake uncontrollably, and my heart immediately drops. She has us all down, but not for long.

"Angel, go to Paris and Jordan. He's okay," I say as I watch Alex stand up.

She gives him one last look of hesitation, and when he nods, she turns to help our friends.

I get up and try to move closer to Christian, who now looks unconscious. What did she do to him? My heart aches as I see the bruises and cuts that decorate his golden, sweat-soaked skin.

Alex stands closer to me while Robin takes a couple of steps our way.

"That's more like it. Just the three of us, the way that it was always meant to be."

"Alex has nothing to do with this. The prophecy says this is between Christian and I against you. This has nothing to do with Alex. Let him and my friends go."

She rolls her eyes. "Typical. You don't even know what the prophecy really is about. God, you are stupid," she snarls at me.

I don't get a chance to ask her to elaborate because right behind her, the throne levitates off the ground and makes its way toward her. Without looking, I know that Alex spelled it while we were talking, and that is why it's coming toward her. But as if she had eyes behind her head, with a whisk of her hand, the throne gets slammed to the wall and breaks into pieces.

"I liked that chair," she jokes.

Without thinking, I look up at the light fixture that stands directly above Robin's head and say, "Cadere," hoping that it will fall and hit her, but just like with the throne, she avoids it.

"Let's face it. You, too, are no match for me, so how about I make you a deal, Alexandra?" She turns to me, and her face is sinister. "I will stab you with this knife, which will not only kill you, but transfer your power to me right after you die. You give me your powers, and I won't kill everyone you, starting with that fleabag you love."

I shake my head. "I can't do that."

Too much is on the line. I can't let her hurt Christian or my friends, but I also can't let her take my powers. I have seen what she has done without them. I can't imagine with them. Earlier, I was willing to risk it all for love, but now I have to fight, and I have to win. Dying is the easy way out. I see that now.

"And here I thought he was your true love."

"What do you even know about love?" I snap at her out of anger.

"It's a weakness and one I'm planning on exploiting." She raises her and points it to Christian. "Don't say I didn't warn you, little cousin."

Everything moves in slow motion. I see the volt leave her hand and try to make its way to Christian. But somehow, I'm faster. I jump in front, completely prepared to take the hit and maybe even die, but nothing happens. My eyes are shut close, and I'm scared to open them, but I know that I have to.

And what I see when I do is unbelievable. Right in front of me, coming out of my own hand, is a shield made out of fire. Actual flames shielding me from her powers. My gift. My grandma always said it would always come in my time, and I guess it did.

"Oh shit," Alex says as he stares at me, shocked, and I can't help but feel the same.

The flames come out of my hand as an extension of me, protecting me from Robin. I feel its warmth, but not enough to burn me, but actually, the opposite. It makes me feel safe, like a warm hug from a loved one.

"That's my girl," I hear Christian say behind me, and even though his voice is low and his eyes are practically closed, I could still hear the pride in his voice.

"Fire and ice," Alex mutter and then look at me. His eyes widened as if he finally put together the pieces of a puzzle. "Lexi, the prophecy, we're fire and ice."

I try to think of what he's saying and how it makes sense. The prophecy said, "Rose and pine, fire and ice." Pine has to be Christian. Every time he's around, that's all I smell. Rose would be a nod to what Christian said I smell like. Fire and ice are Alex's and my gifts. It's all starting to make sense. The way my grandmother always said it was Alex and me against the world, how we can tap into each other's power source. This whole time, I thought that being high priestess meant that I would have to face danger on my own, but looking back at it, I have never been alone. Alex has always been there, my friends and even Christian. I was so focused on whether or not I was capable of taking over my mother's place and facing the world on my own, but that was never the case. I don't have to be high priestess on my own, and I don't have to fight Robin on my own either.

I look back at Robin, and she has a frown on her face, and there's fear in her eyes. She assumed I was weak. She knew that she needed to create a divide between my family, friends, and Christian. She knew that would be the only way she could win. Now she's seeing her plan fall apart.

Robin shakes her head and throws another bolt my way, and when she sees that it doesn't affect me, she throws one to Alex before it reaches him, a block of ice appears from his hand, protecting him like a shield.

The prophecy said that we could do it if it was just us two against her, and now we know it to be true, and by the look on her face, she knows it too. The fire shield disappears in me, and a flame ball takes its place, and this time, I throw it to Robin.

She dodges it once and twice, but the third one hits her right on the shoulder. She falls back on the ground in pain as it hits her. The skin is blistering, and it does look quite painful, and a small part of me feels a little guilty.

"Surrender, Robin. I can talk to my mom and get you a prison sentence instead of death. It's mercy and a good deal compared to what she has done to me and friends."

She scoffs at my words. "Fuck you!" she screams and tries to throw another bolt my way.

I dodge it easily. "I'm really sorry for what your parents had to go through, what you had to go through, but I am not my parents' mistakes. Neither of us are."

That angers her more, so she starts to stand, but Alex turns the ground under her into ice, and she stumbles and falls hard. She lost. We all know it. She just refuses to admit it.

"Don't move," he warns, his eyes follow her like a hawk.

I look at Robin, the woman who grew up without her parents and has handled so much loss, and I can't help but feel sorry for her even after everything she did. But at the end of the day, she is my cousin, my blood.

I can't think of that. I have to think of my people, and Robin will always be a danger to them, including the wolves, if she were out and about. Alex and I have to figure something out.

"Freeze her," I tell Alex reluctantly. If he freezes her, she won't be dead, and it would give us time to figure out what to do with her, at least for now.

Before he gets a chance to do so, she stares me down. "They will come, Alexandra. It's not just me. I am not the only one who doesn't want this alliance to happen. They will come for you, all of you!" she shouts as she motions to my friends.

Her words make me shiver, but at this moment I can't do anything. She said her peace, and although I don't know if I should believe her, if someone were really after us, they will make themselves known soon enough.

"You and Christian, this alliance is unnatural, and I was just a pawn sent out to stop it. But there will be more. More people are coming. More danger are headed your way. Mark my words. You will both die before it's solidified and—" She doesn't get a chance to finish her warning because the ice starts to take over, covering her up until she's a frozen statue of her former self.

I look at Alex, and he just shrugs. "She was talking way too much."

I wish I would have known what she wanted to say next, but it's probably for the best I didn't. For all I know, Robin just wanted to plant seeds of fear.

I can't think of potential dangers when I just got rid of one. It's finally over, and we can breathe. I immediately turn to Christian to untie and set him free. I try to be cautious of the cuts and bruises that cover him up, not wanting to cause him any more pain.

His legs are so weak that he almost falls over me when I get the wolfsbane off him.

His bruises cover his face, his neck, and down his shirt, and I can't imagine the kind of pain he's in. However, he still manages to give me a small smile.

I want to ask him if he's okay, physically and mentally, but he eats up my words as he smashes his lips onto mine. His lips are eager and forceful yet soft. He kisses me as if he didn't know he would ever get a chance to kiss me again. His hands roam around my body, almost like he can't believe I'm standing in front of him.

I kiss him back with the same force and need. Seeing how hurt Christian actually is makes me want to unfreeze Robin and torture her immediately. I push that thought out of my brain and try to enjoy my Christian.

"I always knew you could do it," he says after he breaks the kiss but he still holds on to me for dear life.

"I wish you would have told me," I joke around as I wrap my arms around him and hold on to him. I look into those brown eyes that started everything, and to think it all started from a look in the hallway, and now I can't imagine my life without him.

Earlier this evening, I didn't think that I would make it out alive, but not only did I make it alive. I'm thriving. I am no longer scared of my future. I welcome it and anyone who wants my throne with open arms, my werewolf boyfriend, protective brother, a group of loyal friends, and a fireball by my side. For the first time in my life, I feel ready.

*****

Christian's POV

"Who would have thought that witches would be saving the day?"

Jackson jokes as Devin, Jackson, and I stand in the corner, looking at the crazy witch who tortured us. She is now a completely frozen statue.

"That's your future queen." I nudge him in the ribs. I'm still sore but never too sore to whoop Jackson's ass, and he knows it.

I look over at Robin. I had a feeling in my stomach the first time I met her at Alexandra's party. I knew that she was bad news. It turns out I was right. I should have followed up on it, find her, and see what she was up to. I could have avoided this whole thing.

"Fire out of her hands?" Devin asks, bringing my head out, my thoughts for the third time since I told him what happened just fifteen minutes ago. "How do you feel about that?"

"I think it's badass," I say in all honesty. I couldn't see much due to being in so much pain, but I did see Alexandra shoot fireballs out of her hands. I always knew she was powerful. Now I'm glad everyone got to witness it.

"Until you piss her off and burn you to a crisp." Jackson laughs and nudges me back into my sore rib.

I look up to Alexandra on the other side of the room, talking to Angel and her brother. She's all smiles even though she's bruised and most likely exhausted after today's events. She looks so carefree and happy that I zone out of my conversation with the boys and just pay attention to her and her smile—the way she laughs with her friends and the way that they laugh with her. She looks like she was before all this happened, in those slight moments when she's not worrying about anything but what's going on now.

As if she can feel my eyes on her, she looks in my direction, and I swear every time she looks at me, it's like the first time. The darkness is gone, and the light I didn't know I was missing comes into view.

I see something from the corner of my eye, move lightning speed toward Alexandra, and then leave. I'm pretty sure it was Johan, but my mind is so preoccupied with a series of emotions that I miss him through vampire speed.

I watch as everyone circles around her, rushing to her aid—everyone but me. My feet stay planted on the ground as I become overcome by crippling fear. My mind can't focus on anything but what just took place. The smell of blood has filled the room, accompanied by the sound of yelps and her shallow breathing.

For the first time in my life, I remain frozen, not knowing what to do or how to react. I have been trained for every possible situation:

to always act fast; however, watching the girl that I love get stabbed wasn't something I would ever imagine. My brain can't process a single thought other than the fact that something inside me has broken—my heart, my will, it's shattered. Everyone's hectic voices and pleas for help are like distant echoes in the back of my mind, but one thing is as loud as day. Alexandra's heartbeat gets slower with every second that goes by, and that's when I know, deep in my bones and in the spot where my heart used to be, the love of my life is dying.

About the Author

Daisha Alicea was born and adopted in Cleveland, Ohio. She spent most of her childhood living between Ohio and the island of Puerto Rico with her mother and three siblings. Once she turned eighteen, she joined the military and has since traveled the world and met her amazing husband, Andrew. She is currently still serving in the United States Navy while also being an online college student and a new mother.

Printed in the USA
CPSIA information can be obtained
at www.ICGtesting.com
CBHW022207221124
17857CB00046B/393